FILTHY LITTLE GAMES

A DARK MAFIA ENEMIES TO LOVERS ARRANGED MARRIAGE ROMANCE

NEW YORK CITY MAFIA
BOOK ONE

LANE HART

COPYRIGHT

This book is a work of fiction. The characters, incidents, and dialogue were created from the authors' imagination and are not to be construed as real. Any resemblance to actual people or events is coincidental.

The authors acknowledge the copyrighted and trademarked status of various products within this work of fiction.

© 2025 Lane Hart

All Rights Reserved.

This book or any portion thereof may not be reproduced or used in any manner whatsoever without the express written permission of the publisher except for the use of brief quotations in a book review.

Editor's Choice Publishing

P.O. Box 10024

Greensboro, NC 27404

Edited by AML Editing
www.amlediting.com

Cover Design by Jessica Mohring | Raven Ink Covers, www.raveninkcovers.com

Cover Image: Wander Aguiar Book Club Photography
Model Enrico
https://www.wanderbookclub.com/

Map of New York City Mafia Families by Gabriel Ariza

SYNOPSIS

Zara:

Life has a sick sense of humor. One minute, I'm arguing with my mobster ex while dripping wet in nothing but a towel. The next, he's dead on the floor, and I'm naked, vulnerable, and at the sole mercy of the most dangerous man in New York City.

I've heard the rumors that all the mafia families bow to Creed Ferraro, but I never expected him to drag me into their world.

Creed blames me for his brother's death, and now I'm also a witness to his violent crime.

I know the rules. In the mafia, witnesses and enemies don't get to live.

Creed is unpredictable, though.

I should be terrified of him, but he killed my ex to save my life.

And I can't ignore the twisted sense of safety that comes with being near the ruthless mobster.

Creed:

Someone in my city wants me dead.

The fools missed and killed my little brother instead.

Now, vengeance burns in my veins, and nothing will stop me from hunting down the cowards responsible for his death.

Killing my ally's son in a fit of rage? Not part of the plan, even if he deserved to die. I couldn't stand to watch him lay another hand on *her*.

Zara.

Not only is she responsible for setting me and my brother up, she's also seen too much. One wrong word from her lips, and we're both dead or serving a life sentence.

I can't let her go, but keeping her close is dangerous — for both of us, especially since she's hiding secrets from me that may start a mafia war in New York City.

The more time I spend with Zara, though, the harder it is to remember why she's a threat.

That's why I make her a deal to keep her by my side.

The only way she gets to live is if she agrees to become my wife.

DEDICATION

For the women who would refuse any and all orders from a mafia king, except for this one:

"Now, spread your legs and let me worship you."

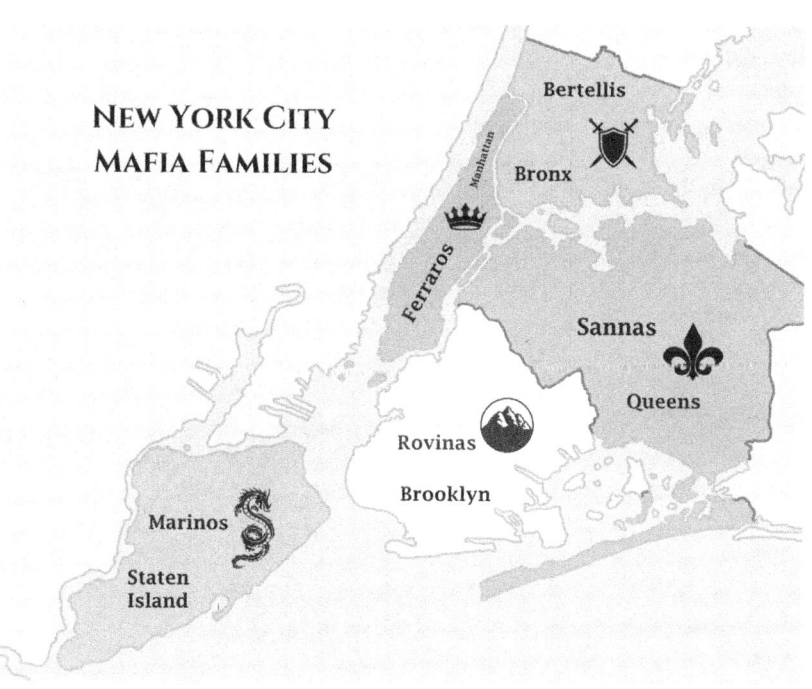

TRIGGER WARNING

This story contains graphic sex scenes, heavy profanity, kidnapping, torture by the enemy, manipulation, references to sexual violence and suicide.

PROLOGUE

Zara Riley

It's close to midnight by the time I walk home from work and get to take a cool shower to wash away the day's dirt and sweat. I comb my fingers through my long, sodden curls and pile the wet strands on top of my head in a messy bun, then wrap an old, nearly see-through beach towel around my still damp body, tucking it into the front of my chest. It's way too muggy to put on clothes just yet, and I'm not yet tired enough to sleep after my twelve-hour shift.

Strolling out into my slightly cooler seven-hundred square foot apartment, I debate killing the air conditioner to open the window and save a little on my electric bill when my bare feet come to an abrupt halt.

"Oh, shit."

A massive, manspreading mobster sits in the middle of my ratty sofa with my broken-hinged laptop on his lap. There's a big-ass gun with a silencer on the muzzle, lying a fingertip away from his thigh on the cushion next to him. He's staring at me over the top of the crooked screen with a clenched, unshaven jaw.

"Hello, Zara."

His deep, rumbling voice and clipped words make it clear he is not messing around.

Tall, dark, and dangerously handsome in his flawless black suit, he stares back at me with nothing but violence brimming in his eyes. With his wavy, shoulder-length jet-black hair and aura of wrath, he looks exactly how I imagine death would look if it was masquerading as a human.

Accabadore.

Beautiful but deadly, he's the Italian mafia's angel of death.

I didn't see the danger in him last week in the dim light of the nightclub, but tonight, there's no escaping it.

Dammit! I knew Izaiah Rovina was going to drag me into deep shit. Not only does Creed Ferraro know my name, but he also knows where I live, and is going to shoot me in the middle of my shitty Queens apartment.

Grasping my towel tighter to my chest, I glance over my damp shoulder at the locked and chained door.

"Wh-how did you get in here?"

Yes, that's the most important question to ask the man who has obviously come to kill you. Like the logistics will help me out of this disaster.

"The window." His voice is tight, his angular face stern. "Do you know why I'm here, Zara?"

I immediately nod as my gaping mouth completely dries up. The way he keeps saying my name, he makes it sound like a swearword or an accusation. Maybe both.

Of course, I know why he's here. His brother is dead, and he rightfully blames me. I blame Izaiah, but I doubt he'd believe that son of a bitch made me do it. Still, I want to try to explain.

Wetting my lips enough so I can try to speak, I tell him, "I swear I didn't know what was going to happen. I-I thought —"

"Bullshit!" he roars. Flipping my laptop onto the sofa next to him, he surges to his feet. When he begins stalking toward me, I retreat until my back hits the closed and locked door.

I have two choices here. I could try to unlock the bolt and chain and outrun the man who is nearly a foot taller than me at five-eight, or I can try to reason with the don.

"I'm sorry," I blurt out, unable to think of anything else to say to a man who just lost his brother.

"You're sorry?" he repeats quietly. I think I prefer him yelling in anger. Just like I knew it was coming, his fist slams into the door right next to my head making me jump. I swear my heart is going to race its way right out of my chest. "No, you're not sorry. Not yet. But you're going to be. And you're not the only one."

1

Creed Ferraro
Three days earlier...

"The next time one of your dealers ends up in Queens, I'm going to send him back to you in tiny pieces like human confetti," Aiden Sanna warns Emilio Rovina while wagging his finger at the older bald man.

These quarterly meetings of the Council are how five Italian mob bosses maintain control of the five boroughs of New York City without constant bloodshed or ending up serving a life sentence. We may not like each other or agree with each other on most issues but wanting to stay alive and out of prison are the two things we all have in common. Together, we've also been able to keep the Irish and Russians out of our territory whenever they try to make a play for a slice of the Big Apple, which means everyone's pockets stay nice and fat.

"Why was your dealer in Queens, Emilio?" I ask with a heavy sigh as I glance at the time on my watch, ready to get the hell out of this meeting. It's Thursday which means playing a few rounds of poker with my brother, two cousins, and consigliere while we drink, light up some cigars, and give each other shit.

First, though, I have to survive the airing of grievances and insults.

My position at the head of the Council means that I'm the tie-breaking vote in these meetings — the voice of reason. And sometimes, it feels like I'm a goddamn babysitter for the most childish men alive, most of whom are decades older than I am.

The Ferraros have been ruthlessly controlling the streets of New York City the longest of the current five mafia families, which is why we've always worn the metaphorical crown of crowns. The other four families only exist because my grandfather gave them a piece of his city and a place at the table with him.

Constantino Ferraro formed the Council forty years ago. As the oldest son, I took over for my father ten years ago after he died of a heart attack just like his old man before him. Two mob bosses dying of natural causes? That shit is almost unheard of in the underworld.

And the older I get, the more I realize exactly why their hearts gave out before either of them made it to the age of fifty.

The lengths I'd go to keep my men alive and thriving would terrify most people. That's the job, though, making everyone fear me enough to think twice about fucking with me or my family. And I'm damn good at it.

Most of the time, it's only petty shit we have to deal with during our quarterly meetings. Meetings that always take place in the Omerta Club, my elite, members only social club on the thirty-sixth floor of the exclusive Park Avenue building. No cell phones are allowed, and every person who steps foot in the door is searched for wires by someone else's guards. It's the only way we can all attempt to try to trust each other.

Emilio Rovina's eventual shrug causes his thick neck to completely disappear before he finally responds to my question. "How the fuck would I know what my man was doing in Queens? Marco isn't returning my calls, and nobody has seen or heard from him in more than a week!"

"Aiden, is Emilio's man dead?" I ask the shit-stirrer.

The pompous man straightens the sleeves of his gray suit jacket that brings out the silver in his beard. "I'm sure Marco will make an appearance just as soon as I have Emilio's word that his dealers will stay off my streets."

When someone begins to barter a man's life to get their way it means we're nearly at the end of our meeting. "Well, Emilio?" I ask to get the ball rolling.

"I'll warn my guys not to stray into Queens to deal, but you do know you can't keep all our people out of Queens forever just for spite, right?"

"He makes a good point, Aiden," I remark with a grin. "How do you know Emilio's dealer was dealing and not just visiting his girlfriend?"

Aiden slams both of his palms down on the glass conference table. "Because he had ten kilos of coke on him with the Rovinas' mountain logo on every goddamn brick!"

I stare down Emilio, who doesn't even have the decency to look ashamed. "Emilio, tell your men not to go to Queens with a shit-load of product on them again, or they may not come back out alive."

"Yeah, I'll tell them," Emilio agrees, slouching lower in his seat. "But Marco wasn't in Queens on my orders! I can't control every motherfucker who works for me."

"Try to keep your men in Brooklyn," I warn him. "I'm sure you wouldn't want Sanna's foot soldiers stomping through Coney Island, right, Emilio?"

"I told you I would handle it," Emilio mutters.

Of the other four Italian mafia families, there are only three that I consider to be my true allies. Emilio Rovina was my father's best friend. He's a pain in the ass, but he's one of the biggest real estate moguls in the state and controls all of Brooklyn. Then there's Gideon Marino, our youngest boss, who handles imports and exports coming into Staten Island. Weston Bertelli, the oldest man at the table in his late sixties, is not someone you want to screw with. He's an arms dealer who also has an impressive hitman for hire organization all over the world and holds down the Bronx.

Finally, there's Aiden Sanna who runs a gambling and transportation empire out of Queens and is always starting shit with the other families.

My family's territory is Manhattan. We've made a fortune investing in and protecting hundreds of businesses, anything from simple street vendors to elite nightclubs. Those business connections are how we distribute literally tons of product a year without getting caught.

"Any other business before we adjourn?" I ask the table.

"I've got a question," Weston Bertelli says. The white-haired man's voice is scratchier than a sheet of sandpaper from a lifetime of smoking. "What the hell are we going to do about this new district attorney?"

"Kirsten Hunt is going to be a problem for all of us," Emilio remarks. "She beat out our guy by running on an anti-drug, anti-corruption platform."

"I still can't believe Edwards lost to her," I admit with a shake of my head.

"I heard she won't take any bribes," Aiden Sanna remarks.

"Weston, if you're so concerned about her, why don't you just do what you do best and have one of your men take her out?" Emilio asks.

The hitman holds up three of his yellowed, wrinkled fingers. "Because one, I don't work for free. Two, she's a female, which I don't know about you, but offing women goes against my personal code. And three, I don't need that sort of heat up my family's ass."

"Fine. We could at least send her a message, try to run her out of town," Emilio suggests.

"Let's not get our panties in a twist until she gives us a reason to," Gideon chimes in. "Sometimes those 'messages' get bloodier than intended and could blow back on all of us."

"I agree with Weston and Gideon, so you don't have the votes yet," I say to Emilio. "For now, we'll wait and see. No one makes a move on her until we meet up again next quarter."

"What are we supposed to do until then? Lie low? Because I don't lie down for anyone," Emilio grumbles.

"Worried your unruly brood will all get locked up now?" Weston's hoarse chuckle sounds like a rake scraping over gravel.

Emilio surges to his feet. *"Vaffanculo!"*

"Seriously, Weston?" I ask when I stand up as well and button my suit jacket. "You crossed a line. Apologize to the man for insulting his family." It's not that Weston is wrong. The Rovinas are a messy bunch of thirty-somethings who could all probably use a month of rehab.

"I'm sorry, Emilio, that your spawn are all worthless pieces of shit," Weston says before he also stands up, going with escalation rather than an apology.

"I will rip your throat out!" Emilio starts around the table. But to do that, he'd have to go through me first. I turn around to face him, six inches and fifty pounds heavier, blocking his way with both of my hands before grabbing his shoulders.

"Calm down. Weston's just trying to rile you up because it's so easy. We all know Bowen leaves much to be desired as an heir too."

I can feel Weston glaring daggers at my back.

"How about we stop talking shit about each other's families and call it a day?" I suggest. "Now, shake hands like you're fucking gentlemen and not children playing dress up in designer suits."

I take a step back and watch the two men. Both grit their teeth and clasp palms directly in front of me, then immediately get into a tug of war over who can pull the other toward them harder using their still clasped hands.

"Enough! Meeting adjourned," I announce, breaking them apart. "See you all in three months unless you get yourselves killed and we have no choice but to deal with your unfortunate heirs."

Everyone hastily makes a move toward the door, except for Emilio, which is probably for the best. The last thing I need is all the city bosses getting into a scuffle on my building's elevator.

"Speaking of...unfortunate heirs," he starts. "You still don't have any, Ferraro."

"My line of succession is secure without needing to procreate," I tell him. "If anything happens to me, I know my men will be in good hands with my brother."

He grins at me. "You're not superstitious? Are you, son?"

I hate when he calls me 'son.' And whether or not I believe in my family's curse...well, our history speaks for itself. Still, putting the blame on some old lady in Italy my grandfather pissed off when he refused to marry her daughter is ridiculous. The women in our family don't have short lifespans because they aren't Italian. They have short lifespans because of our way of life.

The women who have been brave enough to marry a Ferraro have all met the same fate, dead before their thirtieth birthday.

My grandmother was thrown onto the tracks and hit by a train when she was twenty-nine, thanks to the fucking Russians my grandfather pissed off.

My two aunts were tossed overboard a cruise ship. They were

sent away by my uncles to keep them safe from the war with the Irish in the late '80s.

And my mother, she was twenty-eight when she died by my father's hand. She stupidly thought the three of us would be safe in witness protection after she took his money and ratted him and his men out to the feds. She was wrong.

"Your father always wanted our families to form an unbreakable alliance," Emilio says, leading up to his point. "Stella is a strong, beautiful Italian woman. She would make a good wife."

"I'm sure your daughter will make a good wife…for someone else. I'm not interested in marrying a woman who doesn't want to be in the same room with me."

Everyone started calling Stella Rovina the 'viper bitch' when she was a teenager because she's always been a handful. Now that she's thirty-something all that's changed is she seems to be even more hostile toward the entire male species.

There's a rumor that she once gave her older brother's friend a hand job using poison ivy in the bushes at Central Park. The fact she gave a man a red, itchy dick isn't the worst part. The psychotic part is she was willing to let that shit spread all over her palm to fuck him up.

"Oh, Stella's more than willing to marry you," Emilio says, which is surprising since most women fear me. I doubt anything scares Stella Rovina, though. "She also agreed to carry your children. Although, she did say she prefers insemination, but I think you could eventually persuade her to do it the…natural way with the right motivation. We all need to do our part to keep our family legacies going, Creed."

And there it is. Why would I want to marry a woman who refuses to share my bed?

I do like a challenge, but not one that puts my dick in jeopardy of being abused or mutilated.

"Your father would've married a good Italian woman if he

knew what would happen with your mother. Don't make the same mistake your old man did," Emilio warns me.

"I don't need to think about it. My answer is no," I assert firmly. "But I'll talk to Carmine and my cousins," I concede, since it was my father's wish for our two families to unite. And for some reason, even a decade after his death, I still find myself wanting to make the dead son of a bitch proud.

2

Zara

"*Hey, sexy.*"

"I'm busy," I reply from where I'm kneeling on the dirty, rock-hard floor in my ratty jean shorts. I don't bother to look up, because I unfortunately recognize the entitled bastard's voice. Praying he'll take the hint and go away, I continue restocking the discount store's shelves with four-packs of cheap toilet paper without pausing.

Nothing good ever comes from an unexpected visit from Izaiah Rovina, the oldest son of Emilio Rovina, mob boss of Brooklyn. Which is exactly why I live and work in Queens.

From the corner of my eye, I can make out the filthy rich jerk's wrinkled, charcoal designer suit and his black silk tie loose at the neck as he comes closer. His messy appearance was my first red flag that he was nothing but a spoiled, self-destructive, insensitive jerk who loves heroin almost as much as he loves himself.

When his knees are nearly touching my face, he leans a shoulder against the shelves, as if he's too wasted or lazy to hold himself up. He jerks on one of the auburn curls that's fallen from my messy bun. "So, you don't want to go to the zoo with Oriana tomorrow morning?"

My head falls forward, chin touching my chest to free my hair from his grimy fingers. We both know I want to see her and that I'd do anything to spend an entire morning with my daughter. And I do mean absolutely anything.

The Rovina family is one of the richest and most powerful in New York City. Three years ago, the sons of bitches ripped my newborn daughter from my arms when she was only a day old, knowing I could never afford an attorney to fight against their legion of lawyers for custody. I don't even know which of their dozens of properties they're keeping her at, but I'm sure she's locked up behind towering walls and dozens of security guards, safeguarded like Fort Knox.

And their sole reason for taking my daughter from me, refusing to let me spend a minute of unsupervised time with her, is because they deemed me unfit to be a mother. One failed drug test, even though I've been clean since the day I found out I was pregnant.

So, while the Rovinas can spend millions of dollars of their blood money spoiling my little girl, it will *never* add up to my love for her. Love that I've felt since the moment the damn stick turned blue.

Inhaling a deep breath, I get to my feet and finally face the asshole. The first thing I notice is that Izaiah's glassy brown eyes are more bloodshot than normal, and his suit hangs a little looser than usual from his lanky frame. "I wish I could go to the zoo tomorrow, but...I can't." I hate turning down the offer. Taking time off from work is not a luxury I can afford at the moment. "I have to open tomorrow, and I'll be here until closing."

Izaiah stabs his fingers through his short brown hair as if he's growing impatient. "Then how about Sunday?"

Blaring sirens accompanied by red and blue lights start flashing in my head. They're so bright and loud, I can barely think over them. "Why are you being so damn...accommodating today?" I ask the prick.

"Because I need you to do me a favor. An urgent one."

I release the breath I was holding. Thank god. I can do urgent favors all damn day. That's a million times better than having to perform sexual favors in exchange for supervised visitation with my daughter. In the past three years, I've done more of those "favors" than I care to recall.

"I'm off Sunday morning until one."

"Deal," Izaiah quickly agrees. While I wish I could spend the entire day with Oriana, I'll take whatever I can get.

"What do you need me to do?"

The mobster straightens up and shoves his hands into the pockets of his sagging pants. "I just need you to deliver a message to the manager of a nightclub."

Deliver a message? That's it? This is sounding almost too good to be true.

"What's the message?"

He glances over his shoulder to make sure there's no one else in the store. "You need to tell Jasper Burch that his boss, Ferraro, has a bullseye on his head, and there's a sniper coming for him who won't miss."

"Oh."

The name Ferraro is ominous enough that I second-guess agreeing to this favor. Everyone in the city knows that there are five mafia families, one controlling each borough, and that Creed Ferraro is the boss who keeps the other four in line.

If someone wants him dead...well, they obviously have a death wish. The man's nickname is *Accabadore*, the angel of death. While

I've never seen him in person, I've seen pictures on social media of him glowering at cameras, looking as if he's plotting the death of the photographers for daring to annoy him. There's no denying that the mobster is devastatingly handsome, but getting too close to him would be hazardous to one's health.

"So, the message is like a warning? One to keep Ferraro safe from a potential sniper?"

"Something like that."

The only reason I don't bail on this favor is because I long to spend time at the zoo with Oriana on Sunday. She's growing up way too fast. My worst fear is that soon she'll be old enough for the Rovinas to fill her head with lies about me not wanting to be a part of her life. Besides, I don't see what harm could come from giving the mobster a heads-up that could save his life.

"You'll need to deliver the message in person. Tonight. And I want you to text me with updates."

Dammit. I should've known there would be a catch.

"Tonight? It has to be tonight?"

"What time do you get off work?"

"I should be able to lock up and leave a little after ten."

"Perfect." Izaiah eyes the frays on my short denim shorts and then my snug white tee for so long I worry he's going to add more conditions to this deal. "If you dress up slutty enough, you should be able to skip the line and deliver the message to Jasper before midnight."

"That doesn't give me much time to get ready. Where am I even going?"

"To The Vault. It's a club across the bridge."

Great. The commute to Manhattan will take half an hour, if not longer on the subway, which will leave me about thirty minutes to shower, do something with my curls, and find a short enough dress to get me into one of the city's most popular clubs.

"Send me a message when you've delivered the warning and when Creed Ferraro shows up, then delete the entire thread. Understood?" He swipes his disgusting thumb over my lips, watching them intently. "Too bad I'm too wasted to claim this mouth tonight."

"Yeah, too bad," I mutter, not the last bit disappointed, as I pull back away from his reach.

"Next time." His words are a promise, not a request.

Quickly changing the subject, I ask, "What if I can't get into the club before midnight? What if Ferraro doesn't show up?"

"Then you'll never see Oriana again," he warns me before he turns around and staggers out the door, as if he didn't just threaten to cut my heart out of my chest.

Creed

"I fold," I say and toss my cards down onto the green felt table. No better way to unwind after a Council meeting than poker night with the guys.

"Oh, fuck off. Why do you always play it safe, man?" Tristan huffs as he rakes his winnings — a pile of red, white, and blue poker chips — to his side of the poker table. "You've got more money to waste than the rest of us combined."

Every Thursday night, I have a standing game of poker in my penthouse with my second in command and younger brother, Carmine; my consigliere or advisor, Lorenzo; and my two younger cousins, Andrea and Tristano. Although, everyone calls those two by their shortened names. Dre moonlights as an ethical corporate attorney and is third in line to my throne. Tristan is one of our family's main enforcers because he enjoys inflicting pain.

"Maybe I have more money than the rest of you fools because I actually know *when* to fold and not waste it," I reply while Carmine gathers up the deck of cards to shuffle them.

"Tristan was bluffing that hand," Dre declares, his perpetual scowl on his face as he takes a puff from his cigar.

"If you thought I was bluffing, then why did you fucking fold?" Tristan asks him.

"Because you act like a little bitch when you lose," Dre releases a rare chuckle seconds before he ducks to avoid a handful of peanuts in his face from Tristan.

Tristan isn't wrong about me. I do play it safe. Being cautious every second of every day is how I was raised.

Sometimes there's a part of me that wants to take a risk, to go all in. To be someone else, someone who isn't responsible for the lives of hundreds of people. The lives of thousands of people if shit were to go sideways with the other four mafia families.

The stress of maintaining peace keeps me constantly on edge.

"Last hand? I'm ready to call it a night," I tell the guys, wanting to try to get some shuteye before the sun comes up and I go for my daily run.

"Whatever you want, boss," Carmine agrees as he deals the cards.

"Before I forget, Emilio Rovina mentioned earlier today that he wants a Ferraro to marry Stella."

"It's a no from me, dog." Carmine shakes his head.

"Why not? She's hot as hell," Tristan remarks.

I look to Dre, who lifts a single, non-committal shoulder. Before I can ask him what he's thinking, Lorenzo's phone starts ringing.

"You got an old lady we don't know about?" Tristan jokes, but Lorenzo ignores him and answers the call.

"Hello? Jasper? I'm with him now. Here, you can tell him yourself." Lorenzo offers the phone to me. "It's Jasper Burch. He says it's important."

"The manager of The Vault?" I ask as I take the device and Lorenzo nods. "What do you need, Jasper?" I assume it's important if he's calling so late.

"Hey, boss. S-sorry to bother you, but, uh, I just got a message I think you need to hear."

"Great. What's the message?"

"Some girl showed up and said, and I quote: 'Ferraro has a bullseye on his head, and there's a sniper coming for him who won't miss.' It might be nothing, but I wanted to give you a heads up, you know, in case it's legit."

I sigh. "Is this girl still there?"

"Yeah. I think so."

"Have your employees keep an eye on her but keep your distance. We don't want to spook her. I'm on my way over to talk to her myself."

"Thanks, boss," he says in relief.

Handing the phone back to Lorenzo, I stand up and tug my suit jacket off the back of my chair to slip it on.

"What's up?" Dre asks.

"Jasper sounded spooked. He said he's got some girl in the club who had a message for me."

"What kind of message?" Lorenzo asks as he grabs his own jacket and throws it over his arm, ready to tag along.

"Something about how there's a bullseye on my head and a sniper coming for me who supposedly won't miss."

"Fuck. I'm coming with you," Carmine says.

"Me too," Dre agrees as he and Tristan get to their feet. "Why didn't this person just call or text you instead of going to Jasper?"

"I don't know. That's a question we can ask her."

"We should consider bringing in more men, increase your

security," Lorenzo suggests as we all head down the hall toward the elevator.

"It's probably nothing."

"You aren't worried?" Tristan asks.

"Not particularly. She's probably going to ask for some exorbitant reward for providing me with this vital message, and that will be the end of it."

"Well, if nothing else, we can all get drunk and try to get laid tonight," Tristan suggests.

"This shit could be serious, and you're thinking about getting your dick wet?" Dre mutters.

"It's probably nothing," I repeat. "But I'm not paying anyone a dime."

"Are you sure this is a good idea, Creed?" Lorenzo asks. That's what my faithful advisor always does, though. Rather than tell me I'm being an idiot, he'll ask me if I think I'm being an idiot because he knows better than to come right out and say it.

"Jasper's been a loyal associate of ours for six years, Lor. There's no reason we shouldn't trust him, and I don't consider one girl much of a threat."

"I'm not sure how much extra muscle I can have here on such short notice," Lorenzo says while his fingers type away on his phone.

"That's fine. It's late. Don't bother calling anyone in. The five of us can handle this. We go talk to Jasper and the girl, then I'm coming straight home," I tell him, but he still looks doubtful. His concerned frown doesn't lessen an inch as he pauses his typing and stares me down for several more seconds. "And we'll all go strapped just in case," I add to appease him. I don't usually feel the need to wear my shoulder holster and Glock into my own nightclubs, but until we learn more about this so-called threat, better safe than sorry.

Finally, Lorenzo gives me a nod of agreement. "I'll go get a vehicle ready for us while you four strap up."

"Great. And don't worry, Lor. You know most threats are all talk anyway. Plenty of people want me dead, but most are too stupid to try."

"I don't think we should underestimate the stupidity of others, especially the other four bosses," Lorenzo remarks before he walks out the door.

"None of the Council members have been at each other's throats in years. Business is good. Everyone is getting rich. So, I doubt any of them would want to start a war and ruin a good thing. Do you think someone is suicidal enough to try to take my place?" I ask Carmine, Tristan, and Dre, as I lead the way to the walk-in safe in my bedroom, filled with money and firearms.

"Who the fuck knows with those *stronzos*," Dre mutters. "They would probably be the only ones who actually have the balls to try to take you out. But I doubt any of them are stupid enough to talk about coming after you in front of some girl they don't trust."

I'm too damn paranoid about being betrayed or getting caught in a bust by the feds to talk business with most of my own loyal men. It's why there's a particular chain of command. I give the orders to the few I know well — Dre, Tristan, or Carmine.

These are the guys I grew up with and have known my whole life. They then pass my instructions on to our captains, who give the orders to our soldiers who are carefully vetted and have to be known associates for at least eight years before they take our oath.

I've been the capo dei capi, boss of all mob bosses for ten years without anyone challenging me. There's a reason people call me *Accabadore*, the angel of death, behind my back. In the first year after my father died, the Irish tried to move into lower Manhattan, testing me. And that was the last time those sixty-four members were ever seen.

I may be cautious, but I don't take anyone's shit. Disrespecting me or my men may cost you your tongue, getting caught stealing from me will result in no less than the loss of a limb.

And even thinking about coming after me is an absolute death sentence if it proves to be true.

3

Creed

The Vault is packed, which means there are plenty of fish in the sea for Tristan to pick tonight's lucky — or unlucky — lady from the dance floor. While Dre may be the smartest and most ruthless, Tristan is definitely the most depraved.

"What's the plan?" Carmine shouts over the thumping music.

"Let's find somewhere we can all meet down here," I tell the guys. "Jasper's office is too quiet for this conversation." I don't take any chances with people recording meetings.

"Agreed. I'll clear an area," Lorenzo says before he leaves us.

"I'll go find Jasper and bring him down," Dre says to us before he disappears into the crowd and up the spiral stairs to Jasper's office.

"I'll go find out who's down to scream for me tonight," Tristan tells us with a smirk before he stalks onto the dance floor in search of his next victim.

Tristan breaks bones and knocks teeth out of men for a living. He enjoys inflicting pain not just to keep assholes in line but to get off on the sense of well-deserved justice. I'm not entirely sure why he thinks women deserve his wrath.

While Dre can be just as heartless, he doesn't do things to intentionally hurt people. My oldest cousin, a shrewd attorney, is logical nearly to a fault. If someone needs to be put down to protect the family, he'll be the first one to pull out his gun.

"Let's get a drink while we wait," I tell Carmine. When we approach the bar, men and women alike take one look at us, at me, and scatter like mice fleeing a hungry lion.

Accabadore.

I swear I can vaguely hear the word being whispered repeatedly, even over the pounding music.

"Don't pout," Carmine says with a chuckle. "At least now there's no line."

"Right." My brother can always find the silver-lining in anything.

Danny, the bartender sees us and asks, "Good to see you, Mr. Ferraro. Would you like your usual bottle of Dalmore tonight?"

"That would be great, thanks. Six glasses," I tell him.

"Coming right up," he agrees.

Glancing around at the ten feet buffer zone everyone is giving us, despite the fact that the place is slam packed.

"They're trying to be respectful of you in your bar," he remarks.

"Yeah, well, I'm sick of being treated like a walking STD."

Carmine chuckles. "You're actually worse than an STD. A quick death is a whole lot scarier than an itchy dick rash. Nobody wants to make the mistake of getting too close and insulting you in your own club."

"I've never killed anyone for brushing up against me or making me wait for a drink."

"By now, you should be used to the downside of being the

most-feared man in the city of eight million. I don't envy you. It's bad enough that we look so much alike I'm constantly getting mistaken for you."

"How about we just trade places for a day? Hell, I'd be happy with one night."

"No fucking way."

The truth is, it's me who is envious of Carmine. My younger brother has never had to feel the weight of responsibility for our people on *his* shoulders.

And his bed isn't nearly as lonely as mine.

"Do you think I should take Emilio up on his offer?" I ask him, since now seems as good a time as any while we wait for our twenty-five-year-old, single malt bottle of whisky.

Carmine blinks at me silently for several long seconds. "You're not seriously considering that shit, are you?"

"I told him no…but maybe I should give it more thought. It's what our father wanted — an alliance with the Rovinas."

"You're joking, right?"

"Nope."

"You really want to try and wrangle that vicious viper? You two would probably kill each other before your first anniversary!"

"I'm almost forty and not getting any younger," I remind him. "And it's not like I have any prospects lining up for a ring."

"You're thirty-six! That's not 'almost forty.'"

"Close enough. Our father wanted us to both marry strong, Italian woman and have a few heirs — a Ferraro Rovina heir specifically."

"I don't know, Creed. Do you really want to get into bed with Emilio Rovina? He's a greedy man who is always going to want more. And that more is getting his hands on a piece of our empire."

"He was our father's best friend. They rebuilt entire neighborhoods together."

"Our father is dead. Let his plans for us die too. You can do better than trying to survive a marriage with Stella Rovina." Carmine shakes his head. "Where the hell is that bartender? Changing his pants you made him piss?"

My brother doesn't get it. My lack of prospective lovers isn't my choice. I'm not going through a drought. It's a full-blown famine between my sheets. It's been at least a year, hell, maybe longer, since I last had sex.

To run the city and oversee all the bosses, I have to be feared, making me the nightmare mothers and fathers caution their children about. The boys they tell to steer clear to avoid becoming indoctrinated as one of my foot soldiers, and the girls, well they warn girls to stay away from me and my brother because we'll take their innocence, or even worse, they'll be the next victim of the Ferraro family curse.

The truth is, there are plenty of men in this city who would do absolutely anything to become a member of the Ferraro family, so we've never had to recruit.

And more importantly, I don't get off on being feared by women.

I glance around the bar, trying to meet the eye of at least one brave woman, but there's no such luck tonight.

While I don't have any problem with other men paying willing women or men for sex, it's just not for me. I want to fuck someone who wants me without the payday or without me hiding who I am, even if that shit happens rarer than a monsoon in the desert.

As the mafia king of New York City, I'm looking for a fearsome queen, not a doe-eyed, twenty-something gold-digger who bolts at the first gunshot. But no respectable woman in the Family wants to risk their lives by being chained to me. No amount of money can bring someone back from the dead.

Occasionally, I will go home with a willing woman. The sex will be decent, but the next morning, she'll see the invisible blood on my hands, remember that I'm a man who isn't worth the risk, and never be seen or heard from again.

While Stella Rovina may be willing to stick around as my wife, it sure as shit won't be for love. No, the marriage will be more of a business arrangement. A *hostile* business merger that I may not survive.

"You're right," I tell my brother. "I don't want to deal with all the strings that come with Emilio and Stella Rovina."

"Thank fuck," he mutters. "She would only make you even more miserable. And there's no reason to give up on marrying for love just yet. In fact, it looks like you actually have a daring admirer tonight."

"Bullshit."

Carmine lifts his phone and snaps a photo. "Pretty girl, but I think she's more my type than yours," he teases with a grin before he finally shows the image to me.

He's wrong. The woman in the miniscule green dress isn't simply pretty. She's beautiful, tall and *thick* with long, wild auburn curls. And she's looking right at his camera. At us.

I lift my eyes from the phone and search the general direction of where my brother's phone was aimed.

It only takes a moment to spot her. She stares back at me, her gaze unwavering. And the image doesn't do her justice.

She's hands down the most gorgeous woman in the city, and she's…crooking her finger at me?

I can't say I'm not tempted to go over and talk to her.

But I'm not a dog to be summoned by anyone.

"Well? Aren't you going to go talk to her?" Carmine asks as if he's so certain she's interested in me and not himself.

"I haven't decided yet. I don't appreciate being ordered around by a woman I don't even know yet."

Instead of caving, I nod my head to the empty stool next to me at the bar as a counteroffer.

She shakes her unruly head of tight spirals and purses her pretty pink lips together. Shoving her fingers through her hair to toss it out of her face, her eyes dart around the crowded club before she tips her chin up stubbornly as if to say, *get your ass over here right now.*

"Either she doesn't know who you are, or she's got some big brass balls in her panties."

"No shit," I agree with a frown, not a fan of my brother imagining anything in her panties.

When I don't make a move, her gaze scans the club, and she looks exasperated. Once our eye contact is broken, her gaze lowers to the phone in her hands, her thumbs typing away to someone.

I wait for her to lift her head again, but she doesn't, too engrossed with her device.

Carmine shoves his elbow against mine. "You should hurry over before someone tells her who you are and scares her off." When I hesitate, he adds, "Or maybe I'll just go talk to her."

"*Vaffanculo,*" I snap while straightening and buttoning my suit jacket. Realizing exactly why he said that shit. "Well played."

He laughs. "I expect you to thank me profusely in your wedding toast for not taking her home with me tonight."

As I reluctantly begin to make my way toward her, I flip him off without glancing back until the woman's eyes widen when she looks up and sees me approaching her.

Rather than giving my brother the middle finger, I should've been thinking of what the hell I'm going to say to her. First words are important, and I can't seem to come up with any to negate who and what I am.

Before I have a chance to say a single word, she sucks in a deep breath that lifts her shoulders and then blurts out loud enough to be heard clearly over the thumping music, "You and your friends should leave right now, Mr. Ferraro."

Okay, so she knows exactly who I am. And she still called me over? That's…interesting.

Moving in closer, I study the trail of freckles that start between her auburn eyebrows and sweep down her nose before locking eyes with her again.

Eyes that sparkle like light shining through green glass.

"You called me over here, and before I have a chance to even tell you how gorgeous you are, you're telling me to…leave?"

"No. I mean, yes!" She says as she adjusts one of the thin straps of her tiny dress that matches her eyes. "Go!" She points her finger toward the entrance, as if I'm an idiot who can't find my way out. With those parting words, she turns toward the bar, in a clear dismissal of me, which is pretty damn infuriating.

Refusing to let this baffling and infuriating woman slip through my fingers so soon, I grab her bare forearm to stop her. "Wait a second. You're not even going to tell me your name?"

"I can't," she replies just before chaos erupts around us.

When I hear the familiar *pop-pop-pop* sound, rather than reach for my gun in my holster to shoot back, I tackle the woman to the ground, shielding her body with my own, even though I have no idea which direction the bullets are flying from.

Over the sounds of gunfire and people screaming, she clutches my arms and blinks up at me in shock. "I'm sorry. I didn't know…I didn't know…"

There's no time for me to ask her what the fuck she's talking about as a flood of men in all-black uniforms, complete with riot helmets, pour in from the front door. All of them point their big ass guns at the room of patrons.

This is too organized to be some random shooting. It's the fucking cops, and for some unknown reason, they're apparently raiding my fucking club.

Either the cops on my payroll had no idea or they decided to fuck me over.

The place is clean. I know better than to stash any drugs, guns, or money here on a busy night.

"HANDS UP WHERE WE CAN SEE THEM!" the cops yell. "GET YOUR HANDS UP!"

I push my weight off the woman and glance over my shoulder at the bar to make sure Carmine got down.

He's one of the few people in the club still standing. Staggering actually, as he reaches for the bar as if to keep himself upright.

Two officers storm over to me, blocking my view and pointing his weapon right at my face.

"EVERYONE GET ON THE GROUND! HANDS IN THE AIR!" someone shouts.

I don't know what the fuck is going on, but I can't shake the feeling that these sons of bitches are out for blood.

"Get off her! Nose to the ground," an officer says to me as he and his buddy pull me off the woman and shove me facedown to the ground.

"GET ON THE GROUND!" is yelled yet again.

As I'm being felt up for weapons, my fury growing with every second, I lift my head to find my brother still standing at the bar.

What the fuck is he doing?

"Carmine, get down!" I shout at him. He turns towards my voice which is when I see the gun in his right hand. One of my guns.

"DROP YOUR WEAPON!" a voice orders and is immediately followed by another round of *pop-pop-pop*.

"No!" I scream. Carmine drops to his knees and starts to fall forward onto his face.

I'm instantly on my feet and shoving the officers off me to run toward him, but I know I won't make it in time to catch him.

From what sounds like a million miles away, someone says, "HOLD YOUR FUCKING FIRE!"

"Carmine!" I grab his shoulders to lift and roll him over. The front of his white dress shirt and dark suit jacket are so fucking bloody I can't even tell how many times those sons of bitches shot him.

They fucking shot him!

I press my palms to where the bleeding is the heaviest.

My brother's blue eyes are frantic as they blink up at me. He parts his lips, as if trying to speak, but only a trickle of blood slips from the corner.

I lie when I tell him, "You're okay. You're going to be okay."

Cazzo!

I search the room full of people for help. Most are still face down. "He needs help! We've got to get him to the hospital!" I yell when none of the cops move an inch. They just stand there, watching through their helmets with guns raised. "Someone help me get him up!" I don't know whether to try to haul him off the floor or keep applying pressure to slow the bleeding. I've seen plenty of gunshot wounds before, but I've never seen anyone with this many chest and stomach wounds live.

No. No, no, no.

This can't be happening. It can't. Only seconds ago, Carmine was joking with me and giving me hell like usual.

In slow motion, his eyes dull as they sweep over me once like he's checking me over for injuries before they roll back in his head.

"Fuck!" I press down harder on his chest and stomach. "Hang on, Carmine. Just hang on until we can get you out of here," I tell him right before I'm tackled to the floor by what feels like several large bodies.

My head and back slam to the stone ground, and then I'm looking up at a SWAT member who presses the muzzle of his gun to my forehead. I can't see the face behind the helmet, but I warn him through gritted teeth, "Get the fuck off me and get my brother to a hospital right fucking now!"

The cop doesn't flinch.

"Don't do it, Hurley," a voice says from behind him. "Too many witnesses now."

"He's resisting," the cop above me says.

"Bullshit! I'm trying to help my brother!"

Behind him, Dre, Lorenzo, and Tristan all approach and point their guns at the cop's back, even though they're surrounded.

"DROP YOUR WEAPONS!" a cop shouts.

They ignore him.

"Put your guns down!" I command them before they get shot too.

The cop above me scoffs. "You don't fucking give me orders!"

"I was talking to the three men behind you about to blow your head off."

That finally has him pulling his gun back and climbing off me.

As soon as he moves, his less hostile comrade slaps cold metal handcuffs on my wrists, then slips my gun from my shoulder holster. "Creed Ferraro, you're under arrest."

"Where the hell is EMS? Are you just going to let my brother bleed out on the goddamn floor?" I gesture with my restrained hands toward Carmine's unmoving, prone form.

Another cop comes over and places his gloved fingertips to the side of my brother's neck for several seconds before he says, "Too late now."

"*Vaffanculo!*"

The asshole has to be lying, because it can't be too fucking late...

I lunge for my brother. Several hands not only hold me back but start dragging me away from him.

4

Creed

Three days later...

I'll never know if Carmine was still alive or not when the cop checked his pulse. Either way, those motherfuckers let him bleed out on the bar floor and didn't lift a finger to try to save him.

I saw the damage from the bullets and sent two of my guys to the morgue, but I still can't believe he's really gone.

It was my job to protect my baby brother, and I failed him.

When Carmine was born, I was only six years old. One of the first things my father told me was to always watch his back and keep him safe, and I took that shit to heart.

If he got into trouble when we were kids, starting fights at school, or wrecking one of our father's cars in his teens, I would take the fall, along with our father's beating, to protect Carmine.

He was my best friend. The one person who made enduring the burden of this family bearable.

I never should've left him at the bar to go talk to that goddamn woman. She's to blame for his death almost as much as I am because she fucking knew something was about to happen and instead of just coming over and warning us, she decided to play a fucking game with me.

If Jasper wasn't dead too, I would've thought he knew what was about to go down in my club. It was a setup. The warning was a ploy to lure me to the club. Someone baited me into showing up exactly when and where they wanted with the vague-ass threat hanging over my head so I'd come armed.

I can't believe I was stupid enough to fall for it. My father would disown me for fucking up so bad.

And I can't help but think that the reason Carmine's dead is because the *cretino* cops thought he was me. I don't buy that they were threatened by the gun in his hand. Those assholes shot him as soon as they came through the door and kept shooting him.

And now, I'm going to find every fucker responsible for his death and make them pay, starting with the cop who killed Carmine, then the one who wanted to put a bullet in my head.

"*Cazzo!*" I slam my fist into the concrete wall of the holding cell we've been crammed into for three goddamn days while waiting for our arraignment. Now my knuckles are going to be nice and bloody.

"Baxter said he thought he could have us out on bail by this afternoon," Dre whispers from the bench behind me.

"I don't give a shit about bail! Carmine is dead! Jasper is dead! Someone set us the fuck up! I'm going to find them all and snap every bone in their goddamn bodies!"

As soon as we get out of this hellhole, I need to make plans to bury my brother. That's not something I ever thought I'd have to do.

I'm the goddamn boss of bosses. If anyone should be dead, it's me. I'm the one who calls all the shots, who runs the underworld.

If someone wants my crown, they should've fucking killed me to get it, not Carmine.

People already think I'm the angel of death, and I'm about to unleash hell all across New York City.

Once Carmine's been laid to rest, I'll meet with the police Commissioner to find out why the fuck he didn't warn me about the raid, and get the names of every cop at the bar and who put them up to it.

Then…then I'm going to find the fucking woman responsible for setting all of this into motion.

I won't let this insult, this tragedy, go unpunished. Even if it means burning everything my family built to the ground.

∼

"I'm sorry about your brother, Mr. Ferraro." Baxter McMillan, the best criminal defense attorney in the state, sits down at the table next to me in the courtroom.

"Those fuckers came in guns blazing and murdered him!" I tell Baxter, hating that I'm required to sit around and wait for the judge when I should be by my brother's side, saying a final goodbye.

"That's what several witnesses said as well," Baxter remarks quietly. He eyes my orange jumpsuit with a wince. "But I've already seen the body cam footage. It's surprising how the officers' cameras were all recording for once, and for the DA to be so willing to turn it over to me as soon as I filed my Notice of Appearance as your attorney. I'm sorry to say it, but Carmine pulled out his gun clear as day, giving the officers the green light to fire at him."

"It was instinct. When the gunshots went off, how could we know it was the cops? They shot first," I explain, remembering that

I would've pulled out my own damn Glock if not for the woman I was busy trying to cover.

How ironic is it that my first instinct was to protect her when she's the one who's responsible for my brother's death?

"It's all messy," Baxter agrees. "But the DA already has everything she needs to go to the Grand Jury and indict you and your three men for felonies. They have video of you all wearing or holding your guns in plain sight. Guns that are now in evidence with your fingerprints all over them and no serial numbers. You're looking at serving time no matter which way this goes. A plea deal is damn unlikely with this new DA."

"Fuck," I mutter as I have to lift both of my cuffed wrists to shove my fingers through my hair. I don't really give a shit about a felony, but if me and the other three heads of the family are put away for a year, our entire empire will crumble. Not to mention the consequences for Dre who is required to keep a spotless record. "Dre can't lose his law license."

"I know this isn't the best time for this discussion, but there's no point in dancing around the truth," Baxter says. "You four are fucked. Not to mention that you need to watch your back once you're out on bail. Whoever set you up may have wanted to kill you in the chaos, but they had to settle with getting you charged with shit you can't possibly squirm out of."

"Have the others had arraignments? Made bail yet?"

"Tristan, Andre, and Lorenzo have all just been released on a hundred-thousand-dollar bail. I'm expecting the same for you."

Good. I have to get out of these goddamn handcuffs and get to work. "How much time are we talking about?" I ask him.

"The charges are resisting arrest, which we can probably get dropped. But not the second-degree criminal possession of a firearm. That's a Class C felony with a minimum mandatory three-and-a-half years and a max of fifteen years."

"Fifteen years? This is bullshit. Those cops should be in prison for killing Carmine!" What kind of pussy can't face me like a man and pull the trigger himself but sends a woman to set me up? I can't wait to fucking find out.

As if reading my mind, Baxter clears his throat. "Mr. Ferraro, as your attorney, I must advise you that while you're out on bail, if you're brought up on any new charges, you may not get released again until you finish serving time on the gun charges."

"I know." While I wait to say fuck it and blow everyone's heads off, I can't risk jumping to any conclusions.

I owe it to Carmine to do this the right way, to play it smart and take down every single individual responsible for his death in a way that won't ever be traced back to me. My brother wouldn't want me or anyone else in our family to serve a life prison sentence for getting vengeance for him.

"Accidental" deaths happen all the time thanks to car wrecks, fires, plane crashes, and falls from balconies. If done carefully, making murders look like suicides is fairly easy as well.

But apparently, we're going to have to work fast before the four leaders of the family are all thrown in prison for at least three-and-a-half fucking years.

~

Once I'm finally released on bail wearing a white tee and blood-stained suit pants I was wearing when they arrested me, I meet up with the guys on the front steps of the precinct for my first breath of city air.

The sun seems too bright. My skin feels fucking filthy underneath the filthy clothes, and…it feels wrong that Carmine isn't here with the four of us.

The three men stare at me in their own wrinkled clothing, looking like I feel after three days inside, waiting for me to break-down or lash out. Hell, they probably want to do the same.

"I know what you're thinking, Creed. Shit feels...wrong without Carmine," Dre says as he pulls me into an embrace. "I don't know what the fuck else to say. I'm sorry. Fuck, I hate this shit."

"I do too," I agree. "And I'm sorry you might lose your law license."

"I don't give a fuck. It'll be nice to be free for once to do whatever the hell I want with nothing holding me back."

"Right," I mutter, clearly seeing the blatant lie through his tough words. Dre worked hard as hell and went to college and law school for seven years to get his law degree. It's impossible to forget what a pain in the ass he was all those months he was studying for the bar exam.

Slapping his back, I release him, then clasp Lorenzo and Tristan on the shoulder. "We're going to find out who set us up and make them suffer a thousand times over for what they did to Carmine and Jasper."

"Just let us know what you need, boss." Tristan nods, his eyes glassy.

"It has to be one of the other families, right?" Lorenzo asks.

"That's my assumption. But we can't even think about drawing any blood without concrete evidence." I want to play this smart so we don't end up in prison for the rest of our lives or start a mafia war. The rules are simple, no bloodshed between the families without proof of betrayal. "You three get the word out to every single one of our men that they better keep their heads nice and cool until further notice. No retaliation against anyone, even the cops, without my permission."

"Where are you going to start with this mess?" Lorenzo asks.

"First, I've got to..." Clearing the emotion from my throat, I'm finally able to speak the words. "The first thing I have to do is plan Carmine's funeral. Then I have an idea about a few leads." If I can get my hands on Carmine's phone, I can send the image of that woman to one of my private investigators. Failing that, there should be some club footage to go through while Roscoe works on the list of names involved in the raid.

"What do you need us to do?" Dre asks.

"After the funeral, the four of us are going to split up and watch the families. Alone."

"Watch them? Follow them around? All of them? Alone? Do you really think that's smart? What if they see one of us stalking them without backup?" Dre asks.

"We'll just have to be careful and not get caught because I want to know where everyone is going, who they see, and what they're up to. Worst case, we get some blackmail material. Best case, we find our rat."

"Worst case, they finish the job and kill you while you're on their turf!" Tristan exclaims.

"Exactly. Why can't you just hire a few PIs to do that shit for you and report back?" Dre grumbles.

"Because after last night, I'm finding it very fucking hard to trust *anyone* right now," I snap and let that sink into his skull for a moment.

I can't afford to trust anyone. Not even Dre, Tristan, or Lorenzo. Not completely. Not when my brother is dead, and I don't know who the hell is responsible. I doubt it was one of them, but then again, it would be one hell of a way to throw me off their scent if it was with them getting charged with gun possession too.

I know Tristan isn't smart or savvy enough to pull off such a betrayal.

But Dre...he's not only smart and savvy, he's also ruthless. And now that Carmine is gone, he's my underboss. My second in command. My heir if I were to be assassinated.

For the first time in my life, I find myself questioning everything, including my closest friendships with men I thought would die for me. Men who took oaths of not only silence but loyalty until their deaths.

After all, Dre left the main floor of the club right before shit went down, like maybe he was trying to stay out of the gunfire.

Goddammit. I need some sleep and a shower to get my head straight.

I hate even thinking such a fucked-up thing about my cousin, one of my closest friends. But I can't afford to let my guard down around anyone, not when I'll never get to see my brother again. I'll never be able to hear his taunts or teasing voice. He could always find a way to make me lighten up and laugh, no matter what serious shit we were dealing with.

At our father's funeral, after everyone had talked about what a good man the asshole was, Carmine went up last in front of a packed church. Hundreds of people had showed up to pay their respect to the ruthless bastard. He began normal enough with — "Yea, though I walk through the valley of the shadow of death" — which was then followed by him reciting the entire first verse of "Gangster's Paradise," all with a straight fucking face.

I had to walk out of the church, where I laughed until tears soaked my cheeks — the only tears I ever shed for our old man.

A decade later, it's still impossible to think about Carmine's audacity in that moment without smiling.

My brother was a good man, better than me or my father. That much I know for a fact.

So, I don't care how long it takes. I will find every person who was responsible and make them pay.

Pressing my thumb and fingers to the bridge of my nose to dry the corners of my eyes, I mutter, "Fuck. I need to get to the funeral home and start making arrangements. Will one of you get in touch with an employee at The Vault and have them give you the footage of Thursday night? If Jasper wasn't dead, I would've been suspicious of him."

I don't tell any of them about the mystery woman just yet. First, I want to talk to her, then see if she'll squeal and tell me who hired her to set me up.

"It definitely wasn't Jasper. He was shaking like a leaf when I found him and brought him down to meet with us," Dre remarks.

Leaning against the railing, I stare at him for several moments, then say shit I probably should've swallowed. "Funny you should mention that you were upstairs when the shooting started."

"I was on the fucking ground floor when that shit happened! Jasper dropped right in front of my goddamn face. I was wearing Jasper's fucking blood!"

"And I was wearing Carmine's!" I remind him.

"Both of you just chill for a minute." Tristan steps in between us. "Nobody should've died like that, especially not Carmine or Jasper. And now we're also stuck with bullshit charges following us around that might land our asses in prison if we start stirring shit up too much. We all smell like stale garbage and need some decent sleep in an actual bed. It's a lot to deal with in a few days. It could've been anyone who set us up, but it wasn't any of us, Creed." He shakes his head. "I fucking hate that my goddamn face was in a pair of tits when Carmine got popped. I should've been there, should've had his back." He turns to Dre. "We're going to do what the boss thinks is best without bitching. I'm sure none of us will be stupid enough to get caught, especially him, when we should all assume that eyes are on us every second of the day."

Dre gives a nod, and I try to tell my paranoia to settle the hell down. It's the last thing I need right now.

"A ride is on the way to pick us up," Lorenzo says as he slips his phone back into his suit pocket. "From here on out, boss, you should probably keep a few men close to watch your back."

"I don't want any bodyguards lurking around me."

"What do you mean you don't want any bodyguards after what went down?" he asks with a furrowed brow.

"I'm going to the funeral home alone. We'll all work alone when we're watching the families too. It'll draw less attention."

"Then you'll still need a driver."

"I'll go on foot or take a car out myself."

"No fucking way," Dre huffs. "When was the last time you were even behind a steering wheel?"

"Are you insinuating that I don't know how to fucking drive myself around my own goddamn city?"

"It's not as easy as it looks, boss," Tristan remarks. "And your cars aren't exactly…discreet."

"There seems to be some sort of misunderstanding here," I tell them. "This isn't a group decision. It's mine alone. Is that clear?"

"Fine. Just…be careful," As if sensing my distrust in him, Dre adds, "We will get revenge for Carmine."

"I know we will," I grit out. "We start after the funeral. And I want to know everything you three find out. No matter how small."

5

Zara

"Hurry your fat ass up!"

"Ah, honey. We've got to work on your pickup lines, or you're never going to get laid," I coolly inform the rude ass boy standing behind me. The one pressing the muzzle of his gun to the center of my spine through my sweaty tee.

"Shut up and load the bags faster before I put you out of your misery."

"The insults and gun pokes really are unnecessary, Eugene," I tell the masked kid as I continue loading last year's Christmas totes bursting with groceries into the trunk of the car.

"Don't say my name!" he hisses.

"Right. Sorry." I wince, since I really didn't mean to let his name slip. "You know, if you want to speed things along, you could help me load these."

Most people would probably be terrified of being held at

gunpoint, but after enduring the whims of mobsters and working as a cashier at a corner discount store in New York City for the past three years, not much scares me anymore.

I actually prefer being robbed to being visited by sleezy mafiosos and sent on bullshit errands that end in bloodshed.

Two men are dead.

Not just any men, but the younger brother and club manager of the notorious mafia don, Creed Ferraro. Every time I close my eyes, I see that poor man bleeding out on the floor while Creed begged for help that never came.

If I'd known what Izaiah was planning when he sent me with his "warning," I never would've agreed to do it.

Okay, I probably would've eventually agreed, since Izaiah no doubt would've threatened to never let me see Oriana again if I refused. But only then would I have caved.

Finally done with loading the bags of expired groceries and hoping it's enough to get three kids through the week, I slam the trunk closed and give it a pat with my flattened palm. "You're all set. See you next Thursday?"

"If you tell anyone who I am, you'll fucking regret it."

"Yeah, yeah, tough guy. My lips are sealed, just as long as you don't shoot anyone, and you return this POS to whoever you stole it from before the sun comes up. I would hate for you to go down for grand theft auto."

"Fine," he mutters as he shoves his gun into the back of his tattered jeans and hurries around to the driver's side.

"Have a good night. Drive safe. Oh, and keep that gun away from your sisters!" I shout at him before I walk back into the storeroom through the loading dock and lock up.

About three months ago, Eugene came in and tried to rob me while I was working the front register. I explained to him that there wasn't much cash on hand. After all, most items on the shelves are less than five dollars, and everyone uses debit or credit cards nowadays. That's when I explained to him he'd probably be better off stealing bags of groceries.

He finally admitted in defeat that he was a high school dropout just trying to feed his two little sisters.

So, I made Eugene a deal.

Every Thursday, I discreetly round up all the expired products, the loaves of bread going bad, any produce or fruit that's seen better days, frozen goods close to expiring, and "accidentally" opened toiletry items. I toss it all into seasonal bags in the storeroom and then hand them over when he pulls up to "rob" me somewhere between nine and ten at night while his sisters are sound asleep. The gun is simply to keep me from losing my job if my manager finds out what I've been doing. There aren't any working cameras in the store or alley, but I can't risk my paycheck.

Actually, I think it's sweet that Eugene loves his siblings enough to rob shitty little groceries stores for them. He's never mentioned his mom or dad, and I've never asked about them because I know all about having wretched parents.

Sometimes, during the week when Eugene is really desperate, he comes in as a regular customer and walks out with more than he paid for in his pockets to hold him over until Thursday.

Do I feel guilty for giving the kid, who isn't old enough to vote, the store's expired goods or letting him shoplift? Hell no. I do the job of two people, working ten or twelve-hour shifts, seven days a week, as an assistant manager, and I can still barely feed myself after paying rent.

Just like Eugene said, killing me *would* put me out of my misery. Because that's all this life is.

I'm sick of trying to do the "right" thing and be a good person when all that's gotten me is sore feet, an empty bank account, and a life that consists solely of working and sleeping. Oh, and eating obviously. I tend to eat to ease the pain of having such a pathetic existence.

I wish I could say that I made bad decisions that led to my demise. The truth is, I've always been at the mercy of other people's demands, constantly manipulated. Just like when Izaiah made me go to that damn club and set up a don for a morning at the zoo with my daughter.

While the Rovinas like to pretend that I have a choice, I never do. And unfortunately, their constant manipulation is not going to stop anytime soon.

This is the shitty hand life has dealt me, so I have no choice but to play it.

~

It's close to midnight by the time I walk home and get to take a cool shower to wash away the day's dirt and sweat. I comb my fingers through my long, sodden curls and pile the wet strands on top of my head in a messy bun, then wrap an old, nearly see-through beach towel around my still damp body, tucking it into the front of my chest. It's way too muggy to put on clothes just yet, and I'm not yet tired enough to sleep after my twelve-hour shift.

Strolling out into my slightly cooler seven-hundred square foot apartment, I debate killing the air conditioner to open the window and save a little on my electric bill when my bare feet come to an abrupt halt.

"Oh, shit."

A massive, manspreading mobster sits in the middle of my ratty sofa with my broken-hinged laptop on his lap. There's a big-ass gun with a silencer on the muzzle, lying a fingertip away from his thigh on the cushion next to him. He's staring at me over the top of the crooked screen with a clenched, unshaven jaw.

"Hello, *Zara*."

His deep, rumbling voice and clipped words make it clear he is not messing around.

Tall, dark, and dangerously handsome in his flawless black suit, he stares back at me with nothing but violence brimming in his eyes. With his wavy, shoulder-length jet-black hair and aura of wrath, he looks exactly how I imagine death would look if it was masquerading as a human.

Accabadore.

Beautiful but deadly, he's the Italian mafia's angel of death.

I didn't see the danger in him last week in the dim light of the nightclub, but tonight, there's no escaping it.

Dammit! I knew Izaiah was going to drag me into deep shit. Not only does Creed Ferraro know my name, but he also knows where I live, and is going to shoot me in the middle of my shitty Queens apartment.

Grasping my towel tighter to my chest, I glance over my damp shoulder at the locked and chained door.

"Wh-how did you get in here?"

Yes, that's the most important question to ask the man who has obviously come to kill you. Like the logistics will help me out of this disaster.

"The window." His voice is tight, his angular face stern. "Do you know why I'm here, Zara?"

I immediately nod as my gaping mouth completely dries up. The way he keeps saying my name, he makes it sound like a swearword or an accusation. Maybe both.

Of course, I know why he's here. His brother is dead, and he rightfully blames me. I blame Izaiah, but I doubt he'd believe that son of a bitch made me do it. Still, I want to try to explain.

Wetting my lips enough so I can try to speak, I tell him, "I swear I didn't know what was going to happen. I-I thought —"

"Bullshit!" he roars. Flipping my laptop onto the sofa next to him, he surges to his feet. When he begins stalking toward me, I retreat until my back hits the closed and locked door.

I have two choices here. I could try to unlock the bolt and chain and outrun the man who is nearly a foot taller than me at five-eight, or I can try to reason with the don.

"I'm sorry," I blurt out, unable to think of anything else to say to a man who just lost his brother.

"You're sorry?" he repeats quietly. I think I prefer him yelling in anger. Just like I knew it was coming, his fist slams into the door right next to my head making me jump. I swear my heart is going to race its way right out of my chest. "No, you're not sorry. Not yet. But you're going to be. And you're not the only one."

He stares down at me, his eyes a fierce ocean blue, as if waiting for me to name names. When I don't, he says, "I borrowed your phone while you were washing up. While I was *watching* you shower."

Oh god. He was in my apartment this whole time — with the bathroom door wide open. It never occurred to me that a don would sneak through my freaking window!

"I read your text messages back and forth with someone you listed in your contacts as Piece of Shit."

Uh-oh.

He presses his large palm on the other side of my face, caging me in with his much larger body. "I think my favorite message was when you told him I was standing at the bar just moments before the raid. Right where my *dead* brother stood when those cops came in and shot him!"

"I didn't have a choice! He asked me…"

"How much did he pay you to get my family's blood all over your hands?"

"Nothing. And I tried to warn you and your friends to leave!"

"You should've tried harder!"

"I-I couldn't," I confess. "Someone might've seen me if I had just walked right up to you and started blabbing. What I did, calling you over to warn you, he will *kill* me if he finds out…"

"*He* being Izaiah Rovina?"

I nod, since I have no reason to protect that jackass. In fact, it would be a relief if he was permanently removed from my life.

"It was stupid of him to use his actual phone number to text you," Ferraro remarks.

"He's an idiot," I agree. "He-he did tell me to delete the thread afterwards..."

"Why didn't you delete it?"

His voice sounds slightly calmer, his eyes a little less hostile, as if he's genuinely curious, and we're just two people having a normal conversation without a guillotine hanging over my head.

And while I know I should fear him, the man people in the city refer to as the angel of death, it's hard to fear someone so damn attractive. The "angel" part of his nickname is well deserved. Creed Ferraro is one beautiful bastard. I thought so the other night, and that opinion is reinforced by his close proximity tonight.

Shoving all those thoughts out the window, I shrug my shoulders. "In case you climbed through my window one night, and I needed to try to shift all the blame to that stupid piece of shit?"

His eyes narrow. "Cute."

I'm actually not lying. After the raid, I even considered taking the messages straight to Ferraro as an apology, but I was afraid he'd kill me on sight before I could say a word. Hoping Creed Ferraro would kill Izaiah was a longshot, one I couldn't risk if it didn't work out. Rumors say the Rovina and Ferraro families are supposedly tight allies.

The two of us stare at each other. I'm trying to figure out his next move, and if I had to guess, he's trying to decide if he's going to kill me right where I stand, smushed against the wall, wearing nothing but a towel.

Not that Ferraro seems the least bit tempted by what's underneath the cloth, which is unfortunate. I'm used to using my body as a distraction for assholes, but this mobster only has murder on his mind.

A sudden booming thud echoes through my skull hard enough to rattle my entire body. It takes me a moment to realize that it's someone knocking on the other side of my door. Ferraro's men come to help him kill me and dispose of my body?

Leaning closer, so close his open suit jacket brushes against my towel, and I get a whiff of his rich, clean scent, the mob boss whispers in my ear, "Guess who that is."

I gasp in understanding, just before his annoying voice shouts, "Open the fucking door, Zara! What's so damn important it couldn't wait?"

Ferraro must have texted Izaiah from my phone and invited him over. How ironic that he's using the brazen asshole's own tactic against him.

Lowering his voice even more, Ferraro says, "I'm going to wait in the bathroom while you get him to confess to everything."

"Could I at least put some clothes on first?" I implore him in a rush.

He glances down at the towel I'm clutching, as if seeing it for the first time. "No."

With that, he steps away from me.

I suck in a rush of air as I watch him retrieve his gun from the sofa before slipping into the bathroom. He leaves the door open but flips the light off.

Knowing he's in there, waiting to pounce on Izaiah, makes me ecstatic. Creed Ferraro is most likely going to kill Izaiah Rovina, something I've dreamed of doing myself for years, even if his death wouldn't really solve any of my problems.

And for once, being manipulated by a mafioso doesn't feel like a bad thing.

Ferraro is trusting me not to give him away, which makes me feel like I actually have some power for the first time in my life. He must have realized that I hate Izaiah enough or know him well enough to realize Izaiah is no match for *Accabadore*. After all, I saved the texts from Izaiah, proving his guilt and was quick to throw him under the bus. Would I do that if I gave a shit about the man?

It just sucks that once Ferraro kills Izaiah, I probably won't get to live long enough to spit on his grave.

Behind me, the asshole pounds on the door again loud enough to shake it, no doubt waking up all my neighbors.

Closing my eyes, I take a slow deep breath and then spin around to unlock the bolt and chain with a slightly shaky hand.

God, I don't even know what the text Ferraro sent says, so I'll just have to wing this conversation.

As soon as I turn the doorknob, Izaiah pushes past me and into my apartment. He's dressed down in jeans and a tee, as if he's given up trying to look the part of his filthy rich mafia father's heir.

"What's so important you couldn't say it over the phone?" he asks while I shut and lock the door. "And why the hell did you tell me to park half a mile down the road?"

Ferraro is staying one step ahead if he told him not to park in the apartment lot.

Trying to think just as fast, I tell him, "I think someone has been following me."

"What? Who? What do they look like?" he demands.

"I-I couldn't see them. They were in an SUV with dark tinted windows." I decide to keep the description vague. And it works.

"What kind of SUV? Was it a silver Maserati?"

"Maybe. I don't know all the car brands and logos."

"It's car models! Do you know fucking colors?"

"Yes, I know colors," I huff indignantly. "It was…grayish. I think. It was dark and hard to see when I was leaving work."

"Jesus, Zara! What the hell did you do? Did someone in the club see you talking to Jasper?"

"I-I don't know. I don't think so. I gave him the message, word for word like you told me, 'Ferraro has a bullseye on his head, and there's a sniper coming for him who won't miss,' then I left his office and went down to wait for Ferraro to show like you instructed me to do. Was the raid what you were trying to warn him about?"

"Fuck no. I wasn't warning him about the raid, you stupid cunt! The whole thing was a trap."

Yes, idiot, keep spilling all your secrets while insulting me. Maybe Ferraro will let me live if he hears proof it was Izaiah who set up the raid that got his brother killed.

"A trap?" I play dumb.

"You weren't there when the bullets started flying?" Izaiah asks. "Now that I think about it, I didn't see your name on the witness report."

Ferraro and the other men were taken out in handcuffs. Then, his brother was taken out on a gurney, leaving behind a puddle of blood I still have nightmares about. That's when I told an officer it was my time of the month, that I needed to use the restroom to change my tampon. I snuck out the bathroom window into an alley where not a single officer was stationed.

"I, um, I went to the bathroom and then I left the club, so I missed the raid. I did hear about it on the news. Two people died because of you."

"The fuckers were supposed to kill Creed and his brother."

"Oh." Izaiah is so screwed, which makes me so damn happy. "Why?"

"Not that it's any of your goddamn business," he grumbles. "But they're the only two Ferraros everyone trusts to keep shit running right. Once they're out of the picture, my family will take their place at the head of the table."

"And you're not worried about any of those cops that killed Carmine Ferraro, you know, talking to anyone?"

"No, because only two of them knew the full plan, and now they're both six feet under."

"Did you…did you kill them?"

"Suicides. Both left notes about how they were guilt-stricken because of their mistakes during the raid."

"Wow. You thought of everything," I lie right to his face. "Does your dad know about all this? It was his idea, wasn't it?"

When Izaiah doesn't respond but curses and suddenly begins to pace in front of me — his fists clenching, mumbling to himself — I realize why he's suddenly so fidgety.

Izaiah wouldn't have told me all this information if he was going to let me live.

Fucking A.

"I didn't want to have to do this," he mutters more to himself. "You should've been more careful. Gotta clean up the mess you made…"

"What are you talking about?"

"How to do it…how to do it? Here? Now? The clock is ticking…Gotta get the hell out of here."

Oh yeah. He's definitely plotting my death, trying to decide which way is the least messy way to take me out.

For once, I'm glad my apartment is so small. Two steps to the left and I'm standing in front of the drawer where I keep my spoons, forks, and really big, incredibly sharp knives.

Trying to play it off when I open the drawer, I say, "You know what? I just got home from work and I'm starving. Do you want a sandwich?"

Two seconds later, the drawer rattles when I open it. My fingers curl around the first knife I can reach as the drawer slams closed on my wrist. The ache causes me to cry out and drop the knife.

I don't even have a chance to turn around before Izaiah grabs my hair and presses cold steel to my throat.

"It's a shame I have to do this, but it's your own fucking fault," he says into my ear before he rips my towel off me and squeezes my bare breast. "God, I'm going to miss fucking your filthy mouth and cunt."

My heart seizes up in a panic. What if this was Ferraro's plan all along? Let Izaiah kill me, then he only has to kill Izaiah.

"Might as well have you one last time…"

The distinct sound of a gun being cocked interrupts his plans. I feel Izaiah's entire body stiffen behind me, sending one hell of a thrill through my soul.

"Drop the knife, Rovina."

If I thought Ferraro's voice was scary earlier, it's nothing compared to the amount of venom in it now.

Izaiah isn't the smartest man, but he is a vicious don's son and not going down without a fight. He pulls the knife from my neck.

Instinctively, I drop to my knees, getting as low as I can, and scurry away to watch the show.

Ferraro looks like an enraged god when he slams his fist into Izaiah's face, then easily ducks Izaiah's sloppily slashing knife over and over again. His clothes receive a few tears, but I don't see any blood.

What is he waiting for? Izaiah to slice his throat, then mine?

"Shoot him already!" I shout impatiently.

Finally, Ferraro spins around and slips behind Izaiah. With his arm banded across Izaiah's chest, pinning his arms to his sides, he lifts the gun and presses the silencer to Izaiah's temple with the other.

But he doesn't pull the trigger.

Both men are now facing me, and it feels like time is standing still.

Ferraro's eyes meet mine with something like uncertainty in them, while Izaiah's gaze holds nothing but murder and contempt. If I had to guess, Ferraro is either worried about me being a witness or whether Izaiah deserves to die.

"Look away, Zara."

I can't look anywhere but at the final ending of one of my worst nightmares. And Ferraro hesitates a second too long.

There's no time to even warn him before Izaiah slams his knife into the side of Ferraro's thigh once, twice.

The don barely flinches. His gun goes off with one soft puff of air.

When Ferraro releases his hold on Izaiah, he drops. His knees hit the ground, followed by his upper body, leaving his lifeless form lying face down on my apartment floor.

It's over.

It's finally done.

Izaiah Rovina is dead.

If I'm about to meet my end, too, at least I won't have to worry about him touching me or my daughter ever again.

6

Creed

Once we find out who's responsible for Carmine's death, we need to carefully plan our revenge.
Don't lash out impulsively.
Everyone better keep their heads nice and cool, especially with the gun charges already hanging over our heads.

Those were my words, spoken to not just Dre, Tristan, and Lorenzo, but dozens of my hot-headed men over the last few days.

Days passed by in a blur as I held a service, laid my brother to rest, and had to endure the endless line of people offering their sympathy when the only thing I wanted to do was get drunk, crawl into a hole somewhere, and never come out.

I couldn't even shed a fucking tear for him, at least not in public. Dons don't cry or show any sign of weakness. That shit isn't allowed. So, I stuffed my feelings of loss down deep to deal with later. Right now, I'm just angry.

So angry that the day after I buried my brother, I'm standing in the middle of a tiny apartment in Queens with another don's dead son at my feet. His knife still jutting out of my thigh, and a beautiful, completely naked witness staring up at me like I'm not a murderous monster, but her new hero and savior.

Goddamn her!

Why did she have to be involved in this shit? If she hadn't set everything in motion, we never would've gone to The Vault that night, and Carmine would still be alive.

And my brother was wrong about what's in her panties; she has a pretty little pussy, not big, brass balls.

Jesus. Between my grief, fury, and lack of sleep, I know I'm not firing on all cylinders. I should've gone home after finding her at the grocery store, not stalked the parking lot for an hour before following Zara back to her apartment.

But there was something in my gut, telling me she was going to be the key to proving it was Izaiah Rovina and his father who came at me through the club raid.

And I was right.

I have her phone with the text messages from Izaiah and the recorded audio of his confession before he tried to kill her.

So why didn't I let him slit her throat?

She deserves to be punished for the part she played in my brother's death. It's not something I can ever forgive or forget.

My father would've put her and Izaiah down as soon as he saw the texts. He never hesitated to take out anyone who got in his way or threatened his livelihood, not even my own mother, the love of his life.

She stupidly thought the three of us would be safe in witness protection after she took my father's money, ratted him and his men out to the feds, and ran off. She was wrong.

I still remember the day my father came for us. I've never seen him so goddamn furious. He was like a tornado, blowing through the house, smashing and destroying every object in his path until he found the three of us hiding in the attic.

After he unloaded those bullets into her body, he asked me and Carmine if we understood why she had to die. I gave a nod of understanding, even though I didn't really know why. I was still in shock at his violent attack on the woman who loved and raised us, who I knew he had once loved. I saw them together every single day. There was no other way to describe their relationship. My father loved my mother and would've done anything for her. Still, he killed her when she betrayed him.

I've never killed a woman in cold blood, and I'm not entirely sure I could.

Now, here I am with Izaiah dead, and Zara a fucking witness to his murder.

Not that I will ever regret killing him.

That fucker admitted he was responsible for the raid. He deserved what he got for killing Carmine and Jasper. I just hate that I had to do it so swiftly, right in front of Zara, giving her the power to end my life as I know it.

My freedom lies in the hands of an odd woman, who I'm almost certain aided an armed robber earlier tonight.

And if I let her live, she can never leave my sight. I can't have her run off to the police and tell them what I've done, or worse, go tell Emilio Rovina I killed his oldest son before I find evidence he ordered Izaiah to set up the raid.

I hate I didn't get Izaiah to confess to his father's role before ending him. Maybe there will be messages from Emilio in Izaiah's phone. If he was involved, he's dead too. I'll just have to be much smarter about his death if I want to avoid a mafia war. And being smarter means having solid proof he's guilty to show the other families.

But that's a problem for another day.

Right now, I've got a huge mess to clean up or else I'll end up serving a life sentence in prison.

"Now what?" Zara's voice sounds way too calm. I expected crying or screaming, not a simple question. One I don't have the answer to yet.

"Now I have to figure out what the fuck to do with him. And by the way, I have your phone, so there's no way for you to call the police."

Without hesitating, she says, "I don't want to call the police."

"Right."

"I know who his father is, and I don't want that even bigger piece of shit to find out his son died in my apartment. We have to get him out of here, then clean everything fast."

She talks about Emilio like she knows him personally. What the hell is her connection to the Rovinas? And why is she so blasé about Izaiah's murder?

I'll figure that out later.

First, I need to deal with my impulsive, idiotic decision. "Well, this obviously wasn't the ideal location for a hit. Removing him without any residents or the apartment cameras noticing is going to be...challenging," I say, mostly to myself.

Eying the deceased man with lips pursed as if she's annoyed more by the inconvenience of his death than his loss of life, the naked woman says, "There are two cameras at the front of the building, so we could put him in trash bags, roll him up in the rug that's ruined anyway...and send him down the trash chute."

"Whoa. What? You want me to just throw him down the fucking trash chute like garbage?"

"Yes. Fitting for him, right?" she replies coolly. "The landlord is too cheap for a compactor, so you don't have to worry about that. You can drive around back where there are no cameras that I know of, prop open the door, and fish him out of the dumpster.

Unless you have a better idea that can get rid of him within the next few minutes?"

There has to be a better idea, but I'm not coming up with anything right now. Probably because she's still kneeling on the floor buck-ass naked with the heaviest, most delicious pair of swaying tits I've ever seen.

I haven't been alone in the same room with a naked woman in over a year, much less one on her knees. My tightening pants are causing a huge distraction that I sure as shit don't need at the moment.

As if suddenly remembering her nudity herself, or more likely because she caught me staring at her tits, Zara slaps one arm over her chest and the other over her lap. "I'm going to put some clothes on while you make a decision."

"No." The word leaves my mouth before I can stop it. And since I'm still waving my gun around in my hand, it sounds like a command. Grasping for a valid reason to keep her beautiful body bare a little bit longer, I tell her, "You're going to help me get him out of here and clothes are just more evidence we'll have to destroy later."

We? Fuck. I'm not sure when this turned into a team effort, but since I can't bring myself to put a bullet in her head, I guess...I guess we're in this together now.

Besides, I have her phone in my pants pocket, so she can't call anyone. If she tries to run, I'm certain I can chase her down.

And if she's naked, it's an even bigger incentive for her not to take off running down the streets of New York. Although, I would give up my new Lamborghini Urus for a chance to watch her run a naked mile.

Either my reasoning is solid enough, or I look threatening enough, that Zara doesn't get up from the floor.

"Are you going to do something about that knife sticking out of your leg?" she asks rather than argue about the lack of clothing.

"If I pull the knife out, I'm going to bleed everywhere, leaving behind more of my DNA."

"I have an idea. May I get up?"

"Yes," I agree, thoroughly enjoying this power dynamic where she asks my permission. I'm certain that the longer a man goes without sex, the stupider he becomes around women. At least, that much is true in my case. "Don't even think about trying to bolt, though. I can run you down, even with the knife."

Nodding, Zara pushes herself to her feet, then literally tiptoes over, the soles of her feet never touching the floor, to pick up her discarded towel. I'm about to protest her putting it on and hiding her lovely curves when she says, "Could you jump over him?"

Jump over him, she asks, casually referring to the corpse like he's an ordinary obstruction.

She is by far the oddest woman I've ever met, and this is the strangest fucking encounter of my entire life. Those two things are increasingly becoming reasons why I think I want to keep her rather than kill her.

Certain Izaiah is good and dead, I flip the safety on my gun, shove it in the back of my pants, and step over his prone form. Lifting and lowering my left foot sends jolts of pain through my entire limb that I have to grit my teeth to get through. Instead of the discomfort, I focus on following Zara's lead, staying on my toes until I clear the blood pooling around him on the rug, careful not to get any on my shoes.

Once I'm clear of the corpse, she grabs the towel she was wearing and kneels on the floor again within touching distance, her face directly in front of my crotch.

"What are you doing?" I ask her, confused, about to take a step back before I remember the corpse.

"Studying the wound. I'm going to pull the knife out, then quickly wrap the towel around your leg so it won't bleed everywhere. You can move easier without it, right?"

Oh. Knife removal makes much more sense than a blowjob at this particular moment in time. I can literally feel the stupid growing stronger within me.

I need to get my head out of the gutter and take my eyes off her tits before the distraction kills me. This is certainly not the time or place to be horny.

"Well?"

"Fine. Do it fast," I tell her while staring up at the ceiling. I'm not sure why I trust she won't remove the knife then immediately stab me in the dick, but I do. Probably because I know she needs my help hauling the dead body out of her apartment. Without me, she would have two to dispose of.

Before this rash decision, I've always been meticulous and strategic to avoid mistakes, never making assumptions, which is the opposite of this quick-thinking woman's plans that have plans so far tonight.

I'm not entirely sure if her ideas are even good ones, but since time is of the essence, I'm willing to follow her lead. For now, at least, until all my blood returns to my brain so it can work at full strength again. I'm used to being the one everyone turns to for orders that I find it's nice to have someone else helping call the shots for once. That shit gets exhausting.

Zara wraps her fingers around the hilt of the knife still protruding from my thigh and I tell her, "For a moment, I thought you might warn Piece of Shit that I was in the bathroom when you let him in the apartment."

She nods. "For a moment, I thought you might let Piece of Shit kill me to save yourself the trouble," she replies right before she yanks the knife free.

I clench my teeth through the pain as she wraps the thin, frayed beach towel around my leg, then ties the ends tightly over the wound.

"That should hold it for a while. At least he didn't hit anything vital. The wounds look small, the bleeding minimal."

The bleeding is just getting started.

Izaiah Rovina declared war with the Ferraro family when he came after me and my brother. Now, if or when Emilio finds out I killed him, it could be a catastrophic feud where all five families are forced to choose sides.

After years of doing everything in my power to keep the peace, I knew it was only a matter of time before something like this would eventually happen. But if it had been me who Izaiah killed, Carmine probably would've done the same thing. I'd like to think Dre would have, too, if the raid killed me and Carmine both.

Izaiah drew blood first, and now I have the recording on my phone of his confession. Evidence that could come in handy if this bites me in the ass. I'll only use it if necessary. If I'm careful, I can minimize the fallout. Make it look like Izaiah disappeared because he got scared after he failed to kill me.

I'll have to pretend like everything is fine with Emilio until I can prove he gave Izaiah the orders to take me and Carmine out. I don't see Izaiah being ambitious enough to try for the seat at the head of the Council table. His father though…

That son of a bitch was trying his best to convince me to marry his daughter, to solidify our alliance through future generations, telling me it's what my father wanted.

It was all bullshit. Hell, I thought our alliance was rock solid.

My brother was right. I would've been crazy to marry the viper bitch. There's nothing in that deal that would benefit me. It could've been Emilio's plan to have Stella kill me this whole time.

Part of me wants to go tell him I killed his son and blow his head off right now for taking Carmine.

But I have to play this smarter than Emilio.

And I'll need to do it fast, since the gun charges from the raid are hanging over my head. I wasn't planning on adding first-degree murder to my rap sheet, but when Izaiah held a knife to Zara's throat, I didn't have a choice.

I was standing in the bathroom, recording his confession, willing to wait it out to make his death look like an accident when he attacked her. It felt like I was drowning in the blurred haze of my fury, and something inside of me just fucking snapped.

Izaiah was a dead man before he even ripped her towel off. That piece of shit never deserved the right to touch this woman, and he sure as shit doesn't get to fuck her.

Why did she even let him in her life to begin with?

When Zara stands up in front of me, she's tall for a woman, but the top of her head only comes up to my chest. "What's someone like you doing with a guy like Izaiah Rovina anyway?"

"It's not like I ever wanted to be…involved with him." She scowls over at his body. "It just sort of happened one day."

"Is he an ex-boyfriend or what?"

She shakes her head. "Not really. He was a manipulative bastard who knew what buttons of mine to push to get whatever he wanted."

That doesn't sound like a consensual relationship, but more like he was blackmailing her. A tiny smidge of my anger at her dissolves.

"We should start cleaning up, or he's going to bleed through to the floor," she points out.

"One more question before we bag him and roll him up."

Her cautious eyes lift to mine, and she crosses her arms over her chest impatiently. "Okay?"

"Earlier, back at the store, did you wish an armed robber a good night and tell him to drive safe?"

Her eyes widen. "You saw that? How?"

"I was watching you. I even considered intervening when I saw the gun," I admit. "Despite the fact you got my brother killed."

What is it about this woman that made me throw my body on

hers without thinking when there was gunfire, wanting to save her from a gunman, and now…this mess with Izaiah?

Zara winces and drops her arms. "Well, I'm glad you didn't intervene. Eugene is a regular. He's just a kid."

"A regular…customer or robber?"

"Yes."

"You've never reported him to the store or to the police?"

"No. He's only seventeen, and he's raising his two little sisters. I just gather products that are about to expire to give to him."

The fact she didn't run to the police about an armed robber but instead decided to help him on a weekly basis makes me worry a tiny bit less about her turning me in.

Then again, murder and a few bags of expired products aren't in the same league.

"I'm not going to go to the police," she says as if reading my mind. "In fact, how about after we get him down the chute, we load him up in your car and then just forget this all happened? You go…do whatever you need to with him, and I'll go to sleep. I won't ever tell a soul. Besides, I'll be an accomplice after I help carry him out of here, right?"

Zara's naivety is actually cute as she stands before me all confident and sexy, pressing her tits together on purpose. In fact, there's surprisingly only a faint hint of fear showing in her cat-like green eyes.

"This isn't something we can pinkie promise about and go our separate ways. You know I can't let you walk away now, *micetta mia*." I inwardly cringe after the words roll off my tongue.

She shivers, making me feel like a dick for refusing to give her clothes. Slipping off my jacket, I remove my phone from the inner pocket, then hold it out for her to take. It's already evidence, and I can't think with her so close to me, naked.

"Thanks" She shoves her arms through the sleeves, as if she genuinely appreciates the gesture. She's an unusual girl. And I hate that she's covered up all that tempting ivory skin, but it's for the best. "So then, what happens next? After the cleanup?"

"I'm still figuring that out." I unfasten my cuffs and roll up my sleeves. What the hell am I going to do with her? There's no one I can even ask, since I don't want any of my men to know Izaiah Rovina is dead.

When I'm done securing both of my sleeves, I watch Zara button the front of my jacket. And damn, I like the way she looks in my coat that swallows her whole, brushing her knees, leaving only her lower legs bare. She's sexy as hell in my jacket and nothing else over her succulent breasts and incredible ass that I haven't gotten a chance to examine close enough.

I clear my throat. "For now, let's get him out of here. I'll worry about his car tomorrow. Grab some trash bags while I retrieve his keys and phone."

Zara inhales a deep breath. "Oh shit!"

"What?" I ask in concern. Her outburst is so sudden and unexpected, given she's been calm this far. Maybe it's finally hitting her that he's dead...

"You sent him messages from my phone, right? Even if we delete them, won't there be records on the cloud or from the phone company the police can get?"

"Yes," I answer honestly as I go over to search Izaiah's pockets.

"Fucking A!" she mutters. My lips twitch, despite the current circumstances. The swear word sounds hilarious coming from the twenty-something, innocent-looking, Shirley Temple.

"So, it's a good thing I employ some cyber geniuses. They can hopefully make the messages permanently disappear."

"And if they can't and the police suspect me?" she asks. "Oh, right. You would absolutely kill me to prevent me from talking to the cops."

"One step at a time. Now find us some trash bags." I pocket his car keys and begin to scroll through his unlocked phone.

7

Zara

Ferraro deletes my texts to and from Izaiah on his phone and mine, then destroys the device, frustrated that there were no messages tying Emilio Rovina to the club raid.

After that was handled, we covered his upper body in one bag, lower in another, then we rolled him up like a joint, starting with the part of the rug that's stained, along with his knife. To ensure he stays rolled up and spreads the least amount of DNA and fibers possible in the chute or dumpster, I wrapped an entire roll of plastic around him.

Then, somehow, Ferraro deadlifts and holds him in front of his body while I quickly cleaned the floors and even the walls with Clorox wipes. I get on my knees and search for even the tiniest drops. Once that's done, I wipe down my door, window, and laptop, erasing any of Izaiah's or Ferraro's fingerprints.

"That's good enough," he says.

"Okay. I think so too," I agree as I stand in front of the sink and survey the whole room again.

"Let's go, Zara."

I slip on a pair of flipflops, and since he objected to adding clothes, I'm ready to leave wearing nothing but his giant jacket that smells way too delicious for a killer. Not to mention how good he looks in the black button-down with rolled-up sleeves. It's a great choice of color to hide blood stains. Which reminds me…

"One last thing." I wet a kitchen towel under the sink faucet with cold water.

"What now?"

"Your face."

"What about my face?" he huffs.

"There's some blood on it." I have to stand on my tiptoes to reach over the bundle in his arms and scrub at the splatter on his cheek, then his neck before doing the same to the other side. There's even a little drop of crimson on his earlobe.

"Really?" he asks as he recoils.

"I think that's all of it." I swipe the towel over the slice of chest showing thanks to his open collar before my heels lower to the floor again.

Rather than trash the towel with Izaiah's DNA on it, I tuck it under the larger towel I tied on his thigh, so it won't bleed through.

"I'll take his legs, since they're lighter." I grab hold of the rug's end.

Rather than open the door, Ferraro stares me down, his brow furrowed. "Have you done this before?"

"Done what? Disposed of a body?"

"Yes."

"God, no. Why?"

"I think most women would sob and shit themselves if a man was killed in front of them by a don who also wants them dead."

"I've dealt with scarier things than my own death," I confess. "And some people deserve to die."

Ferraro nods. "Unlock the door and check to make sure the hallway is clear. Are you sure he'll fit in the chute?"

"Well, we won't know until we try."

"Go measure," he snaps.

"Measure? With what?"

"You don't have a measuring tape?"

"No, it's in my toolbox I left in my imaginary work shed out back."

He sighs. "This isn't going to work."

"It's going to work!" I assure him, letting go of the rug, since he doesn't need my help holding him up. "And when it does work, you better have come up with a plan that allows me to keep breathing. I could easily grab that gun from your ass and shoot you, you know."

"Why do you think I'm keeping my back away from you?"

Of course, he thought of that.

And since he seems so concerned that our Izaiah blunt won't fit down the hole, I go and grab my laptop from the sofa.

"What are you doing with that?"

"Measuring," I tell him. "My laptop has my phone messages on it, so we should bring it with us to destroy, and it's got a sixteen-inch screen. I'll measure the front of the rug and then go see if it'll fit in the chute."

"A tape measure would be more accurate, but I guess the laptop is better than nothing."

I get the dimension of one end of the Izaiah blunt, then slip out in to the dimly lit hallway and look both ways. At this time of night, it should be clear, so I tiptoe over to the chute at the end of the hallway, pull the door down using the cuff of Ferraro's jacket cloth to avoid fingerprints, and hold up my device.

Hurrying back to my apartment, I open the door and wave Ferraro forward. "It's a perfect fit if you can break the flimsy latch."

"Flimsy latch," he mutters. "If this works…"

"You'll let me live?" I know it's unfortunately not that simple, so I'm only a little disappointed when Ferraro doesn't answer. He slips past me sideways carrying the rug, slowly and carefully so he doesn't scrape it on the door frame, keeping his back to the opposite wall.

When he's clear, I twist the simple lock on the doorknob and shut the door from the outside, wondering if I'll ever see the inside of my tiny little apartment again.

It wasn't much, but it was mine. I busted my ass every single day to have a place of my own. Not that it ever really felt safe thanks to the Rovinas.

I'm so relieved that Izaiah is dead that I'm volunteering to be kidnapped. Because that's what this is right now. My wrists may not be handcuffed, and I may not be gagged while I help Ferraro get his body out of the apartment complex, but I'm not stupid. My fate is in the don's hands from here on out.

There's no one to help me or save me. I sure as shit can't go running to the police. I've heard rumors that half the police force work for the mafia, which would explain why they never get arrested or charged with anything.

Well, except recently with Ferraro. With his money and power, he'll probably find a way to make the gun charges disappear.

I can run, but I can never truly hide from the rich and powerful mafia families. The best I can hope for is to be helpful or tempting enough to convince Creed Ferraro to let me live.

Hurrying over, I use the jacket again to open the hatch, then hold my breath as Ferraro holds Izaiah and breaks the latch off with an impressive yank. Then, he shoves a human burrito through the slightly bigger hole.

A few thuds later and the rug disappears.

"It worked." Ferraro sounds surprised with his hands braced on his hips.

"I told you it would." My words are breathless, since I wasn't entirely sure we could pull it off.

"We'll take the stairs down so you can show me where the dumpster is, and then you're going to wait patiently in the SUV for me, aren't you?"

"Where else would I go?" I ask him seriously.

~

Less than five minutes later, and we're traveling down the dark, mostly empty, city streets... with one smelly-assed passenger.

"I'm going to need to take ten showers to get this stink off me," Ferraro complains from the driver seat. He only pulled Izaiah out of the dumpster and carried him for about two minutes to toss him in the truck, but apparently that's all the time it takes for the stench to sink into every fiber of your being.

"A huge oversight on my part," I mumble through his suit collar, using it to cover my nose and mouth. It should be illegal for a criminal to smell so damn good. I want to suffocate in the leather and cedar scent. "But again, you didn't have any better ideas."

He doesn't respond to my remark. But a few minutes later, he quietly chuckles softly while staring at the road. "My brother would be laughing his ass off at me right now." His good mood evaporates just as quickly as it appeared, a scowl replacing his grin.

I could help him dispose of a hundred bodies, but he's never going to forgive me for luring him and his brother to the club that night.

"So, um, where are we going to dump the body?" I ask to change the subject.

"I don't know yet." Yep, his tone is definitely icier than it was moments before.

"Are we just going to drive around the city with a smelly body in your backseat until you decide?"

"For now, yes. I'm going home to take a shower."

He said he's going home, not that "we" are going to his home.

I did my part. I helped the man clean up the mess he made in my apartment, and now…now I don't know what happens to me.

It was crazy for me to think I could just ask the don to trust me and let me head to bed after we loaded up Izaiah's body in his SUV. Of course, it wouldn't be that easy to convince him to let me go free. Creed Ferraro hasn't survived being one of the city's dons for years by being stupid.

I'm a witness to a murder. Not just any murder, but the murder of a don's son by the *capo dei capi*. At least I assume that's their power dynamic.

If Emilio finds out who killed Izaiah, it *will* start a war. Even if Emilio didn't know about the club setup, he'll want revenge for his son, just as Creed wanted revenge for his brother. It'll be an endless cycle of war that could affect the entire Rovina family.

The *entire* family.

I study Ferraro's profile as he drives. It's possible that we're going somewhere remote where he'll make me return his jacket, then dig my own grave, in the nude, before he shoots me and tosses me in with Izaiah.

And…I can't even blame him for being so ruthless. I know firsthand that people will do anything for the ones they love.

I'd kill anyone who hurts Oriana or go down swinging in my attempt.

I should be terrified of this mobster sitting next to me, but there's only one thing that truly worries me — would Ferraro hurt an innocent little girl?

I'm just about to ask Creed if there are any exceptions to his ruthlessness when he suddenly clears his throat and says, "The way I see it, *micetta mia*, we've got two options here."

Ah, we're finally getting down to the nitty gritty. "Only two options?" Does he mean like firing squad or lethal injection type options? And I don't know what *micetta mia* means, my something or another in Italian. It can't be anything good.

"Yes, only two options that will work for me, since I can't let you walk away now."

"Let's hear these options of yours, so we can get this over with." I steel myself physically and mentally as I clutch the armrest like a lifeline. Sure, I considered trying to jump out, but one look at me in flip-flops and a man's suit jacket, and everyone will assume I'm a crazy homeless person until Ferraro catches up to me.

"The first option is that I give you a swift death and bury you with Izaiah."

"Yeah, no, I'm not a big fan of that plan. I don't want to spend an eternity anywhere near that piece of shit. What's the second option?"

"The second option is much riskier for me, but…it would allow you to keep breathing."

"That sounds perfect. I do enjoy breathing, so I'm all for any plan where I get to stay alive."

Taking his eyes off the road, he turns to look at me, not the smartest thing to do when you're driving around with a dead man. His gaze slowly rakes over his jacket I'm huddling inside, from the collar to the bottom hem before returning to my eyes. "Are you absolutely sure about that?"

"Yes."

"Okay," he replies as his focus returns to the road again. His tattooed knuckles whiten as he grips the steering wheel tighter. "We'll go down to the City Clerk's office tomorrow morning and make it official."

"Great. Okay," I agree, letting out a relieved sigh that I'll get to live and see my daughter grow up. "What's at the City Clerk's office?"

"Our marriage license."

Our. Marriage. License?

He definitely said "our" as in my and his license for *marriage*.

My head pops up from his collar in disbelief. "Whoa! What? Who said anything about marriage?"

Even in the dim car, I can see Creed's jaw ticks. "Would you prefer if I go back to the first option?"

"No. No!" I affirm, even though I know there are some things worse than death. Is this going to turn out to be one of them? "Marriage? Really? Wh-why exactly would we need to get married?"

"Spousal privilege."

"Spousal privilege?" I repeat.

"All communications between spouses remain confidential, and you can't be forced to testify against a spouse in court."

"Ohhh," I mutter. "So, I wouldn't ever have to testify about what you did tonight?"

"You wouldn't have to testify about what happens tomorrow. I think I can get a judge to waive the waiting period and make it all official first thing in the morning. Then, you're going to help me get rid of Izaiah's body, and *that* will be covered by spousal privilege, even if the murder itself isn't, since we're not married yet."

How the hell did we go from discussing my imminent death to...me marrying the man who hates me for causing the death of his brother?

Ferraro must be joking.

Or plotting a punishment worse than death.

My stomach rolls, making me feel queasy, and it's not even because the cabin smells like rotten garbage.

"Well?" Creed asks.

"I'm guessing there's no such thing as a pinkie promise privilege?"

A grunt from him says now is not the time for jokes. "A sudden wedding will look suspicious to the family, but at least it will give us a cover for why you're moving in with me and staying by my side day and night."

"I'm moving in with you?" I blurt out.

"I told you that I can't just let you walk away. This arrangement will only work if I can keep an eye on you and be certain that you're not making any phone calls or speaking to anyone about what happened tonight."

"I can't just move in with you and skip the marriage step?"

"There's no roommate privilege," he replies. "I need a commitment from you if I'm going to try and trust you. What I did tonight...this isn't how I usually handle business. You cannot tell *anyone* what happened tonight, Zara. Not a soul. I don't even want my own men to find out. The family is already all up in arms after Carmine..." When he trails off, the sadness with which he says his brother's name, it makes me feel so damn guilty.

God, I hate Izaiah for not only causing this mess for Creed but making me the bad guy in his story.

My fingernails drum nervously on the door panel. "So, you're saying that if I want to live, all I have to do is marry you, move in, and never tell anyone what you did?"

"Yes."

"Wow. You drive a very hard bargain, Mr. Ferraro."

"Creed," he corrects me. "And...as an incentive for your cooperation, I'll consider opening an expense account for you with a monthly allowance."

"A monthly allowance? Like if I wash the dishes, you'll give me twenty bucks for a new pair of shoes?"

"We can negotiate your allowance later, but it will be a significant amount of money so that you'll be disinclined to betray me, not one you have to do anything to earn."

"Oh, so it's more of a bribe?"

"How much did Izaiah pay you for setting me up?" he asks yet again, his tone frigid.

"I told you — nothing. He said it was a favor."

"Right," he mutters, sounding unconvinced.

"It's true."

"Well, either way, this money isn't technically a bribe. It's an incentive. I'll have to get an attorney to draw up a prenup. Once it's signed, we can start off at a million a month."

"A million dollars?!" I twist in my seat, studying his face in the dim car interior to see if he's being serious.

He nods. "A million a month. Twelve million a year will be well worth it to avoid a life prison sentence. Or Emilio finding out before I take him out."

Holy shit on a stick. I consider telling him that I will marry him for free if he just promises to kill Emilio.

But then he may start asking questions, decide I'm not worth the headache, and dump me in a hole with Izaiah.

"Thanks to my new gun charges," Creed grits out with a pointed glare at me. "I'll probably be going to prison soon for at least three-and-a-half years. After I'm released, we can discuss getting divorced if I can trust you not to run your mouth by then. Just remember that if you tell anyone I killed Izaiah while I'm away, you'll go down as an accessory."

I already know that I'm in too deep to try to turn Creed into the police now. And boy do I have motive for wanting Izaiah dead. A criminal trial would not go well for me.

And if Creed is in prison for three-and-a-half-years, he won't be able to touch me. I'll basically be free.

"So, this would only be a temporary arrangement? For a few years?"

"Yes."

"And you want to take out Emilio Rovina before you go away? If he was involved in the police raid at the club?"

"Yes."

That sounds like a dream come true. I would have a great shot at custody once he's out of the way.

But, if it turns out Emilio wasn't part of the raid, he'll still be a pain in my ass.

"I have a question about you and Emilio," I start, trying to figure out how to ask what I want to know. "How does your…hierarchy work?"

"What?"

"The mafia hierarchy. I've heard that you're the scariest one that the other families answer to. Is that true?"

"I can't discuss the inner workings of the family with you," Creed says. "You already know enough to sink me as it is. Besides, we all take an oath of silence. The *omerta*. It's even the name of our social club because it's the foundation on which we exist."

"You can't just tell me if you're Emilio's boss? Or how you feel about him? You're worried about him finding out about Izaiah, right?"

"I would rather figure out if Emilio was behind Izaiah and the raid first, but if he starts getting suspicious, I may have no choice but to find a way to take him out…surreptitiously to protect my family."

Thank god.

"And the rest of *his* family? What happens to his other children if it comes down to that?"

"If they don't suspect me or cause me any problems, then Saint, Stella, and Cami can stay out of this shit."

I slump a little in my seat, pleased to hear that. "Okay. Good. That's…good to know."

"Why? Are you close with the Rovinas?"

"It's more complicated than that. I don't think the rest of the Rovinas even know I exist. Only Izaiah."

I'm just the Rovina family's filthy little secret they keep hidden.

Izaiah and Emilio only think of me as a harmless, powerless kitten without any claws.

If I marry Creed Ferraro and he really does give me an "allowance," then there's a possibility that I could save enough money to hire an attorney, one who can help me finally get custody of Oriana. Those chances go up with Emilio dead, and Creed is definitely my best bet for making that happen.

"I'll do it. I'll marry you."

He glances at me, then shakes his head. "Did it really take that long for you to decide marrying me was a better option than death?"

"Yes. Because some things —"

"Are worse than death," he finishes for me. Neither of us speak through several stoplights as we reach Manhattan. Then he says without looking at me, "I'm furious at you for setting me up, for being partially responsible for ending my brother's life, but I'm not going to hurt you unless you give me a reason to." His eyes cut to me, and he adds, "Don't give me a fucking reason to hurt you."

"Are those going to be your wedding vows?" I joke, even though there is nothing humorous about the unexpected warmth and... ache that begins to take hold within me, all thanks to the way he's looking at me.

The angel of death.

I just saw him kill a man, so I shouldn't be getting turned on by anything this man says or does.

For the first time since he mentioned the marriage, the word *husband* blares loudly in my head. In a few hours, Creed Ferraro is going to be my husband.

And I'm going to be his wife.

8

Creed

I park the SUV in the garage and lock it up with the harmless-looking roll of carpet in the cargo area before taking Zara up to my penthouse apartment.

She's silent as we take the service elevator to avoid running into people because of my new stench and her lack of attire.

No doubt, she's already second-guessing this decision.

I was stunned she hesitated to choose between death and marrying me.

The woman is a complete mystery. Some of my men wouldn't handle a cold-blooded murder with her amount of composure. They sure as hell couldn't throw out ideas as fast as Zara either. I have to admit they've been good ideas so far.

Still, it's impossible to forget that she played a role in Carmine's death, and I will never be able to forgive her. I can't forget the threat she poses to me if she runs her mouth.

"You'll sleep in my bedroom, so I can keep an eye on you. You'll be free to move around the penthouse when I'm not asleep, but this is still a confinement for you. I don't want to have to restrain you, but I will if you try anything."

"Again, where would I go?" she asks. "I can't go to the police, since I'm guilty here, too, and even if I didn't hate Emilio, he would blame me for Izaiah's death."

"You don't have any family in the city?"

"No. My parents live up in Pearl River. I haven't seen them since I moved to the city seven years ago. I would rather die than ask them for a damn thing. And in case you're wondering, I work twelve hours a day most days, so my only friends are the grocery delivery drivers."

All right then.

"At least you won't have to work twelve-hour shifts anymore," I point out to her.

"That's not exactly the benefit you think it is," Zara replies solemnly. "The only time I've ever been even sort of free is when I'm earning a paycheck rather than depending on someone else to pay my way."

I'm not entirely sure what that means. I want to ask as I unlock the door to my apartment, but I have company.

"Finally!" Dre's voice announces from my living room. "Wake up, shithead. He's home," he says, I assume, to Tristan.

Zara and I turn the corner of the partial wall that blocks off the foyer. I give her a warning look over my shoulder, and she returns it with a single nod of understanding.

Fuck, I hope I can trust her. If not…well, I'll do what I need to do.

And so much for adamantly refusing to marry a woman who doesn't want to be in the same room as me…

"What are you two doing here so late?" I ask when we're standing at the entrance to the living room. I was hoping to make this introduction tomorrow after I had a shower and sleep, but I guess that's not going to happen.

Dre sits up from where he's lounging on one of my sofas in his normal business attire, minus the shoes. He examines Zara carefully, from the messy curls on top of her head to the pink toenails sticking out of her flipflops. "We were waiting for you. Got worried when you didn't show for our poker game or answer any of our text messages."

"I didn't know the game was still on," I admit. Tonight would've been the first game since we lost Carmine. Maybe I just didn't want to ask because I'm not ready to sit at the poker table without him next to me.

"Who's your...*friend*, Creed?" Dre asks.

"This is Zara. Zara, these are my cousins, Dre and Tristan."

She gives them a small wave and a forced smile. I've seen hostage videos with more enthusiasm. "Hi. It's nice to finally meet you."

Finally?

Turning my back to the guys, I lift an eyebrow in question that they can't see. Taking a step toward me, she reaches for my hand as if in answer. The warmth and strength in her sure grip feels so authentic that it makes me momentarily forget my line of thought.

We're not a real couple. This is just a risky little arrangement I came up with on the drive home because I knew I wouldn't be able to bring myself to kill her. I need her to think that I hate her enough to do it, though, if I want her cooperation.

Once we get married and share the news, everyone will be shocked.

Oh. That's what she's doing, trying to pretend as if we've been in a clandestine relationship for a while. One we didn't tell anyone about.

The woman isn't just drop dead beautiful; she always seems to be one step ahead of me.

"She's naked." Tristan sits up and stretches his arms overhead for a better look at her, causing Zara to clutch my suit fabric tighter in her free hand.

"She's not naked. She's wearing my jacket. And stop looking at her like that," I warn him.

"But she's naked underneath your jacket?" Dre chimes in. He tilts his head as if doing so will help him see up the jacket. "Who is she and why is she standing in your penthouse naked, Creed?"

"Stop staring at her!" I yell at the two of them. I really wish this introduction could've waited until Zara was fully dressed. I don't like having anyone else get to admire the view of her beautiful body in my clothing. That pleasure should only be mine.

Not that she'll ever let me touch her beauty…

"Whoa, boss. What the hell has gotten into you?" Dre's eyes lower to the towel wrapped around my upper thigh. "Are you drunk? What the hell happened to your leg?"

I rub my forehead and start to think I'm in way too deep with a woman I shouldn't trust and who will probably end up drowning me. "No, I'm not drunk and my leg is fine. It's just a little cut."

Getting to his socked feet, Dre pads toward us, sniffing the air. He stops abruptly about three feet away, his face blanching as he presses his fist to his nose. "Damn. What's that god awful smell?"

"It's been a long night. Can you two leave us now?"

Despite my warning, and the stink, Tristan gets up and moves closer, watching Zara fidget with the buttons on my suit. He's gawking at her all bleary-eyed and slack-jawed, as if she's the most fascinating creature he's ever seen. "She's a sexy little thing, isn't she? I bet she'll be worth every penny. Hell, I'd like to invest in that ass…"

One second, he's ogling her, and the next, I have the side of his face pinned to the glass coffee table. Lowering to his ear, I say, "Repeat that for me. I must have misheard you. It sounded a helluva lot like you were insinuating she's a whore."

"Fuck, Creed. It was a joke," Dre grumbles from behind us.

"Does it look like I'm laughing?"

"Just tell us she's off-limits before someone ends up dead," he replies.

Dre has no idea someone already did end up dead for touching her. That's how Izaiah signed his own death warrant, and why I made the rash decision not to hold off on getting revenge for Carmine.

"She's off-limits," I say through clenched teeth. Tomorrow they'll find out just how off-limits she is when I tell them she's my wife. Maybe this marriage idea is batshit crazy, but it's better than the alternatives. "Apologize to her."

"Yes, boss," Tristan replies. "Sorry…ma'am."

"Her name is Zara."

"Sorry, Zara. I shouldn't have assumed you were a whore just because of the way you're dressed."

"Fuck off." I press down hard on his face before I release my grip on his scalp.

Tristan straightens to his full height and fixes his tee. "Honestly, boss, she could just as easily be selling thin mints instead of ass. How old is she? Legal age, right? Did you check her ID before she lost her…clothes?"

"Do you want me to throw you out a goddamn window tonight?" I ask him.

"What did I say now?" He looks between Dre and me as if he has no idea why I'm pissed off. "I don't want you getting brought up on any new charges."

"She's not that young," I assure him, although I can't recall exactly how old the background report said she was. "Zara?" I ask, relieved that so far, she's kept her mouth shut, but I hate that I'm blowing her whole plan of pretending we've been seeing each other in secret.

"I'm twenty-seven," she answers.

"See. She's twenty-seven. That's only a nine-year age gap."

"Well, I could *say* I'm twenty-nine, but that doesn't make it true," Tristan remarks. "That's how they get you."

"Get out," I tell him. "Both of you."

Thankfully, Tristan puts on his shoes and strolls over to the penthouse door with a smirk on his cocky face.

Once Tristan leaves, Dre slips on his dress shoes and asks, "You sure you're feeling okay, man?"

"I need some sleep," I declare, something I haven't been getting much of the past week.

"Then I'll go and let you get you some...rest." After a long pause, he adds the last word while biting back a grin.

I let his insinuation go, since everyone is supposed to think we're fucking.

"Call and tell Lorenzo to send someone over to stand watch at the penthouse door."

Dre's dark brow lifts to his hairline. "You want a man on that door?" He points to it.

"Yes. Nobody comes in or out without my approval. Have whoever is available text me when they're in position."

His eyes widen. "Wow." Holding up his palms, he backs toward the door. "Nope. I'm not even going to ask. Good luck, Zara. I mean, good night."

I flip him off in response, right before I remember doing the same to my brother just moments before he died.

"I'm sorry I missed the game tonight," I tell Dre before he reaches the foyer. "We'll pick it back up next week."

"Yeah, next week," he agrees.

After the door closes behind him, I lock up. When I return to the living room, Zara is still standing right where I left her.

"That was...fun," she says. "And while I appreciate you making him apologize, that's not the first time I've been mistaken as a whore."

"Sorry."

"The funny thing is, getting paid for sex seems infinitely smarter than getting fucked over for free."

There is so much to unpack in that last statement, but I can't handle it all tonight. "We're going to circle back to that comment tomorrow," I assure her. "As soon as one of my men comes to watch the door, I'm getting a shower and going to bed." I want to try to get a few hours of sleep before I have to get up, start making arrangements for a marriage ceremony, and expedited prenup paperwork.

That is, if I don't wake up in the morning and realize marrying a woman I don't know is a ridiculous idea. Or she doesn't kill me in my sleep. I'll need to lock my gun in the safe, along with both of our cell phones.

"I could use another shower too," Zara remarks. For a second, I think she's insinuating that she wants to join me. Then she adds, "I feel…gross."

Right.

Just because she didn't flinch when I killed a man doesn't mean she wants to fuck me.

9

Zara

Sitting up in the giant comfy bed within the fancy as hell penthouse, I admire the breathtaking view of the city from the ninety-sixth floor. Last night, it was awesome to see the buildings lit up, romantic even, but today it's even better as I take in the iconic Central Park and Manhattan skyline.

Well, I survived my first night with Creed Ferraro.

His side of the bed is already neatly made as if he was never there.

When Creed told me I had to sleep in his room, I expected the worst and was pleasantly surprised.

He let me shower first, without any gawking, and gave me one of his white undershirts to wear to bed. Then, after I was done, he took a quick shower before turning off the lights and climbing into bed.

There was no pillow talk, no touching, not even accidental. We both just fell asleep.

Despite all that happened earlier with Izaiah, I slept better than I have in years because now I have something I didn't before... hope.

Good riddance to that bastard.

Before I can throw the covers off my bare legs and climb out of bed, the bedroom door opens. Creed strolls in fully dressed in a dark suit with a black shirt underneath unbuttoned and open at the collar, which is apparently his standard uniform.

Here's hoping he hasn't changed his mind after sleeping on it. Losing out on the money that could help me get custody of Oriana would suck almost as much as my death.

"Good, you're awake," he says without even a hint of homicidal intent in his deep voice. "I've made arrangements for us with the City Clerk at ten and have confirmation from a judge who has agreed to waive the twenty-four-hour waiting period. A courier is on the way over from my attorney's office with the prenup. It's standard boilerplate with the details we discussed last night all laid out."

"Okay." So, he hasn't changed his mind. Why am I surprised? It would've been much easier for him to kill me in my sleep than wait for me to wake up.

Creed stares at me as if waiting for me to say more. When I don't, he speaks again. "My offer is more than generous for you, after what you did…"

Wincing at the reminder, I tell him, "It's fine. I'll sign the papers. I'm not going to try and take your money when this… ends."

"I added an additional allowance of fifty million a year for every year I'm incarcerated to… encourage you to maintain your silence."

"Fifty million a year? Wow."

"The penthouse is paid for, so you won't have to worry about losing it while I'm gone. My financial team will keep up to date on all the other bills for utilities."

"You're that certain that you're going to prison?"

"The gun charge has a minimum mandatory sentence. The DA has police cam footage of me possessing the firearm, so my attorney doesn't see a way out of it."

"I thought all you mafia guys bribed judges and DAs to avoid convictions and prison."

"Usually, we do," he replies. "But this DA is new, and she got elected by running on a zero tolerance for drugs and corruption platform. As for the judge, well, there's no bribe that can override a mandatory sentence."

"Hence the name."

"Right." He glances at the gold watch on his wrist. "Can you be ready in half an hour?"

"Do I really have a choice?"

"No, you don't. Be ready to leave in half an hour."

It's odd, but despite his demand, he doesn't seem as angry with me. Deep down, though, I know that hate is still there for the part I played in his brother's death. It's likely festering underneath his tan skin, a wound that will never heal. The best I can hope for is that we'll both try to pretend it's not there.

Nodding my understanding of our agreement, I slip out of bed and make up my side of it, fluffing the pillows and all.

"There's breakfast waiting for you in the kitchen."

"Thanks." I face him again, finding his gaze lowered as if he was just staring at my ass. When his eyes return to mine, he lifts a single eyebrow in challenge.

I'm about to marry him to stay alive, and he's going to give me a million dollars a month as an incentive. Of course, he gets to look at me whenever he wants, and there's nothing I can do about it. He's likely expecting or hoping for more than just looking, since he's a man and that's a whole lot of money.

While the don may be a vicious murderer, I think he'll keep his word about not hurting me or touching me without my permission.

And I can't be upset about his gawking, since I did my own ogling last night when he came out of the bathroom in nothing but a pair of snug, black boxer briefs. It was only for a moment before he killed the lights, but long enough to have his big, muscular, inked body tattooed into my mind.

A hard body carefully sculpted to intimidate his enemies and inflict violence.

The only way Creed could possibly get any hotter would be if he had Emilio Rovina's blood on his hands when he tossed his corpse at my feet.

I'm definitely not the sweet, naïve girl I was when I first came to the city seven years ago, that's for sure.

Creed glances at my bare legs and upper thighs for several more seconds as if remembering I'm not wearing anything under his shirt before he turns to leave. I blurt out, "Wait! I need to make a phone call."

"No. And my IT guys are working on making everything disappear from the Cloud."

"That's good to know, but um, could you at least make a call for me?"

"Make a call to whom?"

"My boss."

"Your boss?" he repeats.

"Yes. Tell him I can't come in today, that I quit. And… um — that I'm sorry I didn't work a notice."

"You're serious?" Creed raises an eyebrow in disbelief.

"I might need that reference for another job someday," I explain to the rich bastard. "Haven't you ever heard the saying about not burning any bridges?"

He stares at me for a long moment. "Fine. What's the number?"

He retrieves his device from his pocket as I tell him, "I don't know his number! It's saved in my phone."

Sighing heavily, he glares at me. Creed then pulls a phone with a purple case out of his pocket. My phone. "What's the name?"

"Steve Ricks."

A few taps of his fingers, and a moment later, my phone is up to his ear.

"You'll probably have to leave a message," I warn him right before he speaks.

"Is this Steve? I'm calling for Zara Riley. She won't be able to make it in today or any other day. That's right. She quits."

"Creed!" I hiss while my fingers fidget with the hem of my shirt. He's rude and abrupt. "Apologize!"

"Zara is...sorry," he grits out while his blue eyes lock onto mine. "It wasn't her decision to quit. It was mine." There's a pause and then. "This is Creed Ferraro. And if she ever needs a reference from you in the future, it better be a glowing one." With that he ends the call. "Satisfied?"

"Yes. Thank you."

"Do you need anything else before I go?"

"Yes." My gaze lowers to his pants. "How are your, ah, stab wounds this morning?"

"Should I say they're excruciatingly painful and ask you to kiss them better?"

"Ha! No. But if you're joking about them, they must not be too awful."

"They're not. Now, will that be all?"

"Just one last question — What am I supposed to wear today?"

"What do you think?" he asks over his shoulder as he turns to leave. "A wedding dress."

"Oh. Is my fairy godmother on her way over to conjure one up from your tees and suits?"

Creed smiles. His lips lift at both corners, making him undeniably more handsome. "A bridal boutique is bringing a few dresses over for you to choose from, along with several pairs of shoes and…undergarments. That's another reason you should hurry."

The door shuts behind him, leaving me standing in his bedroom wearing nothing but his tee and trying to imagine myself putting on a wedding dress and marrying the mafia don in just a few hours.

∽

Thirty minutes later, I'm showered and dressed. My curls are only half dry but pulled up in a tidy bun with a few loose strands hanging around my face.

With more time, I would've liked to let my hair air-dry and have the curls fall over my shoulders and the ivory gown, but I didn't want to keep Creed Ferraro waiting a minute longer than he demanded.

He stands in the living room, waiting for me with an older man, who's wearing a navy suit. When they see me, both of their eyes widen, making me glad I choose the gown that looks like it was poured on me. With the V-neckline, lace corset top, and slit to my upper thigh, I feel like a sexy and fierce bride rather than the innocent and demure girl I was when I first came to the city.

But the long, drawn-out silence is nearly deafening. Maybe I made the wrong choice.

"Well? What do you think?" I prompt the don with a hand on my hip. I stupidly hope that Creed not only approves of my dress choice, but that it makes him have dirty thoughts. Wanting him to want me seems like the only way to regain some of my power in this drastic imbalance.

"You're…it's…perfect," he finally stammers.

I was expecting 'pretty' or maybe 'beautiful' but 'perfect' is even better. I smooth my palms down the skirt while trying to come up with a response to his compliment. "Good. It was the first one I tried on, and it fit."

After a few more seconds, the other man clears his throat. Creed straightens his suit jacket. "Zara, this is Lorenzo, my… advisor and security manager. He's going to be our witness for the ceremony."

"Hi, it's nice to meet you." The man looks ten or more years older than Creed with the same dark hair and a tidy beard. He doesn't stare at me like Creed's pervy cousins, so I feel comfortable enough to offer him my hand to shake.

Or maybe I just feel more confident now that I'm wearing a gorgeous dress that probably costs more than I make in a year.

Made.

I won't miss working the long hours, I will miss the freedom of supporting myself and not depending on anyone else. I'll save the majority of my million a month in a personal account, just in case.

"You make a beautiful bride, Zara," Lorenzo says with a warm smile. "Now, tell me the truth. How in the world did Creed manage to convince *you* to marry *him*?"

He makes it sound like I'm too good for the don, when he's the powerful, ruthless, filthy rich man who could probably have any woman he wants.

"He made me an offer I couldn't refuse," I reply, completely serious.

A big belly laugh bursts from Lorenzo. He doubles over through the cackles that go on and on. Creed shakes his head in warning, but does so with a half-grin on his face.

When Lorenzo eventually straightens and stops laughing, he swipes the tears from his face, then slaps his palm on Creed's back. "She's a good one, boss. Where did you luck up and find her?"

"Carmine," Creed replies, all traces of humor absent from his face and voice. "He actually introduced us."

"Really? Wow. That's such a shame. He should be your witness, not me. I hate he can't be here with you today."

"Me too. Carmine told me to be sure and thank him profusely in my wedding toast for not snatching Zara up first. Somehow, he knew I would end up marrying her."

I know he's lying, but damn, he's really freaking good at it. I make a note to remember that.

"Grab something to eat, and then we'll head out — that is, if you're ready?" Creed asks.

"Yes, I'm ready and I'm not hungry." We may as well get this over with.

I don't remember if, as a little girl, I ever dreamed about my perfect wedding day. Once I moved to the city, all those dreams, along with any others, faded away. I quickly learned hard lessons about trusting men. They're manipulative assholes who enjoy convincing me to do all sorts of shit — things that required self-medication before and afterward.

"We're not leaving until you have breakfast," he demands.

I am starving, actually, even feeling a little lightheaded. I concede and let him show me to the breakfast buffet in the dining room.

That's how I know Creed is going to be…different from the others. I'm different, too, now. I'll never let anyone hurt me that way again, not even Creed Ferraro.

He's the most powerful man in the city. The most dangerous.

And he's going to be my husband.

I'm not afraid of him, even though I know I should be.

10

Creed

Zara in a curve-hugging wedding gown is even more tempting than a naked Zara wearing only my jacket.

I was struck by how perfect she looked, not just in the dress but standing in the living room of my penthouse, about to become mine.

From the high slit showing off her pale, toned legs to the V-neck of her dress drawing the eye down to her succulent cleavage, I still can't look away as we sit in morning traffic on the way to the clerk's office.

But then I remember her crooking her finger at me that night in the club and my desire for her melts away in the blink of an eye.

Forcing myself to watch the foot traffic outside the window instead, I remind myself that this marriage is a business arrangement. Nothing more. It's the only way to keep Zara close and keep my eye on her. She's a witness to Izaiah's murder and partially responsible for Carmine's.

Marrying Zara is only infinitesimally better than marrying Emilio Rovina's viper-bitch daughter.

Oh, and Emilio is going to be fucking furious when he finds out I married someone else a week after our talk.

It's probably best if I keep the marriage license off the public record until I figure out if Emilio put Izaiah up to the club raid or not. There's no reason to incur his wrath before I have evidence and the upper hand.

Which reminds me, as soon as the ceremony is done, Zara and I will have to take the SUV with Izaiah's body and dump him some place he'll never be found. I dread enduring the stench that will have only grown worse a day later in the small, hot, enclosed space. The entire SUV will probably need to be destroyed afterwards.

"I was thinking we could drive out to the Hamptons this afternoon." I carefully choose my words, since Lorenzo is in the front with Aldo, one of my drivers.

"The Hamptons?" she asks.

"You know, for our honeymoon? I have a house there. It's very private."

Turning to me, she nods her head in understanding. "That sounds...great. Do you have a boat?"

A watery grave is exactly what I was thinking as well. Or at least I assume that's why Zara asked about a boat. "I'm sure we could find one to rent when we get there."

"Sounds fun."

Her accompanying smile makes it seem as if she's excited to toss a man in the ocean, reminding me yet again that I know absolutely nothing about this peculiar woman I'm about to legally tie myself to through marriage.

And instead of planning how to dispose of Izaiah without

getting caught, I find myself thinking about how Zara and I should spend a few days away from the city getting to know each other, which is idiotic. Still, I can't seem to shake the thought that since there's no women's apparel at my beach house, I'll get to see Zara in more of my attire. Wearing only my clothes and nothing underneath.

And my ring on her finger.

Rather than publicly shopping in a store with Zara for our wedding rings, I have a jeweler meeting us at the clerk's office with a variety of choices and sizes for her to try on and choose from.

The rings will come after the ceremony, since I'm not paying a fortune for them only to have Zara backout at the last second when we're in front of the officiant.

Would she actually choose death rather than marry me? It's unlikely but still possible for the odd woman.

After all, being married into the mafia won't be a walk in the park. It's potentially a death sentence.

In fact, when we reach our destination, parking near the side entrance, I find myself wanting to be honest with Zara before we go through with this ceremony. "Will you and Aldo give us a moment?" I ask Lorenzo. "Remind him of the importance of being discreet about what he sees or hears about today. And the punishment for failing to do so."

"Sure thing, boss," he replies and jerks his chin at the driver, gesturing toward the sidewalk. They both exit the SUV, leaving it running.

"Before we do this, there's something you should know about me."

"Let me guess...you're in the mafia?"

"I am. And I'm not going to lie. Being by my side will come with its own risks to your life. That's how the Ferraro family curse got started."

"The what?" She smiles.

"Women who marry into my family never live to see thirty."

"Seriously?"

"Seriously. It's our lifestyle, our enemies. I know that it's not just because the women weren't Italian."

"The so-called curse is specific to non-Italian women?"

"Yes. I'll keep our marriage license quiet for as long as I can, but that may only be possible for a few days or weeks."

"Okay."

"Okay?"

"Marrying you still seems like the better option," she replies. "And dumping Izaiah in the ocean during our 'honeymoon' is probably our best bet, right?"

She says "our" honeymoon and "our" best bet because we're already a team, have been since I trusted her not to tell him I was eavesdropping from her bathroom.

And as long as Zara is breathing, I don't have any other choice but to marry her to keep her close to me. I hate that there's an annoying, demanding part of my body that is desperate to fuck the woman responsible for Carmine's death. I need to shut that shit down fast.

"This isn't going to ever be a real marriage. Before the rings or vows, tell me right here, right now that you don't want me and never will."

Zara's auburn brow furrows, drawing my attention to the trail of freckles that lead down her nose. "W-what? Why?"

She wants me to give her a reason why I need her to voice her rejection? Fine. She can have the whole truth. "Because there are already a million and one filthy ideas about what I'd like to do to you, swirling around in my head, and hearing your rejection may be the only thing that stops those thoughts from continuing to multiply." That damn slit in her dress. I can't resist running my fingertips up the smooth bare thigh that's crossed over the other before she tells me to never lay a finger on her again.

Zara covers my hand; I assume she's going to shove it away from her leg.

Instead, she slides my palm up higher, over to where her two legs rest against each other. There, she presses my fingertips about two inches between those tightly crossed thighs before unfortunately pulling them back out again. When my eyes lift to hers, she studies me as she returns my hand back to my lap. The temptress wraps my fingers around the length of my hard shaft, then makes me give myself a squeeze and an agonizingly slow stroke.

I'm staring down at her gorgeous cleavage on the second and third stroke, which is when I groan so loudly that I almost miss it when she says, "I don't want to want you, but I would never say never."

Fuck.

And that is the reason I was late to my own damn wedding ceremony.

It wasn't the partial hand job in the car that had me so strung out, I couldn't wait until later to go rub one out in the clerk's bathroom like a goddamn teenager.

It was the possibility of someday having Zara underneath me that had me so turned on, I couldn't think straight.

11

Zara

The giant sparkling diamond on my finger feels heavy, like a burden rather than an expensive gift. A burden that legally binds me to Creed Ferraro.

I have no clue how much it's worth. If I had to guess, about a hundred grand. That's enough money to live on for months if I ever have to pawn it, and this one was the smallest diamond the jeweler brought with him. I don't blame the man if he's working off commission, but it's going to get caught on everything.

"You don't like the ring?" Creed asks from his seat beside me on the ride back to his building. We had a quick ceremony, even a few photos, and picked out rings all within about ten minutes. It seems like something as life changing as marriage should take longer than the time it takes to order a coffee.

"I'll get used to it," I tell him, even though it's a lie. I'm stashing it as soon as I can to ensure I don't lose something so valuable.

LANE HART

At least our matching platinum bands are simple enough not to cause me any trouble.

Wedding bands.

It's official.

And why in the world did I tell Creed I would never say never while stroking his very long, very hard erection before the vows?

He was giving me an out, a chance to tell him I didn't want him and never would, that sex would not be part of our marriage. But when I asked him why he wanted me to reject him, he just had to go and say, *"Because there are already a million and one filthy ideas about what I would like to do to you swirling around in my head, and hearing your rejection may be the only thing that stops those thoughts from continuing to multiply."*

I like being wanted by the handsome, intimidating man almost as much as I like hearing him openly admit that he wants me. He owned up to his desire for me, but so far, he's been respectful enough not to try to just take what he wants.

Well, at least he was respectful last night and this morning. Guess I'll find out how patient he can be during our "honeymoon."

His words also helped me feel like I have a little more control in this unusual arrangement.

When we pull into the parking garage, Creed tells the driver, "You can let us out here. We'll be driving to the Hamptons alone. Try not to call me, Lor."

"Only if it's an emergency," the older man promises, swiveling around in the passenger seat. "Congrats and enjoy your honeymoon."

"Thanks for being there today," Creed tells him before he opens his door and slides out. I meet him behind the SUV where we finally head to the vehicle of doom.

"I'll roll the windows down and let it air out before we leave. Not that it will help much."

"How long is this trip going to take?" I ask.

"You've never been to the Hamptons?"

"No. I can't afford the bus ticket to get there from here, much less a place to stay."

A giant diamond on my finger and a vacation in the Hamptons are things I never even thought to dream of because they were so unfathomable.

When Creed holds his breath while opening the driver door, releasing the stench, it definitely grounds me back into reality.

Sure, my life includes unexpected and expensive things now, but it comes with a few downsides like dead men in rug burritos.

This is my life now.

No matter what happens in a month or a year from now, last night changed me in a way that I won't ever be able to escape.

Maybe that's why I feel a weird sense of camaraderie with Creed rather than fearing him. He hasn't done anything I haven't wanted to do myself.

Once all the windows are rolled down, he steps out of the vehicle and opens all the doors while sucking in a deep breath of fresh air. "That's…even worse than I imagined."

"We could stop at a gas station and get some air fresheners to hang."

"A few dozen may make it slightly more bearable. Ready?"

"Yes," I agree before glancing down at my beautiful ivory dress.

"What?" Creed asks when I don't go around to get into the passenger seat.

"My dress is going to be ruined. There's no way the smell will come out."

"So?"

"So, it's too pretty to treat it so badly."

"It's not like you'll ever wear it again."

"True, but it's supposed to be a keepsake, something to pass down to my daughter."

Oh shit.

I didn't mean to let that little truth slip. Not that it matters now that we're married. I'll have to tell Creed at some point that I'm a mother.

Thankfully, he doesn't seem to catch on that I meant my actual daughter rather than a hypothetical one in the future.

"I'll buy you a new dress just like that one," he says.

A replacement dress won't be the same because it won't be the one I wore for the actual wedding. But I decide to just get in the smelly SUV and let it go.

~

An hour later, even with every variety of car freshener the gas station had, hanging from the rearview and vents, I still think I may throw up.

"We should've done this last night," I mutter, my voice nasally because I've resorted to holding my nose.

"We weren't married last night. Spousal privilege can't be backdated." Creed is leaning to his left, half his head out the window.

"You couldn't have worked your mobster magic and convinced that drunken judge who performed the ceremony to backdate the paperwork?"

"He may have refused," Creed replies tightly. "Besides, it's over and done now."

Reaching for one of the air fresheners hooked to the vent, he pulls it off and tosses it into the backseat. It's soon followed by a few hanging ones too.

"Like that will help?"

"We just need a distraction, something else to think about." He turns up the satellite radio tuned in to a rock station loud enough to hear it but still talk to each other. "Why don't you tell me what you were referring to last night when you said you get fucked over for free?"

"I'd rather talk about you."

"What about me?"

"How smooth you are at lying."

"When have I fucking lied to you?" he snaps, sounding offended.

"It wasn't to me, but that was a nice little fictional story you came up with earlier when you were telling Lorenzo how we met."

I probably should've chosen anything else to talk about rather than bringing up Creed's brother.

"It wasn't a lie," he says softly. "Carmine convinced me to go over and talk to you that night. Of course, he didn't know what you wanted at the time, but he did say to thank him in my wedding toast for not taking you home."

"Really?"

"Yes."

"He even snapped a photo of you. That's what I used to have a PI track you down."

"Oh."

"I could've used the club video if I needed to, but the photo was better quality, much clearer. After I was released from jail, it only took a day for a private investigator to give me your name, address, and employer. I waited until after the funeral to track you down."

So that's how he found me. From a photo his brother took just moments before he was killed.

And I know that this is it, the perfect opening for me to explain to Creed why I did what I did that night. We're married now. He should know.

I just hope I can trust him with all the information he needs to destroy me.

12

Creed

"Creed, there's something I need to tell you," Zara declares.

Her serious tone and the use of my name, possibly for the first time, momentarily distract me from the stench coming from the cargo area.

The sight of her in that sexy as fuck dress is also distracting, which is why I keep stealing glances at her.

I can't help but try to lighten the mood by using her own words from earlier. "Let me guess. You're also in the mafia?"

With a puff of laughter, she says, "Ha! Funny, but no. I'm just married to the mafia."

I know without looking that she's staring down at her new ring with a frown like she has since we got in the SUV. She hates it. And I'm not entirely sure why. Because it's heavy? Because it ties her to me?

"I should've told you sooner. I know..."

She makes it sound like it's something awful. When she leaves me hanging, I grit my teeth and take a guess with the worst thing I can think of at the moment. "You knew Izaiah was going to try to get me and my brother killed that night?"

"No, it's not that."

I make another guess, relieved she said she wasn't in on Izaiah's plan. "You've helped killed someone before?"

"Izaiah was definitely the first."

"Then what are you so afraid to tell me, wife?" Using that word for a woman I just met feels strange but right for Zara. "It can't be that bad, since nothing is worse than murder."

"The reason I didn't tell you before the marriage ceremony was because I thought you may change your mind and go with the easier option."

"Okay." My curiosity may kill me if she doesn't spit it out soon. "So just tell me now. I can handle it."

"I have a daughter."

"You what?" The SUV briefly swerves to the right when I glance over at her too fast. Wrecking the vehicle with a dead man in the back would be less than ideal.

It takes me several long moments to straighten the SUV and come to terms with just finding out that Zara has a daughter.

I recall a birth certificate in the document file the PI emailed me, but I barely glanced at it as I scrolled past, assuming it was hers and not giving a shit about what day she was born.

"You have a daughter?"

"Yes."

"What's her name? How old is she? Where is she?"

If she has a daughter, then now that we're married, I guess that makes me the girl's stepfather.

"Her name is Oriana," Zara informs me. "She just turned three on July fourteenth. She's bossy and loves Disney princesses, but that's about all I really know about her. Bringing her into this world was the best day of my life, the most amazing reward for surviving the hottest summer ever when I was gigantic. But..."

When I glance over, Zara is staring down at the diamond ring she's spinning around and around her finger. *My* ring that makes her all mine now. "But?" I prompt after she abruptly halts her explanation.

"The Rovinas took her from me the day after she was born, when we were both released from the hospital."

Jesus H. Christ.

"The *Rovinas* have sole custody of your three-year-old daughter?"

"Yes. Although, it's nothing official that I know of. I never tried to fight for custody because I can't afford an attorney, much less one to go up against theirs. I don't even have visitation rights. I-I'm only allowed to see her for an hour or so per month with their permission. Permission that I usually had to earn by fulfilling *favors* first..."

Fuck. That explains her connection to Izaiah Rovina. I thought they were lovers and hated the idea. I had no fucking clue they shared a child, a daughter.

"I never knew...they've never mentioned he was a father..." I trail off.

"They keep Oriana and me both a secret. I don't think the rest of the family even knows about us, just Izaiah and Emilio..."

I'm so hung up on the fact that she has a kid with Izaiah that it takes several moments for the last part of her previous comment to sink into my skull.

Favors? She said she had to earn visitation by fulfilling favors. "You...you had to fuck Izaiah to spend time with your daughter?"

As soon as she nods, my eyes return to the road in front of me, not really seeing the lines or other cars through the rage.

I welcome the stink of that bastard now and wish I had killed him slower for Carmine and for Zara.

"Oriana is the reason I did what Izaiah asked me to do that night at the club. He told me that if I gave the manager the message warning you and let him know when you showed up, then I could spend that Sunday morning with her at the zoo. I swear I had no idea it was a setup to try and kill you or arrest you. If I did, I wouldn't have agreed to do it, not even for a morning with her when I barely get to see her once a month."

"Jesus, Zara. Why didn't you tell me about this shit before?"

"I wasn't sure if you would want to marry me because it complicates things with the Rovinas. And I know you could still change your mind even now, but I wanted you to know, to understand why I did it."

"I wouldn't have called off the marriage for anything," I admit to her. "I manipulated you into marrying me..."

"It was a fair offer after what I did," she says, making me feel like shit.

"You should've told me you had a daughter the second you saw me sitting in your apartment."

"Have you forgotten how furious you were with me last night before Izaiah showed up? Do you really think you would have believed me if I had told you then?"

"I don't kill mothers. That's one of my hard and fast rules. No exceptions."

"There was no way for me to know that, or to know if you were cruel enough to hurt her just because of the Rovinas!"

"I don't hurt or kill children either," I tell her. "Fuck, Zara. That's what you think of me?"

"Do you blame me after I watched you put a bullet in Izaiah's head without flinching? People call you the *Accabadore*, the angel of death."

"Izaiah was a piece of shit who deserved to die for killing my brother!"

"For all I knew, you could've enjoyed killing just for fun."

"I don't kill for fun. Most of the time, I even hate myself afterward."

"Oh," Zara whispers.

Neither of us speak for several miles. Eventually, she asks, "Do you hate yourself for killing Izaiah?"

"No. I'll never regret that decision or feel guilty."

"Good. Because I don't regret it either," she whispers.

"You don't?" I ask in surprise.

Leaning her head on the window, most likely to gulp down some fresh air, Zara smiles when she says, "I can't wait to throw him in the ocean and watch him sink to the bottom."

Looking at this beautiful, happy woman in my passenger seat, wearing her satin and lace gown, her loose auburn strands of hair blowing in the wind, I can't help but feel that despite our many differences, we share plenty of common ground.

The enemy of my enemy isn't just my friend.

Now, she's my wife.

I killed for Zara when I hated her. Before I ever knew the reason why she lured me to the club that night, I protected her.

Hearing what she's been through, that she has a daughter she loves and would do anything for, I know I won't just kill for her again.

I'd go to war for her.

13

Zara

Several hours later, Creed and I are relaxing in the Adirondack chairs on his deck facing the ocean with a glass of red wine in our hands, celebrating the day's accomplishments.

Now, the sea holds our secrets.

The don had a boat ready and waiting at the dock for us when we got to his thankfully secluded beach property, so Izaiah is finally out of our hair for good. He's literally swimming with the fishes, as they say. The thought puts a smile on my face and almost makes me giggle.

"What are you going to do about his car?" I look to Creed. His head is leaning back against the chair, his eyes closed. I'm not sure where he lost his suit jacket, but it's gone now and the sleeves of his black dress shirt are rolled up his arms, the top buttons undone to reveal his muscular chest.

"I decided to leave it where he parked it," he answers.

"Are you sure that was wise? Leaving it so close to my apartment? I don't want to end up on a suspect list!"

"Since my text that he thought was from you instructed him to park half a block away from one of Aiden Sanna's taxi companies, I thought it was best to leave it be instead of trying to move it and get caught on a surveillance camera or leave behind a trace of my DNA."

"You think Emilio will blame Izaiah's disappearance on Aiden Sanna because his car was found in Queens near his business, and they hate each other?"

"Yes. The two had an argument about Emilio's drug dealers in Queens just the other day."

"Smart of you to think of setting that up when you were furious and texting him."

"Don't forget, I was also watching you bathe."

Taking a deep sip of wine from my glass, I mutter, "I've tried to forget how you invaded my privacy so brazenly."

"Getting to watch you shower may have saved your life." Creed grins. Lifting his head, he reaches over and takes my left hand in his. His thumb swipes the protruding diamond. "We can get you a different ring when we're back in the city."

"I'll get used to this one. Eventually."

"You can still keep this one. It's worth over three hundred grand, you know, in case you decide to pawn it. I would hate for you to get swindled."

"How did you know I was thinking about pawning it?" I ask, pulling my fingers free from his in surprise. Then, I instantly regret severing the innocent contact with him so soon when he looks away from me with a sigh of defeat.

"You're not used to having a safety net. I get it. The first thing my mother pawned when she left my father was her diamond. We lived off the money from it for months while she looked for a job."

"Oh. I'm sorry your parents split up."

"They loved each other, but she didn't want me and my brother to grow up and take over the family business for him. She thought she was protecting us from the violence by giving him up to the feds and running."

"But your father found you?" I hazard a guess.

He nods. "The charges didn't stick, and he found us. My brother and I came back home with him."

I don't need to ask what happened to his mother to know that it must not have ended well for her. Ratting out the mafia is a death sentence. It's why I never considered going to the police to report the Rovinas. They have men on the inside to protect them from not only charges but rats too.

And I can't help but wonder if Creed is not so subtly giving me a warning about what will happen to me if I betray him in such a way.

To change the subject, I ask him, "How is your leg feeling?"

"It's fine," he says while straightening the long limb out in front of him. "The cuts were shallow."

We also dumped Izaiah's bloody knife, his car keys, and my old laptop into the ocean with him. Creed promised to buy me a new one once he trusts me.

"Are you hungry?" he asks, glancing over at me. "You must be starving by now. We could get something delivered."

"I'm actually not hungry. The scent of garbage is still lingering in my nostrils."

"Mine too. Our appetites will hopefully return tomorrow. For now, showers?" He stands up.

"Showers," I agree as I get to my feet as well.

I follow him back through the wide-open French doors to the sitting room that has an ocean view. Guess he's not concerned about the electric bill and is wealthy enough to let all the cool air escape.

"This place is beautiful. Do you come here often? I would live here if it were mine."

"It is yours now," Creed says when he stops and faces me. "You can come here whenever you want."

"As long as you're with me, right?".

"For the time being. I hope I can trust you one day."

"Me too," I admit. "And it would be nice to have a phone again."

"Why?" he asks, his words suddenly harsh. "Someone you need to call?"

"No. I just have photos of Oriana on my phone, along with some others."

"I'll think about it," he says before he turns and walks off down the hall.

"I need something to wear!" I call after him.

"Help yourself to my closet."

I'm guessing his closet won't have any panties or bras. At least, I hope it doesn't. Even though we've not even been married a full day, I don't like the thought of my husband bringing some woman here so often that she has a whole wardrobe waiting for her.

Curious, I slip into the master bedroom just as the hot water turns on in the en suite bathroom. Going to the closet, I open the double doors and flip on the light. On the left are rows of various dark suits. On the right are more casual pants and button downs. Along the back wall are drawers below a wall safe.

I head for them, pulling the top drawer open expecting to find skimpy lingerie. Instead, there are socks. The next drawer is underwear. Men's boxer briefs in various dark colors. And the third drawer is full of white cotton tees.

I grab one of those, since they're the most comfortable thing in the closet to sleep in, then browse the hanging clothes on the way out. I've just stepped into the bedroom again when Creed strolls out of the bathroom completely freaking naked. Head to toe, there's nothing covering his flesh but ink.

"Ah...I'm...I was just...Sorry! I'm sorry..." Why am I apologizing profusely for busting in on him, when he's the one who is wandering around the room with his dick swinging this way and that way? Yes, it's long enough that it swings around like a pendulum on its on volition. And he's just standing there while I stare at it, at him, unable to remove my eyes from his massive, gorgeous body. Thankfully, the knife wound in his upper thigh looks to be healing.

"Yes, my blushing bride?"

"I was...need...a shirt." I hold up the tee like an idiot, unable to speak in complete sentences.

Grinning, he says, "I was...need...a towel," before he walks toward the hallway, giving me an unobstructed view of his bare backside and muscular ass.

I hear a closet open and close, then he returns with a blue towel in his hands and his pendulum in full swing again.

Something blue flies at my face, hitting me and falling to the floor before I can react. A second towel.

"For your shower and your drool," Creed says with a smirk as he swaggers back to the bathroom.

Oh, he's never going to let me live this moment down.

Without turning around, he calls out over the running water, "I guess we're even now, for me watching you shower and having to jerk off in the city clerk's bathroom."

A laugh bursts from my lips as my brain eventually catches up to his comment.

I knew Creed disappeared into the restroom before the marriage ceremony, but I had no idea that he was in such a state from a few teasing strokes I gave him in the car.

I had only intended to have his hand make one taunting pass down his length. And then when I felt how long and thick he was, I couldn't stop myself from doing it again and again before my common sense returned to me.

Oh, this is going to be a long night if Creed insists I sleep in his bed again but refuses to touch me.

Not that I think he'll refuse tonight.

And having sex with Creed Ferraro, because it's our wedding night and he's most likely expecting it, won't be the worst thing I've ever had to endure.

It could even be great.

Besides, the closer Creed and I get, the more likely it is that he'll help me get Oriana back after he kills Emilio Rovina.

14

Creed

"*I don't want to want you, but I would never say never.*"

Those are the words Zara told me earlier today. I thought she was referring to the possibility of wanting me in the future, not hours after we were married.

But there's no denying the way she was looking at me earlier.

My wife couldn't peel her eyes away from my cock, which was so damn hot.

It's been over a year since I've had sex, since a woman has seen or looked appreciatively at my naked body.

I need to get ahold of myself and calm down before I make a fool of myself by coming on her thigh.

Trying to calm my dick down after my shower and second hand job of the day, I dry off and wrap the towel around my hips, then retrieve Zara's phone from my discarded pants pocket.

Other than asking me to call into work for her, she hasn't tried to make any calls or even get her hands on the device, which is surprising.

Entering her easy code, I unlock the phone and start snooping around, wanting to learn more about my new bride.

I start with her text messages.

Other than Izaiah's that I deleted last night, there are a few conversations that seem to be with people she works with, talking about shifts and store shit.

Moving over to her photos, I open the album, expecting to see mostly images of a little girl who looks like her mother in the recent images. Instead, there are photos of people and places in the city, mostly Queens. Random things, all in black and white which makes them seem sad. I go through pictures of a train, an old man sitting alone on a bench, an ice cream truck, women pushing kids in strollers, and a cat sitting in the doorway of a bodega before I finally get to an adorable, smiling, curly-haired girl in full color.

The first image is a photo of the back of her head. In the next several shots, she's standing in front of glass with greenery and rocks behind her. If I had to guess, I'd say the images are from the zoo.

Right, that was Zara's reward for setting me up and getting my brother killed.

There aren't many different settings behind the girl, just tons of her looking and pointing at different things, a few of her eating a melting ice cream cone. The pink dessert is literally dripping down the sides of the cone, over her fingers, and running down her messy, cherubic face. Every photo of Oriana is brightly colored, a contrast with the images of dark and gloomy city life.

Knowing why she helped Izaiah lure me and Carmine to the club that night, I don't feel nearly as angry with her. If anything, after learning what Izaiah has put Zara through, I want to hold her and kiss her until she forgets that bastard ever existed. And I want to be the one who returns her daughter back to her arms, to make her world bright and happy every second of the day.

Fuck, I hope Izaiah is rotting in hell where he belongs.

While I don't trust Zara enough to return her phone to her yet, I order up a compromise for her online and have it shipped to the penthouse.

After I'm done with her phone, I check mine and follow up on a few messages before I walk out of the bathroom.

The last thing I expected was to see Zara sitting in my bed underneath the covers, wearing my white tee.

God, I want her so damn much, it hurts.

I wish I could climb into bed, grab her, and kiss her to see where it goes. After all, it's our wedding night, and she's waiting for me in my bed.

But I can't do that.

Not after what she told me about fucking Izaiah Rovina and his "favors."

Not until I know if she actually wants me and doesn't feel obligated to fuck me because she thinks she can't say no.

"What are you thinking about so hard?" Zara asks when I continue standing there like a statue, my fingers gripping the two phones in one hand and the doorway in the other as if trying to hold myself back.

"You want the truth?"

"Yes."

"I was just thinking I've never wanted anyone more than I want you, and I don't know why. What it is about you?" I find myself being brutally honest with her, probably telling her more than I should, but I can't seem to stop myself. "And it's not just because you're beautiful, and now you're my wife. That's what makes you so dangerous."

"I'm dangerous?" she replies with a huff of laughter. "No one's ever been afraid of me. I don't have any scary nicknames, either. That's all you, Mr. Angel of Death."

"Just because I have scary nicknames doesn't mean that you owe me anything. In this marriage, it's you who holds all the power."

"I wish that were true," she replies with a sad smile.

"I killed a man in a fit of rage *for* you before you were even mine."

She blinks at me as if in surprise. "That's...that's why you killed Izaiah?"

"I couldn't stand seeing him near you, and when he held that knife to your throat I...snapped. I know you were concerned I might let him kill you so I wouldn't have to, but the thought never crossed my mind. It should have, but it didn't."

Leaving her with that truth, I go into the closet and lock up my cell and hers in the safe. When I return to the bedroom, Zara says, "Izaiah...that wasn't just revenge for your brother?"

"I don't make stupid, spontaneous mistakes like I did last night. After he confessed, I should've waited, come up with a foolproof plan, and made his death look like an accident once I found out if Emilio was involved. But I couldn't wait."

"Oh." Her cheeks redden, and I have no idea why. So, it's my turn to ask, "What are you thinking about?" I pull the covers back to climb into bed next to her.

"Nobody's ever done anything like that for me before," she says softly. "Even just being spoken to with respect is new. Most of the time, Izaiah was drunk or high or both when he came over, and he had other plans for my mouth rather than talking to me like a person."

Fuck.

Now, I'm unfortunately thinking about her on her knees for that piece of shit.

"Our conversations were short, usually him giving me orders."

"Orders?" I ask, then instantly regret it.

"Orders, you know, like telling me to suck harder, swallow like a good girl. And my least favorite of all, he would make me tell him who I belonged to."

I loathe hearing what Izaiah did to her, with her. It seems so one-sided, I ask her, "Was he always a selfish bastard? Did he ever give you what you needed?"

"No. It was always about him. Izaiah barely touched more than the back of my throat."

Jesus Christ.

"How about we make a deal that neither of us will ever say that fucking *stronzo*'s name again?"

"Deal. I prefer Piece of Shit anyway."

"And that piece of shit never got you off?"

She shakes her head, her curls still damp and pulled up off her delectable-looking neck. "Never."

"That's a shame, *micetta mia*. I would give anything just to make you moan for me." Moan, scream, rake her fingernails through my hair or down my back. The list of things I want to do to her is long. And there's no point in pretending I don't want her when she's married to me and sharing my bed.

"Anything?" Zara asks. Before I can answer, she reaches for my hand and places it on her thigh, and I'm beyond stunned. Even more so when she slips my palm up underneath the hem of my tee she's wearing. "Would you kill another man for me?"

"Just tell me his name."

Fucking hell. I'm certain I'm dreaming when she lets my fingertips brush over her bare pussy because she's not wearing any panties.

And while this almost feels like another set up, I plunge headfirst into it again as she presses harder against my hand.

"Being married to the mafia has some nice perks."

"You have no idea how nice the perks are yet," I assure her. "Want me to show you a few of them?"

"Please." Her soft whisper nearly undoes me.

I watch Zara's face, her eyes holding mine as I glide my middle finger through her slit, then slide it inside of her slickness. She's so damn wet for me, making me rock hard.

When her lips part on a gasp, I swoop in, claiming her lips. Her hand tightens over mine as it fucks her nice and slow. At the sound of her first moan, I shove my tongue deep into her mouth, tasting her for the first time.

She's fucking delicious.

Both of us swallow each other's groan from the teasing sensation of our clashing tongues, knowing exactly what the thrusts really represent.

Wanting to hear her cry out, I pull back and say, "I don't like the idea of letting my new wife go an entire day without coming for me. Especially not on our wedding night."

"Was…was the ceremony…just this morning?" Her back arches when I add a second finger. "*Oh god!*"

"Yes." It's so hot hearing her scream. I don't think I could ever get enough of it.

"It-it feels like…a lifetime ago."

"It's been a long day." I press my lips to her neck, and my fingers keep pumping in and out of her. "And you deserve to be worshipped, not only for being brave enough to marry me, but for helping me throw a man's body into the ocean."

Rather than recoil from the mention of the asshole I murdered, her silky walls tighten around my fingers and her thighs clench around my arm. All it takes is pressing my thumb to her clit, and Zara cries out even louder.

I don't dare cover her mouth again, even though I ache to keep kissing her. No, I just watch the ecstasy spread across her beautiful face, her pretty lips parting wide on a silent scream. Her eyes are closed tight while her hips buck, riding out the waves of pleasure. She drenches my fingers in her arousal, making my mouth water.

When her grip on my hand between her legs relaxes and her eyes open again, finding mine watching her, I pull my fingers free. She keeps gripping my hand even as I lift my fingers to my mouth, sticking them inside to suck them clean. "Mmm," I groan. "You taste so damn good, *micetta mia*." Knowing how drenched she is between her thighs, my dick gets heavier. I lift the hem of her tee to see her glistening for me and nearly come right then and there at the sight. "Can I lick you until you come on my tongue, Zara?"

"Ah…" she trails off, her eyes still hazy from her orgasm.

"I don't expect anything in return," I clarify as I run my tattooed hand up the inside of her thigh. While I'd love nothing more than to climb on top of my wife and claim her, make her mine in every possible way tonight, there's something holding me back.

Carmine.

It doesn't feel right for me to be here with this beautiful woman, receiving even an ounce of relief for myself while my brother is dead. But I could pleasure Zara all damn night. Even if she's partially at fault for Carmine's death, I know I need to let that go.

She's my wife now, and I want to treat her right in and out of my bed, give her anything and everything she needs. "This is just for you tonight."

"Just for me?" she repeats, her voice skeptical as if she doesn't believe.

"Yes. Just for you. I don't deserve any pleasure."

15

Zara

I've never been as wet as I am at this moment, and Creed is asking if he can go down on me?

He claims it's just for me tonight, but I find that hard to believe.

I don't deserve any pleasure, that's what he said. And I'm not entirely sure what he means.

"You don't want me to…do anything for you? Even afterward?" It's not that I'm opposed to taking Creed in my hand or mouth. I just want to prepare myself.

"All you have to do is lie back and let me worship you."

It's impossible to refuse such an offer when I'm still feeling all nice and tingly from coming on his fingers. I'm a little nervous but curious to see what his tongue will feel like. "I guess we can try it. I don't know if I'll like it or not."

His fingertips on my inner thigh freeze, and his handsome face looks incredulous as he arches a single dark eyebrow. "You don't know if you'll like having your pussy licked?"

And now I feel embarrassed.

"I mean, I've had a man's tongue down there before, but only like a few swipes if I wasn't wet enough for him. I've never been close to…finishing that way."

"Wait. Iz…he fucked you, even though you weren't wet for him?" he asks, his voice getting louder. I don't fail to notice that he didn't finish saying his name.

"He wasn't the only one."

"He wasn't?" Creed repeats. "These… *stronzo*s couldn't take the hint that you weren't wet because you didn't want them?"

"They didn't care."

"They hurt you?" When I don't give him an answer either way, he asks, "What are their fucking names, Zara?"

Shaking my head, I tuck a damp strand of hair behind my ear and try to explain without going into details. "It's not as bad as it sounds. It was consensual." I never technically refused. If I had, I'm not sure it would have made a difference, though. It was easier if I took something to help relax me right before, pills they both gladly provided, which is why I failed the most important drug test of my life.

"Consensual but not…enjoyable?" Creed asks for clarification.

I nod, even if it's a lie. The older I get, the more I realize that what happened was wrong even if I didn't try to stop it. Sometimes I wish I had at least tried, although I doubt it would have mattered.

"One day, you're going to tell me who else hurt you, and I'm going to kill them," Creed promises.

"You already killed one," I reply with a small smile.

"Piece of Shit."

I nod and he tosses the covers off me so he can move his big body between my legs. Lying down on his stomach, his large, tattooed hands curl around my thighs, pulling me down the bed toward him until I'm lying flat on my back with my legs draped over his broad shoulders.

"Between the manipulation and selfishness, no wonder you weren't sad to see him go," he says. And seeing this larger than life, intimidating mobster's face between my legs makes me feel cherished for the first time in my life.

"I'll go slow." Creed gazes up at me, the sides of his hair tickling my thighs. "If you don't like it, just tell me to stop. If you give me a chance, though, I promise I'll have you forgetting all about those other assholes." His lips gently press against my inner thigh, stealing my breath. "Twenty-seven-years-old and you've never come on a tongue?"

"No. Never."

"Then we've got some catching up to do."

The first long swipe of his warm, wet tongue is all it takes to erase the last of my inhibitions. Each kiss and lick after that makes me melt a little deeper into the mattress. I cradle Creed's head to my body, my fingers buried in his hair, urging him to keep going, to never stop.

"Creed!" I scream when the tip of his tongue flicks rapidly over my clit. Nothing has ever felt so good.

I'm right on the edge for this mobster, this cold-blooded killer, my new husband and... "Oh god! Creed!" The pleasure bursts free and my body trembles through the wonderful spasms.

I think I temporarily lose consciousness.

There's no time to even recover. He just keeps licking me like his sole purpose in life is to make me come.

So, he does, again and again.

Creed said he wanted to worship me.

I didn't know he meant it so literally.

There's no other way to describe what he's doing to me as I ride out the waves of pleasure, my hips bucking against his face for what is the third or fourth time.

I'm a hot, sweaty mess, barely able to open my eyes.

God, what is this man doing to me?

Anything he wants is the answer because it all feels so good.

His lips, his tongue, his fingers begin pumping inside of me, sending me over the edge again.

After that, my clit is so sensitive the air hurts.

It takes a great deal of effort to make my fingers tug on Creed's hair hard enough to lift his face from between my legs.

When he does, his blue eyes look feral. For a moment, I think he's angry at me until he removes his fingers from inside me and shoves them into his mouth, licking them clean.

Seeing this powerful, mostly naked man sprawled between my thighs would be a turn on all on its own any day of the week. But Creed Ferraro watching me while licking up my arousal is almost too much to handle. My pussy spasms around the emptiness, wishing there was something filling me again.

While I thought I couldn't handle any more orgasms, I'm wondering if I could take one more if it was Creed's long, hard inches stretching me.

With a cocky smirk, he sits back on his heels and swipes his forearm over his damp chin and lips. If I had the strength, I'd sit up and run my nails over his tattooed, muscular chest and down his carved abs.

I'm not sure if I'll ever really believe that this man is my husband.

"From the way you gushed all over my tongue multiple times and screamed my name until you went hoarse, is it safe to assume you enjoyed me eating you out?"

"That was...fucking A."

Chuckling, he asks, "Is that a positive review?"

"God, yes."

"Well, I would be happy to make it a daily ritual. Twice a day until you come at least twenty-two more times."

"Twenty-two?" I ask in confusion.

"You deserve to receive at least twenty-seven orgasms, at least one for every year of your life before I get to come. I counted five tonight."

"Oh," I say in surprise. "Do you really want to...do that so many times without, you know..."

"Getting anything in return?" he finishes. "Trust me. I get plenty of things out of this deal. I get to taste you, to make you scream and squirm for me, to watch your back arch in that sexy fucking way when you're riding the pleasure the hardest. Those memories are all I need to finish when I'm fisting myself in the shower." Leaning back, he presses his palm over the giant bulge straining the soft fabric of his black boxer briefs.

I'm transfixed at the sight and wonder what he would feel like inside of me, so it takes me a moment to catch back up to our conversation.

Creed doesn't think he deserves any pleasure from me, the woman partially responsible for his brother's death, which hurts.

But watching him touch himself is so freaking hot.

"Can I watch?" I blurt out, wanting to see him come even if he won't let me touch him.

"Hell yes. That's what the glass walls in the shower are for, *micetta mia*," Creed says before he drags the pad of his thumb through my damp slit, making me squirm. Then he puts his thumb in his mouth to suck it clean.

"I still don't know what la mia meeseeta or whatever means, since I don't have access to a phone or a laptop..." I remind him. Instead of responding, he suddenly pumps not one, not two, but three fingers deep inside of me several times in a row, making me whimper.

Creed withdraws his fingers from me. "You probably won't like it, so I think I'll keep it to myself for now." He shoves his hand down the front of his briefs and pulls his erection free, distracting me from what we were talking about.

God, he's big. Like scary but please let me try to take it all big. And he's stroking himself with his fingers slick from being inside me.

"I deserve to ache, but I can't hold off any longer. You make me so damn hard, I can't help myself."

I glance up at his face. His blue eyes are still wild as they stare down at me, at my face, my breasts in his thin tee, lower to where my legs are still spread wide. That's where he stares the longest with what I think is longing on his face.

Rather than climb on top of me to slam inside, he groans as if in agony while milking himself until his thick release runs down his tattooed knuckles. Apparently, he's left-handed, since it drips over his wedding band.

When I swipe my tongue over my dry lips to wet them, Creed swears to the ceiling and squeezes his shaft tighter. "If you keep licking those pretty pink lips like that, I'm going to paint them white."

I make sure he's watching me when I do it again, then bite down on my bottom lip.

"Fuck," he shouts before releasing himself. Grabbing my chin in his right hand, he presses his knuckles to my mouth, smearing his release across my lips, so the next time I lick them, I taste his salty flavor on my tongue.

"Missed a spot," I tell him when I grab his hand. I hold it close enough that I can swipe my tongue over the platinum band, up his fingers and stick his entire thumb in my mouth. I like seeing the proof that he's mine on his finger more than I should.

I feel Creed's growl rumble through my entire body. "I knew you were fucking dangerous."

I'm not dangerous, but I'm playing a dangerous game — one with a vicious don.

While I'm still trying to tempt and tease my new husband, he's already figured out how to make me scream.

16

Creed

Somehow, I managed to sleep on my side of the bed last night and keep my hands and all my other body parts off my wife while she was sleeping.

I'm waiting for her to wake up, so I can go down on her a few more times when I hear what sounds like my cell phone ringing from the closet safe. It stops for several seconds only to start up again. I relent, crawling out of bed and retrieving it from the safe by punching in the code.

Lorenzo's name lights up the screen.

I press the button to answer and put it up to my ear. "What?"

"Sorry to bother you so early," he begins. "But I just got a call from Emilio's people. He's having a dinner party tonight."

"So?" I don't give two shits about a dinner party at the Rovinas when I have my sexy wife in my bed wearing only my tee.

"So, he's invited all the families to his estate. Apparently, his oldest son Izaiah is missing."

"Fuck," I mutter, shoving my fingers through my messy hair, unable to forget how Zara pulled on it last night when she was humping my face. I want more of that this morning. I need more of her. "Emilio's missing drug addict son requires a sit down with all the families?"

Dammit. I was hoping it would take a few more days before Emilio realized his son hadn't been seen or heard from in a while.

"He's got some nerve calling a meeting like that without asking you first," Lorenzo says. "What do you want me to tell him?"

I can't shut down or miss the damn dinner without raising suspicions, even though I would love to spend at least a few more days here alone with Zara. "Tell him I'll be there. I want Dre and Tristan to come with me whether Emilio likes it or not."

"I'll tell his staff to put out two more place settings."

"You do that. I'll be back in the city by five. Tell Dre and Tristan to meet us at the penthouse. And I want you to stay with Zara while we're gone."

There's a long pause before he says, "Will do," and ends the call.

When I return to the bedroom with my phone still in my hand, Zara is sitting up awake, half of her curls loose and falling in a tangled mess.

"Everything okay?" she asks.

"We're going back to the city this afternoon."

"Oh. So soon? Why?"

"Emilio is having a 'dinner party' for all the bosses, which isn't really a dinner party but likely going to be a bloodbath where he blames everyone for Izaiah's sudden disappearance."

"And knowing that, you're still going? Do you think he found out Izaiah is dead? That we did it?"

I'm growing to love when she uses the term 'we' more and more each time.

"Guess we'll find out soon. If I don't show, it'll make me look like a suspect."

"True," she replies. "He couldn't know what we did already, right? Or that we're married?" When she chews on her bottom lip, it's impossible for me to not think about her licking my cum off them last night.

"No, I doubt he knows anything we did, and we're going to keep it that way. Our marriage license is staying off the record for now," I tell her, glad I made that decision, since I'm not ready for the Rovinas to know I married Izaiah's baby mama just yet. "And we're not leaving here until I have breakfast." I throw the covers off Zara and straddle her clasped lower legs. "How about you take that shirt off and spread your legs for me so I can eat my fill?"

Without hesitation, Zara lifts the tee up and over her head, revealing her perfect, heavy breasts. Why the hell didn't I have her get naked for me last night? I could've watched them jiggle with every orgasm.

"I need to devour those big, beautiful tits of yours first," I warn her as I run my palms up both of her legs.

Squeezing her breasts together, Zara asks, "Only after you finish on them."

"Only after I finish on them?" I repeat, surprised by her ballsy demand and loving the challenge all at the same time. "You think covering them in my own cum would stop me from sucking those titties dry?"

"Would it?"

"Hell no."

"Then prove it."

"Spread your legs," I order her, knowing eating her pussy will have me ready to explode in no time.

Sliding her legs up from where I'm straddling them, she bends her knees and opens them wide, holding on to her ankles. While I enjoy having her thighs clamp down on the sides of my head, this way will work just fine.

Lying on my stomach, I slip my palms underneath her ass cheeks to lift her pelvis and dig into the delicious buffet before me.

∼

Zara

Creed doesn't seem too concerned about Emilio's little meeting, so I'm trying not to worry about it either. It's nearly impossible to worry about anything after he went down on me, getting me off three times before he sprayed his release on my breasts and then licked them clean.

It was the single hottest thing I've ever done to make this beautiful, dangerous man taste himself after pleasuring me, while all I had to do was lie back and watch him.

The blissed-out state combined with the intoxicating sense of control over the mobster is definitely going to my head.

I like having him at my mercy more than I should.

I don't think I stopped smiling the entire ride back to the city. Thankfully, we're in a brand-new SUV Creed rented to drive us back while leaving the garbage one in the garage to deal with later.

I'm yet again wearing nothing but another one of his suit jackets, since my dress was smelly, and Creed said a tee would be too revealing for me to wear on its own in public.

Soon we're going to have to talk about letting me pick up some of my clothes.

"Lorenzo is going to stay with you tonight," Creed tells me as we slow down for a stoplight near his building.

Well, that brings me back down to Earth.

"I need a babysitter?"

"It's for your own protection in case things go badly at Emilio's," he says without looking at me, and we both know it's a lie.

It doesn't matter how many orgasms Creed Ferraro gave me last night or this morning — I think it was eight in total — he still doesn't trust me.

"I know what you're thinking," he says in the long silence. Reaching over to take my hand, he kisses my knuckle right above the diamond ring and wedding band. "It's nothing personal. I just can't afford to trust the wrong people. There are too many lives at stake."

"I can't tell anyone what happened without screwing myself over," I remind him.

"I'm well aware of that, so make my life easier by not giving me any reason not to trust you," Creed says before releasing my hand. "In fact, I'll put this call on speaker for you to hear." The light is still red when he pulls out his phone and calls someone, letting me hear it ring.

"A little busy here, boss," a man answers.

"Just need a few minutes, Roscoe," Creed snaps back.

"Hold on." There's some rustling on the other line before he returns. "I guess you heard about Izaiah Rovina?"

"Yeah, what the hell is going on?"

"He didn't come home last night, so his father got worried. A traffic cop found his car in the eighty eighth block of Queens with no sign of him or any foul play. His phone went dead at the same location. Nobody's seen him. Detectives are checking area cameras for a lead, but so far, nothing's come up on them."

"So, then what the hell do you think happened to him?" Creed asks, playing up the lie that we don't already know where the asshole is currently decomposing. "Do you think him going missing might be connected to the raid that killed Carmine?"

"Nah, I don't think it's connected. You didn't hear this from me, but the rumors at the station are that he was a big-time H-addict. Most likely it was either a drug deal gone bad or the Sannas grabbed him for dealing in their neighborhood without their permission."

"Wow. Okay. Thanks for the info. Give me a call if you hear anything else, okay?"

"You got it," the man says before the call disconnects.

"So, you have officers in the NYPD working for you?" I ask Creed.

"Not just any officers. That was the Commissioner. He swore he had no idea what SWAT was doing that night. The two in command are dead, not by me, and the rest are pointing fingers at each other, saying they were just following orders."

"Well, hopefully he's right, and Emilio blames this on a drug dealer or the Queens' don."

"I'll find out soon enough."

~

Creed spends all his spare time in his office until he has to leave while I hang out in the living room flipping television channels.

I don't see him again until he comes through to answer the door, letting in Lorenzo, Dre, and Tristan. All three are dressed in various fitted suits, complete with colorful pocket handkerchiefs. I notice Creed has changed too.

"She's still here?" Dre asks as soon as he steps into the living room. "Without any clothes?"

"Do you want me to put your face through that glass coffee table?" Creed asks.

"I just meant that I'm surprised you still have company."

I guess that means Creed hasn't told his cousins we're married.

Slipping my left hand with the rings underneath my leg, I wave to the men with my right. "Good to see you all again too."

While they're all staring at me, Creed quickly twists off his ring and slips it into his pants pocket. I don't know why, but seeing him hide away the symbol of our odd little marriage is like a punch to the gut.

When Creed walks toward me, I get to my feet and give him a hug.

"What was that for?" he asks.

"For luck?"

"Fuck," he grumbles, lowering his eyes from my face to my chest visible in his jacket. "What am I going to do with you?"

"I don't know. What are you going to do with me?"

He reaches out and rubs his thumb across my bottom lip to part them, making me fairly certain of what he's thinking about doing to me. And I sort of hate myself for looking forward to the day he lowers me to my knees.

"Why is it so hard to leave you behind?" he asks.

"Because you don't trust me?" I whisper so only he can hear.

"We both know it's more than that."

I do know it's more than a little trust issue. He wants me.

Creed is a handsome, powerful man who could have anyone he wanted, and he wants *me*. More than just wanting me, he made me his wife.

And the look in his dark eyes...it feels like he's obsessed with me.

I love that. Nobody has ever looked at me so intensely. Ever.

Creed's mouth covers mine without warning, his kiss urgent and demanding, with no restraint as if he forgot or doesn't care that there are other people in the room with us. When I moan into his mouth, Creed pulls away, his lips lowering to my neck. "Wait for me out in the hallway," he says to his friends.

As soon as the door shuts, he lifts my arms, loops them around his neck, then turns us around. His lips are still on my neck when both of his palms cup my bare ass cheeks underneath the jacket and squeeze. He groans low and loud right next to my ear.

Finally, he lifts my feet off the ground with his grip on my bottom and then sits down on the sofa, gently guiding me down on him so my knees straddle his lap. Bringing his face to mine, he says, "I dreamed about this ass last night."

"Oh yeah?"

"I'm surprised I didn't wake up humping a pillow."

His comment makes me smile.

"Don't laugh at me. My blue balls are a very serious, very painful condition."

"Uh-huh. You're the one who refuses to let me help relieve the ache..."

"Not yet. I need to know you actually want me, that it's not an act," he says. "For now, just let me hold your perfect ass for a few minutes, and then I'll go."

"Okay."

There's a whole lot of information to unpack in his remark. Creed doesn't think that I want him?

He kisses me again, this time slower. Our tongues tangle as if we have all the time in the world.

"Fuck. If I don't leave soon, we'll be late. I'll send Lorenzo back in. Tell him to call me if you need me."

Creed lifts me up and sets me down on the sofa. When he stands and starts to walk away, I grab his hand. "Be careful. Even if there's no proof yet that he was involved in the raid, you shouldn't trust Emilio."

The mobster towering above me smiles down and pulls his hand away. "Emilio just wants to bitch. He won't touch me tonight or any other night."

And I really hope he's right.

17

Creed

I hate having to leave Zara alone at the penthouse, but this meeting is important. And I need to discuss part of my plan with my cousins, even if I can't tell them the entire truth.

"What's this shit at Rovinas even about?" Dre asks.

"Izaiah Rovina is missing," I explain from the front passenger seat of my Maserati SUV as Aldo drives us over to the Rovina estate in Brooklyn.

"And? Why should we give a damn about his nasty ass son going MIA?" Tristan asks.

"It could be connected to Carmine," I tell them, which is partially true. "And I want to look every family in the eye to see who might be responsible for setting us up."

"Wait," Dre replies. "*Every* family is coming to this dinner tonight?"

"Yes."

"Did you sign off on that?" Tristan asks.

"No. I didn't. But I'm going to let it slide this time, since Emilio is a distraught father. We'll hear him out, see if anyone acts shady, have a nice meal, and then leave. Calm and cool, understood?"

"Yeah, boss. We'll be cool," Tristan agrees. "So, about that girl. Zara was it?"

Here we go. "What the fuck about her?"

"Well? Is it serious? Where did you even find her?" Dre asks in a huff.

"Carmine introduced us. And as for whether or not it's serious." I glance over my shoulder at their faces in the back seat. "Can I trust you to keep your mouths shut?"

They look at each other, then both give me a nod of assurance.

Slipping my hand into my pants pocket, I pull out my wedding band and hold it up. "Zara and I got married yesterday."

"You did what?!" Dre exclaims.

"Are you high?" Tristan asks. "Trippin' on pussy, boss?"

"I have my reasons, more so than being pussy-whipped. It's nothing you two need to worry about right now. But I do need one of you to help me out with something tonight."

"I can't believe you got married without telling us!" Dre grumbles. "Who else knows?"

"Only Lorenzo. He was our witness. The clerk's holding the license, so it's not even on the public record yet."

"Damn. You picked Lor over us?" Tristan mutters. "That's fucked up, Creed."

"We were in a hurry and wanted to keep it under wraps for the time being," I explain to them. "So, can you two keep your mouths shut? Aldo?"

"I won't say a peep, boss," Aldo replies, his hands firmly gripping the steering wheel. It's not news to him, since he drove us to the clerk's office and back yesterday.

"Tristan? Dre? I need you two to accept this, accept Zara. Don't give me or her any shit. I didn't have a choice but to marry her."

"What the hell does that mean? You're Creed fucking Ferraro. Nobody makes you do anything," Dre remarks.

"It was solely my decision, but…necessary."

"Is she knocked up?" Tristan asks.

"No, she's not knocked up," I reply, then decide to quickly change the subject, since I like the idea of putting my baby in her way too much, and we haven't even had sex yet. "The reason I'm telling you this now is so you'll understand why I can't marry Stella Rovina, but I don't want Emilio to know about Zara yet. Which means I need one of you to agree to marry Stella instead."

"Whoa, buddy! Didn't see that one coming," Tristan chuckles. "Hell yeah, I'll let the viper bitch sink her fangs in me any day of the week."

"Don't even fucking think about it," Dre grumbles. "Her fangs aren't going anywhere near you."

"So does that mean you're in, Dre?" I ask.

"Yeah, I'll do it," Dre says with a heavy sigh.

"I'm sure Stella will love your enthusiasm."

"Could you at least tell me *why* I have to marry her?"

"We need to distract Emilio, and the best way to do that is by promising his family an alliance with ours. There may or may never be a wedding."

"So, I'm just supposed to pretend that I'm going to marry Stella?"

"For now," I reply.

"Fine."

"Try to find her tonight and see how she's doing," I order him. "I'm sure she's also worried about her brother."

"That viper bitch probably hopes Izaiah is dead so she can move up a notch in the family succession line," Tristan remarks.

"How far do you think we'll have to take this distraction?" Dre asks.

"I don't know yet," I admit. "But set a date. Pick out a cake, start planning that shit anyway."

Focusing on the wedding will give Emilio something to think about other than his missing son. And keep the heat off our family.

If Zara were here, she'd probably laugh and say something like, *"That's a great idea. He'll never suspect that you suspect him and killed Izaiah if you're busy rushing your cousin down the aisle toward his sister. Only a psychopath would do something so messed up."*

"Did you just call yourself a psychopath?" Tristan asks since I must have said that last part out loud.

"Why not? That's what we all are," Dre murmurs as he stares out the window, watching the busy New York streets scrawl by at a snail's pace thanks to traffic. "And just in case you forgot, Stella hates me. She's never going to agree to actually marry me."

"Yeah, well, I doubt Emilio will give her a choice. Since I refused to marry her and Carmine is dead, you're the next best option."

It should've occurred to me sooner that the setup at the club happened hours after I rejected Emilio's offer. So much happened that night with Carmine dying, going to jail, planning his funeral, and then dealing with Zara that I haven't had a chance to think about the meeting earlier that day.

"And why was Stella not good enough for you? Her hair not curly enough? You didn't think she would look as cute as Shirley Temple, sitting nearly naked in your penthouse and waiting for you to return?"

"Watch it, Dre," I warn him. "In fact, don't mention Zara again. She's my wife now, and you will respect her. And trust me, she's more dangerous than she looks."

"Seriously? I bet she couldn't smush a spider." Tristan remarks.

"You'd be surprised by what she's capable of," I tell them. "I know I have been."

"Did she sign a prenup?" Dre asks.

"Of course she did," I confirm.

"Just making sure. It would be a shame if she took everything from you while we're all in prison."

"That reminds me, try not to start shit tonight, since we've already got charges hanging over our heads. Don't be surprised if Emilio calls out Aiden."

"What's his problem with the Sannas now?" Tristan asks.

"I heard from one of our NYPD contacts that Izaiah's car was found in Queens."

Tristan whistles. "Damn. So, we might get to witness the beginning of a war tonight?"

"Let's hope it doesn't come to war. And we're going to try not to choose sides."

"But if we had to choose, it would be the Rovinas, right?" Dre asks.

Fuck.

I wish I could tell them it was Izaiah who set up the raid and that Emilio might be behind it as well. But I can't, or they'll figure out I had something to do with Izaiah going missing and that Zara is involved.

"Of course we would side with the Rovinas," I tell him. "Emilio and Aiden have never gotten along because they share a border. They went off on each other at the meeting last week because one of Emilio's dealers ended up with product in Queens and Aiden snatched him up."

"Jesus. So, tonight is not going to go well," Dre remarks.

We finally pull up to the Rovina residence. Cars line the curb up and down the lot. It looks like everyone came rolling deep with multiple cars, most likely a few capos and bodies for security. Hell, it might be time for us to increase our numbers when we're out in public. After what happened to Carmine, nobody would bat an eye if I increased protection. But I just don't want anyone else getting in the line of fire if Emilio or someone else tries to take me out.

I can handle myself, but Zara? Sure, she's tough, but she's also weaponless. I can't even give her a phone. Pulling out my device, I text Lorenzo to have him bring in two men to help him keep an eye on the penthouse.

"What are we waiting for, boss?" Tristan asks.

Lorenzo texts back with a thumbs up. "All right. Let's go in. Keep your mouths shut. Dre, do some sucking up to Stella. And Tristan, you haven't been here as often as Dre and I have, so I need you to do me a favor."

"What's that, boss?"

"Get lost."

"Huh?"

"Wander around aimlessly like you're looking for the bathroom or kitchen or whatever lie you need to come up with. And while you're wandering, I want you to look for a little girl."

"A little girl?" he repeats, glancing from me to Dre in confusion.

"Don't fucking ask me. I have no clue what he's talking about," my cousin mutters.

Even though I've known Dre and Tristan my entire life, my first inclination is to not trust anyone with Zara's secret. Not yet. It's too…precious.

"Don't worry about it. Just let me know if you see any little kids, about three years old. And if you do, don't mention it to anyone. Snap a photo, send it to me, then delete it from your phone."

"You want me to take a picture of a random kid like some pedo?"

"Yes." I don't tell them that once I find her, we're going to plot to kidnap her. I haven't even mentioned my plan to Zara yet. I don't want to get her hopes up in case it fails.

How the hell did I become such a fool for this woman in less than two damn days?

"Jesus Christ," Dre grumbles as he slips out of the car. "He's lost his fucking mind."

"I haven't lost my mind," I say to him when I get out. "Now shut up and go find your new fiancée."

"This is going to end badly. I can already feel it going to hell," Dre remarks before he walks away.

"He's not wrong, boss. You know we wouldn't be busting your balls if we weren't concerned about what's going on with you. It's just, after Carmine was killed, we all got hit with the fucked up gun charges, and then you married this random chick. Even you have to admit that you haven't been acting like yourself."

"Because everything is fucked up!" I yell at him. "My brother is dead! Someone wants me dead or at worst, spending years in prison. And it's got to be one of the fucking families coming for me."

Or someone in my own family.

I keep that thought to myself, because they'll think I really have lost my mind.

I trust my men with my life. I've taken every precaution to make sure we induct only the most loyal bastards around. Every member of our family must be an associate with close ties to an actual member for at least eight years with provable Italian heritage before they take the oath.

These rules have kept my men out of prison and on the streets earning for our family for over ten years now.

And it may all be crumbling around me.

If Emilio gave Izaiah the orders for the raid that killed my brother, he's going to pay for it. I just need to find proof so that the other families won't bat an eye when we retaliate.

If I can't resolve this soon and it's found out I killed Izaiah, the five families could decide to take me out, hell, or my entire family, to replace me as head of the Council.

Since my father set up the Council, a Ferraro has led it. The boss of bosses, capo dei capi, the deciding vote and voice of reason. It's how we've managed to keep the peace in New York City.

And if that peace is shattered, a lot of people are going to die a bloody death, including my family.

∼

Dre beats us to the front door, where four of Rovinas guards are waiting. He appears to be arguing with them, arms flailing around.

While he's preoccupied, I quietly say to Tristan, "If anything happens to me, get Zara out of the country with a new identity and make sure she gets access to my money."

My cousin stares at me slack jawed. "What the hell are you talking about? You think we would let someone take you out during dinner?"

"Just tell me I can count on you to keep her safe and you won't let anyone hurt her, no matter what you might hear."

"I mean — ah… yeah, boss," Tristan finally stammers just before Dre comes stomping back.

"They say we either hand over our phones and guns at the door or leave them in the car."

"Are you fucking kidding?" Tristan asks.

"It's nothing we don't ask of the Five Families when we have a Council meeting at Omerta."

I can't say I'm all that surprised that Emilio is being cautious after his son suddenly went missing.

The three of us head back to the car to drop off our weapons and devices with Aldo, who will stay with the vehicle.

"If they lay a hand on me, I'm going to break it," Dre warns.

"They won't lay a hand on you. They'll probably just wave a security wand over us and let us through."

Sure enough, once we step inside the foyer, a guard does just that. Since all three of us emptied our pockets and holsters, they immediately clear us to go inside.

Gideon Marino and his brother, Zaven, are chatting up Aiden Sanna and his two sons in the front receiving room, which is... odd. Emilio is huddled up with Bowen Bertelli while his father, Weston, and adopted sister, Serafina, talk a few feet away.

All conversations stop, though, when we enter the room.

Ignoring the eyes on us, I head straight for Emilio to get this over with. Either he suspects I had something to do with Izaiah's disappearance, or he doesn't have a clue. Time to find out.

Bowen nods at me and then goes over to join his father and sister.

"Creed. Glad you could make it on short notice. I apologize if I stepped on your toes, but time is of the essence." Emilio offers me his hand.

"I was sorry to hear Izaiah's gone missing. If there's anything I can do..."

"You can press your men at the NYPD to get off their asses and find my son!"

"Done," I agree. "I've instructed my inside guy to let me know if he hears anything." I don't mention that I'm in the Commissioner's pocket since he probably assumes as much. "Do the detectives have any leads yet?"

"No. I don't know what the hell Izaiah was thinking. He never should've gone to Queens so late."

"What was he doing there?"

"Between you and me, I know exactly what he was doing in that part of town."

"Yeah? What's that?"

"Visiting a *puttana* who lives there," Emilio explains. "Now she's gone, probably skipped town with whatever piece of shit helped her grab Izaiah. I think the Sannas put her up to it..." He glares over at the family. "When I find her, I'll get the truth out of her. I need you to press Aiden. They're probably holding Izaiah where they had Marco."

Great, he doesn't suspect me. But, Jesus, I think the *"puttana"* or "whore" he's talking about is Zara.

"Is that what this meeting is about? Seeing if the Sannas offer up any information?"

"They want something for him. I just don't know what yet. I had hoped to find the *troia* before they got here tonight."

"You got people still searching for her?" I mutter, having to grind my teeth to keep from jumping to Zara's defense. I hate that he already suspects her and that he's put together that she had help making Izaiah disappear.

Clearly, there's no love lost between him and Zara. I bet Emilio is the reason that she rarely gets to see her daughter.

"Regardless of how our meeting goes, I won't stop until I find her," he grumbles. Then, he nods his head at someone, calling them over to us. I'm not surprised to see Saint Rovina, the second oldest son, appearing at his side. Unlike Izaiah, the thirty-something kid looks sober and carries himself well. His pinstripe suit is an odd choice, though. All he needs is a matching hat to fulfill the mobster stereotype.

"If you need to reach me, do so through Saint. He'll be learning the ropes, but I'm sure he'll be able to handle himself soon enough," Emilio says.

"Sorry about your brother." I offer Saint a handshake. He looks at my palm with disgust, but after a glare from his father, he reluctantly shakes it.

It's clear that Saint isn't going to have any love for my family, but I don't really give a shit. His father is still running things for now. Until I decide if I need to take him out.

To lighten the mood, I tell them, "Dre was hoping to talk to Stella. Is she around tonight? He's agreed to that alliance you said you wanted."

"Really? Well, I'm glad to hear our families will finally be united," Emilio remarks. "Stella's around here somewhere."

"We can postpone the wedding for however long Stella needs while we look for Izaiah."

"No, no," Emilio replies. "I think they should go ahead and make it official, decide on a date. It'll be a nice distraction for my Martha. We could all use something nice to look forward to." Which is exactly what I thought as well. Martha Rovina has non-Hodgkin lymphoma. The last I heard, her prognosis isn't great, since this is the second time it's returned in five years. Curing cancer is, apparently, still one of the things money and power can't buy.

If I feel a tiny shred of guilt, it's because the woman is dying and I killed her son, making her last days on this Earth even more miserable.

"By all means. Dre is ready whenever Stella wants to move forward," I assure him, pushing aside the hint of remorse. At least Martha will be able to see one of her kids get married before she passes.

"Stella's not going to go down the aisle willingly, but I guess that won't be a problem for the Ferraros," Saint grits out.

I'm not sure what he's implying. "Dre won't rush Stella into anything. We're well aware this wasn't her idea, and it may take time for her to…come around."

"Stella will marry Andre before the end of this year, and that's final," Emilio informs me and his son, leaving no room for argument. "We don't know how much longer your mother has, since she decided to stop the chemo and radiation."

"I'm sorry to hear that," I tell him honestly. His wife isn't my enemy. She probably never wanted to marry his sorry ass in the first place.

Rushing the wedding means we'll have an opportunity to spend more time together and convince them we're not responsible for Izaiah going missing while keeping an eye on what news the Rovinas receive about him from their sources.

Not to mention, it'll give us more time to flame the fire, urging them to look in the direction of the Sannas.

"Help yourself to some appetizers. Dinner should be ready soon," Emilio says. "If you'll excuse me, though, I should try to speak to everyone and thank them for coming on short notice."

"Of course," I agree.

"You can drop the act now," Saint says as soon as his father walks away.

"What act?"

"The one where you pretend to give a shit that my brother is missing."

"I do care. I care more than your father knows."

"Bullshit."

"I think whatever happened to Izaiah could be connected to whoever hired those cops to kill my brother and try to take me out."

Saint blinks at me in what I think is surprise. And judging by his face, I don't see any sort of hint that he was involved in the raid. "You think that was a hit? At the nightclub?"

"I know it was," I assure him. "The cops came in firing at Carmine before they even saw that he had a gun. It wasn't a drug bust or whatever bullshit the press release said. It was a takedown. And when they failed to kill me in the chaos, the one in charge had to settle for arresting me and my guys after another cop talked him down. That cop and the one who killed Carmine either committed suicide before we posted bail, or someone made it look like they blew their own brains out."

"No shit?" Saint mutters as if he's now considering a connection too. "I didn't know all that."

"We haven't been broadcasting the details while we're conducting our own investigations. I won't point any fingers until I have evidence. So far, everyone we've looked into is clean."

"It wasn't us," Saint says, his words crisp with confidence.

"I didn't say it was, did I?"

"Well, I'm just telling you that if some shit like that were going down, I would've heard about it."

Fuck. I actually believe him.

"I crossed your family off my list after I heard Izaiah went missing," I lie.

Either Saint had nothing to do with the setup, or Emilio and Izaiah kept the younger brother in the dark.

Could Izaiah have pulled it off on his own without his father's connection? Probably not. Emilio didn't act suspicious at Carmine's funeral or tonight, though, so who knows?

Maybe Izaiah was trying to prove something to his father, who I heard was reconsidering him as his heir.

As soon as Saint wanders off, I go find Tristan to see if he's seen Zara's daughter. I hate that he won't have his phone to snap a picture of her if he does, but at least we can begin the search.

"Anything?" I whisper when I spot Tristan coming from a room down the long hallway that leads to the kitchen.

"No. Not on this floor. Too risky to go up right now." He glances toward the receiving rooms at the front of the house, all the people coming and going.

"Another time," I agree with a nod. "Let's find Dre. We're getting out of here as soon as we finish dinner."

We find Dre in another sitting room, talking to Stella. We're just in time to watch the show. She starts to walk away from him. Dre says something too soft to hear in the same moment he grabs her wrists. "Don't fucking touch me!" she yells as she lifts her other hand holding a full glass of red wine and throws it right in his face.

There are several hushed gasps from the other guests while I try to hold in my laugh. Tristan turns his back to the room as he chuckles quietly into his fist.

A moment later, Emilio storms into the room, grabs Stella by her arm, and drags her away while apologizing to Dre.

My cousin's face is so red underneath the wine that he looks like he might explode. A passing waiter carrying a tray of appetizers offers him a cloth napkin. Dre mops off his face, muttering what I have no doubt is a slew of swears. When he sees me and Tristan in the crowd, I tip my chin toward the hallway.

Once the three of us are alone, Dre continues swearing under his breath while wiping his neck where the crimson liquid drips onto his white shirt collar.

"What the fuck did you say to her?" I ask him.

"Nothing! I told her I was sorry her brother was missing and wanted to know if she was okay."

"Wow," Tristan remarks. "She really does hate you."

"No shit," Dre mutters while glaring at me.

"Too fucking bad. I told Emilio you agreed to the wedding, and he wants it to happen before the end of the year."

"Before the...that's only five months away!"

"Best get your bachelorhood shit out of your system fast because you're about to be a married man," I warn him. "And I get the feeling that Stella wouldn't put up with a wandering eye."

"You are so fucked," Tristan tells him with a bark of laughter.

18

Zara

Sitting in the penthouse with a silent Lorenzo watching me like a hawk is awkward.

The only time he'd moved was to accept a small package delivery from the doorman. That's when I got up and asked him if he wanted some of the Caesar salad already prepared and ready in the fridge, but he declined.

Once I eat, I return to the living room to continue watching reruns of *Bones*. One of Lorenzo's legs is propped on his knee. His arm is stretched across the back of the sofa several feet away from me, and his body is turned to watch me instead of the flatscreen.

After two more episodes, I've had enough. "Are you staring at me because you think I'll suddenly vanish or is there something on your mind, Lorenzo?"

"There's something on my mind," he replies without even denying his creepiness.

"Oh yeah? What's that? Are you wondering why Creed married me after you pretended to be happy for him yesterday?"

The Lorenzo I first met seemed easy-going and like a sort of father figure to Creed. It must have been an act on his part.

"No. It's obvious why you two got married."

"Is it?"

"Yes. Love at first sight. I'm not doubting that for a second. It happens and can't be helped."

"Love at first sight?" I repeat. "You're exactly right." There is no love on either side of this marriage. "So, if you've got me and Creed's relationship all figured out, then what's up? Why have you been staring at me for hours? It's starting to creep me out."

"Ever since I heard Izaiah Rovina was missing this morning, I've been thinking how odd it is for him to disappear on the same night that you came home with Creed for the very first time, wearing nothing but his jacket — according to Dre and Tristan."

"Okay." I guess Creed still hasn't told anyone about the murder, even his closest friends. And I'm not about to spill the beans either. I like having this secret with my husband and him alone.

"Not only did you show up on the same night, but Izaiah also went missing from Queens. I looked into you today, and I have it on good authority that your apartment is in Queens, only a few streets away from where Izaiah's car was found by Emilio. It was almost as if his old man knew exactly where to search for him."

"Wow. That is a quite a coincidence," I agree. "Guess it's a small world after all, huh?"

"Did you know Izaiah Rovina?" he asks, no longer beating around the bush.

"Did you know that you just asked that question in the past tense? Do you know something the rest of us don't about Izaiah's disappearance, Lorenzo?"

He stares at me, refusing to look away. I stare right back, holding my ground without cowering, and trying to figure out if

Creed put him up to this whole conversation like some sort of loyalty test.

The older man gives me a half smile. "You're not going to answer my question?"

"How about we wait for Creed to get home and ask him? If he tells me to answer your questions, then I will. Creed is my husband. I don't answer to anyone but him now."

"Who did you answer to before Creed came along the other night?"

I hold his gaze, refusing to look away or say another word.

Lorenzo doesn't scare me even if we are alone in Creed's penthouse, and I don't have a phone or a weapon. He doesn't put off any psycho vibes like other men I've known.

How did Creed refer to him? As his advisor and security manager? I doubt Lorenzo is a hardcore killer unless he's defending himself.

And since I'm not threatening his life, we can just sit here and stare at each other for the rest of the night if he wants because I'm not saying another word to him.

The time for being intimidated by men is over and done for me.

I'm Creed Ferraro's wife now, and I'm not scared of anyone.

~

Creed

Our Council dinner gets off to a rocky start.

While Martha Rovina never made an appearance, and Stella didn't join us at the table, Serafina Bertelli did, and Emilio can't hide his disdain for the blonde.

"Stop glaring daggers at my daughter," Weston Bertelli grumbles before salads are served. "Serafina is staying."

"She'll have to leave before we discuss any business," Emilio tells him.

"The rule of excluding women from our business is antiquated bullshit," Weston responds. "Sera is just as smart and tough as any man at the table. She could kill you with nothing but a fork before your guards could stop her." The blonde woman doesn't say a word or smile but shoots a wink at Emilio.

"Damn that's hot." Tristan's comment, thankfully, isn't overheard by anyone but Dre at our end of the table and is drowned out by snickers.

"I don't care if the girl stays," Aiden Sanna says.

"I care," Gideon Marino replies. "Not because she's female, but because she's unvetted like your brood. They can leave with her, along with my brother, after our meal."

Guess my assumption about a Marino and Sanna alliance was wrong.

"Creed?" Emilio asks, since I'm the tie-breaking vote once again.

"This isn't an official Council meeting, so everyone can stay for the discussion. Whatever is said will be shared with our own non-members before we get off the street anyway."

"Fine," Emilio grits out, but he's clearly not happy about it.

"Do you really think she can kill a man with just a fork?" Tristan whispers to me once the rest of the table resumes small talk again.

"Probably," Dre answers for me. "She's trained with his assassins since she was like fourteen."

The rest of the meal, thankfully, goes by without any further disputes. Although I can feel the tension growing with each bite.

And as soon as dessert is brought out by the staff, plum cake with honey mascarpone, Emilio starts his spiel before we can enjoy a single bite. "Well, you all know why I called you here tonight. It's no secret that I blame Izaiah's disappearance on Aiden, since he went missing in Queens."

"Your son shouldn't have been on my turf, but I told you. I didn't have anything to do with him going missing, Emilio. I didn't even know his car was there until you found it."

"You're lying!" Emilio pounds his fists on the table so hard, all the plates and utensils rattle.

"You would accuse me of lying no matter what I say," Aiden replies. "But do you think I would've shown up tonight with my sons if I had laid a hand on your boy?"

"Maybe I'll insist that Kai and Raiden stay here with me and my family until my son reappears."

"Emilio," I start. "You know the rules. Unless you have some sort of proof that ties Aiden or his family to Izaiah's disappearance, then you can't act against the Sannas in any way."

"Exactly," Weston chimes in. "For all we know, your son could've been snatched up by whatever dealer he was there to see."

"You mean one of Aiden's dealers or that corner store *puttana* of yours!" Emilio exclaims. I have no doubt that the "corner store whore" he's referring to is Zara, which makes me want to stab my fork through the asshole's eyeball. The only reason I don't is because it would be an admission of guilt and start a war.

"First of all, I don't have any whores. Furthermore, my dealers haven't seen Izaiah or done business with Izaiah in months," Aiden declares. "Yes, he was coming to Queens for H, but when I found out, I put a stop to it because I didn't want him to OD on my supply and have you blame me for his stupidity."

Oh fuck.

Emilio shoots to his feet. "Get the hell out of my house before I blow your head off!"

"Gladly. I'd rather have a falafel from a street vendor than another bite of this garbage you're serving," Aiden mutters as he and his two sons toss their napkins on the table and walk out the dining room.

I listen for the front door to open and close without gunfire from the guards then breathe a sigh of relief.

Fuck.

That could've ended badly, and it would've been my fault. I need to do damage control to calm Emilio down before he does something stupid.

"I thought the meal was delicious," I tell him. "And I know I speak for everyone here when I say that we hope Izaiah turns up soon, unharmed and unaware of how worried you've been for him. It's probably best if we call it a night before more tempers flare."

"If Aiden's responsible..." Emilio seethes.

"Then I'm sure you'll have no problem finding the proof," I finish for him. "Just as I plan to find the proof of everyone who was responsible for Carmine's death."

~

None of us speak a word until we're in the car, pulling away from the curb.

"That was a goddamn disaster," Dre grumbles from the backseat.

"And you're about to marry into that disaster," Tristan reminds him.

"Emilio is worried about his son. We would be, too, if we had a kid who went missing," I tell them. "Let me know if you hear anything about what may have happened to him."

While Emilio doesn't seem the least bit inclined to suspect I played a hand in Izaiah's disappearance and murder tonight, I know that could change in a heartbeat.

Nowadays, with surveillance cameras everywhere, all it would take is one of them recording an image of me or my license plate to blow up my life and Zara's.

While killing Emilio before he finds that evidence would be the best way to cover my ass, if he dies right now, it would be too suspicious.

So, for now, I'll let my father's former best friend live and hope he never finds his proof.

19

Zara

I heave a sigh of relief as soon as Creed walks through the door. Lorenzo goes to meet him in the foyer. "Everything okay?"

"Yeah. Thanks for staying. I'm keeping the guards on the door for the night."

"Should I be worried?" his advisor whispers.

"No." It sounds like Creed claps him on his shoulder or back. Then I hear the door open and close.

I get up as soon as Creed walks into the living room. "How did it go?"

"Emilio doesn't suspect me," he replies as he grips my waist and walks backward to the sofa. He slumps onto the cushion, pulls me onto his lap, and kisses me, picking things up where we left off. I wrap my arms around his neck, relaxing at his touch, the taste of him, even his rich scent.

"That must be a huge relief, right?" I eventually ask when I pull away.

"Yes."

I study his face, his tightly clenched jaw, and his lowered eyes. "Why don't you sound happier?"

"Because...I wanted to be able to tell you that I saw your daughter. Tristan wandered around the lower level of the house, but we didn't see her."

"Oh," I say in surprise. "Well, thanks for trying to check on her for me," I tell him sincerely. "She probably doesn't even stay in the main residence. In fact, does Emilio seem like the type to put up with a whiny three-year-old in his pristine home?"

There's no way in hell Emilio would ever let Oriana in his house. I know this for a fact, but don't tell Creed.

"Probably not," he agrees. "I'm sorry, *micetta mia*. I can't imagine how awful it must be to not know where your daughter is or be able to see her whenever you want."

"It's not easy. It feels like...like part of my soul has been missing for over three years now. July fourteenth is my favorite and saddest day of the year. That was the one day and night I got to spend with her. I held her the entire time. She didn't cry even once. She just stared up at me like she was the happiest girl in the world." I blink away the tears. "Sorry. I know you were probably expecting more ass grabbing tonight when you got home, not my sob story."

"I can handle both," he says as his big palms slip underneath his jacket to grab my bottom.

"You're going to have to give me something else to wear eventually."

"Not yet."

"At least a fresh suit jacket tomorrow?"

"We'll see," he replies with a quick kiss on my lips. "What have you been doing while I was gone?"

"Just sitting here watching television. It sort of feels like I'm on vacation. I can't remember the last time I had a chance to just sit around and do nothing all day. The worst part is that I have too much time to think."

"About your daughter?"

"Yes. And you," I admit.

"What do you think about me?"

"I just wonder what happens next. With us."

"We're married. What else is there? I like this marriage of ours so far, even if it's less than ideal for you…"

"It's not so bad." I feel safe with Creed.

"I missed you tonight. I missed having my tongue between your legs."

"I-I missed that too," I admit. Even though it feels selfish to let him keep going down on me without offering him anything in return. I love it.

"Good."

Lifting me off his lap, he stands up holding me like I weigh nothing and then gently lowers my back to the chaise end of the sofa, so I'm lying flat. He kneels on the floor and grabs both of my legs, pulling me until my ass is right on the edge.

Creed slips both of my knees onto his shoulders and then leans forward and swipes his tongue from my asshole to my clit. Before I can fully recover, the tip of his tongue flutters rapidly over my clit.

"Oh god!" I groan.

"You taste even better than I remembered," his deep voice rumbles from between my thighs. His tongue batters my flesh again as I squirm and gasp. "This is exactly what I needed. Now scream my name when you come for me."

He's so damn good at oral that it should be illegal. I imagined that a rich, powerful man like Creed Ferraro would prefer women to get on their knees for him, not the other way around.

But the way he laps at me leaves no doubt in my mind that he isn't just doing this out of obligation. He thoroughly enjoys it. His grunts and groans every time I wiggle or moan sends me flying so high.

When I reach down to grab his head and pull him up after the last of the tremors, he resists. Instead, he keeps at it, making me come for him again. The second time, I do shout his name to the ceiling. It's a plea both for more and for him to stop because I'm so sensitive down there...and empty. I want him in me, stretching me, filling me up.

But he doesn't even shove his fingers inside me. He just keeps licking me until I come a third time.

After that, I'm incapable of doing anything except trying to remember how to breathe as my limp arms rest over my head.

"I can't...no more."

But Creed doesn't move from between my legs. His damp lips press soft kisses to the insides of my thighs. Eventually, he says, "Seventeen to go."

"Seventeen?"

"More orgasms for you." With another kiss to my thigh, he says, "I thought Emilio would kill me on the spot today."

"I'm glad he didn't." I lower my arms and run my fingers through his hair. He leans into my touch like he craves the non-sexual intimacy.

"I wish I could trust you not to tell him the truth. But now more than ever, I know I can't."

Sitting up in concern, I tighten my fingers in Creed's hair, lifting his face as I try to reassure him. "You can trust me not to speak a word to him. Why would I want to tell Emilio the truth when he's only going to blame me either way?"

"Because you could give me up in exchange for your daughter back."

I'm momentarily speechless. "That thought never occurred to me," I admit. "Not only because I don't want Emilio to kill you, but because it would never work. There's nothing I can say or do to get custody of Oriana, not while Emilio is alive."

"I want to believe that," Creed says as his sad eyes remain locked on mine.

"Since we're talking about honesty…did you put Lorenzo up to the twenty-questions tonight?"

"Twenty questions?"

"He was asking me about my connections to Izaiah."

"Fuck," he mutters as he gets to his feet, then offers me a hand to help me stand up as well. "What did you tell him?"

"Nothing. I told him I wouldn't answer his questions unless you told me to."

"Good," he says with a sigh. "He may be suspicious, but at least you didn't give him any details."

"So, you didn't put him up to it as, like, a way to test me?"

"No. I haven't told him, Dre, or Tristan anything about you and Izaiah. All they know is that we're married."

"Well, Lorenzo obviously suspects there's some connection. Do you trust him enough to tell him what really happened?"

"I don't know who the hell I can trust with this shit," Creed grumbles. Pressing a kiss to my forehead, he says, "I'll talk to Lorenzo and make sure he comes to me with any questions from now on rather than putting you on the spot like that."

"Thank you."

While my life has been anything but easy, I realize that it's not all champagne and caviar in Creed's world either. Well, he probably does have plenty of both of those things at every event he goes to, but he also has to live his life without knowing who he can or can't trust.

Nobody pretty much sums up who I think he should trust.

He considers Dre, Tristan, and Lorenzo to be loyal enough to never doubt, but probably not many others.

For some reason, I want to be one of the few people Creed cares for and believes in.

Stroking my fingers through his hair, I tell him, "How about we call it a night and go lay down? You can sleep cozied up to my ass you dreamed about all night."

"Not sure if I could do that and resist you, even though it sounds fucking amazing."

He's basically saying he doesn't think we can cuddle without having sex. And while I could say to hell with it and let him inside me, I like where things stand right now — with me getting all the orgasms and him aching, demanding nothing for himself from me. I've never been on this side of the fence before, and I like it.

"Then how about you tuck me into my bed, and we both get some sleep?" I suggest.

His fingers slide down the side of my face until his thumb brushes over my bottom lip. "I'll tuck you in, but first, have you had enough to eat today?"

"Yes. Your refrigerator is full of food."

"Good. Let's have breakfast together tomorrow. I'll have my chef cook for us."

"Deal," I agree. "What else do I have to do in the morning or during the day?"

Taking my hand, he leads me down the hall to the bedroom where he even throws back the covers for me to climb into the giant bed.

"Thanks for tonight," he says as I settle in.

Does he mean… Wow. I should be the one thanking him.

Creed grabs one of his fresh white tees from the closet and offers it to me. "Get some sleep. I'll join you shortly." He places another kiss on my forehead, and then he just walks out, leaving me sitting there in his bed alone.

I'm puzzled because I shouldn't want to spend more time here with Creed. That wasn't part of our deal when I agreed to marry him. But he makes me feel…safe, as crazy as that sounds.

And I'm baffled but hopeful that one of these days, after he licks me so good, he'll drag me to his bed and finally have his way with me.

20

Creed

For the fifth time today, I pull out Zara's phone and read the text from "Even Bigger Piece of Shit." The one that came in the night after the dinner at the Rovinas and says: WHERE'S MY SON? *I'm going to find you and make you regret this, you stupid little slut.*

It didn't take but a few seconds to confirm that the number was, of course, Emilio texting Zara. The way he insults her infuriates me. While I may not know my wife well, I do know that she is not stupid or a slut.

And I haven't told her that Emilio suspects her and is searching for her. There's no need to worry her.

She'll never need to know she's in danger or be afraid of what he'll do to her daughter because I'm going to get Zara's daughter back to her safe and sound as soon as possible.

It's an idea that I've been chewing on ever since she told me about Oriana, but now I'm ready to make it happen. Which leads me to the second part of that plan that I'm fucking dreading. One I've tried to figure out a better option but can't.

Once Zara has her daughter back, I'm going to have to send them both as far away from New York City as possible.

I don't like it. In fact, I fucking hate the thought of being away from her for even a few hours a day. But I don't see any other choice.

Taking out Emilio is not something I can make happen overnight without serious casualties in my own family. And as long as he suspects Zara of having something to do with Izaiah's disappearance, she's not safe in this city or even this country.

When he finds out her daughter has been taken, I'm certain he'll ramp up those efforts to find her.

Which means I need to get them both out of the country and I need to do it fast.

The fact that I'm not spending every waking minute trying to find the girl makes me feel like an asshole.

But I like having Zara in my penthouse, in my bed, having meals with her, and making meals out of her. I think I could stay between her legs forever.

Which is ridiculous and doesn't make any sense. I barely know her. We haven't even been married a week.

Every night I go to bed still horny as hell for Zara after eating her out over and over again with no relief for myself, and I find her sound asleep.

That's how I know it's official – I'm a fucking idiot.

I should've taken her up on her offer to come to bed with her. I could've had her amazing ass against my lap all night without thrusting inside her. Probably. But I haven't tried to do so yet. I let her sleep and I stay on my side of the bed.

Something is holding me back from taking her.

I have to let Zara go soon, and I already fucking miss her.

There's no reason to make it even worse by giving in and doing everything that I want to do to her and have to live with only the memories for the rest of my life.

I need to focus on making sure Emilio doesn't find out I killed Izaiah, determine if he was involved in having Carmine killed, and get Zara her daughter back all without it blowing back on me or my family.

I don't trust private investigators who aren't part of the family enough to pull them into tracking Rovina or finding where he's keeping Oriana, so I'm just going to have to do it myself.

And as for my men who all want to be doing something for Carmine, well, I guess it's time to ask for backup. I'll have them keep an eye on the other families. Otherwise, they'll start getting suspicious about why I'm not doing more to find out who is responsible for killing my brother and Jasper.

I want to find and punish every single person responsible for my brother's death. I owe that to him.

But I also hate the reminder that Zara is one of those individuals.

Even though we're married and she's now my wife, I'm not sure if I'll ever be able to forgive her or fully trust her.

~

"How is your leg?" Zara asks during breakfast after I watched her barely pick at the fruit on her plate and fidget with the hem of my white tee for half an hour.

"Healing."

She nods. "That's good," she replies while pushing a loose curl behind her ear.

"What's up, Zara?" I say, since she obviously wants to say more.

She lifts her eyes to mine. "I know I'm a pain in your ass, but could I ask you for a favor?"

"Of course." I sip my glass of orange juice. "And you're not a pain in my ass." I assume she's going to ask me if I could help her get custody of her daughter.

Instead, she says, "Tonight…it's Thursday."

"Okay?"

"Thursday is when Eugene, the armed robber, comes to the store."

"Oh. Right," I reply in understanding. "You don't want him to show up and fake rob your replacement?"

"No. I don't want him to get arrested, and I don't want him and his sisters to go without food for a week either."

The woman's heart is bigger than the entire state, and despite all the reasons why I shouldn't, I still wish I could own a little piece of it someday.

"I'll handle it," I promise her.

"You'll go meet him? Between nine and ten tonight?"

"Yes. I'll meet him in the alley before he pulls out his gun and give him enough money to get by for the week."

"Thank you." She smiles. "Despite how it looks, he really is a good kid doing the best he can for those he loves."

"I get it," I tell her. She'd do anything for her daughter and respects the kid for helping his younger siblings. I don't blame her. In fact, he's the type of man I wouldn't mind having in our family.

Glancing at my watch, I realize I need to leave now if I don't want to be late for my meeting. I toss my napkin on the plate and go around the table to give Zara a kiss on her forehead. "See you tonight?"

"See you then," she replies. Grabbing the front of my suit jacket, she pulls me closer to kiss me.

After that, it's nearly impossible to leave. But I make myself walk away, heading down to Omerta, where I've called an emergency meeting.

It's rare to have all my family in one place at the same time, but it'll be easier to talk to everyone at once.

As is our usual procedure, every man drops his phone and weapon in a box as soon as they come off the elevators and are searched for wires before being allowed in the conference room, which takes up nearly a quarter of the social club on the thirty-sixth floor. Most will have to stand, since the space isn't big enough for a group meeting this large.

Once everyone has been checked in, I take my place at the front of the conference room. Buttoning the front of my jacket, I can't help but think about Zara in a similar one.

"Thank you all for coming," I start. "I'm sure you already know what this is about. We have to figure out who is behind Carmine's murder, who is responsible for setting us up at The Vault. There has to be some loose end either in the PD or in one of the families. Have your associates put out feelers, listen to gossip, and report anything you hear to Lorenzo, no matter how small or unimportant you might think it is. Any questions?"

"Do you think the missing Rovina son could be connected?" a thirty-something delivery driver asks.

"It's possible," I say. My men don't need to know what I did to Izaiah unless we get dragged into a war for it.

"So should we also listen out for details on Rovina?" another one of our street soldiers who runs a food truck asks.

"Yes, absolutely. Everyone stay armed and alert."

Once Dre finishes up with some bookkeeping matters, calling out those who still haven't paid their dues this month, we adjourn.

"I'm starting to think we're never going to figure this shit out," Tristan says half an hour later once it's just me, him, and Dre left in the conference room.

"Every secret comes out eventually," I assure him. Hopefully, that's not true about my own secrets. There is one secret I think I can finally trust them with.

"So, about Zara," I start. "I know you think it's too soon for me to marry her, but I told you I have my reasons."

"Right? And?" Dre asks.

"And she probably won't be staying with me much longer."

Tristan and Dre exchange a look before Tristan says, "What do you mean, boss?"

"You know the little girl I had you look for at the Rovinas?"

"Yeah."

"She's Zara's daughter. I'm going to get her daughter back from the Rovinas and then get them both out of the country, somewhere off the map where she can live without fear of…my enemies." I start to say the Rovinas before catching myself.

"And let me guess, then you're going to keep them up financially for the rest of their lives too?" Dre asks.

"Yes."

"Not to sound like an asshole or anything, but why? Why go to all the trouble of marrying and helping this woman?"

"Because she's my wife and I put her in a tough spot," I admit. I don't want them to know about her part in Carmine's death. They'd never forgive her.

Nobody will know where she ends up either. I don't plan to trust even my own family with that information.

Ready to change the subject because I already feel like a dick for keeping secrets from them, I ask Dre, "Any reconciliation in the works between you and the missus yet?"

"You think Stella returns my calls after throwing a drink in my face? Fuck no," he grumbles. "And I'm not trying to speak to her again until she fucking apologizes."

"Hell might freeze over before that happens," Tristan mutters.

"Her brother is missing and likely dead," I remind him. "Give the woman a break. Let her have a free pass this time and try to make amends. Emilio wants a wedding soon before his wife dies, so buy her a big-ass ring to show off to her friends."

"Right, I'm sure the rich mafia princess will warm right up to me after I give her an expensive ring her daddy could have bought her."

"Then figure out some way to get on her good side. While everyone else is spying on the other families, you keep an eye on Stella. See what she likes, her hobbies and interests, then try to use that information to win her over. We could use an inside man in the Rovina family. Or woman in this case."

"Right. I'll do all the work to win her over just in time for us to find out her family killed Carmine."

"We don't know that it was the Rovinas who set us up."

"All signs seem to point to them, boss," Tristan points out.

"And if it was the Rovinas, we have to take them out, right?" Dre says.

"Right," I agree. "Not Stella or Cami, but Saint if he was involved."

"And Izaiah? Why did you dismiss his involvement so fast?" Dre asks, sounding suspicious.

Fuck.

"Izaiah being a part of it or not won't matter if he never turns back up."

"And what exactly are we going to do about these charges hanging over our heads?" Dre huffs. "It's like you've forgotten we're all headed to prison soon. Who's going to run shit? How will we keep the Ferraro empire from falling during those three or four years?"

"I've been trying not to dwell on it too much, since my attorney doesn't seem to think we can get out of it. It's…inevitable."

"No, it's not. I'll find a way to get us out of the bullshit charges," Tristan declares.

"How the hell are you going to do that, Tristan?" Dre sounds as skeptical as I am. "You can't kill the DA."

"Why not?"

"Because we would be at the top of the suspect list!" I remind him.

"Oh. Fuck. Well, I'll figure something else out. I'm not letting our family's empire fall apart."

"Good luck with that," I tell him seriously before I walk out of the conference room. It's only been a few hours, but I'm ready to head back up to the penthouse.

While I know I shouldn't spend any more time with Zara than necessary, I can't seem to resist. I'm addicted to that woman and feel the need to spend as much time as I can with her before I have to let her go. And I want to spoil her too.

With everything that's been going on, I had forgotten about the gift I bought her. The one in the box that's been sitting on a table in the foyer for days now. I'll give that to her and get her off a few times before I go meet her robber tonight.

21

Zara

Creed, thankfully, comes home earlier than usual around lunchtime. And he's holding a package, the box that's been sitting unopened in the foyer.

"Hi," I say in greeting, unable to help my smile. When I see the man now, it's an automatic response. I'm sure it has something to do with the fact that he's worked his way down to only three orgasms remaining of the twenty-seven he said I was owed.

"Hey. I bought this for you when we were in the Hamptons and forgot about it," he says as he pulls out a knife from his pocket and slices open the tape. The box isn't very big, just about three inches thick and the size of a sheet of paper.

"You bought something for me…and left it sitting unopened on the table for nearly a week?" I accept the opened box from him without getting up from my seat on the sofa.

"Sorry. I've had a lot on my mind."

The worry lines between his brow have been obvious, but I don't ask him what he's worried about. His brother just died, and he killed an ally's son and married me in a matter of days.

Instead, I open the flaps of the box to see what's inside.

It's a…digital photo frame?

"I thought I could upload the photos from your phone to the frame so you could still see them."

"Oh."

He bought the frame so I could look at my pictures, which is sweet, but he did it because he still doesn't trust me with my phone.

In fact, every day when he leaves the penthouse, he has two guards stay here with me at the door. They may not leer at me from the sofa like Lorenzo, but I know that they're there, ensuring that I don't leave and reminding me that I'm really just a prisoner who gets to enjoy lots of oral sex.

"Thank you," I add, since it's a sweet gift. Sort of.

"I wish I could trust you. You know that right?" Creed sits next to me on the sofa.

"And I don't blame you," I admit. "I do appreciate the gift and your help with Eugene tonight."

"I'll start transferring the photos over now." He lifts the frame box from my lap and opens it. When he removes my cell phone from his pocket, he remarks, "You have a lot of photos on your phone."

"Yeah, it's sort of a hobby."

"A hobby?"

"I've always loved capturing life through the lens, even if the lens is my shitty little phone's camera."

"I like the photos. They're good shots, capturing the essence of city life."

"Thanks," I say, since that's the way I'd describe the images as well. "I actually came to the city because I thought I had a shot at modeling."

"Really?" Creed looks up at me.

"You don't have to sound so shocked," I tease him.

"No, I mean, you're gorgeous. I can see you on the runway or on a giant perfume ad in Times Square."

Laughing, I tell him, "You are so full of shit."

"I'm serious. Why did you give up modeling?"

"I ended up in some campaigns that I didn't feel completely comfortable with and decided the industry wasn't for me. Oh, and I got pregnant."

"Right. Well, I wish it had worked out for you, but I'm glad I don't have to share you with an audience." Creed gives me a small smile that quickly disappears before he returns to working on the frame.

I don't say much to him the rest of the afternoon until he leaves to meet Eugene in Queens, too lost in the memories of those first few years in the city. I regret them. In fact, Oriana is the only reason that I'm glad I came to the city seven years ago.

Well, Oriana and now, Creed.

I'm so glad I met the mobster, despite the shitty circumstances. I just wish he felt the same.

~

Creed

I've been waiting in the alley behind the discount store for about ten minutes when an ancient blue Cutlass comes squealing. Last week he was in a different vehicle, but I have a feeling it's the same boy. I stay hidden in the shadows until the car stops just beside the store's back door.

The familiar-looking scrawny kid that's nearly my height climbs from the driver side with a ski mask covering his face, leaving the vehicle running. He goes to the door and lifts his fist to pound on it.

"She doesn't work here anymore." My voice startles the kid. He whips around to face me while pulling out the gun tucked into his rear waistband of his baggy jeans. "And if you're smart, you'll throw that damn thing away before you end up with a three-and-a-half-year mandatory prison sentence."

"Aw fuck," he mutters, then turns back around and reaches for the car's door handle.

Stepping out of the shadows and into the glow from the car's headlights, I tell him, "Wait a second, Eugene. Zara sent me. She'll be pissed if I let you leave empty-handed."

The boy pauses. "Zara sent you? Are you a cop? I don't know what she told you —"

"Do I look like a fucking cop?" I gesture with both hands toward my custom suit, letting him also see that I'm not armed.

"Guess not."

"I'm Creed Ferraro."

With another swear, he scurries into the driver seat as if to leave. So, I take a seat on the hood. "Get out of the damn car. Either you're a wannabe gangster or you're a pussy. What's it going to be, Eugene?"

After a long moment, he opens the squeaky car door and steps back out.

"What do you want from me? Did you hurt Zara?"

"No, I haven't and wouldn't hurt Zara. But she is staying with me now. And she sent me to give you the envelope full of cash in my suit pocket. I'll give it to you if you put your gun on the hood."

"How much money?" he asks curiously.

"You'll find out after you give up the gun."

"Fine," he huffs. "It's not loaded anyway. Can't afford bullets." He places the weapon down on the hood near the windshield wipers, as far away from where I'm sitting as possible.

Standing up to face him again, the boy tenses as if he's about to take off on foot. I reach into my jacket to retrieve the envelope and hear his exhale of relief when I offer it to him. He snatches it from my fingers and immediately starts thumbing through the bills.

"Holy shit! How much is this?"

"Ten grand. And it's just the start. You can keep that cash with no strings attached. If you want more, you'll get that much in cash every week in exchange for agreeing to work for me."

His fingers tighten around the envelope. He looks up at me through the eyeholes of his mask. "I don't get it. What's the catch?"

"The catch is that you do what I say, stop pretending to rob stores, and keep your mouth shut about my business."

"That's it?"

"That's it. There will be risks involved in the work, but you'll also have my protection. What's your last name, Eugene?"

He only hesitates for a moment. "Gallo. It's Eugene Gallo, sir."

"Gallo? Your family have any Italian in your blood."

"Uh, I don't know. Maybe?"

"Find out. If so, in eight years, if you've proven yourself to be loyal, then you can move up the ranks, become one of my men."

"But...why me?"

"Because Zara says you're a good kid, doing what you need to do to raise your sisters. And if you keep doing that shit on your own, one day, probably not too far in the future, you're going to get caught, thrown in prison for life, and never see them again."

"Is that a threat?"

Chuckling, I tell him, "No, kid. It's a fact. Not everyone is as amenable to being robbed as my wife."

"Your wife is Zara?!" I shouldn't have let that shit slip like that.

But I can't seem to help myself. I want everyone in the fucking world to know who my wife is, even though it's too risky to announce.

"That's your first test, Eugene Gallo. Nobody knows Zara and I are married, except three people who, without a doubt, would take a bullet for me. If anyone else finds out, I'll know it was you, and I won't be happy."

"Fuck, man. Who would I tell?"

"I don't know. Who would you tell?"

"Nobody," he replies. "I don't talk to anyone."

"Good. Keep it that way. Give me your phone number, and I'll call you when I have a job for you."

"I...um...I don't have a phone."

"You don't have a phone?" I say in surprise.

"No, sir."

Jesus. I should've realized that if the boy was fake robbing a discount store, then he doesn't have the money to pay for a phone and monthly plan. It's a good reminder not everyone is as lucky as I am. I guess I have my wife to thank for that reminder as well.

"Buy yourself a phone with that ten grand, even if it's the cheap, pay by the minute kind, then call this number and tell him you're our new errand boy," I say as I pull out my wallet and hand him one of Lorenzo's business cards.

"Okay," he agrees. "Thank you, sir. Tell Zara...tell her I appreciate her help."

"I will. Stay out of trouble," I warn the kid. "You're no good to me if your ass is in prison."

"Yes, sir."

And for some reason, I know not only will this kid be an indispensable employee to me, because he's desperate to keep a roof over his sisters' heads and food in their bellies, but I also think he's got the kind of grit that will make him one hell of a man someday.

22

Zara

For the past two weeks, I've been lounging around Creed's Park Avenue penthouse, bored out of my mind without any access to a phone or laptop. All I have is the television with every streaming app under the sun, and a digital photo frame that makes me sad every time I see my baby girl's face without knowing when I'll get to hold her in my arms again.

Oh, and I also now have a closet full of expensive clothes I'll probably never wear, since Creed won't let me leave the building.

That was a funny conversation with my husband when he told me he was going to have some clothes sent up for me. I said, *"Finally. Although, I have gotten comfortable in just your jacket or tee. It'll be nice to put on panties again."*

And his response? *"Who said anything about panties?"*

He did provide me with various undergarments, most of which are very lacy and sexy but not uncomfortable to wear.

He could've bought me two pairs of leggings, two tops, a few sports bras and a package of panties from Target, and I would've been happy to have a set of comfy clothes to wear while washing the other set.

Not that I'm allowed to do laundry, any cleaning, or cooking. There are daily staff who come and manage those chores. They all glare at me like I'm a threat to their positions whenever I offer to help.

Being waited on was nice the first week or so, but the longer I'm here, the more it reminds me of the months when I was spoiled and pampered, living in one of the Rovinas' apartments before and while I was pregnant with Oriana. Until the evil assholes took my daughter and kicked me out on the street.

I can't shake off the sense of dread that this little vacation as Creed Ferraro's secret wife might end just as badly.

And each long day I go without seeing him, I worry that it's one where Emilio succeeds in his next attempt on Creed's life.

While there might not be any evidence of Emilio's involvement in the club raid yet, I know he had a hand in it. Izaiah couldn't tie his own shoes, much less try to take out the head of the mafia without significant help or acting on his father's orders.

Creed has to know that much as well. Soon, I'm going to tell him the truth about Oriana's father rather than let him go on assuming. But I've barely seen the don this week, and it feels like he's avoiding me on purpose. I lie awake in bed, waiting until he finally comes in around midnight or so. Then he's gone before I wake up the next morning.

Of course, I'm worried he's distancing himself because he still doesn't trust me. How can he after what happened to his brother?

If Creed trusted me, he'd let me use electronics by now. And he'd let me touch him since he's reached those twenty-seven orgasms he promised me before it would be his turn.

One thing is for certain: if I can't spend time with Creed, then

I'll never have the chance to earn his full trust before he's sent off to prison.

That's why I've decided I've had enough waiting around and am determined to seek out my husband tonight.

"Where's Creed?" I ask the guards at the door. The two large, imposing men in suits both wince at my direct question but neither respond.

"Is he out? Is he in the building? Is he alive?" I huff.

"The boss is downstairs in his office in Omerta," one of them finally remarks.

"Where is his office? Which floor?"

"Don't," the other, surlier guard warns the younger man.

"I'll take her down and watch over her."

"Really?" I say in surprise.

"Boss won't like that."

"Getting some ass will do the boss good," he replies to his fellow bodyguard, then turns to me. "That is why you want to see him, right?"

I guess his guards assume we're hooking up, since I live here now and sleep in his bed, even if they may not know we're legally married yet. I wish those things were true. But Creed hasn't even gone down on me in several days.

Not that I need him to or anything. And I do want to return the favor, dammit. Creed is the scariest, deadliest man I've ever met, and by far, the sexiest. But he won't let me touch him.

"That's exactly why I want to see him," I assure the guards and myself. "Just give me a moment to change."

Creed seemed to have a hard time resisting me when I only wear his suit jacket, so I slip into his closet and find one to throw on after removing my leggings and tee, along with my bra and underwear. Since I showered less than an hour ago, all that's left is to run my fingers through my curls to untangle a few, and I'm ready.

It seems like it takes us three days on the elevator to get from the ninety-sixth floor to the thirty-sixth. The whole time, I have my arms wrapped around my waist to make sure the suit jacket keeps everything important covered.

"After you." The guard waves his arm forward for me to exit the elevator first.

I do and find dozens of men playing cards or billiards, drinking at the bar, and milling about, staring at me, or more specifically, my attire. I begin to have second thoughts, wishing I had remembered that this place is also a literal boys only club.

I fidget with the jacket button, hugging myself tighter in it. "Maybe...maybe I shouldn't bother him, you know, in case he's busy."

"He'll be happy to see you." The man steps off the elevator and lets the doors close behind him, removing one of my escape routes.

"How do you know that?" I ask. "What if you're wrong, and he takes his anger out at you for bringing me down here?"

"Do you know how many women the boss has brought up to his penthouse?"

"Not sure if I want to know the answer to that question."

"You're the only one I've heard he's been with in over a year," he tells me anyway. Over a year? I doubt that. Then, he points straight ahead. "Down the hall past the check-in desk. You can't miss his office, since it's the big one on the left at the end of the hallway."

"Oh. Okay. Thank you." I head in that direction, if for no other reason than to get away from all the prying eyes of strangers.

I quickly bypass the man working the check-in desk, who barely gives me a glance.

All the lights are out in the rooms that I pass until I get to the last one on the left.

If I didn't know he was the don of all dons, I'd assume the handsome man with his black dress shirt sleeves rolled up his arms, typing away on his laptop, was a successful businessman, catching up on his correspondence. The crease between his black eyebrows and his scowl makes me think that whatever he's working on isn't pleasant.

Before I can turn around and leave, he lifts his eyes and catches me standing in the doorway

"How did you get down here?" he snaps. I can't tell by his tone if he's happy surprised or angry surprised.

"The elevator," I answer and attempt a small smile. Hopefully, my comment reminds him of a similar response he once gave me after I asked him how he got into my apartment, and he told me. "The window."

Getting to his feet, Creed strolls around his giant wooden executive desk and approaches me, his jaw tight, eyes hard. He hooks one long finger into the V of the suit and gives it a tug to reveal the tops of my breasts all while holding my gaze. "Are you wearing anything underneath my jacket?"

"No."

"Good." He pulls me inside his office with that single finger until he can reach around to close the door. He turns the lock, sealing us alone inside.

Some of the tension leaves my shoulders as he crowds me back against the door. When I'm completely plastered to it, Creed braces his left palm next to my head. His nose brushes mine, and he peeks down the front of the buttoned jacket that his finger still holds open.

"My wife is so damn gorgeous," he whispers down into the cavernous space. "I've always been an ass man, but these beauties?" Creed crouches down a few inches to swipe his hot, wet tongue over one swell, then the other. That's all it takes to have me dripping wet. "I want to bury my face in these tits until I fucking suffocate."

Dropping to his knees in front of me, his fingers quickly work to undo the two front suit buttons. I slump down a little, knowing exactly what he wants. As soon as he parts the two sides of the jacket, his mouth clamps down on my right breast.

"*Creed*," I whimper. My mouth falls open on a gasp, and my eyes slam shut. My fingers sink into his long hair, holding his face to my chest. He licks, sucks, and gently bites down on my flesh as his palms grip my hips tight enough to leave bruises.

Sliding his hands up my ribs, he cups my breasts and squeezes them together. As he runs his tongue up the middle, his dark blue eyes lift to mine.

"Why are you avoiding me?" I blurt out the question because every second I'm near this man, I get even more confused about if he wants me or not.

Between kissing my breasts, he says, "I'm not *just* avoiding you...I've also been busy." His admission doesn't make me feel any better.

"Too busy to come upstairs or to bed until you're ready to pass out?"

"I've been trying to keep my hands off you. It's not fucking easy..."

"Sorry?" I mutter and maybe tug on his hair just a little harder.

"It's not your fault that I want to fuck you so badly, I can't be in the same room as you for more than five seconds. I barely sleep at night with you so close, smelling delicious. The ache I have for you keeps me awake for hours."

"I don't...I don't understand." If he wants me so badly, then why hasn't he pounced on me yet? We're freaking married. I don't understand his holdup, other than it's a trust issue.

"I've spent the past two weeks trying to figure out if Emilio was behind the raid and stalking each of the Rovina properties," Creed tells me. "They're all over Brooklyn, and a few in Manhattan. During the day, I've been watching them on my own or with Aldo or Lorenzo occasionally driving me, so I can try to get some work done on my laptop while we wait."

"You're still trying to find evidence that Emilio put Izaiah up to the raid?" I knew he was determined to get vengeance for his brother, but I had no idea he was obsessing over it day and night.

"I am. And I've been looking for Oriana."

My daughter's name coming from his lips stops my heart mid-beat, mostly because I've only said it a few times and can't believe he even remembered it. "W-what?" Maybe I misheard him.

"It takes a few days to observe each property before I'm confident enough to cross it off the list and move on to the next. I don't trust anyone else to look for her, or even know she exists, except for Dre and Tristan. So, I've been spending my days out on the streets of New York City and my nights either catching up on family business or avoiding ravaging you."

"But...why?" I ask in confusion.

"I'm determined to return your daughter to your arms, Zara."

I shake my head because it seems insane. I even tug on his hair to pull him back up to his feet. Having Creed Ferraro kneel before and offer to give me back my world is too ridiculous to be real.

But his stern face says he's serious.

"No. It's too dangerous. Emilio...he won't let her out of the caretakers' sight. And he may already want you dead because of what happened with Carmine, then Izaiah..."

"I can handle it. In fact, I think I'm getting pretty good at this kidnapping thing, since it worked out so well with you. I didn't even need to use handcuffs to keep you from running off, which is a little disappointing if I'm being honest."

"Creed..."

"I won't get caught."

"He'll come after me if she goes missing," I remind him. "So, how do you think this could ever work?"

"Because I typically don't do anything without coming up with a flawless plan. Izaiah was the exception," he says while slipping his hands underneath the hem of the jacket to grab my ass. "And while I wish I could lay you out on my desk and devour you right fucking now, Emilio is on his way here for a meeting."

"Emilio...he's coming here? R-right now?"

Creed removes one hand from my ass cheek to glance at his watch. "Any second."

"Shit! He can't see me here!"

"I know, *micetta mia*."

I push Creed away and then begin to panic, wondering if I should try to make a run for the elevator or hide in the office under his desk.

"You can stay in here. I'll wait for him in the lobby and take him to one of the conference rooms."

"Okay. Okay." I nod a little too much, not all that reassured by his words.

"He won't know you're here. I promise. He still doesn't know we're married either. I don't want him to suspect I might try to come after Oriana for you," Creed says as he grips my shoulders and places a kiss on my forehead.

"Okay," I say, even if I am anything but okay.

"Emilio probably just wants to talk about wedding details."

"Wedding details?" I repeat in confusion.

"Dre's supposed to marry Stella before the end of the year."

"Oh."

Strolling over to his desk, Creed picks up his cell phone and starts back to the door. "I shouldn't be long if you want to wait here for me."

"You don't think he knows, do you? About what we did to Izaiah or about you sitting outside the properties?"

"I guess we're about to find out." He reaches around me to open the door.

"Wait!" I grab his arm to stop him. "You need more men with you. Armed ones!"

"I don't need any backup. I'll be fine. He has to leave his weapons and phone at the front desk. Besides, I'm sure whoever brought you down is still waiting out there, right?"

"Y-yes."

"Good. I'm glad you came down here tonight. When I get back..." he runs his thumb over my bottom lip, down the center of my chest to my stomach. "When I get back, I want to hear you scream my name at least three times."

As soon as Creed slips out the door and shuts it behind him, I slide down the wooden panel and slap a hand over my mouth to keep quiet as tears fall.

Creed's been putting his life on the line for me, for Oriana, and I haven't even told him the truth.

If something happens to him...I'll never forgive myself.

But no matter what, at least I know I'm finally free of that fucking man once and for all.

I'll never have to endure having a Rovina's hands on me again.

Creed won't ever let him lay a finger on me.

I repeat those assertions to myself over and over again to try to calm myself.

23

Creed

I was right.

I can't be in the same room with Zara for longer than a few seconds without needing to get my hands and mouth on her.

Of all times for her to come down here and literally bring me to my knees, I have to leave her to go talk to Emilio Rovina.

I didn't want to worry Zara, but when he asked for the late-night meeting on short notice, my first thought was that he knows I've either been following his family, watching his properties, killed his son, or married her in secret.

At this point, there's not much I can do but see how it plays out. If it comes down to it, barehanded I'm sure I can kill the old man before he kills me.

One of my more easy-going guys and recent penthouse guard, Matteo, is waiting in a chair near the reception desk. He gets to his feet when he sees me.

"Thank you for bringing Zara down," I tell him. "Escort her anytime she wants."

"Yes, sir. Do you want me to wait for her?"

I sigh. "No, go back upstairs." Even though I could probably use the backup. The kid is Gianni's nephew, one of my capos, and only in his mid-twenties. He's got his whole life ahead of him.

Once he's gone, I lean against the receptionist desk, scrolling through my phone while I wait for Emilio to show.

He finally does a few minutes later. He steps off the elevator with two of his men, no Saint tagging along, which is surprising, since I thought he was supposedly showing him the ropes.

"What's so important it couldn't wait until the morning?" I ask, trying to act like my usual cranky self.

It's funny that I have to even try with all that's going on. There's something about being around Zara that instantly brightens my mood. It doesn't matter that I was dog tired or frustrated when she walked into my office. As soon as I laid eyes on her, everything else in my head got shoved out of the way to make room for only her.

In some ways, she reminds me of Carmine with the way she so easily makes me feel lighter, happier. It's strange how quickly she stepped in and filled that space he left.

"This isn't something I wanted to discuss over the phone," Emilio replies tersely while swiping his palm over his slick head.

"Fine. We can talk in one of the conference rooms after you hand over phones and weapons."

He reaches into his jacket, pulls out a cell phone, and tosses it into the box on the desk. "No weapons," he says as Jace, our receptionist, pats him down. "The guards will stay here."

Once Jace gives me a nod, I lead the way down the hall, giving Emilio my back to literally try to stab me in it if he so chooses.

I'm not suicidal. I don't *want* to die. But the risks outweigh the reward of finally figuring out if Emilio wants me dead, so I can get retribution for Carmine.

"Why not your office?" Emilio asks, nearly making me flinch before I catch myself.

"Because there's a half-naked woman sprawled out on my desk, waiting for me to return," I tell him, which is partially true. I'm going to have Zara in that exact position as soon as this meeting of ours is over.

Emilio grunts what may have been a scoff or a bark of laughter as I walk in and flip on the lights for the smaller conference room that can accommodate six people.

I take a seat at the head of the table, and Emilio shuts the door, then pulls out the chair to sit at the other end.

"Any updates on Izaiah?"

"That's why I'm here."

Well, fuck.

"It's not…it's not looking good. There's no sign of him. If Aiden had him, he would've folded by now and made demands, which makes me think he's most likely dead."

"I'm sorry, Emilio. That's shit, not having any closure, can't be easy. I know there's nothing I can say to help."

"Right," he agrees as he folds his hands together in front of him on the table. "There is something you can do to help, though."

"Oh yeah?"

"I want your permission to, ah, question a few dealers in Queens, possibly in some of the other boroughs as well."

"Dealers?"

"It's possible Izaiah was killed by an H dealer, someone that *puttana* was probably fucking on the side."

It takes all the restraint in my body not to launch myself across the table and wrap my fingers around his throat for calling Zara a whore yet again.

I take a slow deep breath and focus on the rest of Emilio's

words. He doesn't suspect me. Or, if he does, he's damn good at pretending he doesn't. He, no doubt, plans to pick up and torture all the drug dealers in the entire fucking city until someone confesses to killing Izaiah.

"Do you really think any of those pieces of shit would admit to what they've done if it was one of them?"

"I just want to question them."

"Question and release them while they're still breathing?"

"Yes."

"Fine," I agree, knowing it's fucked up, but at least if he's busy chasing down a drug dealer, he won't look closer at me as a suspect. "On one condition. You release every single one, and I mean they walk out on their two feet, not on a gurney or in a wheelchair. If or when you find the person you think is responsible, we bring in the boss of their borough before ending him. Deal?"

"Deal."

"I'll let the other bosses know what you'll be doing and to notify me if you don't keep your word."

"Fuck that!" Emilio's face turns red. "If you tell them, they'll warn their guys, and they might run or try to cover for them."

"Then I'll also warn the bosses to keep track of their men, and if any run, we'll assume they were in on it and do what we need to do to settle the score."

Emilio settles deeper into his chair. "Fine. I have to find who did this, for my reputation's sake and for Martha."

"I know you do. Just like I have to find who lured me to the club, killed my brother, and had me and my guys arrested."

I study his face with every word spoken. He doesn't give anything away if he was behind it.

"Has Andre made any progress on the wedding?" Emilio asks, changing the subject, which is fine with me.

"Not that I've heard. Stella still seems...reluctant to speak to him."

"She'll marry him. I know a guy who can probably fit us in for the Tribeca Rooftop by the end of the year. I'll tell him to put down a date, and that will be that."

"Good. I'll let Dre know you've got it handled."

With a final nod, Emilio pushes his chair back and gets to his feet.

"I appreciate you meeting me so late. Time slips away from me lately," he says as I open the conference room door to escort him back to his waiting guards at the elevator.

"Glad we could keep it short," I mutter. "Now, if you'll excuse me, my dinner is getting cold."

This time, Emilio does chuckle. I don't wait for him to get on the elevator, but I take my time walking back down the hall to my office.

By the time I reach for the door handle and glance back over my shoulder, the three men are stepping onto the elevator.

Thank fuck.

When I try to push the door open, though, it jams. Glancing down in the two-inch opening I see Zara on the floor, crawling away.

"Sorry," she says, scrambling to her feet and swiping at her cheeks. Her damp cheeks.

"What's wrong, *micetta mia*?" I close and lock the door before wrapping her in my arms.

"There's something...something I haven't told you," she says through hiccups, her face pressed to my shoulder.

"Okay. Are you going to tell me now?" I whisper.

"Izaiah wasn't...he wasn't Oriana's father."

That's the last fucking thing I expected her to say. "What do you mean?" I ask as I take a step back to see her flushed, damp face.

"Izaiah...he *thought* he was her father."

"You're telling me that Emilio Rovina didn't demand a DNA test before taking her from you?"

Zara shakes her head. "No. Emilio did a DNA test, but he had someone fake the results, letting Izaiah believe he was her father because the piece of paper and his father said so."

"Then why the hell did Emilio keep her from you?" I must be more exhausted than I realized, since I can't figure out why the mobster would take Zara's daughter if he knew his son wasn't the kid's father.

Zara stares up at me, her green eyes brighter from the tears. "Creed, are you really going to make me say it?"

"Say what?" I ask in confusion, right before one of the missing puzzle pieces slides into place.

"No." My hands fall away from Zara because I want to ram my clenched fists into a fucking wall. "Jesus Christ! *Emilio* is her father?"

Zara scrubs her palms over her face. "I'm sorry I didn't tell you. I try not to think about it. I know that sounds stupid, but it's true."

Pacing away from her, I press my fingers to my forehead, trying to wrap my head around this shit while not wanting to think about it either, but goddammit I have to. "You fucked Emilio? At the same time, you were fucking Izaiah?"

"Yes."

My feet finally come to a stop as my soul breaks in half for her. "Did you…did you want either of them?"

She shakes her head emphatically. "Absolutely not."

"Then how…"

"It's a long shitty story."

"Tell me. Please, Zara." It occurs to me that when I stopped touching her, she probably thought it was because I'm repulsed and no longer want her. But nothing could be further from the truth.

I still want her, more than ever. I need to wipe both of those sons of bitches out of her mind forever.

Closing the distance between us, I gently cup her face in my palms. "I want to know, *micetta mia*; I just want to understand. I'm not angry at you for keeping this secret from me. It's none of my damn business."

"You told me you've been going to all this trouble to find Oriana, and I knew you deserved to know the truth. Even if you change your mind about helping me get her back, since her father's not dead. He's very much alive, and one of the heads of the Five Families."

"Of course, I'll still help you get her back! That's all I've been doing for weeks. She's your daughter. She deserves to be with you. That's all I care about."

"Thank you," she whispers, visibly deflating. She bites her bottom lip. "Could we maybe sit down for the rest of this conversation?"

"Yes, of course. Sit." I turn each of the two chairs in front of my desk to face each other, and once Zara takes the one on the left, I take the right.

"So, I first came to the city with Emilio seven years ago. I was only twenty, not even old enough to drink yet."

"How did you meet him?" I ask, wanting to know everything.

"Through my parents."

"Your parents?"

"I'm not close with them anymore. I haven't been, since they sent me to the city with him that first weekend. If they know they have a granddaughter, well, it's not because I told them..."

"Your parents encouraged you to what, date Emilio?"

"They knew I dreamed of moving to the city, to try and make it as a model, you know? Emilio was one of their customers, a rich customer who came in whenever he was traveling through Pearl River. Our, their brewery was struggling. He convinced us that he had contacts that would help me get signed to an agency. So, at first, I went with him to the city on weekends. They had to have known what he did to me when I stayed in one of his apartments for free. My mom told me I was *lucky* to have caught such a wealthy, important man's attention, one who could help me chase my dreams. I had never even had a boyfriend or dated anyone before he came along."

"Emilio Rovina was your first?" The words taste bitter on my tongue.

"Yes. And when he helped my parents with a loan to save their brewery and helped me get hired with one of the best modeling agencies, I was sent to live in the city with him permanently. It felt like my body was part of the whole transaction, a 'buy a struggling business, get our daughter free' kind of deal. So, I lived in one of his properties for almost three years. He paid for everything while I got to do some photo shoots here and there, making a little money but not enough to pay rent or anything, especially not in the city. Emilio visited me whenever he wanted, which was…often, usually two or three times a week, all behind his wife's back."

"Jesus. Even while she was sick the first time?"

"Yes. Especially then," she says. "She was getting treatment when I got pregnant. Since Emilio didn't want anyone to know he had a bastard, especially his wife who was fighting cancer, he introduced me to Izaiah."

"He gave you to his son, so he could fuck you and lie about him being Oriana's father?!" It's impossible not to raise my voice with that question, the infuriating absurdity of it.

Zara nods. "When Emilio first found out, he threatened to drag me in for termination. I warned him I would kill myself if he did that, and he caved."

"You wanted to have his baby?"

"No, I didn't *want to* but it was too late. I considered it, sure. I already loved her, though, even if she was his. It wasn't her fault that he was her father. And I needed...I guess I thought she would be my salvation. That I could love her enough to drown out the hatred."

I nod even though I can't even begin to understand the position he put her in.

"So, after that was settled, Emilio moved on to a new plan." Shaking her head, she says, "Izaiah was such an idiot. He didn't even notice Oriana would've been born two months early if she was his. Emilio made me tell him I was pregnant after a few weeks, then forced him to do a DNA test. He showed him the paperwork, stating there was a 99.9% chance he was her father, and that was that. I don't think any of the other Rovinas know they have a sister..."

Jesus. Fucking. Christ.

No wonder Zara hated Izaiah so much when he blackmailed her, like that night he had her set me up and killed Carmine. It wasn't even his goddamn child that he was using against her, but his own sister.

"Weeks after the stick turned blue, I gave up chasing modeling gigs. I lived in the apartment Emilio owned and barely left throughout the rest of the pregnancy. I was used by them both whenever they wanted. Emilio didn't care if he was my only lover. All he asked was for me not to kiss him on the mouth if his son had been in it the same day."

"Jesus," I mutter in disbelief.

"Izaiah visited me more often than Emilio, since he wasn't, you know, married. I still don't know why either of them wanted me. Because they knew I wouldn't refuse? If I did in the beginning, my parents would've lost everything, and I would've been thrown out on the streets of New York with nothing. It's not like I could go back to my parents. They practically gave Emilio their blessing. Then, after Oriana was born, well, Emilio kicked me out of the apartment, knowing I'd do anything for her..."

"You were his captive," I mutter in understanding.

"Yes."

"And I've done the exact fucking thing to you."

Zara shakes her head. "No. That's not...this is not the same."

"Isn't it? I kidnapped you, refused to let you go, forced you to marry me, touched you, kissed you, wanted to fuck you on my desk tonight..."

"It's not the same, Creed!" she says again. "I wanted you too. I want you. I'm the one who came down here wearing nothing but your suit jacket tonight, remember?"

"Because you felt...obligated?"

"What? God, no. I didn't...I didn't even know what you've been busy doing these past few weeks, day and night, until I came down here. I thought you were tired of me or regretted it..."

"I will never regret you, or us. And I am going to get Oriana back for you."

"You don't have to do that. If you get caught..."

"I told you I'm becoming an expert at this kidnapping thing. I'm sure I could handle a three-year-old girl."

"It will be nearly impossible. Even if you managed to take her, Emilio would hunt me down to get her back."

"I've already killed one Rovina. Emilio is next on my list," I tell her, leaving out the part that he's already out for her blood. He'd kill the mother of his own damn child if given half a chance.

"No, Creed. He's not worth it."

"If he's gone...you said you don't think Saint, Stella, Cami or Martha know she exists, right?"

"I-I don't think they know. If they found out from Izaiah, they would think she's his daughter. But I'm serious, Creed. I don't want you to kill him."

"Why not? Do you care about him?"

"God, no. I just don't want his filthy blood on your hands."

"His blood won't be on my hands. I'll make sure it doesn't come back on me. It may take some time, though. I can't be hasty like before with Izaiah. I'll need to set it up carefully. But if I'm able to get your daughter back in the meantime, I will."

"But...why? Why would you do that for me?" She looks genuinely puzzled. "It can't be for sex. We haven't...I haven't touched you."

"Because you're a good mother," I tell her. "And you endured that *figlio di puttana* Izaiah just to see your daughter. You obviously love her. She belongs with you."

"Thank you," she whispers, then leans forward to place a soft kiss on my lips, followed by another. As the kiss deepens, my restraint lessens. But I can't do this, not right after everything Zara just told me.

"I didn't offer it so you would fuck me," I assure Zara when I grip her upper arms to reluctantly push her away.

"I know." A small smile lifts her lips. "And I was just kissing you, not fucking you. Get Oriana back, and you can do anything you want to me for the rest of my life."

Fuck. I want to take her up on that offer so bad.

But I won't ever take advantage of her the way the Rovina assholes did.

And worst of all, I know I can't keep her much longer.

24

Zara

I'm falling in love with my husband, a murderous mobster.

I think I'd love Creed just for giving Eugene a job if for nothing else. It would be an understatement to say I was surprised when the teenager showed up at the penthouse with a bouquet for me from my husband.

Eugene told me Creed gave him ten thousand dollars with no strings attached and a job the Thursday night I sent him to the store. While I know the 'work' Creed will have Eugene doing for him may not always be legal, at least the boy will have someone to watch his back and bail him out of trouble if he needs.

Now that I also know where Creed is spending his days, it's impossible not to want him so much, it hurts.

There's no way I could ever repay him for what he's trying to do. He's not just risking his life to get Oriana back to me. He's risking everything.

There's nothing I can offer him for such a gigantic favor but my body. I'd offer it up on a silver platter for him to do whatever he damn well wants with it every night, but he hasn't touched me since the night in his office.

Even if he can't pull this off, I won't be upset or disappointed with him. Creed has been kinder to me than anyone ever has been before.

Maybe it's stupid, but I actually believe he will succeed in this impossible task, despite the odds. Creed Ferraro doesn't seem like the type of man who doesn't back up his talk.

After all, he's the king of kings. The other mafia bosses answer to him and fear him and his family.

That afternoon, when he walks into the penthouse hours earlier than usual, I get my hopes up.

As if he can see the hope written on my face, he says, "Sorry, *micetta mia*. There's not been any sign of her at the apartments on Union Avenue either."

"You don't have anything to be sorry about. I'm sorry," I tell him. "I hate that you're spending so much time out there alone." I keep offering to go and sit with him, but he refuses without an explanation. So, I've just been sitting around the penthouse waiting. "I wish I knew where they keep her. Whenever I do get to see her, it's at Central Park or one of the playgrounds in Brooklyn. They never invite me over to the house. I've never seen her bedroom or read her a story before bedtime. I've never had a chance to tuck her in."

"You will," Creed promises as he takes a seat on the sofa and grabs my arm, pulling me onto his lap. "I won't give up searching for her. It could take weeks to find her or maybe even months."

"I've waited years," I remind him. "I can wait however long it takes. Being able to raise her on my own...it's not something I ever thought would be possible."

"I'm going to make it possible," he says. "But tonight, how about a little distraction?"

"A distraction?"

"I know you must be bored, sitting around here all day."

"Only a little," I lie with a smile.

"Well, tonight, I'm taking you out."

"Out? Out where?"

"I chose some dresses and several pairs of shoes for you. They're being brought up right now in case you wanted to change..."

"You picked out clothes for me?" I say in surprise. "What about the ones from a few weeks ago?"

"I had a little help from the stylists."

"Thank you." I give him a quick kiss on the cheek to show my appreciation, wishing he'd accept more.

"You're welcome. Now, go get ready. I'll be waiting for you here in, say, half an hour?"

"Sure," I agree, since I've never been the type to take hours getting ready. What you see is pretty much what you get with me.

∽

Thirty minutes later, I'm dressed in the most gorgeous long golden gown with draping neckline that I've ever seen. It matches my strappy heels. My hair is down and natural, flowing over my shoulders. I feel pretty damn good about myself for the first time in years. That is, until I step into the living room where Creed is waiting in a pristine black suit, and he frowns at me.

"What?" I ask him.

"You look stunning, but I think you look even better in my jacket."

"I love long dresses. They hide all the...imperfections, the baby weight I still haven't lost in three years..."

"I love every inch of you, *micetta mia*."

Love. I know I'm probably reading way too much into that simple statement because it's how I'm starting to feel about Creed. It's crazy and doesn't make sense after only knowing him for such a short time, but there's been something drawing me to the don from the moment we met. Part of me thinks he may even feel the same.

"Where are we going?" I ask, forcing myself to push aside those ridiculous thoughts.

"To the stairs."

"The stairs?"

"I should've mentioned that we're staying in the penthouse."

"Oh."

"I hope you don't mind," he says.

"No, of course not. I'm just glad to spend an evening with you for once."

We take the narrower stairs next to the elevator up to the building's rooftop.

It's not just a flat, mundane rooftop either. The sun is setting in the sky, making the city glow around us. There's a cozy sitting area and tiny lights draped along the lattice work overtop to provide a soft, romantic vibe. And food, lots and lots of food spread out on a long table.

"We can't eat all of that," I tell Creed.

"Sure, we can." He slips his arm around me, and his fingers tease the bare skin along my upper back. "So? What do you think? Slightly better than staying in and watching old shows?"

"It's...stunning," I admit. "You didn't have to do all this or have someone else do it, but it's sweet."

"You deserve to have a life like this, one with peace and freedom. And I want to be the one to give you those things."

"Thank you." I turn and cup his face in my palms. Rising to my toes, I place a soft kiss on his lips. "Thank you for this, and for trying to find Oriana."

"Oh, I will get her back to you."

Smiling at his bravado, I add, "I should also thank you for protecting me that night at the club when the bullets started flying and for what you did to Izaiah. If you hadn't shown up, he would've either killed me or I would've spent the rest of my life indebted to that family, missing my heart and soul and knowing there wasn't a single thing I could do to change anything. But you...with one impulsive decision, you changed everything for me while risking everything for yourself."

"No matter what happens, I'll never regret stopping him. Izaiah got what he deserved."

I nod my head because those are not the worrisome thoughts that have been consuming me during the days Creed is out. I have zero regrets about Izaiah's death.

"What's wrong?" he asks, poking my bottom lip with his fingertip, so I stop biting it.

"I don't know, I've just been thinking..."

"Never a good thing but do go on." He grins.

"I've just been thinking that I've never been a mother to Oriana before, not a real one. What if...what if I'm horrible at it, like my parents were? What if Emilio was right to take her from me because I'm not cut out to raise her?"

"You are going to be an amazing mother." Creed grasps my chin between his thumb and forefinger. "I know because I can *feel* how much you love your daughter. That's all that matters. That's all that it takes to be a good mother. Even if you make a few bad decisions along the way, like my own mother did, it doesn't make you a bad parent. Not if you make those decisions to try and do what's best for your daughter."

"Your mom must have loved you and your brother fiercely to risk her life to try and give you a safer one away from your father."

"She must have. The day my father killed her in front of us was the day I started hating him. He loved her, but he cared more about his fucking pride than he did about letting her live her life in peace."

"I'm sorry he killed her and you had to grow up without a mother. You know she would be proud of the man you are today, don't you?"

"Since I followed in his footsteps and became the don, I highly doubt that."

"You wouldn't kill anyone just for your pride, only those who deserve to die. Was your father like Emilio?"

"Yes. They were best friends," he admits.

"Maybe if your father had lived by the same code as you, your mother would've respected him and not left him."

"I've never actually considered that before, if I'm a better man than my father was or not. It never felt that way to me, since I picked things up right where he left off."

"I didn't know him, but I know you. You protect the people you care about. There's nothing wrong with that," I say. "I would do the same. That's why I can't help but worry that the Rovinas have filled Oriana's head with bullshit about why I'm hardly ever around, making her think I don't...that I don't *want* to be with her, when nothing could be further from the truth."

"I know, *micetta mia*." Creed swipes away one of the tears on my cheeks with his thumb.

"You know that I still don't have a clue what *micetta mia* means. It's not like I've been allowed near a phone or computer to look it up. I guess I could ask someone…"

Smiling down at me, he says, "It means my...pussycat."

"Your pussycat?" I repeat, followed by a gasp of understanding. "You mean your pussy, don't you?"

"Maybe at first that's how I saw you, wanting every inch of you to be mine, especially that part of your body. But you were also pretty damn cute and feisty like a feral kitten from the moment we met."

"You mean I was weak and powerless?"

Lifting my right hand, he places it on his cheek. "You are neither of those things. You're not weak or powerless. I told you what you are — you're dangerous. All I've wanted since the second you crooked your finger at me, like I was already yours to command, is your claws carving into my skin. Only my skin."

Shaking my head, I mutter, "*Your* pussy. You're such a dick."

"*Your* dick," he replies with a grin to match my own.

"Right," I agree as I slide my palm down his face, over the suit fabric and dress shirt covering his chest and stomach, and stopping when I palm his erection through his soft pants. "I think it's finally time for me to meet this dick of mine, husband."

Creed closes his eyes and makes a sound between a grunt and a growl as he covers my hand with his much bigger one. "Zara...I didn't bring you up here because I expected anything tonight."

"I know." I press my palm against his chest, walking him backward until we reach the patio sofa. "Sit down. Let me thank you properly for everything, but especially for all the time you have spent on your knees for me."

Slowly, Creed lowers himself down onto the cushions.

I lift the skirt of my dress as I kneel in front of him. When I reach to undo the front of his pants, he whispers, "I don't deserve any pleasure."

"Yes, you do."

I unzip and tug his pants and boxer briefs down far enough to free his long, thick erection.

"Fuckin' A, you're big," I say as I wrap my fingers around his shaft as much as I can to stroke him, making him get even harder in my fist.

With a puff of laughter, Creed slips his fingers into the side of my hair, not urging my mouth lower but giving me a sweet caress

I place a soft kiss to his blunt head while glancing up at his face, holding his gaze. "Is this how you became the boss of bosses, capo dei capi? Because you have the biggest dick?"

"Something like that," he replies, but his smile doesn't reach his dark, hungry, blue eyes. This man is horny as hell and has been for weeks.

More than ready to finally put him out of his misery, I part my lips and lean forward, letting his length slide along my tongue and fill my mouth so damn good.

"God, yes," Creed groans. His fingers tighten in my hair as I take him to the back of my throat and suck.

Already I can taste just how excited he is from my mouth. This man who doesn't think he deserves any pleasure is so close to giving in to it.

My gag reflex is long gone, so I don't take it easy on him. I bob my head faster and suck him harder, wanting to see Creed lose control.

"*Fuck!*" With a roar, he finally loses it.

Both of his hands cup the sides of my head as he thrust his hips up, shoving himself deeper. His eyes are near feral as he watches my nose ram into his pelvis over and over again.

I love how good it feels to be the one who causes him to let go, who gets to taste his beautiful cock when it swells and erupts down my throat, to hear his shout of ecstasy and claim it as my own prize.

My husband may be a murderous mobster, but that won't ever stop me from wanting to worship him.

25

Creed

Since the incredible blowjob Zara gave me on the rooftop, I've been making excuses at night, such as I'm too tired for anything before the two of us lie down and go to sleep.

Of course, it's a lie.

Zara's mouth is so damn amazing that, while it pisses me the fuck off, I know exactly why Izaiah and Emilio couldn't stay away from her.

I hate myself for being no better than those assholes, taking advantage of Zara after giving her no choice but to be my wife. I don't want to use her like that, no matter how good it feels. That's why I've done my best to keep my hands off her, which also means I don't get much sleep. How can I when I know she's lying right next to me, looking and smelling too damn good to be true?

And it's not just my craving for her body that worries me.

I'm falling for her a little more each day. And I feel guilty for not getting her daughter back yet, as if I'm intentionally dragging my feet to keep her with me a little longer.

But the truth is, the search is just a slow process. It's not like I can ask if anyone has seen Emilio Rovina with a curly-haired girl. All that would do is raise suspicion. For this kidnapping to work, it needs to be completely unexpected. I have to catch him off-guard.

I'm considering sending my new employee, Eugene, with fake food deliveries to each door to scope out the apartments one Friday when two young women and four big men come walking out of a building on Park Avenue. It's the third to last property on the long list and not far from my own penthouse.

On the blonde woman's hip is a tiny girl with auburn curls blowing across her face. The girl is identical to the one in the photos on Zara's phone.

Oriana is beautiful, just like her mother.

Finally getting to see her in person almost feels like a dream.

"That's her," I say to Aldo. I'd reluctantly let him drive me today, so I could review the discovery files my attorney sent over for the possession of a firearm charge. "You see her, too, right?"

"I see *a* little girl, boss. How can you be sure it's the right one, though?"

"I just know it. Follow them. Discreetly."

I can't believe that I wasted so much time watching all the Rovina Brooklyn properties first, when I should've started with the one closest to me.

When the group walks into Marcus Garvey Park, I have Aldo park the SUV on the side of the road. I climb out to get a closer look even though it's risky.

But I'm glad I did it a moment later. I would've hated to miss seeing the tiny girl, bouncing around like she's a rabbit. When the brunette gives her a container of bubbles, she runs over and blows them right into one of the guard's faces with a giggle.

She's a little troublemaker like her mother, and I already know I'd protect her with my life.

I make sure to zoom in and take photos and videos to show Zara and confirm it's her daughter, even though I'm almost certain.

For the next hour, I watch the girl play until they leave, heading back toward the apartment while I return to the SUV.

Aldo follows the group, and we watch them disappear inside. "We're going to do this tonight."

"Tonight?" he repeats in surprise.

"I'll ask Dre and Tristan to help us."

"Just those two?"

"Yes. Just those two. Four of us are more than enough to draw attention. We'll go inside in pairs and take out the guards. We'll need to wear Kevlar vests under long coats, gloves, and hats to make sure we're not identified on any cameras."

"You got a plan on how to handle the four guards and two women?"

I've considered this potential scenario for weeks now. "Stun gun batons. They won't be easy to procure, but I want gunfire to be a last resort. Not only are they loud and messy, but I don't want to hurt or terrify the girl. If she screams and fights on the way out, it'll draw too much attention. If we go late enough, hopefully, she'll be asleep, and we'll catch the guards dozing."

We don't know for certain what the inside of the apartment looks like or if there are more than four guards. But that's a risk we're going to have to take. I can't postpone in case Emilio decides to move her somewhere else. And I can't put this reunion off for Zara any longer either.

That's another reason why I haven't touched my wife since the night on the roof.

I don't want Zara to fuck me as repayment for anything, especially not for returning her daughter to her. I'm just trying to right a wrong by the Rovinas. What they did to Zara was evil. How could anyone think she'd be anything other than a loving mother, giving the girl a safe and happy home?

It's something that I've gone without most of my life. There's no amount of money or power that can buy love. Not the real kind that Zara has for Oriana.

It's the unconditional, unwavering love I've started to feel for Zara, even if it will never be returned.

I can't keep her. I won't. Because of Emilio, Zara and her daughter could only remain in New York locked up like prisoners.

I'm going to kill that son of a bitch one of these days, but until then, Zara is going to get the peace she deserves.

*

Zara

Creed returns home earlier tonight than usual. Once again, I'm lazing around his penthouse after spending the day doing nothing. It was nice to not have any obligations at first, to not have to go into work and stand on my feet for twelve hours. But lately, I've been getting so damn depressed. I need something to do. An actual purpose.

I go meet him in the foyer, happy to see him, to have his company again. "Hey." I miss him when he walks out the door every day after we have breakfast together.

He dismisses his watchmen before turning to me. "Hey. I've got something to show you." He gives me a kiss and takes my hand, guiding me back to the sofa. It's one of the rare times when he's actually touched me.

I thought that things would change between us after our date on the rooftop, but Creed still refuses to make a move at night or in the morning before we get up and share the only meal of the day together. It's frustrating to want him so much and not have the sentiment returned.

If anything, Creed seems to have pulled away even more after the night on the roof as if he didn't enjoy it and didn't care for a repeat. And there haven't been any occasions of him kneeling between my legs lately either.

"Here." He offers me his phone. "There are photos and videos. Just keep scrolling until you've seen them all."

"Okay." I accept the device, wondering what he's found, and assume it's something that connects Emilio to the raid.

I couldn't have been more wrong.

The first photo is a zoomed in image of Oriana, grinning from ear to ear and standing in what looks like a park.

"How did you..."

"I found her."

If he says anything else, I don't hear him. I'm too captivated by the images and especially, the videos with the sound of her happy squeals even from some distance away.

Once I've replayed every video at least three times, I lift my drenched face and stinging eyes to Creed. "I'm sorry to be blubbering and all, but I haven't seen her in over a month. She's grown so much!"

"We're going to get her tonight."

"Tonight?"

"Why does everyone suddenly question my every word?" he mutters.

"Sorry, it's just...that's so soon. Are you sure you're ready?"

"Yes."

"I don't know, Creed. I don't want her to get hurt during a

shootout. Or for you to get caught by Emilio's men. There are at least four, right?" I saw the big burly dark-haired men in the photos as well.

"It won't come to a shootout," my husband says. "And I didn't see Emilio or any of the Rovinas today, just two nannies and four guards, so that shouldn't be an issue."

"How can you be so sure? About the shooting, I mean."

"We're going to have our guns on us, but we'll use stun guns on the guards."

"And the women?"

"What do you think we should do with them?"

"Don't kill them," I exclaim. Then, realizing that sounded like an order, I add, "Please. They probably don't know who they work for, or that he took her from me for one failed drug test."

"Okay, we'll leave them alone if we can." Leaning forward, he kisses my cheek and says, "I know it doesn't seem like a great, well-thought-out plan, but we knew it was going to be risky, regardless. And we expect casualties — the guards, I mean. If you can't handle that, then we can call it off. We could try to wait…"

"No. Do it. If you think it's safe for you and Oriana, then I trust you."

"Good."

"The guards…" I start when I have an idea.

"You don't want me to kill them either?"

"I was just wondering if maybe you should question them first, see if they know anything about Emilio being involved in the club raid with Izaiah."

"That's not a bad idea. I doubt they'll know anything, but it's possible his guards rotate and aren't assigned solely to watch over Oriana." I nod my head as he continues, "I'm going to go get changed."

"Wait." I stand up with him and grab the front of his suit jacket to stop him. I throw my arms around his neck, holding him tight. "Thank you. And please be careful. If it's too dangerous…"

"It won't be. Oriana will be safe, I promise, *micetta mia*." Creed gives me a quick kiss on the lips before he walks away.

What I meant was that I wanted him to be careful and not get hurt. But it doesn't seem like he's concerned about his own safety.

26

Creed

In my office, I decide now is the time to meet with Lorenzo, Dre, and Tristan and tell them the whole truth before asking them to risk their lives.

"First off, Dre, I've got news for you. Emilio has picked out a venue, so we're just waiting for a date."

"Fuck," he grumbles and scrubs his palm down his face, taking the news about as well as I expected.

"Now, I hope you three don't have any plans tonight. I need your help pulling off something important. Tristan and Dre will need to come with me while Lorenzo stays here with Zara. That is, if you don't walk out after you are all up to speed…"

"Well, don't keep us in suspense. What's the super-secret mission going on tonight?" Tristan asks.

"That's what I'm wondering too," Lorenzo replies. "And why do I have to stay here again and babysit?"

"Because I said so," I snap at him. "But, fine, I'll start at the beginning. I didn't give Zara any choice but to marry me. If she refused, I was going to kill her."

"Huh?" Tristan mutters.

"You forced the woman to marry you by threatening her life?" Dre asks.

"Yes. And we didn't date before the night you met her. I saw her for the first time the night Carmine died at The Vault. He encouraged me to talk to her, and he actually did tell me to toast him at our wedding..."

Lorenzo's forehead wrinkles. "Why was Zara at The Vault that night? I don't remember seeing her."

Here we fucking go. "Zara was there at the club, giving Jasper a message — the warning for me."

"Fucking hell," Dre grumbles.

"And after the funeral, you tracked her down?" Lorenzo guesses. "Who put her up to that shit?"

Crossing my arms over my chest, I ask him, "Who do you think?"

"Izaiah isn't really missing, is he?" Dre catches on quickly.

"In a sense, Izaiah is missing. I just might happen to know where he could potentially be found..."

"Jesus fuck, Creed!" Dre huffs.

"How?" Tristan remarks.

"I went to Zara's apartment to confront her. While she was in the shower, I went through her phone and laptop. She really needs a better passcode. Anyway, I saw her texts about giving Jasper the message and even where I was standing in the club right before the raid. The texts were to and from Izaiah. They had a...relationship where he manipulated her into doing shit for him. So, I texted him to come over."

"He showed up at her apartment, and you killed him, right then and there?" Lorenzo asks.

"I had to, for Carmine, and because he was going to slit Zara's throat."

"You mean he was going to slit the throat of a woman who set us up? Who got Carmine fucking killed?" Dre rages. "You went after her to kill her, right? And instead, you end up killing Emilio's son and saving her life? No, not just saving her, but you strong-armed her into marrying you!"

"The only other choice I had was to let him kill her. But I...I couldn't let him hurt her."

"You love her," Lorenzo declares, a statement not a question.

"I do," I admit. "She holds the power to end me in her hands, and I love her. I have for a while now."

"Why are you telling us all this now? It's too late to ask our opinions, not that you would have heeded them," Lorenzo remarks.

"I'll still give you mine," Dre grumbles. "She doesn't deserve your forgiveness or ours."

"I'm not asking you to forgive Zara. I'm coming clean with you three now because things are about to get worse with Emilio. I'm going to kill him too. Eventually."

"Do you have proof he put Izaiah up to the raid?" Lorenzo asks.

"No, but I'm going to kill him either way."

"Could you at least tell us why Emilio needs to die? Why you feel the need to potentially start a bloody war?" Lorenzo demands. "Just to prevent him from finding out you killed Izaiah?"

I nod my head. "That's one reason."

"What's the other?" Tristan asks.

"He's the father of Zara's daughter."

"Holy shit," Dre whispers, burying his face in his palms.

"Emilio...and your *Zara*? No fucking way! He's old enough to be her grandfather!" Tristan shouts.

"She says it was consensual, but I don't believe her. He manipulated her into coming to the city. He's been taking advantage of her for seven years."

"Do we need to point out the irony here?" Lorenzo asks.

"Right! You're doing the same damn thing, Creed!" Dre agrees. "You manipulated the woman so she would marry you. You bought her silence with millions of dollars when you should've killed her for Carmine. Are you that pussy-whipped?"

"I haven't fucked her."

Lorenzo scoffs. "I find that incredibly hard to believe. She runs around half-naked most of the time!"

"I haven't fucked her. We've fooled around but..."

"But you feel guilty?" the old man supplies.

"Yes. Like you pointed out, I forced her to marry me. She's the reason Carmine was killed. I know that, but I can't stop myself from wanting her."

"Does she love you?" That's an odd question, especially coming from Tristan of all people.

"I don't know. I think so." *But I'm not sure, and it's driving me fucking crazy.* I can't tell her how I feel. She holds enough power over me as it is. I don't need to go and tell her that I would burn the world to the ground with myself in it for her.

"You're talking about killing Emilio and going to war with the Rovinas, Creed. Are you sure about this? Do you really think she's worth all the trouble?" Dre asks.

"Yes."

"Then I hope you're damn well prepared for the fucking consequences," he replies.

"I'm not just doing this for Zara. I'm doing it for Carmine," I explain. "And it doesn't matter how I feel about Zara or if she returns those feelings. I'm going to send her away."

"Good," Dre replies.

"I don't want to, but I don't have a choice. Emilio suspects Zara had a hand in Izaiah's disappearance. He wants her dead. I got the judge to hold off on filing the marriage license, but I can't hide that she's my wife forever, especially not after I get her daughter back for her. For all I know, Zara may even be...relieved to be rid of me."

"If this woman has been manipulated by the Rovinas for years and forced into this marriage with you, then I would guess she only wants one thing — her freedom," Lorenzo points out. "You're doing the right thing."

"I know that. I just fucking hate it."

"Sometimes when you love someone, you have to make sacrifices to keep them safe. This is one of those times, Creed," Lorenzo says.

"You think so? Even about Emilio?"

"You're going to kill him anyway, right? It's just a matter of when," he replies.

"I will wait, play it smart, make his death look like an accident. That way shit won't blow back on our family," I assure them. "You know I don't apologize very often, but on this, I'm sorry I was so damn reckless with Izaiah."

"You know I'll back you up on that decision anyway, no matter what."

"Thank you," I tell Lorenzo. "What about you two?" I ask Tristan and Dre, who have gone quiet. "Tonight, I need help getting Zara's daughter away from Emilio's guards. Are you with me or not?"

"Of course we're in, for you and for Carmine," Tristan says then looks at Dre. "Well, I'm in at least. You're the boss. We follow your lead. Even when your plans are nuts. Right, Dre?"

"We follow your lead, even when you do some crazy fucking shit," Dre agrees. "What do you need me to do tonight?" Dre asks, making me smile in relief that I'm forgiven for not only making mistakes but hiding them from my family.

27

Creed

"You and Aldo are going in alone? You can't be serious," Dre says from where he and Tristan lean against the SUV in the parking garage. His arms are crossed over his chest. I've just told them my plan for how to get this party started. Of course, Dre wants to bitch about it.

"I know what I'm doing." Nothing and no one will stop me from going after Zara's daughter tonight. "If I storm into the building with an army, it'll raise the alarm."

"Oh, it's going to raise the alarm no matter what. Missing kids have a tendency to do that," Tristan says with a chuckle. Still, he comes over and holds out his palm to me. When I take it, he pulls me in for an embrace, slapping my back. "Good luck, boss. Call us if you need us."

"He's going to need us," Dre mutters.

"Just follow behind us, wait until we're inside, and get a look at the place before you do anything."

With that, I open the door and climb into the SUV. Aldo has already changed the license plates to fakes and loaded up both vehicles with weapons, armor, and zip ties, so I tell him, "Let's go."

∽

"Can you hear me?" I ask into the earpiece an hour later after Aldo and I have suited up and staked out the apartment, searching for any changes since we last left.

"Ready, boss," Tristan replies from the car parked a block away. "Local wi-fi has been jammed so any personal security cameras inside the building should be offline until someone notices."

"Good. Aldo and I are going in now. Wait where you are until you hear from us."

I've pulled a lot of jobs before — murders, heists, robberies, teenage punk bullshit — but I've never wanted any of them to go off without a hitch as much as I want this one to be flawless.

I wish Carmine was with us. My brother loved kids, wanted a dozen of his own. He would've been on board with this plan even if it was half-cooked.

Since Emilio's apartment is on the sixth floor, Aldo and I slip into the stairwell and start the trek upward while keeping our heads down and baseball caps pulled low to avoid being identified on any cameras.

We step through the door to the floor when I hear the elevator ding. Before the door can shut behind Aldo, we backpedal. I keep it cracked to watch the hallway and see who exits the elevator.

My heart drops to my stomach when an entourage strides past, surrounding a single, bald, older man.

It's fucking Emilio.

Of all the times for him to visit...I guess Friday night is one of them. If I had waited and done more recon for another week, I would've known that too.

And of course, he also had to bring a small army with him.

"What do we do now, boss?" Aldo whispers as I let the stairwell door shut softly.

We sure as shit can't walk out any of the main doors right now, since there could be more guards downstairs or a car waiting at the curb. Glancing around, I jerk my chin up and begin climbing the steps as quietly as I can.

Over my shoulder, I whisper to Aldo, "We'll go up two floors and try to find a custodian closet to wait him out in."

The eighth floor doesn't have such a closet, so we go up to the ninth. There, we find a maintenance room, but the door is locked. Aldo rams his shoulder into it a few times, and it buckles.

Once we're inside, I press the earpiece to inform Dre and Tristan what's going on, then have them pull around, so they can watch the front of the building and tell us when Emilio and his entourage leave.

"Good thing we waited a few minutes, huh, boss?" Aldo remarks.

"Yeah, good thing," I agree, turning over a bucket to sit on top of it.

I refuse to let this setback kill our plan, though. Zara would be so damn devastated if I returned home without her daughter tonight. I refuse to let her down.

Loving her apparently means wanting to do everything in my power to make her happy. It's like her feelings matter more than anything else in the world.

And that's exactly the problem. I'm starting to make Zara a priority over everyone and everything else, even all the people I'm responsible for protecting.

"We wait until Emilio leaves. If he takes the guards with him, we do what we planned to do tonight."

"You still want to do this tonight?"

"Yes, tonight!"

"That could be hours from now, boss."

"Yes, Aldo, it could be. So, have a seat, get comfortable. We're not leaving unless it's with that little girl."

∼

Tristan finally tells us that Emilio has exited the building with his guards a little after ten. I assumed the girl would be asleep by now and was wondering if he was going to stay overnight. That definitely would've fucked everything up.

Once we confirm that all his cars have pulled away, we wait another thirty minutes for Emilio to get out of Manhattan before putting our plan into action.

Stun gun baton out and by my side, I pull the brim of my Yankees hat down over my eyes and lead the way down the stairs back to the sixth floor.

"Ready?" I turn to ask Aldo at the stairwell door.

"Let's do this, boss."

For a long moment, I wonder if I'm about to send this man, my cousins, and myself to an early grave.

But I didn't force any of them to be here. They could have walked away when I told them what we were doing. And with the Kevlar vests, we're as protected as we can be. We also have the element of surprise on our side too.

I open the stairwell door and slam my baton into the camera above the lens to bust it, hoping it's the only one on the floor. Then I walk straight to the apartment. I knock rather than try to sneak in. It'll look less like a kidnapping if the door isn't broken down and the lock is still intact. Here's hoping the guards assume it's their bossman returning or one of his henchmen and answer without thinking.

The meatheads are too confident. I hear the stride of boots on the other side of the door, then the turn of the lock. They didn't bother glancing out the peephole. Thank god they're morons.

As soon as the man opens the door, Aldo is ready. Standing off to the side where he can't be seen, he reaches around and shoves the stun gun directly into the man's neck before he can open his mouth and ask what we want.

The guard barely makes a sound as he clutches his throat and stumbles backward. I strike him on the top of his head with the blunt end of the baton, putting him down. Aldo grabs his phone as we move past him.

We run right into the second guard on his way to check on his buddy. He throws up a gargantuan-sized forearm to block my baton coming down toward his face. I shove the weapon into his dick instead, dropping him to his knees. A few hits to his head with the baton have him down and out too.

Only two more to go if there are, in fact, only four.

The interior of the apartment is mostly dark, only two lamps glowing softly next to a sofa. With quiet steps, we cross the living room and wait. I tell Dre and Tristan through the earpiece, "Get up here."

"On the way," Dre replies.

As soon as they join us, it's time to finish this. "We find the other guards, disarm them by stuns or blows only, get their phones, and then you two zip tie their wrists and ankles to take them with us," I instruct. "Can't have them telling their boss what happened as soon as we leave."

"You want them alive?" Dre asks.

"Yes."

"Why? The dead don't speak," Aldo remarks.

"Not that I owe any of you a reason, but I want to question them. Make sure at least one survives. Two would be better."

"You've got it, boss," Tristan replies, and Dre nods his agreement.

"How do we get them out of the building without the cameras catching us?" Aldo asks.

Taking a play from Zara's book, I tell them, "Let's see if they'll fit down the garbage chute, then fish them out of the compactor."

"Brilliant," Tristan chuckles.

"It is," I agree. "And it was Zara's idea."

I really hope this building has a giant chute or things will get tricky. We don't have time to waste dragging off four big men, but we can't leave them alive either.

"You ready to proceed, or would you like to debate every single move I plan to make first?"

"Sorry boss," Tristan responds.

"Won't happen again," Aldo promises.

"Let's go," Dre agrees.

I give them a nod just as the other two guards barrel down the hallway, probably having heard our voices.

Aldo and I each take one on while our backup slips around and stuns the back of one's neck and the throat of another.

Now, we just have to secure the guards, find the girl, and get the fuck out of here.

I tip my head toward the closed doors, telling Aldo to start checking the rooms on the right while I take the left. There could be more guards, but the odds are good that only the four we took down are in the apartment.

The closest door to my left is cracked open. I push inside and see a dark and empty bedroom.

I continue through the luxury apartment, until from the doorway of the last room in the hallway on the right side, Aldo says, "Here, boss." Smart of Emilio to put the girl furthest from the door in case of a situation like this.

Unfortunately, the dumbass has his gun out and is pointing it inside that goddamn room.

"Put that away," I growl while shoving him aside.

That's when I see why he has his gun out.

Two women who look just as sweet and harmless as Zara, maybe a few years younger than her, have their own small-caliber handguns raised and pointed right at my head.

"Good evening, ladies," I say, lifting my hands up in front of me, so they can see I'm only holding the stun gun baton. I jerk the earpiece from my ear to concentrate without hearing Dre and Tristan's updates on restraining the guards.

One of them, the blonde, looks like she's prepared to pull the trigger if I breathe wrong. I search the room for Oriana, but don't see her. She must be in a room off from this living area.

"Ladies, we're in a bit of a hurry, so I'm going to make this quick. We will not harm Oriana. We're here to get her back to her mother. Do either of you know Zara? Maybe you've even been along on some of her supervised visits, where she spends maybe an hour at a time with Oriana at the park." I probably should've asked Zara if the women looked familiar.

"I've met her. Mr. Rovina said she's an alcoholic whore," the blonde replies.

"Well, Emilio is lying to you. Did you know that the Rovinas took Oriana from Zara when she was only a day old?"

The two women exchange a look, one that I hope means they're softening to the idea of handing over the girl to us.

"Put the guns down and let us take Oriana back to Zara tonight. *Please.*"

"We need to hurry this along, boss," Aldo says from behind me.

Dammit, I know.

"What will it take for you to give her to me?" I ask them. "Name your price. Anything. But I can't leave this building without her. I don't think Zara would ever forgive me for getting her hopes up about getting her daughter back and then failing so spectacularly."

"You're not taking her," the blonde snaps.

"Paige," the other woman whispers. "Maybe he's telling the truth."

"And what if he isn't, Bethany? No telling what could happen to her!"

"I am telling the truth. And Zara made me promise not to hurt either of you. She knows you're the girl's nannies, that you've been caring for her daughter while she couldn't. So, name your price. Because you see, Zara doesn't have to know what actually happens here tonight. The guards are all down. There are four of us to you two. My guys are trained shooters. So, while you might land the first shot, my money is on us landing the last ones. Is this girl worth dying for to keep her from her sweet, gentle mother?"

"Who are you?" the blonde huffs.

"I'm Zara's husband."

"He's Creed fucking Ferraro," Aldo announces from behind me.

"That too," I agree with a wince since sharing my identity wasn't part of the plan. Too late now, we'll have to roll with it.

Now the women exchange another look, and their faces tighten with concern, clearly having heard my name before.

Some sort of silent conversation passes between them, and then the blonde says, "Oriana doesn't leave this apartment without us." Before I can object, she adds, "We're all she knows, who she trusts. You'll terrify her."

"Okay, so then you two will come with us quietly. I have plenty of room in my penthouse for you to stay and help Zara get reacquainted with her daughter who she's barely seen in three years."

"He knows a lot about her to be lying," the brunette, Bethany, remarks.

"When's Oriana's birthday?" the blonde, Paige, asks.

Her birthday? Zara has told me twice, hasn't she? Hottest summer ever, and she was gigantic, nine months pregnant. Best day of her life and favorite day of the year, even if she doesn't get to celebrate with Oriana.

"July fourteenth," I answer. "She was born July fourteenth and taken away from Zara on the fifteenth."

"Boss..." Aldo warns, having obviously heard from our backup that we need to hurry.

The blonde finally nods and tells the brunette, "You pack a bag, and I'll get Ori."

Ori. I wonder what Zara will think about the abbreviated name some other woman gave to her daughter. But at least it seems like these two women really do care for the girl. To hold us at gunpoint and be willing to die for her means that they love her too.

"Make it fast. Put your guns and phones down on the floor first and leave them here. You have two minutes," I tell the women.

They both lay their guns on the carpet in front of them, then their cell phones. The blonde slips into a back room while the brunette runs around the living room area and kitchen, gathering up toys and cups and shoving them into a giant shoulder bag.

"How are things looking for our exit?" I ask Aldo without taking my eyes off the women.

"Tristan and Dre thumped the guards on the heads again to knock them out and have got two shoved down the garbage chute."

"Good," I say in relief.

～

It turns out that the chute could accommodate all four large men.

Leaving the removal of the guards to Dre and Tristan, Aldo and I hurry the women along down the stairwell. I'm not too concerned about them being caught on any street cameras, since our faces won't be seen, and Aldo and I are close enough to the size of the guards. Once we're out, the women will live under my roof, under constant surveillance, unable to tell Emilio or anyone else what's happened.

The small, curly-haired little girl is half-asleep on the blonde's shoulder the whole time we hurry to the vehicle. Only when we're waiting turns to pile inside the SUV with the overhead light on does Oriana finally lift her head.

I'm standing behind the women, waiting on the brunette, when Oriana's sleepy eyes blink open to take in me and the dark street. And in that moment, I'm struck by the same protective instinct as the night I watched Izaiah hold a knife to Zara's throat.

This girl is precious and innocent, just like her mother, and I know I'd risk it all to keep her safe.

I rack my brain, trying to remember what Zara told me about her. She said her daughter is bossy and loves Disney princesses. That's why I whisper, "Hello, princess."

The blonde stiffens in concern that Oriana is not only wide awake, but she's also lifted her head from the woman's shoulder to stare at me, a complete stranger.

"You don't have a car seat," the nanny remarks as she slides into the backseat with Oriana on her shoulder.

"I think we have bigger concerns right now." I take the seat next to them. Then to the girl, I say, "My name is Creed, and we're going to go see your mommy."

"Zara," the blonde corrects me. "She doesn't know…"

"Seriously?" I mutter with a disgusted shake of my head. She doesn't know Zara is her mother? What the hell is wrong with these people? "Ori, you're going to see Zara and tomorrow we're going to find you the prettiest princess crown in town."

The girl gives me a sleepy smile, then lowers her head to the nanny's shoulder, shutting her eyes again.

I hold my breath until all the doors of the SUV close with us inside, the other nanny in the front passenger seat.

When Aldo pulls away, heading the short distance to my penthouse, I finally breathe a sigh of relief.

We actually fucking did it.

28

Zara

Creed has been gone for so long that I've worn down his carpet from pacing across his living room, looking out into the dark city and wondering what's happening. It's times like this I wish I had a phone, but I don't because he still doesn't trust me.

I thought he'd be home by now. It's been over three hours since he left, telling me that the apartment was just down the street.

Something must have gone wrong. That's the only thing that could be the holdup.

"Have you heard anything yet?" I ask Lorenzo, who seems tense on the sofa. Wearing a dark gray suit with a burgundy button-up underneath and a matching handkerchief in the suit pocket, the older man dresses even better than Creed. Although, I think Creed just asks his tailor for black everything.

"No, ma'am. Nothing since the last time you asked two minutes ago."

"Sorry," I tell him. "It's just..."

I hope he didn't get caught or hurt. I shouldn't have let him even attempt this. Emilio Rovina is an evil, ruthless man.

And while I know Creed is too, maybe even more so, I know for a fact that Creed still has a good heart deep inside that mafioso tattooed exterior.

"It's just what?" Lorenzo asks when I pause. "A fool's errand that may get him killed?"

"I didn't ask him to do this," I explain. "In fact, I asked Creed if he was sure his quickly hatched plan would even work. He seemed to think so, and then he went off to do it. Can anyone talk that man out of doing something when he sets his mind to it?"

"No, no they can't," he mutters. "If he succeeds, and that's a big if, you're leaving the city with her ASAP, right?"

"What?" I ask, since this is the first I've heard about leaving the city. "What do you mean, 'am I leaving?'"

He blinks at me. "Creed hasn't told you?"

"Told me what?"

He drops his gaze to his knee where his fingers drum along it. "You should ask him when he gets back. If he gets back alive."

"I'm asking you, Lorenzo. What hasn't Creed told me?"

He sighs. "Did you really think you could stay in New York once he takes your daughter from Emilio Rovina?"

"I...I guess I haven't really thought about it."

"Obviously not. You can't stay."

"Because Emilio would eventually find out Creed took Oriana?"

"And because Emilio knows you had something to do with Izaiah going missing. He's been searching all over for you. He wants you dead, girl."

"He does?" I say in surprise. "Creed...he hasn't said anything about Emilio knowing..." Of course, Emilio knows I'm involved, since Izaiah's car was near my apartment. An apartment Emilio has visited plenty of times after he kicked me out of his place. And Creed didn't tell me because he didn't want me to worry. "I have to leave the city."

"Exactly. And I asked you if you were leaving as soon as you get your daughter, assuming Creed doesn't die trying."

"Yes. I'm…I'll make plans to leave as soon as possible."

"Good," he says with what sounds like relief. "Because you're not good for him."

"I'm not good for Creed Ferraro? Really?"

"He's been through a lot lately. I don't know why he's latched onto you, but he's not thinking clearly, hasn't been since the raid when Carmine died."

"Creed feels guilty, like he should've died instead of his brother," I say in understanding. "He has to work that out in his own time."

"I'm well aware he needs time to come to terms with what happened. But Creed is responsible for hundreds of people. You know that, too, don't you?"

"I didn't know how many."

"Hundreds of people depend on him to pay their bills and support their families."

"And you depend on him as well to earn your big paydays for those fancy suits, right?"

"I would be just fine if Creed walked away from being the head of the Five Families or gets thrown in prison. Financially, I mean. I'll be right there with him in prison. But he's also my friend, first and foremost. Yes, he's made me a very rich man, but I would trade every penny to keep him alive."

"Then, you're a good friend."

"He's the reason Dre went to law school after he got out of the military. Do you know why?"

"No?"

"Because Dre knew Creed would need a damn good attorney,

not just for his business dealings, but to at least have someone with criminal defense attorney associates who could keep him out of prison. And for the past ten years, he's done his part to keep him alive and free. Creed was always rational, which helped. But then you came along. Now Dre will lose his law license because of the charges from that raid you dragged them into. I just know that it's only a matter of time before you bring about Creed's downfall. That's why you need to go."

"I think you're giving me way too much credit. Creed won't even touch me anymore."

"What?" Lorenzo asks, his brow furrowed.

"We're not sleeping together," I tell him. "We share the same bed every night, but he hasn't touched me in weeks."

"Why not?"

His question makes me cough out a laugh. "I wish I knew the answer to that question, but I'm afraid I'm at a complete loss. We've never even had sex."

"Then, what the fuck?" Lorenzo asks. He rubs the back of his neck as he thinks it over. "Creed said you two hadn't, and I thought he was full of shit. I could've sworn the man was so pussy whipped, he wasn't thinking clearly, and now you say that's not even happening..."

"He's still upset about Carmine. He doesn't think he deserves anything good in his life," I explain. "Yes, he's trying to get my daughter back to me, but as for the rest, it has nothing to do with me."

"Oh, it definitely has something to do with you. The man risked everything when he killed his ally's son for you, when he didn't even know a damn thing about you, except that you were responsible for his brother's death."

"That was not my fault. I had no idea what Izaiah was planning to do. Am I glad that Creed killed him? Hell yes, but I *never* would've asked Creed to do that. His death doesn't really solve any of my problems. Yes, I hated his visits and constant blackmail, but I was enduring it just fine. And now... now Emilio thinks I killed him. That's why Creed won't let me leave the apartment, isn't it?"

"Well, the man's car was found near your apartment in Queens. It wouldn't take a genius to put two and two together."

"Fuck," I mutter, covering my face with my hands. "I should've realized. Creed hasn't told me but, I should've known that Emilio would blame me. I hate that son of a bitch."

"We all do, too, but he's a useful ally. And his father's best friend." Lorenzo's phone dings, and he pulls it out of his pocket. "They're on the way up."

"Thank god," I sigh. "Did he...did he say anything else?"

"No. It was just Dre saying they're back."

Lorenzo and I both go out to the elevator to wait for them. "Thanks for the talk," I tell him. "It was a nice distraction from going out of my mind worrying about them."

"No problem."

The doors open and Creed steps out first. There doesn't appear to be any tears or blood on his black clothing, which is a relief.

Dre and Triston exit after him.

"You couldn't..." I start, trying to swallow down my disappointment. At least he tried. That's more than anyone else would ever do for me.

But then he turns around and says, "Paige and Bethany meet Zara, Oriana's *mother*, just as I promised. That's how you'll refer to her from now on."

A blonde woman I see once a month with Oriana steps up beside Creed, and on her shoulder is the most beautiful girl in the world.

I slap my palm over my mouth to keep from crying out. My daughter is dressed in bright pink fleece footie pajamas with little unicorns on them, her head resting on the woman's shoulder, sound asleep. She looks so tiny and peaceful. I've never even seen her in pajamas before, since I was only allowed short visits during the day.

"H-how is she?" I quietly ask the woman, holding her when I place my hand on her back just to feel her warmth, to feel her breathing.

"She slept through most of it," she replies, narrowing her eyes at the man behind me. "He never told us you were her mother."

On playdates, I didn't spend much time talking to the nannies who would sit and glare at me the entire time. Oriana's only ever called me Zara, never Mommy. I should've insisted, but having them badmouth the woman she sometimes sees isn't as terrible as them telling her how awful the woman who gave birth to her is.

"What the fu-hell?" Creed asks. "They look just alike!"

"We assumed but knew better than to ask Mr. Rovina any questions." The woman cups the back of Oriana's head, her fingers trailing through her curls just like mine. She hefts her up higher as if she's getting heavy.

"Could we... why don't we find a room to tuck her into bed?" I suggest.

"Do you have a toddler bed? Or a bed with rails? You can't put her in a normal bed, or she'll roll off," the woman explains in a quiet rush.

"Don't," Creed warns her. "You're free to offer suggestions, but you won't tell Zara how to care for her daughter, or I'll throw your ass out."

The blonde woman, Paige, lowers her eyes. The brunette, Bethany, is relatively new. She steps forward and says, "How about you show us to a room, and we can work on setting it up to keep Ori safe?"

"Ori?" I repeat. "You call her Ori?"

"Yes."

"How long have you two been caring for her? I know Paige has been with her for a long time..."

"I've only been her nanny for four months, but Paige has been with her every day for almost a year," the brunette, Bethany, says.

No wonder the blonde seems more protective of her.

"Thank you both for taking care of her. I wish it could've been me, but I'm glad she had two people who love her so much."

Creed's arm comes around my chest, hugging me to the front of his body before kissing the top of my head. "Feel free to choose any room you think she'll like best," he says quietly in my ear. "And tomorrow, I promised her a princess crown."

I cover his hand on my shoulder and kiss it to thank him. I'll have to show him my full appreciation later.

For now, though, I have to put my daughter to bed for the very first time.

~

After she woke up and we decided she needed a bath, the nannies and I picked one of the guest rooms with a king bed for Oriana. Paige reluctantly hands her over while she and Bethany build a wall of pillows around the center of the mattress.

My sweet girl doesn't make a sound after that. Her little breaths warm my neck as she dozes.

After the pillows are in place, Paige props her hands on her hips and studies me in the glow of the soft bedside lamp. "You know he's going to kill the guards, right?" she grumbles.

I nod in understanding but not approval.

"He would've killed us, too, if we had refused to come with her."

"I'm sorry. Really," I say as I rub circles over Oriana's back. "But it was the only way. I'm not sure if you know much about your employer. Emilio Rovina is not a good man."

"We know," Paige replies. "But Ori deserved someone kind to take care of her. And it was a complicated process to get hired for the position of nanny. Mr. Rovina ran background checks on us, called almost everyone we knew, demanded we turn over passports if we had one — that sort of thing. He's very protective of her."

"No kidding," I mutter. "All he had to do was let me stay with her too. At least at night, when I wasn't working. He didn't think I would be a good mother to her."

"He once mentioned that Oriana's mother was a drug addicted w-h-o-r-e."

"That's not true. I failed one drug test, the first one when I went to the doctor after I realized I was pregnant. Pills I got from Emilio. I haven't touched any since then. And I've never taken money for s-e-x."

"What are you to Mr. Ferraro?" she asks.

"It's complicated."

"He said he's your husband," Bethany chimes in. "Before he even told us his name."

"Like I said, it's complicated. Creed's just trying to help me out. Despite all the rumors about him, he's a good man."

"A man who probably just put four men in the ground tonight," Paige remarks.

"Were they good men? The guards who worked for Rovina?"

Paige shrugs. "I don't know. But it isn't up to Creed Ferraro to judge them."

"I hate that. I do. I never wanted anyone to get hurt. But there was no other way for me to get Oriana back. I couldn't fight Emilio in court, not with all the money he has. Please, just stay here, and don't try to tell him what happened. That's all you both need to do to be safe. Creed won't hurt you. I promise."

Paige's lips purse. "We should put Ori to bed before she wakes up and starts running laps around this whole place."

"We should...it might be best if Paige and I stay in here with her tonight," Bethany suggests. "We can sleep on either side of her, and if she wakes up, we'll make sure she knows she's safe before she worries about where she's at."

"Okay," I agree, even if I wanted to be the one to sleep beside her tonight.

"Tomorrow, after she spends the day with you, you can take one of our spots," Bethany offers.

"That sounds like a good plan. I don't want her to wake up and get upset. As you already know, we haven't spent much time together. And the things I had to do for that time...well, I would do anything for her, just so you know. Despite what Emilio may have told you about me, I would *never* let anything happen to her. I love her so much and have missed her every second."

Blinking back the tears, I kiss the side of her head and lower her to the mattress. I pull the sheets around her, tucking them in tight, so she feels safe, like someone is holding her. Then, I leave her with the two nannies.

It's easier this time because I know they're not urging me to leave out of spite, but because it's really what's best for Oriana, letting her sleep with the women she's spent every second of the day with for months.

29

Creed

I'm lying flat on my back alone in bed, staring up at the ceiling in the darkness and straining my ears to hear what's going on down the hallway. Thankfully, I don't hear any screaming, so I assume that means that Oriana is still sound asleep.

Now that Oriana is with Zara, I need to make travel arrangements to send them as far away from New York City as possible.

And I fucking hate it.

As soon as we got home, I received a message from Dre and Tristan, saying they'd question the guards in one of our empty warehouses and save me the trouble. Then I sent Gideon Marino and Weston Bertelli a message, asking if they could meet with me tomorrow. Both have already responded with times that work for them.

I'm dreading saying goodbye to Zara and never seeing her again. The thought of losing her hurts almost as much losing my brother because I love her. It's a different type of love, but just as strong. Zara feels like a part of me that's been missing my entire life. I want to wake up every day and see her and come home to her every night. I've never thought about having kids before I met Zara, but since I have, I'd give anything to be a father and for her to be the mother of our children.

And I know that happy little family I'm suddenly craving is nothing but a pipe dream.

My bedroom door opens quietly, spilling the light from the living room in, before it shuts again. I sit up in surprise and reach over to turn on the bedside lamp before she hurts herself wandering around in the dark. "Is everything okay?"

"I just tucked Oriana into bed." Zara moves to her side of the bed and starts undressing. Removing everything, even her bra and panties.

"You're not going to stay in her room tonight?" I ask when she climbs up on the mattress next to me — completely naked.

"No." I can hear the disappointment in her voice from just that one word. Even worse, I can see it on her beautiful face, the sadness in her eyes.

"Why not?"

"The nannies want me to spend some time with her tomorrow before she wakes up with me next to her."

"I'm sorry." I can't imagine how much that hurt for Zara to hear. "And I'm sorry she doesn't know you're her mother."

"It's okay," she lies as her fingertips reach over to stroke my arm and then my stomach before she climbs on top of me, her legs straddling mine. Her fingers thread through my hair, bringing her lips down to mine. My arms wrap around her. I groan at the feeling of her bare skin, from the top of her back down to her sweet ass.

"What are you doing, Zara?" I ask, since I know she's excited, sad, and a million other things tonight.

"I want to thank you," she says as her mouth moves lower to kiss my neck. "I want to thank you with my body and my mouth, because I can't possibly find the words."

She grips the waistband of my boxer briefs to tug them down, but I grab her hand to stop her, sliding her palm back up to my shoulder. "You don't owe me anything, baby."

"Oh," she whispers, her eyes studying mine. "Is…is everything okay? Do you not want to…"

"Yes, god, yes I want to." I hold her to me even tighter.

"Then what's wrong?"

What's wrong? I think it would be easier to give her a list of what's right. Her. Us. That's all that's right at the moment.

I want her so much, but not like this. So, I tell her the one thing that's most likely to make her hate me. "I'm going to have to kill Emilio's four guards. Otherwise, they could run and tell him everything."

Her hands grip my shoulder tighter. I brace myself for her rejection.

"I'm sorry you have to do that, especially for me."

"What? No. That's not…I don't blame you," I assure her. "But this is who I am, who I'll always be. And I hate…I fucking *hate* being this person sometimes, the kind of man who has to kill anyone who is a threat to me or my family."

"Well," Zara starts with a heavy sigh. "Even when you hate yourself, I will still love you."

Her words steal all the air from my lungs.

She loves me?

How? How the fuck could someone as good as her love me?

And why did she have to tell me this now when it won't change anything? Sending her away while breaking my heart is nothing, but I can't stand the thought of sending her away while her heart breaks.

Zara presses a kiss to my cheek. "You do what you have to do to protect your family. There's nothing sexier than seeing you do whatever it takes to keep everyone safe. Do you want to feel how much I love your ruthlessness for me, for Oriana?" Taking my hand, she places it between her legs, brushing my fingertips over her clit, then lower to her entrance.

"Jesus," I groan before easing a single finger inside of her. "You are soaking wet, *micetta mia*." I add another finger, making her gasp. "Soaking wet just for me."

"Yes. Only for you," she whispers in my ear before she slides down my body, kissing my neck and chest. "Only for my big, scary husband."

"What are you doing, baby?" I ask her again as my fingers slip free from her.

"I haven't been worshipping my angel of death nearly as often as he deserves. Tonight, I want to spend hours pleasuring you," she tells me as she tugs down my boxer briefs, this time without my intervention, freeing my half-hard shaft.

Resisting Zara has become nearly impossible. With her mouth moving down to my cock, I'm not sure if I can stop her this time if she goes any further.

"Jesus, baby. You don't owe me anything...especially this." I tell her again just before her lips place a kiss on my head. Her tongue swipes along my slit. I gather her long curls into a makeshift ponytail as her mouth lowers halfway down my shaft and comes back up again. I try one last time to let her know I'm not expecting anything from her — ever — before I lose the ability to form coherent words. "You don't have to do this or anything else to thank me. I told you...I don't deserve any pleasure."

When Zara's mouth leaves me, I want to shoot myself in the face for encouraging her to stop.

"Yes, you do deserve it. Now shut up and let me do this. Unless...unless you don't want me and are trying to be nice by saying *I don't deserve any pleasure.*" She lowers her voice in imitation of me, making me smile. "Creed?" she asks, when I don't respond.

"Of course I want you, especially your mouth, but —"

"Then shut up." She reaches up and slaps her palm to my lips. After shushing me again, the gorgeous woman's mouth resumes its descent again. Up and down, she licks and sucks me so damn good.

I'll never be deserving of her pleasuring me, but I let her keep going while I hold her hair. My fingers tighten in the strands the closer I get to release. Just when I can't take another second of her incredible mouth, I grab underneath her arms and haul her up until she's straddling my lap again. Grasping the sides of her face, I bring her lips to mine in a crushing kiss.

I don't want to finish in her mouth. I can't.

We both know where this is headed. I need to finally have her, take her, fill her up just once and make her mine in every way. Hell, I don't even know if she's on birth control, and I don't fucking care. I hope she's not.

Getting her pregnant before sending her away, before I go off to prison for three years, is the last thing I should be thinking about, but I can't help myself. I could endure all of that, even die a happy man if her belly were to swell with my baby.

Zara seems just as eager to finally have me inside of her. Our hands get in each other's way, trying to shuck my boxer briefs all the way off my legs so Zara can line me up.

"No condom?" I whisper before it's too late, rather than be the selfish asshole I want to be.

"No condom," she agrees as she sinks a few inches down on me. "*Ohh!*" she cries out in pleasure and then huffs a laugh. "That's... a lot. Wow. Give me... give me a minute."

I give her a minute or ten to work her sweet pussy all the way down. Her whimpers and constant commentary about my size bring me close to the edge before she finally starts to ride me.

"God. Damn. Zara. Nothing has ever felt as good as your tight, slick pussy clenching around me."

I love watching Zara's face, staring into her eyes while our bodies begin to move together a little faster. It's perfection. Her arms tightly wind around my neck to hold on. My own curl around her back, as if neither of us can get close enough.

"*Tu sei mia. Tu sei mia.*" I have to let her go tomorrow, but tonight, she's mine.

After the warm-up her mouth gave me, it doesn't take long for me to ache for a release. I hold off for as long as I can, trying not to thrust up into Zara, but allow her to take me as deep or fast as she needs to find her own pleasure.

When her mouth opens against mine on a gasp, I feel her spasm around me, taking me over the edge with her.

"*Uh! Oh! Yes!*" she whispers as we ride out the tremors together.

She gushes all over me, and I realize what an asshole I was for not licking her first.

Not wanting to let even a drop go to waste, I lie down flat on my back and pull Zara's body up my own until she's straddling my face.

My greedy tongue lashes against her flesh, licking up my cum and hers combined. Then I focus just the tip on her clit until her entire body quakes above me. Holding onto the top of the headboard, she cries out my name as her thighs clench around my head.

My wife is so fucking sexy. I'll never get enough of her. Never. Even if I could keep her.

Lifting her off me, I lay her back on the mattress and hover over her. "How does your pussy feel?"

"Tingly." She smiles up at me.

"Good tingly? Or are you sore?"

"You mean...to go again?" she asks. "Like right now?" Her eyes widen in surprise when they lower to my swollen cock. "I thought you finished."

"I did," I say while kissing her lips, letting her taste us both on them.

"I'm not sure if I can move yet," she replies.

"Then I'll do all the work."

Without warning, I flip her onto her stomach, pull her up onto her knees, and use my thumbs to spread her ass cheeks apart. "Fuck, yes. That's what I've been craving."

"Creed," Zara mutters, her face pressed to the mattress.

"What? I want to look at this beauty for a few minutes before I turn the whitest ass I've ever seen red." I run a finger down her slit, making Zara moan. While she's distracted, I swat her cheek with my other hand, loving her gasp.

"God, that's so damn sexy, watching your ass jiggle for me. I swear it's calling to me, wanting my hands and mouth on it."

Leaning down, I sink my teeth into the meaty part, not hard enough to hurt or leave a mark, but just to taste the perfection.

"Creed!" Zara huffs in annoyance.

I tease her clit with the brushing of my fingers to make her squirm, then take myself in my hand, lining my head up to sink into her heaven again.

I easily glide inside her wet heat, all the way to the hilt.

"Fucking hell, you take every inch of me so damn good, baby." I swear it feels like I'm deeper than I was when she was riding me.

I give her a moment to adjust to my size at this angle while gathering her hair again. Tugging her head back, I lean forward and kiss her cheek. "Let me see you work that ass up and down a few times before I pound you into the mattress."

"Yes, sir," she replies before her walls clench and she begins to move. I watch my cock disappear and reappear from her depths three whole times before I lose it.

Gripping her hip with my free hand, I hold her in place as I slam in deep, over and over again, loving the way her ass moves. "God, yes." I slap her cheek. "I would fucking kill for this ass."

"You...already...have." Zara sounds nearly as out of breath as I am.

Needing her to get there with me again, I reach around and press my palm to her pelvis, holding her still as I pump my hips faster. My fingertips barely graze her bundle of nerves, and she explodes in a cry of my name and god's.

My fingers tighten in her hair as I shove deep one final time before spilling inside her. The tremors are more intense this time than before. When they begin to lessen, I swivel my hips, trying to wring out every last drop of pleasure.

I'm soaking wet, cum dripping off my balls from our releases. It's by far the messiest round of sex I've ever had because I've never been stupid enough to shove inside a woman without a condom.

But I trust Zara. And I think she trusts me as well. I want to put my baby in her so damn bad.

I press my lips to her shoulder, then her neck as she lies still underneath me, head down, ass still up in the air. "Are you okay?"

"So...good," she replies in a slur that makes me smile.

Fuck. I'm so damn screwed.

I'm falling for Zara, have been since the first night I saw her and then convinced her to marry me. And I think she may feel something for me too. She told me tonight that she loved me, and I want to believe her.

But it doesn't really matter, since I have to let her go soon.

I got her daughter back for her like I promised. Now it's time to make travel arrangements to get them out of the city and away from Emilio.

"Why haven't we...done that before?" Zara asks.

Because you started out as my captive, and I threatened your life to make you my wife.

If I'd fucked her before, I'd have been taking advantage of her.

But how is it much different now when she's only in my bed,

underneath me, because she thinks she owes me for getting Oriana back?

"I needed to fuck my wife at least once." I place one last kiss over a freckle on her shoulder. "Now, I can let you go."

There's a long pause before Zara says, "Let me go?" Turning over, she looks up at me. "When were you planning on telling me you think Oriana and I have to leave the city?"

"I thought it was obvious," I say, even though the truth is I've tried to avoid thinking about it.

"Obvious. Right."

"I'm going to try to get you on a ship tomorrow."

"A *ship*?"

"A cargo ship is the safest way to get you out of the country without detection."

"And it has to be tomorrow? You're not even going to ask me what I want?"

"It doesn't matter what you want, *micetta mia*."

Zara scoffs as I move to sit with my back against the headboard.

I watch as she slides off the bed and stumbles around, pulling on her clothes. Her cheeks, face, and ass are the brightest shade of red I've ever seen from sex and her fury.

Fuck.

I don't want her to leave, especially not right now. I want to hold her all night, possibly for the last night, which is exactly why it's best that she should go. I don't like upsetting her, but it'll be easier to convince her to leave if she hates me.

Zara slips out the door without another word, softly shutting it behind her. I'm guessing she wanted to slam it as hard as possible, but she didn't because her daughter is sleeping down the hall thanks to me.

30

Zara

After the most humiliating night of my life, I was up and showered, listening outside the door to Oriana's room at six a.m. Of course, she wasn't up that early, but I wanted to be prepared to spend every waking minute with her today. I'm going to focus on getting to know my daughter and not think about my husband who cruelly kicked me out of his bed last night. After waiting so long for something so amazing, the prick told me that he just wanted to fuck me at least once before I left.

Creed didn't even ask me how I felt about leaving the city, possibly the country, or offer to figure out another solution with me. No, he made it clear I'll be getting on a ship any second now whether I like it or not. He's pushing me away, and I don't know why.

Because he fears what Emilio will do to me? That he will try to find Oriana? I don't want that man to ever get his hands on me or

Oriana again either, but there has to be some way to keep her safe other than giving up the only man I've ever wanted. The only man I've ever loved.

I told him I loved him last night. I thought Creed loved me, too, and that he was finally starting to trust me when we were together last night. But he didn't say the words back.

Now…well, I don't know anything, including what this means for our so-called marriage. Will he mail me divorce papers once I'm shipped off to wherever he decides is best?

And speaking of leaving, has Creed even considered making arrangements for Paige and Bethany to come with me and Oriana? While I think I'd be fine with her on my own, I know she'd probably like having some familiar faces with us until we get better acquainted. And getting them out of Creed's hair, away from where they could tell Emilio who took Oriana, is best for the don too.

I still don't have a phone, since Creed apparently doesn't trust me even after everything we've been through, so I approach the guards at the front door.

"Could you please tell your boss that I would like for Oriana's nannies to come with us if that's at all possible?"

The two men stare at each other before the one on the left tells the other, "Do it. Boss said to give her anything she wants."

"Creed told you to give me anything I want?"

"That's right. Screw it. I'll just text him myself," he says as pulls out his device and begins punching in the message.

"Thank you so much. You hopefully won't have to put up with me much longer."

"That's not a good thing," he says when I turn to leave to go back and listen at Oriana's bedroom door.

"What do you mean?"

"When you're gone, the boss isn't going to be happy. And when the boss isn't happy, shit goes sideways."

"I'm sure Creed Ferraro will be just fine without me."

"Oh yeah? Well, someone wants him dead, and yet, he still refuses to take bodyguards with him."

"Shut your mouth, Matteo," the first guard warns.

But now I'm curious. "What do you mean, Creed doesn't take any bodyguards with him? Isn't someone with him now?"

"Aldo is his driver. He makes him stay in the car. Tristan wanted to go with him today and he caved. The only time the boss has asked for help was last night with the...you know, nabbing."

"Why doesn't he want anyone watching his back?"

"Because he doesn't want anyone else to die or go to prison because of him."

My heart sinks into my stomach. "Because of Carmine?"

"That's right. Boss thinks it was some sort of mistake that his brother took bullets, and he didn't. But we all work for him because he deserves our loyalty. Carmine wouldn't have blamed his brother for a second. Any of us would gladly take a bullet for him because Creed takes care of our families, even if we're not around. He helped my grandma get into this crazy expensive nursing home when we couldn't leave her alone anymore or afford a nurse to stay with her. And Maurice here, the boss paid for his father-in-law's chemo and surgery. He's been in remission for what, five or six years now?"

"He just had his cancer free scan for the fifth year."

"That's...wow, very sweet of him."

Creed doesn't just pay his employees' wages; he takes care of everyone in Manhattan who needs it. Or at least he tries to. Even if it might get him in trouble.

"One of our men went to prison for killing the guy who touched his little boy. And you know what Creed did?"

"What?"

"First, he bitched him out for not coming to him to help kill the son of a bitch, and then" — the guard leans closer and whispers — "he actually helped him escape, so he could be with his family."

"That's...amazing." I can't say I'm surprised. Creed is a good man, even if he can't see that himself.

"The boss can make anything happen. That's why he's the capo dei capi."

"Right. King of kings."

I assumed Creed Ferraro ruled over the other families with fear before we met, but now I know that's only a small part of it. He rules because he's earned it through the respect of all the people he helps, doing what's right even when it may be legally wrong. He loves and protects those loyal to him and would do anything for them.

Creed

"So, what information did you and Dre get out of the guards last night?" I ask Tristan as we sit in morning traffic. He's in the back while Aldo drives and I ride in the passenger seat. Since this wasn't a conversation that I trusted to have by phone, I decided to kill two birds with one stone.

Besides, it's best not to show up alone when meeting with the other bosses.

"The four we picked up are all bachelors who live there in the apartment to watch the kid for Emilio day and night with the nannies. The boss visits several times a week, almost always on Fridays with the same four men — the ones who were searching everyone at his house. Izaiah would visit maybe once every few weeks with his father on Friday nights, but never on his own. They also said that other than Izaiah, his family doesn't know about the kid. Or if they do, they've never been to visit. The guards were surprised and thought we were lying when we told them Emilio was the girl's father."

"Good." If nobody knows, then once Emilio is dead, nobody will be trying to track down Oriana and take custody from Zara. "Did they give up any information about the club raid?"

"No. They were with the kid and swear they didn't know anything about it."

"Tell Dre to get rid of them tonight after you question them again for anything else they know about Emilio's entourage and schedule."

"Will do. So, where exactly are we going?"

"I've got a meeting with Gideon," I tell him just as a text comes in from Matteo, who is standing guard at the penthouse. Zara asked if the nannies could go with her, which makes sense.

"Gideon Marino?" Tristan asks.

"Do you know any other Gideons?"

"No, but why are you meeting with him? The Marinos aren't as seedy as the Sannas, but they're not exactly trustworthy by any means."

"The Marinos run the majority of the exporting out of New York. Either they pay for the cargo ships or know who does. I need a favor from them."

"What favor?"

"Putting Zara and her daughter on one of his boats along with a few of our men to make sure there's no trouble getting them somewhere far away."

"You sound so excited by the idea."

"I don't have any other choice. At least this way Zara gets to live her life. I'm sure Dre will celebrate when she's gone."

"You know, he's just a grumpy bastard who is trying to protect you from yourself. He's not wrong in this case, either. The woman is not only a liability, but she also had a hand in Carmine's death."

"I know. I just wish Dre could understand there's more to her than that one mistake. He probably wishes I would go with her."

"What the hell? Why would you say that?"

"Dre is next in line," I mutter aloud before I can stop the words from leaving my mouth. The thought of going with Zara and Oriana has crossed my mind. Leaving the country would also be one way to avoid prison...

Tristan is silent for several long seconds. "You can't be serious."

"He's my second, the underboss to our entire family now."

"I meant about you leaving! And I'm your third. Do you think I'd ever want you and Dre out of the way?"

"No. But he's not wrong. I've been making bad decisions, ones that put our family in jeopardy."

"Just because he's pointing out problems doesn't mean he's about to try and push you out."

"So, you don't think he could've had anything to do with the raid?"

"What? No." Tristan shakes his head. "Absolutely not. That was all on the Rovinas, right?"

"I only have proof Izaiah was involved, not Emilio. Izaiah had to have been working with someone. That someone could be anyone."

"You probably should've asked Izaiah before you killed him."

"Right, like I could've strung Izaiah up by his ankles and asked him about what he and his father or whoever else have been up to, and he would've just confessed."

"He might have. What if we string Emilio up by his ankles and see if he confesses to anything?"

"Our alliance with Emilio is hanging by a thread, one that Dre is going to sever if he doesn't hurry up and convince Stella to marry him. We need that wedding to happen while we bide our time until we can take out Emilio."

"You don't actually think Dre is dragging his feet to hurt you, do you?"

"Maybe."

"It's only been a few weeks since you told him he had to marry her. And I know for a fact Dre wants Stella so bad, he would crawl across Manhattan in the nude, on his hands and knees, for a taste of her."

"What?" I ask, since nothing he just said makes any damn sense.

"You really didn't know?"

"Know what?"

"I thought that was why you pushed him toward Stella. It's why I intentionally tried to rile him up by acting like I wanted to hit it."

"You were messing with him just to get him to agree to the marriage?"

"Trust me. He doesn't want Stella to marry anyone else. He lost his fucking mind when he thought I might swoop in and agree to the wedding. I was sure he was going to blow my brains out."

"Because you joked about fucking her?"

"Yes! He wasn't about to let that happen."

"Why not?"

"Because he's been trying to hit that for years now.."

Twisting around to look at him, I ask, "Stella has turned him down for years?"

"Repeatedly."

"Wow. How did I not know this?" I face forward again.

"Because you're too busy, sitting around and thinking the worst about people instead of actually getting the details. Dre is a good soldier. He wants to keep you alive, make you proud, and fuck Stella Rovina's brains out."

"He never told me." Is that why he was so pissed at me for

killing Izaiah? He's afraid it'll fuck him over with Stella if she finds out?

"Do you go around telling everyone about the women who reject you?"

"If I did, it would be a long list. Zara was the first in a long time to let me touch her. Even if I was just a gratitude fuck."

"A what fuck?"

"Zara was happy and excited after I got her daughter back, so fucking me last night was her way of thanking me. It was our first time, only time..."

"You don't think your wife is hot for you?"

"Zara is used to doing men she doesn't really want to get what she needs."

"I'm gonna have to call bullshit."

"You can call whatever you fucking want," I tell him while staring out the window. Now, I'm seeing the entire city in black and white like Zara's photos. It's all...colorless without her.

"Zara reminds me of the heart-eyed emoji whenever I see her looking at you. She's head over heels in love with you. But is she wrong to have held off because you forced her to marry you and threatened to kill her? Now, you're shipping her off to who the hell knows where, right? Why start something you can't finish?"

"I tried not to give in, but last night...I couldn't refuse her."

"For the first time, right?"

"Yes."

"And? How was it?"

"I'm not giving you details and shit," I warn him. "But it was...better than I imagined it would be. The best I've ever had."

"So that's why you're so pissy today. Last night you got the best fuck of your life, and today you're arranging for her to leave, talking crazy shit about Dre having it out for you."

"My head hasn't been right since the raid," I confess.

"No shit, boss. Everyone knows that. It rattled us all to lose

Carmine and Jasper and not have anyone to take our grief out on. At least, none that we knew of…"

"I don't know who I can trust anymore, and it's driving me insane." It's not like I've ever been all that trusting, but at least we've had peace for the past decade, only a few minor scuffles with the other families. The raid was an assassination attempt to replace me at the head of the table. I know it, and it wasn't just Izaiah behind it…

"Honestly, boss, I think it could be anyone."

I turn around to glare at him, and he quickly adds, "Anyone in one of the other families. That shit didn't come from ours. Emilio was probably in on it with Izaiah. I could see Bertelli, Marino, or Sanna coming for you like that."

"It wasn't Bertelli," I declare.

"Why do you say that? Weston craves power. He built an empire on having the ability to murder anyone, anytime, to keep everyone scared of him."

"He's too old, and he's not going to let his shithead son, Bowen, lead all the families. He's smarter than that. And Serafina isn't his biological daughter. She doesn't have any Italian in her blood either. He knows she would never be accepted at the top of the food chain, not to mention she's a woman, and Italians are sexist assholes. If it'd been Weston, he wouldn't have missed taking me out."

"Okay, those are good points. It wasn't the Bertellis. Who else have you eliminated?"

"The Marinos, obviously. Do you think I would ask Gideon for this huge of a favor if I thought he wanted me dead?"

"Why can't it be the Marinos?"

"Because the only potential leaders in their family besides Gideon is Gia, who is probably going to marry one of the Sanna boys. They were chatting it up at Emilio's dinner. Then there's the younger brother, Zaven, who is less serious than even you are about running things. Gideon wouldn't make that big of a play when he knows he's barely holding on to his own house."

"Fine. So, it wasn't the Marinos either. That just leaves Sanna, who hates Emilio Rovina, so I doubt they would work together to take you out. Hell, who knows? Maybe Aiden Sanna and Emilio Rovina only pretend to hate each other and were in on the attack together. Team ASER."

"Aser?"

"Aiden Sanna and Emilio Rovina."

"Right." I roll my eyes. "But it's possible, I guess. I don't fucking know anything anymore, and it's driving me fucking insane."

"That's all that's driving you insane?" Tristan chuckles.

"Zara will be gone in a few days, and it'll be like she was never here," I assure him, wishing I believed that lie myself.

∼

Gideon Marino was only twenty-five-years-old when he took over the family business after his father died. He's handled himself well enough these last five years, expanding their shipping business all over the world. The Marinos can get you anything from anywhere and can send anything wherever you want it to go.

"Gideon, thanks for meeting with me," I say as I approach him and his crew just inside the harbor warehouse. I hold out my hand for him to shake.

"No problem, it sounded urgent, and I felt bad for not checking in on you after the funeral."

"You were low on my suspect list."

"Good to know," he says. Pushing up the sleeves of his button down, he reveals the tattoo of a sea serpent that takes up his entire forearm. I swear this family thinks they're a bunch of pirates. Every made man in their crew is required to get the ink on a visible part of the body. To not openly show off the sea serpent is a sign of disrespect to their family, like they're ashamed of their association with one of the largest importers in the world. Legal and not so legal drugs.

"So, what's up?"

"I need a favor from you."

"How big?"

"I need three women and a child out of the country, and as many of my guards as you can cram into a boat to accompany them on the voyage."

"Do you have a particular destination in mind for this large group of individuals?"

"No. Just the further away, the better."

"Will the women and child have papers?"

"I'm working on that. I'm hoping to have the documents by morning."

He nods. "Then you're in luck. I've got some cargo headed to Lisbon tomorrow. It's one of the...shorter destinations."

Portugal would be a great place for Zara, and the shorter the trip, the better. Fuck. The country feels a million miles away from New York, though. I know a flight would be easier and faster, but that requires more documentation and is easier to track.

"Deal. Name your price. How many guards can you take to escort them?"

Rubbing his chin, he says, "I'll have to look at the manifest, but three or four should be fine. Is that going to be enough protection?"

"Do you think it's enough protection for three women and a child on a cargo ship?"

"I think your women and kid would be fine without any, but that's your call."

"None of them are mine," I lie. Since Zara is leaving, there's no reason for anyone to ever know we're married.

"If you say so."

"And I need them to not be seen by anyone while boarding, if you can help it."

Crossing his arms over his chest, he asks, "How deep in shit is this going to get me if it blows up in my face?"

"Here's all you need to know, the honest to god truth — she's a good woman, a good mother, who had her daughter taken away when she was a day old. Now that she's got her back after waiting for three years, she shouldn't have to deal with anyone else fucking with them. The other two women are twenty-something nannies."

"Okay. Well, make sure they all have docs because once they leave the boat, they're on their own. And it'll cost you a million a head plus a future favor."

"That won't be a problem," I agree. I was expecting at least five million a head and was willing to pay it. The favor I would've done for him for free.

I hold out my hand again, and Gideon shakes it with his right. The sea serpent looks like it's moving underneath the muscles.

"Since you don't want any of my crew to see them, how about I have them picked up at your building two hours before departure?"

"That will work."

"Send them down with my fee and luggage at four p.m. tomorrow."

"They'll be ready and waiting," I assure him. "I appreciate this, Gideon."

Tristan thankfully doesn't speak until we're back in the SUV. "So that went well. Now where to?"

"We're going to go see Bertelli."

"Great. Why are we paying that ancient asshole a visit?"

"Because he's going to get the travel documents Zara will need."

Tristan whistles. "Damn, boss. This is turning out to be one expensive bitch. I mean the favors alone —"

Surging up between the seats, I grab his neck and squeeze before he can finish his sentence. "What did you call my wife?"

"Sorry," he wheezes out.

"You won't speak a negative word about Zara again, will you?"

"No sir, boss."

"Good. Now let's go to the Bronx," I tell Aldo.

∽

Weston Bertelli runs a hit man for hire organization across the world. Anywhere Marino can ship to, Bertelli will hire someone to kill for you, if the price is right.

His services are not cheap. His reputation is of the utmost respect. After all, who would dare disrespect a man with over two dozen snipers on his payroll? Nobody who wants to live a long life. We only have one long-range sharpshooter in our entire family.

"Weston, Bowen," I say when the two men finally come out to the lobby. Their Concourse Plaza office in the Bronx serves as the front for their business dealings.

I didn't know Bowen would be a part of the meeting, and it's too rude to ask him to sit it out. If his old man trusts him, then I guess I'll have to trust him too.

"Creed, Tristan. How have you been?" Weston asks, his voice scratchy from a lifetime of smoking. "Well, other than the near-death experience a few weeks back?" His chuckle sounds like a rake scraping over gravel.

"You know, if I were dead, I would have pinned the raid on you, old man."

He chuckles again and gestures toward his office. "Come. Sit. Have a drink. Because of course it wasn't me or my people. We don't fucking miss."

Inside the spacious office overlooking his territory, Weston has his secretary pour us all a scotch, and then we settle into the sitting area as if this is all an informal little get together.

"Have you found out who killed your brother and was trying to kill you?" he asks, getting straight to the point. That's one of the things I always liked about him. The old man doesn't beat around the bush. He's a straight shooter, which is rare in this city where everyone wants to dance around shit to see what they can get out of you before doing actual business.

"I have a few suspicions, but nothing more just yet," I admit to him. "Have any of your people heard anything?" I ask, since not all his assassins are men. His adopted daughter is just one of the many women who kill men for a living. That's why he's so good at taking out the target. Men are usually stupid when it comes to women, underestimating them to their own detriment.

"Not a peep," Weston replies. "The culprit didn't use a professional, obviously. Why would they think the cops could get anything done right around here?"

If I have a handful of men in the station on my payroll, then Weston has probably no less than fifty. He has to pay law enforcement well if he wants to keep his business lucrative and not end up in prison.

"No gossip from the NYPD either?" I ask in surprise.

"No. My guys and gals had no idea that you and your crew would even be in the club that night. They were told it was a drug bust set up by a confidential informant."

"Well, that was obviously a lie. And the two cops who led the men into the club put a bullet through their own heads."

"Did they?" Weston asks. "Or did someone want to make it look like suicides?"

"Either way, they're not going to be talking," I remark, since I don't see why it matters.

"Right," he agrees. "So, what is this business deal you need from me?"

"I need the best identification, documents, and passports that money can buy, and I need it today or tomorrow at four at the latest."

Since Weston's employees need to get in and out of countries regularly without being noticed, he has one hell of a forgery team creating documents. I've heard he even has plastic surgeons and all sorts of makeup and costume artists as well to change the looks of hit men and women as needed.

"How many individuals are traveling on such short notice?"

"Three women and a child."

"Do you have their photos?"

"Yes." I asked the guards to get the photos after Zara requested the nannies accompany them, and they didn't let me down.

"I can try and ask my... representative at the State Department to expedite your request, but it's going to cost you."

I have no clue if he actually has someone working for him in the State Department, or if he's just saying that to cover his ass. Either way, I don't care as long as he gets it done.

"Name your price."

"Twenty million that Andre is going to invest and turn into fifty million."

"I can't make any promises about investments," I admit. "But I can make you as much money as possible."

"Why not just make him pay it now?" the son, Bowen, asks.

His father raises an eyebrow in his direction in warning making me assume that he's supposed to be seen but not heard in this conversation.

"I apologize," Weston says. "Bowen has a thing or two to learn about how to clean money and make it multiply."

"Right." While twenty million in his hand right now might be nice, he needs the cash to be laundered through legit means like investing.

"Do we have a deal?"

"Do you have any sort of time limit for when you want to make this fifty million?"

"Let's say a year?"

"A year," I agree. That should give Dre plenty of time to invest and get great returns on Weston's money. He can get it all set up, hopefully, before our prison sentences begin.

As I get to my feet, I offer the old man a handshake, but not his idiot son.

"I'll have the documents hand-delivered by four p.m. tomorrow. Not a minute later."

"I appreciate your help."

"Of course," Weston says. "And if you find out who is behind the failed attack on you, I hope you'll share their name with me. I don't want to be in bed with amateurs."

I nod my head in agreement, and then Tristan and I are shown out of the office. On the elevator, Tristan opens his mouth to say something, but I shake my head in warning. God knows Weston has video and audio recorded in these elevators.

Once we're back on the ground and enclosed inside the SUV, Tristan asks, "Did Bertelli just offer to off whoever came after us?"

"Yes. At least, that's how I interpreted his comment."

"Even if it's one of the other families?"

"I'm sure he's considered that possibility. He's obviously offended that someone's assassination attempt in his city failed. He doesn't want anyone thinking it was him. Weston would rather be the one who took down the fucker responsible to send a message than to let his reputation take a hit."

"Even if it starts a war?"

"Respect is more important to some men like Weston Bertelli than bloodshed. He would go to war with one of the other families just to prove he's still good at what he does, what he promises his high-paying clients all over the world."

"Good thing he's on our side," Tristan mutters.

"Do you see why I didn't suspect him? Now, his son, on the other hand, I wouldn't trust him as far as I could throw him off the top of a flight of stairs."

"You think Bowen is shady?"

"I think Weston may need to skip over him in the line of succession unless he wants his entire empire to be spent on whatever pops up in that idiot's mind. He's too impulsive."

"Says the guy who killed another man for a woman he didn't even know."

"Zara and I had met, briefly," I correct him. "And that may have been impulsive on my part, but it was still the right thing to do. I don't regret it."

Tristan sighs heavily. "And I thought love at first sight was a bullshit myth."

"I didn't fall in love with Zara the second I saw her," I assure him. "It took a few days."

"Right. How many seconds did it take for you to put those bullets in Izaiah?"

Unable to help my grin, since he's not entirely wrong. "I waited almost five minutes before interfering."

"So, roughly three-hundred seconds? Excuse the fuck out of me."

"You and Dre have both been a little too...opinionated since I brought Zara home."

"Since you killed a man, an ally's son, without planning it all out or asking for our help, and then kidnapped and married a random witness, one who fucked us all and could take us down with you? Huh, I hadn't noticed."

"Smartass. One of these days, I bet you'll fall in love with someone who you would kill for without knowing her name too. Here's hoping the kill shot won't actually be necessary in the same five minutes you're alone with her."

31

Zara

My first full day with my daughter is nothing short of magical. Oriana threw a tantrum at breakfast when her toast wasn't exactly the way she wanted it, too dark and crispy. I prepared another slice, one that looked identical to the first, and she devoured it. I know her fit was just about having control when she feels like she doesn't have any, waking up in this new place with new people and not many of her toys or things.

After breakfast, she seemed happier as she played with the bags of toys Creed had sent over from FAO Schwarz. Her favorite, of course, was the three different princess crowns.

Oriana loved them all and wore them one on top of the other at the same time.

Creed stayed out all day, and I assumed it was because he's not fond of screaming kids. Still, it was sweet of him to send toys for her to play with and luggage for me to pack it all into to take with us, along with the clothes and things he bought me.

While I have no idea how I'll make a living wherever it is we'll be sent to, it doesn't really matter. I'd clean toilets or scoop giant elephant poop, anything as long as I get to be a part of my daughter's life as she grows up.

Nobody is ever going to take her away from me again. I was weak before when they stole her from my arms. I knew Emilio was an asshole when he got me pregnant, but I never thought he'd take my daughter from me. I won't make the same mistake of trusting the wrong people again.

∼

Creed finally returns home late that night, after Oriana has been tucked in. I'm going to stay with her tonight, but I wanted to talk to my husband first.

"Hey," I say in greeting. "Busy day?"

"Yes. And we have a few things to discuss." He avoids looking at me as he removes his jacket, hanging it in the foyer for someone to come along and take it to be laundered for him. "I'm starving. Let's talk while we eat," he suggests, heading straight for the kitchen to give the chef his late order for dinner.

I go on to the dining room to wait for him, sitting not so patiently and trying not to think about what happened last night and how amazing it was until he kicked me out of his bed.

Creed enters the room with a wooden board full of cheese and crackers, some already in his mouth as if he couldn't wait the few minutes for dinner.

"Are we going to talk about last night?" I ask him quietly.

"No. I've got everything arranged for you to leave tomorrow," he says as he takes a seat at the head of the table, completely brushing aside what happened between us. It takes a long moment for his words to seep into my skull because I'm so annoyed with him.

"Tomorrow?" I repeat in surprise. "Wow. That was fast."

"The sooner the better." He focuses on piling cheese atop another cracker rather than look at me.

"And were you able to find space for the nannies too?"

"Yes."

"Good. I mean, thank you. I think I would be fine with Oriana, but I know she would be happier to have them along until we get more comfortable with each other."

"How did she do today?"

"Great. She was a little fussy at breakfast, but after she got some food in her belly, she had so much fun playing with the things you had sent over. Especially the princess crowns. Thank you for doing that."

He nods but doesn't respond. He just continues snacking on the cheese and crackers as if they require his complete attention.

"So, where are we going?" I ask to fill the silence.

"Lisbon, Portugal."

"Portugal? Fun," I say, meaning it. I've always wanted to travel but never thought I'd be able to actually afford a trip out of the country, since I can barely afford the gas to drive to New Jersey.

"You'll need to make sure all your things are packed and you're downstairs, waiting for your ride, at four o'clock tomorrow afternoon."

"Oh. Okay. Four tomorrow."

There's a long pause where neither of us says anything. The only sound is the crunching of crackers, one right after another. Unable to take another second of the awkwardness, I reach for Creed's tattooed hand that's resting on the table. "Thank you for everything. I wish... I wish you could come with us."

He quickly pulls his hand from underneath mine. "You're welcome. Another thank you fuck tonight isn't necessary."

"A what?" I ask, his rejection so badly stinging throughout my chest that I don't think I heard him clearly.

"Last night when you thanked me with your mouth and pussy. A repeat is unnecessary."

"You... don't want to be with me again? Is that what you're trying to say to me so crudely?"

"I don't want you to fuck me because you feel obligated to do so."

I shake my head, swallowing past the knot in my throat, my eyes burning. "That's not..."

"Don't lie to me, Zara." The don's tone is harsh, cruel, just like when we first met, and he wanted to kill me. And even after weeks together, he still doesn't trust me. I don't think he ever will because of Carmine.

"I'm not lying, Creed! You're the first man I've ever been with who I chose!"

He lifts his dark blue eyes to hold mine. He blinks at me, as if in surprise, but there's still some distrust in them. "You choose me for the wrong reasons."

"What?"

"Emilio and Izaiah ruined you. And I hate them for that. But I forced you into a marriage to keep you close, which isn't much different. It was wrong, and for that I'm sorry. You don't owe me any obligatory pussy."

"Obligatory..." I can't even finish repeating that offensive remark.

"There are plenty of women who would give it to me for much simpler reasons."

"You are so full of shit!" I push my chair back and get to my feet. "There are no other women, because you're *Accabadore*. If they are, it's only because they're gold-diggers with ulterior motives."

"Maybe so, but I guess I don't find gold-diggers quite as deceitful. At least they're honest about what they want from me, whether it's my credit card or a giant diamond ring."

"And you don't think that I've been honest about what I want from you?"

"No, I don't, Zara. I think you've been hurt, victimized for so long that you can't stop trying to please people, even the ones who use you. It's as if you think all you deserve is the abuse. You don't even get why Emilio and Izaiah were manipulating you by using your daughter's wellbeing."

"They did it because they were sick bastards who would take whatever they wanted whenever they wanted it without caring about how I felt. I guess you're not that much different from them, Creed."

The muscle in his jaw ticks. "Other than the marriage, I haven't made you do anything. Did you forget that you're the one who came to my bed last night and climbed on top of me?"

"Don't worry, I will *never* make that mistake again," I tell him before storming out of the dining room.

"Good! I'm glad we finally understand each other!" he calls after me, his words so cruel that I nearly run into the staff bringing out the asshole's dinner.

I hope the son of a bitch burns his fucking tongue on every bite of the steaming dishes.

∼

Creed

I fucking knew it.

Zara just admitted that sleeping with me was a mistake.

Last night, she didn't really want me, but I didn't stop her

And I fucking hate the scalding fire burning up my stomach, into my lungs when she walks out of the dining room.

I wanted to share a meal with her, one last meal with my wife before she leaves tomorrow. And I had to go and run my mouth, antagonizing her until she gave me exactly what I wanted from her — the truth.

But if I had asked her to stay with me, to sleep in my bed with me again tonight, I'd be no better than Emilio or Izaiah, forcing her to pleasure me out of manipulation, rather than doing it because she wants me.

While I'm angry at myself for losing out on spending more time with her, a small part of me is also relieved. Relieved I won't have to worry about being inside her and doing something those *stronzos* did, triggering her and hurting her even more than using her body. Zara would've done anything I asked because she's so grateful to me for bringing her daughter back to her.

While I haven't seen her with Oriana today, I had Matteo and Maurice send me reports and photos of them together all day.

Zara is a good mother. It's a shame those monsters kept her from her daughter for so long and used the girl as blackmail.

I'm glad I killed Izaiah, and I'm looking forward to killing Emilio.

I'll be ready to deal with the fallout when I do, whatever it will be, just as soon as Zara and Oriana are out of the country. I want them to get as far away from me, from Emilio, and the violence of the mafia once and for all.

32

Creed

"So, Zara's leaving today?" Dre asks when he finds me brooding in my Omerta office.

"Yes," My brow furrows. "How did you know?"

"I just came from the penthouse. There were suitcases sitting at the door."

"They're leaving this afternoon." I glance at the watch on my wrist. "In about fifteen minutes, actually."

"And you're not going up there to spend your last few minutes with your wife?"

"No."

"I find that hard to believe, since you were willing to ruin your life and the rest of ours for her just a few days ago."

"Do you want me to shoot you in the face? Is that why you came in here talking shit?" I grumble.

"I'm just asking a valid question."

"She's leaving. I thought you of all people would be happy to get rid of her, since you think she's a liability and blame her for Carmine's murder. You said she had to go and you're right. It's safer this way."

"And if you listened to me instead of yourself and what you feel about her, then you're a fucking idiot."

"That's it. I'm definitely blowing your head off." I get to my feet, open the left drawer of my desk, and pull out the spare Smith & Wesson I keep there.

"Oh, shut the fuck up with the tough guy act. And put the gun away. You won't kill me," he says. "I know you better than anyone but maybe Tristan. And I know that this whole pouting thing you're doing isn't going to end any better than the impulsive decision to kill Izaiah. You care about Zara. So much so that you threatened to kill her to make her marry you, and now you're sending her away to protect her and yourself. If she's gone, then you won't have to actually trust someone not to shred your shriveled black heart."

Clenching my molars, I grit out, "Her staying with me was never an option. It was stupid to insist she marry me. Sending her away was always the best solution. I just didn't want to face it before."

"You could see her again. She's not going to disappear after the boat leaves the harbor, you know. But you're too scared that she doesn't love you or accept all of you or whatever bullshit to even try."

"Do you want me to go chasing after her so you can take over for me?"

"*Vaffanculo.* I don't want to be the boss of bosses. I doubt I could pull it off, even if all the heads of the family were replaced. What I'm trying to say is that maybe I was wrong."

"About?"

"About Zara being bad for you and your awful ass decision making! My first reaction when you told us about her setting us up with the raid was to hate her, to think she's the enemy because what she did got Carmine killed and all of us arrested. If the Rovinas had her little girl, then it's easier to understand how they convinced her to screw us over. She's a victim here too. And that's why you married her instead of killing her, right?"

"That's where I fucked up. We were never an actual couple in a real marriage. She was never anything but my captive and then a woman thankful for someone helping her get her daughter back after she was wrongly taken from her."

"Yes, how could any woman love the asshole who went out of his way to risk his life to save hers and give her the best gift ever?"

"You're an asshole."

"Creed, isn't it possible that Zara loves you for the things you did for her, the way you treated her, and that she wasn't just fucking you as some sort of unspoken requirement? I mean, I've been with women who aren't into it, and I don't know how shit went down with Zara, but unless she just laid on her back, staring at the ceiling, counting the seconds until you finished, then she probably wanted to be with you. Is that what happened?"

"She rode me the first time."

"There you go. She was an active, dare I guess, enthusiastic participant?"

I narrow my eyes at him. I can't help but give him some shit too. "Do the women you sleep with really just lie there?"

"I'm only the underboss to the capo dei capi. That doesn't seem to get them all hot and bothered. Who knows? I sure as hell don't. Maybe I'm the problem…"

"So, all your complaining about Zara being bad for me was coming from a man who screws women who have less energy than a blowup doll?"

"Basically. Yes."

"No wonder you're so damn grumpy all the time."

"You would be, too, if you could never touch the only woman you want," he blurts out, then quickly glances away.

"Stella Rovina, huh?"

His fingers pause halfway through shoving them in his hair. "How did you know?" He slumps into a chair.

"Tristan."

"Him and his fat fucking mouth."

"You're marrying the woman by the end of the year, so I would say that your chances of getting inside of her are somewhere around like fifty percent now."

"It's zero if she kills me before the wedding."

"True. Best watch your back. I don't trust anyone in that damn family. How could Emilio and Izaiah take a baby girl from her mother right after she gave birth?"

"They're cruel sons of bitches," Dre agrees. "That, unfortunately, doesn't change the fact that I want to bend Stella over every surface in New York."

"So, it's just a physical attraction to her?"

"I guess. But no other woman seems to get her out of my head, no matter how beautiful or kind they are to me."

"Have you had them throw wine in your face in public? Maybe that would do the trick."

"Ha, you're not fucking funny," he mutters.

"So, what is it then?"

"I don't know. There's just something about Stella… maybe the fact that she hates me and doesn't want anything to do with me is why I find her so infuriatingly sexy."

"You like the challenge she presents?"

"I hate the goddamn challenge! I don't want to want someone who loathes the sight of me. I sure as shit don't want to chase her either. Screw it. I'm not marrying her. That just sounds like the worst kind of torture imaginable, calling her my wife and not being able to touch her without losing a hand."

"Oh, you're going to marry her," I assure him. Now, it's not just about our alliance with the Rovinas. I think the only chance Dre may ever have of changing Stella's mind about him will be if she's forced to live under the same roof as him as his wife. "I don't want Emilio to see what's coming when we set up his accidental death."

"*Vaffanculo.* If I marry Stella, you have to get off your ass and tell Zara that you're in love with her, then give her a chance to be honest with you about how she feels without assuming the worst."

"Me and Zara, it's not that easy."

"It is easy, Creed. It is," he says again. "It's you who is making shit hard. There has to be some other option for you to keep your wife here with you. If not now, then at least in the future — a few months from now when Emilio is dead."

Fuck. Maybe he's right.

"What time is it?" I ask before I glance at my watch. "Three-fifty-six." If I hurry, maybe I can say goodbye to Zara before she leaves and ask her if she wants to see me again. "I need to get downstairs." I head for the door.

"No shit, man. I was wondering how long it would take for you to wake the fuck up."

Dre follows me to the elevator, and I press the down button no less than five times to call the damn thing.

"Won't make it come any faster."

I glance at the door to the stairs. We're too high up to try to run down all the steps.

Finally, the elevator dings, the doors open, and we squeeze on with the rest of the passengers. It feels like an eternity before we pile out at the lobby floor.

I jog out the door to 56th Street but don't see her, so I hurry around to 57th, knowing they were going to be picked up at the corner of Park Avenue.

"Where is she?" Dre asks when he catches up.

"She's gone."

"To Marino's harbor, right?"

"Yes."

"Then let's go."

"There should be time," I agree. "Marino was going to load them a few hours before departure to keep most his crew from seeing them."

"Then call up Aldo with a car, and we'll head over to the harbor."

I shoot a text to Aldo to come and pick us up. He replies that he just loaded Zara and the rest of the group, so he'll be around to get us soon.

While Dre and I are waiting, a long black suburban rolls up to the curb. The passenger window rolls down, and the driver with a shaved head waves, showing the sea serpent ink on his forearm. "Mr. Ferraro?"

"Yes?"

"I'm Jimmy, picking up your passengers for Mr. Marino."

"What?" I walk up to the window, getting closer so I can hear him better.

"You had some travelers that needed to be picked up today at four, right? Sorry, I was late. Traffic. You know how it is. But Mr. Marino said we'll get boarded up with plenty of time to spare."

"What? No." I shake my head. "I don't understand. I thought they had already left." Aldo just told me he loaded their luggage. I look down the street as my stomach sinks to the sidewalk. "At least, I thought they had left."

I call Aldo.

"Hi, boss."

"You said you loaded up Zara and the others?"

"Yes, sir." That was about, ah, ten or fifteen minutes ago."

"Are you sure it was Marino's SUV?"

"Yes, sir. Well, I assumed it was his…"

"Fuck."

"Maybe she just got in someone else's Uber," Dre suggests.

But the odds of that are slim. It'd have to be one hell of an Uber to carry Zara, her daughter, two nannies and four guards plus some luggage.

"I need to call Bertelli," I say as I end the call with Matteo and find the number in my contacts.

"Creed," Weston says when he answers. "I trust the documents were to your satisfaction."

"When did you drop them off?"

"My messenger handed them to a woman with long curly hair matching one of the photos about…fifteen minutes ago."

"Did your messenger also give her and the others a ride by chance?"

"No."

"Are you certain?"

"Yes. He was on a scooter."

"Fuck!"

I end the call without another word, too furious to speak.

"We'll find her," Dre says, his phone already to his ear, calling someone he must think can help. "Hey, Anthony. It's Dre. Do you have the street camera footage for the past half hour? Yeah, the boss and I are coming to take a look. Thanks."

He hangs up. "Let's go to security, find out the make and model of the vehicle, and try to get a license plate. Ask Gideon to let you know if they show up at the harbor in case it's just an Uber mix up."

"Yeah, okay." My entire body is numb as I somehow get my fingers to type out the text to Gideon. Then I send a group text to the entire family to be on the lookout for them, including my men with Zara, who I ask to contact me immediately.

I hear several notification pings right after I hit send coming from nearby. Heading toward the sound, my heart sinks to the sidewalk when I see a pile of cell phones and guns inside a planter near the building's entrance.

I don't even have to look to know they're my guys who are as good as dead, along with Zara, if we don't find them fast.

33

Zara

I thought it was odd for the driver and passenger of the long white passenger van to insist everyone leave their weapons and cell phones behind; although, I know Creed is strict about those things in his club. After all, only his guys had devices and guns.

But then when the van drives over the Queensboro Bridge, heading the opposite way to the Staten Island harbor, I know that something is definitely wrong.

I try not to panic, not wanting Oriana, who is sitting on my lap in the middle row with the nannies, to worry.

While I pull off my rings and slip them into my jean pocket, I whisper to the guards squeezed into the two back rows and the nannies next to me, "This isn't the right way."

"Sure, it is," says the driver. He even meets my gaze in the rearview mirror, a grin on his face. He, unfortunately, looks familiar.

If I had to bet, I'd say he's one of Emilio Rovina's men. I don't know how the hell that's possible, though. Maybe I'm just being paranoid.

Clearing the worry from my throat, trying to keep my voice calm, I ask, "Where are we going exactly?"

"Right where you need to be," he replies ominously. "If anyone tries anything, I'll run this vehicle into a brick wall. Me and Danny will survive, since we have airbags."

Oh shit.

Emilio somehow knew when and where I'd be waiting, or someone saw me standing outside the building with Oriana and told him so he could have us picked up. I honestly don't know what's going on, but whatever it is, isn't good.

After we pull up to an unfamiliar building and park in a double garage, the driver says, "Everyone out. Slowly. Try anything, and we kill all the women right now."

Creed's men are good guys. They wouldn't let us die just to save themselves.

How do I know?

Because once everyone climbs out of the SUV, they all lift their hands in the air. They allow the three approaching armed men to pat them down. Those same men come and do the same to me and the nannies. I take one of Oriana's small hands while Paige takes the other.

"Mr. Rovina expected better than this from you girls," the driver says to Paige and Bethany.

"We were held at gunpoint. There wasn't much we could do, but at least we stayed with his granddaughter," Paige tells him. She still doesn't know Oriana is his daughter, not grandchild.

"Right," the man mutters with a roll of his eyes. "I'm sure Mr.

Rovina will understand. Now, in an orderly fashion, everyone start walking over to that door." He points the way.

I wish there was another option. Any option other than letting my daughter return to this son of a bitch. While I could try to grab her and run, I have no doubt his men would fire at me, and one of the idiots could accidentally hit Oriana.

"Too risky," Paige says, as if she's thinking the same thing.

"I'm sorry. I'll figure a way out of this," I promise them.

"You should worry about yourself, not us," she whispers back.

I'm worried about us all, actually. Especially Oriana. She doesn't seem to realize that we're marching most likely to our deaths as she swings from between me and Paige. At least, I know she'll be safe for the time being. Emilio won't intentionally hurt her. No, he'll wait until she's older, so he can control her like he does his other children.

Our procession into what I'm thinking is Rovina's construction office, since there's a big truck with their logo in the garage, stops as the man in the front speaks to someone in the doorway. "Boss says only the women are going inside."

No, no, no.

"Please!" I beg them. "These men...they were only sent to protect Oriana. That's all they're meant to do."

"We know they're part of the Ferraro family," one of the men says. "Now get inside!"

"I'm sorry. I'm so sorry!" I tell the guards left behind as we're ushered into the building. It's a normal-looking office with cubicles, conference rooms, printers, and computers. For once, I want to see Emilio. Maybe I can beg him to let the nannies and the guards go.

The door to the garage barely closes behind Bethany when we hear the rapid gunfire, making us all jump.

No! Fuck.

I'm too late.

Now four of Creed's men are dead.

"What was that?" Oriana turns around and asks, her green eyes wide as she looks back at the door.

"Fireworks," I blurt out. "Right, ladies?"

"Uh-huh," Bethany agrees, her face pale as she nods too vigorously.

Paige seems to be holding it together better than me and Bethany. She gives Oriana an explanation and everything. "I bet someone left fireworks from the Fourth of July in their truck, and when they get too hot, they go pow-pow-pow."

"Can I see the fireworks?" Oriana bounces on her tiptoes.

"No, honey. The show is over now. There's just yucky smoke left behind," I tell her as I guide her by her shoulders to face forward.

I swear, one of these days, I'm going to kill Emilio Rovina.

The fucker himself finally strolls out of one of the rooms. "Sanzio, take the nannies upstairs to my office with little Ori," Emilio directs his men. "Hi, doll." He smiles at his daughter, then his face reddens. All that fury is directed right at me. "Zara's staying with the rest of us down here."

Knowing this may very well be it, the last time I ever see my daughter, I kneel and give her a big hug, holding her tight, inhaling her orange and vanilla scented shampoo. Her arms hold me tight like she's afraid, too, even if she doesn't know what there is to be afraid of yet.

"I love you so much." I kiss her cheek, then her forehead. "Miss Paige and Miss Bethany love you too. Behave for them, okay?"

She nods, and then each woman takes one of her hands to lead her to an elevator with the door standing open. Oriana glances over her shoulder at me once before they disappear.

"Take her to the back and put her on the table," Emilio orders his men.

I don't know what the "table" is, and I don't really want to find out.

"Please, Emilio. I'm her mother!" I yell at him as his men grab either of my arms. He doesn't respond when they begin to drag me down the hall into a room in the very back. Inside, there's nothing but a long wooden workbench with a table saw on the end and a wall of toolboxes. I have a really bad feeling that the tools aren't just for building houses.

The men drag me over, wrench my arm around, and zip tie my right wrist to one of the legs, so tight, I can't even move it an inch. Then they yank my other arm across, forcing me to lean or risk pulling it out of socket. Once my wrists are tied, there's no point in trying to resist as they lift my legs to tie my ankles to the lower table legs with the table saw sticking up right between them.

Still, I try to kick them in the face as they grab my legs, but they ultimately have my ankles secured, within seconds.

Emilio won't kill me quickly. He's going to take his time, draw it out, and make it hurt.

Why else would he go through all the trouble of strapping me to the table?

"Leave us," he tells his men. "Make sure the nannies don't try to go anywhere. They're going to pay for their fuck up soon enough."

"It's not their fault. The women didn't have a choice," I tell him.

Ignoring me, Emilio goes over to the workbench. He pulls something from inside a toolbox, then leans over me, holding a long knife. He slashes it across my chest, making me cry out as it easily slices through my shirt and into my skin.

"You're in for a world of pain, Zara," Emilio says in my face. "How long you stay here on this table depends on how quickly you tell me what I want to know. Did you kill my son, or was it Creed Ferraro?"

Of course, he thinks it's me. Why should I bother dragging Creed into this hell?

"It was me," I confess.

"I know." His knife lowers, my blood staining the tip already. And this time, the sharp point scrapes across my chest. I scream through the pain, and only vaguely recognize that he just carved a giant capital I into my chest, inches above my right breast.

"Tell me what part Ferraro had in my son's death. I know he was involved. Why else would he have come after your daughter and hid you both in his penthouse?"

"It was...it was all me. I shot Izaiah. In the head. Then threw him down the trash chute."

His knife drives into my skin again, this time carving the letter Z without lifting the blade even once until he's done. The burning pain is like nothing I've felt before. I can't lift my head enough to see it clearly, but I feel my blood drip down my torso.

"You're lying. Admit it was Creed Ferraro who killed my son, and I'll stop."

I don't respond at all, which earns me a big capital A.

I close my eyes and clench my teeth for the next half hour or five minutes — however long it takes for him to carve Izaiah's name into my flesh.

After he finishes the H, I'm shaking so badly, it's hard to even take a breath. Emilio returns above me with a different tool. I'm not sure what it is until he shoves it into the I shape, and it sizzles.

Smoke rises into the air with the scent of my burning flesh right before the icy sting has me slipping into darkness.

Creed

"He has her. Emilio has her!" I tell Dre and Tristan while clenching my fists and staring out the view of the busy, crowded city from my office window. Zara could be anywhere.

"We don't know that yet," Dre says.

"Then where the fuck else could she be?" I shout. "Gideon's boat left the harbor an hour ago, and she wasn't on it!"

"There are still plenty of places —"

"Shut the fuck up! I don't want you to give me a list of places Zara *could* be. I want to know which of Emilio's properties he took her to."

I don't have weeks like before to stake out each building and wait. Zara and my men don't have that kind of time. Emilio is going to kill them and her for Izaiah's death. He's spent weeks searching for her, plotting his revenge.

I feel so fucking helpless, even more so than I did when Carmine bled out on the club floor. That night...at least I knew what had happened to him and why. But this...I can't stand not knowing where Zara is or what he's doing to her, wondering if I'm going to be too late.

No, I can't let myself think like that. I have to believe that she's still alive, that she may be in agony, but she'll be able to hold on until I find her.

We may not have spent much time together, but I love her and can't bear the thought of losing her. Especially not to that son of a bitch.

Zara took a piece of me I can't live without, a heart that I never knew I possessed because she's had it this whole time.

The night she came to the club, it was fate. Carmine recognized it right then and there. I know now that I'm meant to be with Zara. My brother likely saved my life that night by giving me shit, convincing me to go talk to her.

And I'm glad I did, even though that decision meant Carmine dying alone instead of with me by his side.

That night in her apartment, I waited outside Zara's window for her to turn on the shower before slipping inside. And like a pervert, I watched her as she threw her head back, washing her long hair and scrubbing her beautiful body clean.

Maybe Tristan was right, and it was love at first sight.

All I could think about in that moment was I'd give anything to be in the tub with her. When she got out of the shower wearing nothing but a towel and found me sitting on her sofa, well, it was hard to hold on to my anger instead of telling her whatever she wanted to hear to convince her to let me kiss her.

And then Izaiah put his knife to her throat and ripped that towel away when he didn't deserve to be in the same room with her, much less be that close to her body, touching her.

Trying to push aside my emotions and think rationally, logically, I tell Tristan and Dre, "Get the list of Emilio's properties. Send at least three of our men to every single one of them. They don't leave until I give the order. Tell them to take listening devices, binoculars, whatever spy shit they have to look for Zara and the others."

It may be impossible for me to be in twenty places at once, but I have the manpower to cover every property. If I asked them to sit on them for days, these men would because they're loyal to me.

Pulling out my cell phone, I call Roscoe.

"What do you need?" the NYPD Commissioner asks, skipping the bullshit so we can get right to the point.

"I need you to trace a phone."

"Okay. Text me the number. I'm driving right now, but I can pull over and run it when it comes through."

"The number is Emilio Rovina's," I warn him, so he knows what he's getting himself into.

Roscoe whistles through his teeth. "Then the search will probably get flagged by someone on his payroll when I type it in. I can try to get someone in IT to delete it…"

"I know and I don't care. You don't need to worry either. He won't be a problem for you or me as soon as I find him."

"Understood. Get the number to me. I assume you want to try and pinpoint his location?"

"Yes. How small an area can you narrow it down to?"

"Ten blocks at best."

Ten blocks of New York are still a lot of ground to cover. But it's better than the entire state, since I don't even know for sure if he's crossed into New Jersey.

"That'll help. Thank you." I end the call.

Tristan and Dre are bent over my desk, going through the list of properties and splitting them up into groups of our guys.

"Roscoe will try to narrow it down. The three of us go with ten others to whatever property is the closest to where the cell phone tower pings. While you're handling the assignments, I'll go upstairs and grab us more firepower. Be ready to leave when I get back."

"We'll be ready." Dre nods.

34

Zara

My head rocks to the side as if something struck me during my sleep. I try to lift my palm to cup my throbbing cheek but can't. That's when I remember where I am and what's happening to me.

I blink my heavy eyelids open to find I'm still restrained to the workbench. Emilio's smug face stares down at me.

"Last chance to confess that Creed Ferraro killed my son before I put you through even worse hell. This table saw goes right through bone, you know. It's so messy, though."

However long I've been here, Emilio has carved his son's name in my skin, slowly burned every line of each letter, and broken several of my fingers and toes. Oh, and how could I forget when he covered my mouth and held my nose for several minutes over and over again until I was certain my lungs would explode, and I'd never take a deep breath again.

Now, simply breathing is agonizing. Every part of my body hurts, and I just want to go back to sleep.

But torturing me is no fun for him if I can't stay awake. And threatening to use the table saw...I don't even want to know what he plans to do to me with that damn thing.

I thought I was ready to die, to never see my daughter again, or Creed.

But there's still a part of my soul kicking and screaming, yelling at me not to give up. Not yet. That if I hold on a little longer, Creed will burst into the room, killing Emilio and his men to save me.

Only, there's no fucking way Creed will find me in time.

And there's no point in dragging him down with me.

"Just kill me...and get it over with," I tell Emilio.

"Kill you?" Emilio laughs. "Why would you think I want you dead? This is just the beginning of your long, drawn-out punishment. One where you will never see Oriana again." He runs a finger down my nose, over my lips, and lower between my breasts, right through the burnt lettering, making me whimper. "I enjoy fucking you too much to ever get rid of you, though. It'll be even better when I don't have to worry about knocking you up. I have a surgeon who owes me a favor. He'll tie your tubes to avoid any more accidents, since Izaiah's no longer around to take the fall. I don't want to have to share you with Saint to cover another mistake."

There are some things worse than death.

And this is definitely one of them.

Leaning his scowling face over mine, he grabs my chin. "You don't like that idea, do you? Too fucking bad. You can't do anything about it now. Why don't you just admit Creed Ferraro killed Izaiah, so you can keep all your limbs intact?"

"I killed Izaiah. And I don't regret it."

"Why are you protecting him?!" he shouts.

"I'm not protecting anyone."

"You lying cunt! There's only one reason you'd lie for that son of a bitch. And he did go to an awful amount of trouble for you... How long have you been fucking him, huh? Was it before or after he killed Izaiah?"

I don't like where his thoughts are going. He's already rightly assumed it was Creed who killed his son and guards. And if he didn't know for certain about Oriana, I'm sure the nannies will fill him in, since they don't owe any loyalty to Creed. Hell, maybe they already have while I was passed out.

And the nannies may also tell Emilio Creed is my husband.

"It was just sex. We had an agreement — he wouldn't kill me for setting him up, getting his brother killed, if I let him fuck me. I hate him," I lie.

"Creed wouldn't kidnap my daughter and kill my men for pussy. Do you think my guys didn't notice you slip something into your pocket on the ride over?"

Reaching his hand down into my jean pocket, he pulls out my huge diamond and my wedding band. "You married him, didn't you, you stupid whore?"

He sounds jealous, even more so than when he'd find out Izaiah had visited me on the same day as him. It was always more painful on those days.

When I don't respond, Emilio smirks. "Let's find out if I'm right, shall we?" His phone is in his hand a moment later.

Fuck.

If he's going to make me call Creed and beg him to find me or some shit, I should at least try to get something useful out of him first.

"We may be married, but Creed doesn't give a shit about me," I assure Emilio. "He threatened to kill me if I didn't say the vows and sign the application. So, whatever you're plotting will just blow up in your face when he kills you. Creed still has more allies than you in the other families, who will come after you if you kill him to take his place."

"Who are his allies? Those slum pirates, the Marinos?" I shrug in response but he just huffs, "I already knew that, you dumb bitch."

"And the Bertellis," I add, hoping that revealing this information won't bite any of them in the ass.

"Now that's not necessarily true," Emilio immediately replies. He squeezes my jaw, and it feels like he could crush the bones with his bare hands. I close my eyes to fight the pain and nearly miss the vital information in his next statement. "How do you think I knew to be looking for you at that exact place and time, huh?"

How did he...

Oh fuck.

Weston Bertelli betrayed Creed?

This is the information I wanted Emilio to spill before he calls Creed. I need to tell him. I have to warn him about Bertelli before I never get to talk to him again. It's also been driving Creed insane that he can't find evidence Emilio was behind the club raid that killed his brother.

"Was it... did you set up the raid at the nightclub...with Izaiah?" I ask Emilio, figuring there's no reason I shouldn't try to get the mouthy asshole to keep spilling his secrets.

"No. That was all Izaiah's idiotic idea," he says, his outrage obvious in his tone. "He was trying to take Creed and Carmine out. He wanted to prove to me I should make him my heir after I told him he had to get clean, or I would pass him over for Saint."

Well then, it wasn't Emilio after all.

"He had a little help but not enough," Emilio continues ranting. "Too bad it failed, or Izaiah would still be alive. Fucking Bowen Bertelli." He practically growls the man's name. "If he had the balls to hire one of his father's men, it would've gone off without a hitch. But Bowen is a fucking pussy."

So, it wasn't the head of the Bertelli family, but the son, Bowen, who was stupidly working with Emilio.

"My son did his part perfectly," Emilio says. "Bertelli is the one who fucked everything up. Izaiah was on the right track. He was finally getting clean."

No, he wasn't.

I don't say that to Emilio because it will only anger him. But I knew Izaiah, and he *never* would have given up the drugs. Not as long as he had access to his family's fortune.

I'm surprised he didn't overdose before Creed killed him.

The fucking idiot was so braindead he died still absolutely certain he was Oriana's father.

And Bowen Bertelli must be a gigantic idiot as well, to not only go against Creed, but his own damn father.

I need to give Creed all of this information, so he'll finally know who was responsible for Carmine's death and make them pay.

For weeks, he's felt like it was his fault his brother died. That's why he was so determined to find who was behind it, to have someone else to hurt and blame.

I only need one last thing from Emilio.

"What are you going to do to Creed?"

"I'm going to convince him to put a gun to his own head and pull the trigger," he says simply. "Just like Izaiah did to those two cops."

Over my dead body, I think before it occurs to me that's exactly what Emilio is going to use to convince Creed to do it — my life for his.

35

Creed

Roscoe's information wasn't as useful as I hoped. He did help us narrow down Emilio's list of properties to four instead of twenty in Brooklyn by tracking his phone. I've moved most of my men but kept two at the other locations, just in case all the cell phones were abandoned in one area and Emilio took Zara and the others somewhere else.

"So, what's the plan here, boss?" Tristan asks as we sit a block away from a property. "Take four teams and bust in guns blazing?"

"I wish it were that easy." I shove my fingers through my hair to avoid looking at the time on my phone yet again. It's been hours, and I know we're running short on time to make a move. I just don't know which move will save Zara and which ones might doom her.

"We'll need to take out all the security cameras around each building," I explain. "There are probably plenty of guards, watching over each, who will sound the alarm to everyone as soon as they spot us. At best, we might sneak up on them at one location, but not all four. And I don't fucking know which one to choose!"

My cell phone dings with a new text message I almost ignore, so I won't see how much time has passed since I've been debating this fucking decision.

But I do cave and look.

The words turn my world upside down.

"What is it?" Dre asks from the driver seat when I keep staring down at the screen.

"It says...it says: 'Your WIFE wants to tell you goodbye. She wishes you well and doesn't want you to do anything rash.'"

"Bullshit," Tristan huffs from the backseat. "There's no way Emilio would just come out and admit that he has her in a text message."

I click on the notification to read the entire message again and again.

Leaning up between the seats, Tristan reads it over my shoulder. "He's setting up a trap, boss. You know that."

"I don't care. If she's still alive..."

"You can't believe a word that fucker says," Dre remarks. "There's no way to know if she's alive just because he says so in a text."

"I'm calling him." I pull up the number and dial it before anyone can protest. I was expecting a smug Emilio to answer. That's not what I get.

"*Creed?*"

Hearing her voice say my name makes me glad I'm sitting down. If I had been standing, it would have dropped me to my knees.

"It could be a recording," Dre whispers, since he must have heard her voice as well.

"Zara, baby, are you okay?"

"I'm...I'm alive," she replies, which isn't very comforting. "Your men are not. I'm so sorry."

"I didn't think they would be." Rafael, Shawn, Carlo, and Gino were good men. Loyal to their deaths. And I'll make sure their families never want for anything.

"Prove this isn't a recording. What do I call you?"

"*Micetta mia.*"

I cover up the speaker at the bottom of the phone to tell Dre and Tristan, "It's her. She's alive." To her I say, "I'm coming to get you, *micetta mia.*"

"Izaiah and Bertelli's son, Bowen, were the ones responsible for the raid. Bowen also told Emilio when and where to pick us up," she blurts out in a rush while Emilio curses in the background. Emilio must have admitted all that shit to her, which was stupid of him. Or Zara got him to run his mouth.

God, I fucking love her so damn much. Even when he's doing no telling what to her, hurting her, she mined for the answer to a question that's been eating at me for weeks.

There's a loud *smack* as if he hit her before his voice comes over the line. "You stupid *Mignotta!*"

"Zara!" I shout. "Don't fucking touch her again, or I will slaughter your entire fucking family!"

"Your *wife* is pretty beat up with broken bones and my son's name branded across her chest that will be a permanent reminder of him. Things will only get worse unless you end it yourself and make it look realistic."

I close my eyes, not wanting to even picture the horrible things he's done to Zara in such a short amount of time. And it's all my fucking fault.

"Well, Ferraro? Are you willing to trade your life for hers?"

"No fucking way," Dre whispers.

"Don't do it, Creed! Just find Oriana and take care of her for me. Please! We're in Brooklyn at the construction office with only five guards!" The call ends in complete silence, her words still echoing in my ear.

"*Cazzo!*" I clutch my phone in my fist, wanting to throw it out the fucking window.

"It's a setup," Tristan says. "He'll kill you and her both as soon as you walk through the door. It may be too late for her after she told you…"

I shake my head. "Emilio knows we're married, that I love Zara and that I would trade my life for hers. But I know something about him too. He may never let her go, but he'll never kill her."

"You're certain about that?" Dre asks.

"I am. So, let's proceed as planned. She said he only has five guards with him. Just watch out for Zara, Oriana, and the nannies if bullets fly."

"He'll have them out of that place in seconds, before we even figure out which of the locations he's at," Tristan remarks.

"No, he won't," I tell him as I text the others to move. "Because we're moving on all four right now. Try to take his men alive to protect the women and girl. They're outnumbered, so this should be easy."

Once we're out of the vehicle and checking our guns, I turn to Dre. "If this all goes to hell, I know you'll make a damn good boss, even if you are a grumpy son of a bitch."

He flips me the finger, which is both ominous and familiar all at the same time.

Zara

"We're leaving. Now. Bring them down and get them out the backdoor," Emilio orders into his phone. As soon as the device is tucked into his pants pocket, he grabs a knife from the workbench and starts cutting through the zip ties on my wrists and ankles.

"If you try to fight me, I'll drag you out of here by your hair," the asshole warns.

I wish I had more strength in my body to fight him, to try to slow him down until Creed gets here. Unfortunately, I can barely lift my bare foot to try, much less kick him in the face hard enough to do any real damage with several broken toes. And who knows where Creed is or how far away? It could take him half an hour to get across the bridge.

But I know this is the only chance I'll get to slow Emilio down.

So, once my second wrist is undone, I make a fist and punch him right in his throat despite my throbbing bent-wrong fingers.

Emilio cries out, clutching his neck and gargles what sounds like, "Bitch."

I slide off the table on weak, shaky legs, dizzy and feeling drunk on the adrenaline caused by hours of his torment. Every little movement makes my raw, burning chest wounds scream in agony.

Instead of aiming for the door, which is where he wants me to go so that we can leave, I turn toward the workbench, grabbing the first object I can reach while he lunges for me.

The blow of what I think is a wrench to his forehead barely slows him down as he grabs a handful of my hair and slams my face into the sharp corner of the workbench.

Every muscle in my body goes slack, dropping me to my knees. The entire room is edged in darkness as I fight to keep my eyes open. I blink to try to clear my murky vision with no luck.

I hear muffled voices coming from the hallway, and assume they're more of Emilio's men he called for backup.

"Guess we'll see if he loves you or not," it sounds like Emilio says with a jerk on my hair, pulling me to my feet. I try to swallow, but there's something pressed against my throat.

It's like a bad case of déjà vu — the night Izaiah died.

That's when I realize Emilio must be out of time, and he's hedging his bets because Creed and his men are here. I just hope they get Oriana out safely, without any of Emilio's idiots hurting her.

"Stupid fool," I slur. "Creed would rather kill you than save me."

"Let's find out," he pants next to my ear. "I think he cares for you more than he wants my death."

"You're wrong. I can't wait to see you in hell when you find out."

"Why else would Creed Ferraro marry you? Why would he risk his life to kidnap Oriana and let you both stay with him if he wasn't in love with you? He'd never do that for any amount of money, not that you had any to pay him. And he certainly wouldn't do that for a cheap *puttana* he could fuck for free."

We don't have to stand there long before I see a blur of men in dark clothes, dark hair. I think it's Creed, but can't be sure until he says, "Like father like son, you brought a knife to a gunfight."

God, I missed his growly threatening voice. And I have no doubt he's holding a gun, but it's all blurring together.

"Is Oriana safe?" I ask him.

"She's safe. The nannies too."

"Thank you," I whisper in relief. Whatever else happens, at least my daughter is going to be okay.

Creed wouldn't actually be willing to trade himself for me, would he? Does he honestly think Emilio will just let me walk away from him with a few broken bones and a giant scar of Izaiah's name? No, I'd rather die by Emilio's knife than ever have him inside me again.

"You and your men better let us leave, Ferraro, or I'll slice open her throat."

"No, you won't," Creed asserts.

"Before you can kill me, I'll take her life! Or you can put your guns down and let us both leave here alive. I won't give you the choice again."

"You were Zara's first, weren't you?" Creed asks, making me wonder if I'm hallucinating. "When you brought her to the city?"

Emilio must be as surprised as I am by the random remark, since his knife presses even harder against the thin flesh of my throat.

"What about it? I put her up in a beautiful apartment, helped her get modeling gigs she was so desperate for, and gave her anything she wanted for years. She thanked me so hard for it all and thanked me often."

"I hated you every fucking second, and you knew it!" I tell him. "Do not let him leave here alive, Creed."

"But you *never* denied me, did you? Such an obedient girl, a loyal daughter to parents who sold her off to save their dreams while she chased her own in the city."

My husband just stares at us, at me, and I can't tell for sure what he's thinking, what his plan is here.

Emilio's mouth is right against my ear when he says, "A sweet, innocent girl from Pearl River. I'm guessing you haven't met Samuel and Rita Riley, Zara's parents yet?"

"No, I haven't," Creed grits out.

"Nice couple. They run the Main Street Brewing Company in Pearl River thanks to my generous investment."

"I don't give a shit about her worthless parents. I know that you care about Zara," Creed says. "That's why you haven't killed her, isn't it? You wanted your daughter's mother to suffer, but you were never going to give her up, not even to death. And you're angry that she prefers me, that she married me, the man who killed your oldest son because he killed my brother!"

"I knew it was you!" Emilio bellows.

Okay then.

It looks like these two mob bosses are playing a game of 3D chess, and I'm just a spectator.

I'm not sure what Creed is up to, but I really hope his plan is working.

36

Creed

"I wish I could've been the one to enlighten Izaiah with the truth about Oriana being your daughter," I say to the psychotic monster. "I'm surprised Zara never informed him of what you were doing to her."

"She didn't say a word because I threatened to never let her see Oriana again if she told a soul."

I fucking hate seeing Emilio Rovina touching Zara, holding his knife to her throat like it's all that's keeping her upright. My beautiful wife looks like she's barely hanging on, so weak she's about to fall apart. I can't tell how bad her injuries are from ten feet away.

I have to keep my gaze solely focused on her face instead of the bloody, burnt mess spread across her chest. I can't afford to think about how much pain she must be in right now when I need to finish setting up Emilio, but I have no doubt she's in agony and trying not to show it.

"She'll do absolutely anything for her daughter, and I do mean *anything*." Emilio chuckles while every word out of his mouth is sealing his fate.

Keep talking, motherfucker. You're going to be dead soon enough.

"Those first few months after Oriana was born, Zara was enthusiastic in performing any act I demanded," Emilio says, driving the knife he's holding to her throat into my chest. "And when she was a week late delivering, well, we had a marathon of fucking until she finally went into labor."

"You're a disgusting son of a bitch," I tell him.

"She's just as filthy as I am. Do you really think she's worth starting a war with my family? How many of your men do you think will die for her? You've already lost your brother and four men. I've lost a son and four men as well. We're even. Let me walk out the door with her, and we'll call a truce."

"You're out of your fucking mind. And you're a pussy for using a woman as a shield. And I know for a fact that you won't ever slit her throat. Just like you could never slit Martha's."

Emilio visibly flinches at the mention of his dying wife.

"Does Martha know about Oriana?" I ask him. "How about Saint, Stella, or Cami?"

"Will you enjoy telling my Martha and my children about my bastard before or after Zara's funeral?" Emilio asks.

"I'll make you a deal, Emilio. Type up a little goodbye note to your family, slit your wrists with that knife instead, and I swear to you that Martha and your children won't ever learn the truth. Your wife can die in the dark, without knowing you're a nasty piece of shit. Wouldn't you rather she thought you died from the grief of losing Izaiah rather than trying to save your dirty little secret?"

When he doesn't respond, I continue, "You've got three seconds to choose. Either you go out by your own hand and keep your secret, or I'll make sure they all know exactly why I put a bullet in your head while we're at war. Of course, I'll have to kill Saint first to end it before he comes at me."

Lifting my gun, I line up my shot, aiming for the center of his head, and start counting down. "Three, two, one —"

"Wait!" Emilio shoves Zara toward me and holds up his palms, the knife still clutched in his right hand. Zara drops so hard, I can hear her knees hit the floor, making me furious. But I don't go to her just yet. With her on the ground, I have a better shot at Emilio. "I'll do it. Just don't tell them about Zara or Oriana. Promise me you won't hurt any of them, that this bloody feud ends here."

"I won't hurt them. There won't be any more bloodshed between our families," I agree. "Now, where's your phone?"

"In my pocket."

"Put the knife on the table and keep your hands up." Once he complies, I yell out, "Dre!" When he's next to me, I tell him, "Give me your gun, go type out the message in an email, and have it sent to himself."

"Yes, sir," he agrees, handing over his Glock to keep it out of Emilio's reach.

Since Dre is wearing leather gloves, he grumbles, "Fucking mother fucker," when it takes him a moment to retrieve the phone from Emilio's pocket. Holding it in front of Emilio's face, he unlocks the device, then it takes several more minutes of him tapping the screen repeatedly to pull up the mail app thanks to the leather.

"Okay, I'm ready."

I begin slowly dictating, "To my loving family, I'm sorry for any pain I've caused. I wish I had found Izaiah the help he needed to get him sober. He was taken from us too soon because of his addiction, and for that, I cannot ever forgive myself. To my Martha, live out your final days in peace, knowing our son and I are both waiting for you, darling. Saint, take care of our family and your sisters. I know you're strong enough to handle whatever may come. Stella, I have no doubt you'll do your part to protect our family as well by strengthening it with an unbreakable alliance. The Ferraros will help you get through hard times. Cami, I hope you find happiness in whatever you do. I love you all. Please forgive me, Emilio."

"Does that sound like something you would write?" Dre asks the *stronzo* as his fingers finish typing in what will be the man's final words.

"Yes."

"Send it."

"Done," Dre agrees once it goes through.

I have to give it to the bastard; Emilio doesn't shed a tear as we wind down the end of his life. Despite all the awful shit he's done, the fact that he actually loved his family and didn't want his wife to learn his secret or his last son to die, will make my life easier by framing his death as a mourning father's suicide rather than vengeance.

"Can we trust you with the knife or do you need help with that too?" I ask the bastard.

"You swear they won't find out?"

"I swear it on my father's grave." While I could easily break that promise, since I don't give a shit about my old man, I won't tell his family. Only hurt will come from the disgusting truth. Not to mention, it would raise more questions about Izaiah and Emilio's death possibly causing them to point fingers at Zara.

"Then do it already," Emilio grumbles.

"Dre?" I ask, since he's already over there. "Will you do the honors?"

"The honors of slicing up my future wife's asshole father? Sure, why the hell not," he mutters, sounding more put out about this than Emilio.

"Make it look real."

Nodding, Dre picks up the knife in his gloved hand, then wraps

Emilio's right hand and fingers around it. As he places the sharp edge to the man's wrist, Zara turns around on her hands and knees to watch.

"Good riddance," she says, having the final word before Dre makes the cut with one hand, then the other. All that's left is to wait.

"Oriana?" Zara asks me, as if we're not watching the life drain from the son of a bitch. Dre lets go, and he drops to the floor, the knife clattering.

Putting the guns down on the table, I take out my phone and check my messages from Tristan as I go over and kneel in front of Zara, glad I can give her more good news. "She's on the way to the penthouse with the nannies, Tristan, and several of my men."

"I'm so glad the nannies are okay too. And the guns…?"

"Not a single shot was fired in front of her."

"Oh, thank god. No, thank you, Creed. I knew you'd save her for me."

"You can see her safe and sound back at the penthouse soon."

"Good. Thank fuck you were nearby."

"I had a cop trace Emilio's phone, narrowing down the location," I explain.

"I hoped you were coming…but wasn't sure how long it would take."

I gently grasp her face between my hands. "How badly are you hurt? What the hell did he do to you, baby?"

"He wanted me to admit that you killed Izaiah. I didn't, though. I wouldn't…"

"God, I'm so fucking sorry, *micetta mia*."

It's my fault he hurt her. And my sweet, beautiful wife refused to give in, to give me up, even though she knew he'd keep hurting her, knew he already suspected me. That's how damn strong this woman is; she refuses to let anyone break her.

Zara takes a deep breath and winces. "It's just a few broken fingers and toes." Holding up her right hand, it's clear two digits are curled in the wrong direction. "This is the worst, only because it may never heal." She gestures to her tattered shirt, revealing her mangled chest... and that son of a bitch's name written, *burnt*, into her skin.

"Fuck, baby. Fuck," Tears well up in my eyes now that it's all over. I blink them away, refusing to cry for her when she's the one who endured the pain and survived it. And I sure as hell don't want her to know how much I loathe seeing Izaiah's name on her beautiful, perfect body instead of her cute freckles.

"We'll find you a doctor tonight. Then get a plastic surgeon to fix the damage. Or a tattoo artist. We could get a design drawn to cover it."

"You don't want to touch me while his name is on me, do you?" she whispers.

"Oh, *micetta mia*. I'd want to touch you if his name was written in your skin a million times over. I'm just so damn relieved you're alive. I'm so sorry, baby. I wish I could kill Emilio and Izaiah over and over again for all the pain they caused you."

"Thankfully, it's all over now." Her shoulders slump, and my entire body tenses.

"I wish it were that easy."

"What...what do you mean?" she asks.

"We're going to make this look like a suicide, but if anything goes sideways, it will start an all-out war. I hope not, but if it comes to that, the bloodshed may never end until all of us are dead. I don't want you or Oriana anywhere near that shit."

"So...what does that mean for us?"

"I'll make new arrangements with Gideon to get you and Oriana out of the country. I'll try to get you on a boat first thing tomorrow morning."

"So, after everything, you're just going to send me away? That's it? It was all for nothing?"

"All for nothing?" I repeat in confusion. "You're alive. Oriana is going to be with you. The safest thing I can do is send you away. You know it's not because I don't love you."

"If you loved me, then you would want us to stay."

"It's not safe. I'm going to prison soon, and if anything like this happened to you again while I was away..."

"It wouldn't be your fault, Creed. Why can't we talk about this? Why can't it be my decision too?"

"Because you don't know how fucked the streets of New York could get."

"And neither do you! Maybe the Rovinas will buy the suicide and not question it."

"We both know that's probably not going to happen. Saint already hates me. And it's not just the Rovinas. If Bowen Bertelli is a traitor, then his father might still protect him when I try to take him out. Don't you see? My life is going to be dangerous all the damn time now, and it always will be until I'm dead."

"I understand the risks."

"No, Zara, you don't. And if anything happened to Oriana, you would blame me, and you'd be right to do so. I don't want that to happen. I couldn't stand it if you hated me. So please, baby, just let me make the arrangements for you to leave."

A tear slips down one of her cheeks and then the other. "You promised me you'd *never* force me to do anything I didn't want to do. Well, I don't want to leave you. If you send me away, I will *never* forgive you."

"Good," I reply, even if her words feel like daggers shoved between my ribs. "Don't forgive me. You shouldn't. I don't deserve to be with someone like you. And you, you deserve to have a peaceful life where nobody manipulates you or forces you to do anything to be with your daughter. I'm so sorry you've spent all these years being under Emilio's thumb. But you're free now. Take it. Enjoy it."

Her shoulders slump. "You still don't trust me, do you? Or is it you still don't think you deserve good things because you blame yourself for your brother's death?"

"Zara, I trust you and love you more than anyone else in this world. That's why I'm letting you go." Even though my next words will no doubt hurt her, I still say them, wanting to make this separation easier for her. "You got exactly what you wanted from me all along — I stole back your daughter for you and killed Emilio and Izaiah. You're free now; you don't have to keep pretending you want to be with me."

Pressing her palms to the ground, she pushes herself up, wincing and gasping in pain to get to her feet. Then she hobbles toward the door.

And I don't try to stop her, even though I want to chase after her and beg her to forget everything I just said and stay with me.

But I can't do that.

Not after all she's been through the past seven years. It wouldn't be fair to her to convince her to stay when I know the future is going to be rocky, starting with three and a half shitty years behind bars.

"You good, man?" Dre asks.

"Yeah. I'm good," I lie as I get back to my feet and glance over at the corpse on the floor. "Thank you for taking care of him. I'm sorry it ended this way."

"Me too," he agrees. "But I'm relieved we found Zara in time. You can relax now." He pats my shoulder before picking up his gun from the table.

It was stupid for me to ever doubt Dre, to think that he wanted me out of the way, so he could take my place.

Nobody in their right mind would want my job as the capo dei capi.

This lifestyle is so fucked up, it constantly has me questioning who I can and can't trust to kill me or rat me out to the cops. Or who will die next because of me.

"How is Zara?" he asks.

"She'll have some scars, some bones that need to heal, but she'll be okay."

"Well, you look like someone just ran over your puppy instead of scooping it up and saving it from the middle of the street. You're serious about sending her away after everything?"

"I hate it. I do. Of course, I want her to stay. But I can't. Our necks are all on the line now. Shit is going to be tense for a while, then we're all going to be locked up."

"Yeah, I doubt Stella will take the news of me killing dear old dad very well either."

"She won't find out," I assure him. "We're taking the guards with us. Emilio's death will look like a suicide. As long as we don't leave any breadcrumbs behind, we might be okay."

"You're not going to be okay without her, man. Admit it."

"Zara's been through hell. It's time for her to be free and live her life on her own terms for once. She told me..."

"Told you what?" he asks when I hesitate.

"She told me I was the first man of her choosing she'd ever slept with."

"Fuck. That's brutal. Especially when you didn't believe she actually wanted you."

"No, I didn't. I should've, but everything was so fucked up. Even with him torturing her, she was determined to make sure I knew Bowen Bertelli helped Izaiah with the raid and gave her up today."

"That fucker's funeral is next on the agenda," he remarks.

"We'll have to be careful about how we handle it. The last thing we need is to have two families coming after us. One is plenty."

"That little *figlio di puttana* is going to pay for killing Carmine and Jasper one of these days, though."

"Yes, he will," I promise him. "I'm sure we can come up with something in a few months to make it look like an accident once all this dies down."

"Of course we can."

"Just as soon as things are settled with the Rovinas. And before we go to prison," I tell him. "For now, we need to clean up any trace of Zara in this building and get a doctor to the penthouse to clean those wounds."

37

Zara

The family's doctor on call was already at the penthouse when we got there. He examined my burns, treated them, and set my fingers. There was nothing to be done about my toes other than taping them to the others. Before he left, he gave me antibiotics and pain pills along with all the bandages and supplies I'll need for the next several weeks.

I could barely keep my eyes open after, so that night I didn't think twice before I climbed into bed with Oriana. My arms wrap around her, as if I might fall asleep and she'd disappear again. I couldn't handle it if she were taken from me again.

Which is why I hate to admit that Creed might be right. She'll be safer if she's far away from him and the mafia world, which means both of us will be far away from him, since I'll never leave her side again for another second.

Paige and Bethany were, thankfully, okay and not too traumatized after Tristan and Creed's men grabbed them.

Nobody was shot, or at least that's what Tristan told me. I know what will happen to Emilio's guards. They'll probably end up in the ocean with Izaiah.

I'll be forever grateful to the two women sleeping soundly on the other side of the bed. I hope wherever we're going they stay with me and Oriana. The three of us could share an apartment and help each other with all the other finances, so it wouldn't be so bad, taking turns watching Oriana.

It sounds like a pretty good life, except Creed won't be there, and we won't ever see him again after we leave New York City.

The life of a don will always consist of violence. That reminder is now etched across my chest.

The only option would be for Creed to come with us, which I know he won't do. He can't walk away from all the people who need him here, running things in the city. Even the occasional visits would be too difficult because eventually the distance would cause us to drift apart until we both decided to give up.

It's best if we have a clean break.

My heart just needs to heal like the rest of my body, even if it feels like an impossible feat.

Unfortunately, there are no pills to make that ache go away.

Creed

I've been at the docks for hours this morning. Long enough to watch Zara, Oriana, an entourage of men and nannies, board a few minutes after sunrise with their documentation we found in the van in the construction site's garage.

This morning, I left the penthouse early, unable to even attempt to say goodbye. I hope Zara is cussing me out right now for the slight. The sooner she hates me, the better off she'll be.

As their boat slowly disappears out of sight, my lungs tighten when I try to take a deep breath. I try again with the same result. Grabbing my chest, I know I fucked up, and I'm probably having a goddamn panic attack.

I'm a fucking *cretino*.

I should've said goodbye, kissed Zara, and held her in my arms one last time. But she was hurt and had been through hell. Now, the last time I saw her will always be with Emilio's body cooling nearby and the horrors she endured at his fucking hand.

Instead of hating me, Zara thinks I was so disgusted by seeing Izaiah's name on her body that I don't want her anymore.

Nothing could be further from the truth.

Behind me, one of the doors of the idling SUV opens. "Meeting time," Dre says, interrupting my breakdown when he stands beside me.

I nod and press my palm to my chest even harder, trying to will the ache away.

We're about to go face the music for last night, and I need to get myself together. Lives depend on me selling this load of horse shit to the rest of the families, especially the Rovinas.

～

"Thank you all for meeting today on short notice," I say to the men gathered at the table in Omerta. "I want to offer my condolences to you, Saint. I'm sorry you lost your father so soon after losing a brother."

The next words out of his mouth will seal our fate — either the family bought our lie, or I'm their top suspect.

Saint nods while gritting his teeth. "The police said there was no foul play, that they're certain it was a suicide, since he sent himself a note. But my father *never* would've left without putting up a fight. Taking his own life is not his style, and you know it. We don't even know if Izaiah is dead yet, so it doesn't make any fucking sense!"

"I can't imagine how hard it must be to not have closure for Izaiah and now all this..."

"Do I really have to say it?" Saint asks. "Someone killed my father and made it look like a fucking suicide. Whoever is behind it is a dead man walking!"

"You know the rules," I remind him. "You need evidence before the Council will allow any sort of revenge." Knowing that standard applies to me as well, I'm glad I still have the recording on my phone of Izaiah confessing to killing Carmine. "The medical examiner will have a report soon. They'll be able to tell if the wounds weren't self-inflicted," I say, trying to reassure him.

"My family will interrogate each and every one of our assassins," Bertelli quickly adds. "If it was murder, and one of my people were behind it, then it was done without my permission or knowledge."

"I won't let the police close this case until we're certain what happened," Saint grumbles.

"You're right. It's only a matter of time before we find out if it was a suicide, what happened to Izaiah, and if either of those things was connected to someone killing my brother and trying to take me out too," I agree. "Everyone should keep a low profile until then. We don't know who the next target might be. That means underbosses too, Bowen. They might try to hit you to hurt your father," I say as a thinly veiled warning to the traitor. "That goes for you, too, Gideon with Zaven, and Eiden with Kai. Or is Raiden going to be your heir?"

"I haven't decided yet," Eiden replies quietly, giving me a stern look that says he doesn't think it's any of my business. Or perhaps he noticed that I was subtly pointing a finger his way for Izaiah, Emilio, and Carmine's deaths.

"Right, well, just keep your families close until this is all resolved. Let's keep in touch. Meet again next month?" I suggest.

Everyone gives a nod of approval, so I adjourn the emergency Council meeting.

When Dre approaches Saint before he can walk out the door, I want to fucking throttle him.

"Hey, man, tell Stella we can put wedding plans on hold for however long she wants. Or if, now that your father is gone, she doesn't want to go through with it —"

"The wedding is still on," Saint interrupts him.

"It is?" Dre's eyes widen in surprise.

"It's what my father wanted for her. It was his last request in his…note."

"Really?" Dre sounds shocked, as if he wasn't the one who typed the damn words.

"My father said he wanted the wedding to happen by the end of the year, so we're moving forward, making plans off the ones he started."

The way he says "making plans" sounds a little ominous before he slaps Dre's shoulder and walks out.

When we're alone, Dre turns to me. "What the hell do you think that means?"

"I think it means you're still marrying the woman you're obsessed with, and I think I know why."

"Why?"

"Because the Rovinas still suspect us, but are playing it cool, waiting like we're doing with Bowen, pretending everything is perfectly fine and we're not about to have a bloody massacre in the streets of Manhattan."

"Fuck," Dre mutters while rubbing the back of his neck. "She's never going to let me touch her now."

"Probably not," I agree, then feel like a dick for being glad that I'm not the only one who will be pining for a woman he can't have.

38

Zara

Creed is such a piece of shit.

I can't believe that after everything we've been through, he didn't even say goodbye to me.

Not a word, a kiss, or a hug.

The first contact I had from him after three long weeks was the damn divorce papers I received by courier this morning. Oh, and how could I forget the box that came with it that had a professional digital camera inside, like it was supposed to be some sort of parting gift.

I guess Creed was just glad to finally be rid of me and all my baggage. Ever since I came into his life that night at the club, things have been fucked up.

But I wasn't the one who pulled the trigger when he killed Izaiah.

I didn't ask him to orchestrate Emilio's death either, even if I'm relieved that him and his son are dead and can't touch me or Oriana ever again.

Emilio was never a good father to her, but he did make sure she had everything she needed, along with protection. I doubt the man loved her, but he considered her his property, so he did what he could to keep her safe.

I should be happy that I get to raise Oriana outside of the busy city. But the estate Creed set up for us is ridiculous. I knew it would take weeks, maybe even months, for us to secure employment and find a place of our own, possibly a three-bedroom home with two bathrooms. That would have been a dream come true while living in Italy, since we missed the boat to Portugal, and starting over.

But where did Creed's instructions left with Marino's men lead us? To the Umbrian countryside that includes two houses, eight bedrooms, eleven bathrooms, a badminton court, and not one but two freaking swimming pools.

Every morning I wake, it's like we're living on a movie set too perfect to be real.

The main villa was an 18th-century farmhouse that was restored several years ago. But that's not where we stay. The four of us have been just fine, living together in what was formerly the stables with three bedrooms and five bathrooms, which is more than enough.

"How are you doing?" Paige asks when she sits on the pool steps next to me.

"I'm great. She loves to swim." I smile, nodding to my adorable girl, splashing with her pink arm floats in the shallow end. I've spent the past three hours swimming with her and am beat. I don't know how the little princess has any energy left.

"Are you really great?"

"Yes. Mostly. Honestly, I've never been anywhere except New

York City, so it's nice to get to live someplace new, to see more of the world, free to come and go as I please."

"But?"

"But what?" I glance over to ask Paige.

She shrugs and scoops up a mosquito from the water to toss out of the pool. "It just sounded like there was a 'but' at the end of your remark."

"I love getting to spend all this time with Oriana, finally having a chance to really get to know her…"

"But?"

I groan. "But I guess I'm still angry at Creed."

"You're still angry, or you still miss him?"

"Both. It's for the best how things worked out. I mean, I spent seven years of my life being tied to a mobster."

"But Creed is different from Emilio, right?"

"He's still a mob boss. Boss of bosses, actually. You were angry at him for what he did to Emilio's guards, remember?"

"Yes, he's a lethal mob boss, but he risked his life to save your daughter when he barely knew you. A lethal mob boss who risked his men to not only save Oriana a second time, but me and Bethany, too, when he could've told his men to leave us behind."

"He's a good man who does bad things sometimes, like kill people. And that's why I shouldn't want to be with him. His lifestyle constantly revolves around violence. I don't want Oriana to grow up with all the bloodshed and rivalries."

"If Emilio could protect her from his enemies, then I'm sure Creed Ferraro can too. Oriana could use a decent male role model in her life."

"And you think Creed Ferraro would be a decent role model for her? After everything that has happened?"

"Ori was born a mafia princess and she already bosses everyone around like they live to serve her royal majesty."

Laughing, I admit, "She does do that. I had no idea how much you and the Rovinas had spoiled her. She deserves to be loved, not given whatever money can buy to appease her at the moment."

"Ori is young enough that she probably won't miss Izaiah and Emilio as much if she had another father figure to help you raise her. Hopefully she won't remember them in a few years. She needs a male role model to help love her and show her what a healthy relationship looks like. I doubt there are many men who could handle such a firecracker without dousing her flames completely."

"Well, you've certainly thought a lot about something that's never going to happen," I point out to her, wishing she hadn't painted such a sweet picture in my head of the three of us as a happy family. Swiping the tear drop from underneath my eye, or maybe it's just a drop of rain, I remind her, "Creed didn't even come to tell me goodbye before we left. He's done. That ship that I was literally on sailed away from him at his direction."

"You don't think it's possible that he didn't come say goodbye to you because it would've been too hard to let you go? I doubt a man like Creed Ferraro has much experience being vulnerable around another human being. I doubt his parents gave him many hugs when he was growing up or told him that they loved him. He's probably emotionally stunted because he was raised to be the meanest motherf'er in New York City, to always show his strength and power, not openly share his feelings."

"I'm sure he wasn't raised in a very loving home. His mother tried to take him and leave when he and his brother were kids because his father was too angry and violent. She gave up his father to the feds. Eventually, though, the charges were dropped, and his father found and killed his mother in front of them."

"That's awful. Other than his mom and brother, you're probably the first person who has ever loved him, the man, not just his money or the power. He'll need some time to wrap his head around all that. To allow himself to trust that you won't leave him or hurt him like they did, even though it wasn't their choice."

"Again, this is all a moot point. I can't even call him, since he never gave me his phone number. Not that I would call him if I had it."

"God, you're so damn stubborn. That's where Ori gets it from, not just on the Rovina side."

"I'm not stubborn. I'm only being realistic," I tell her. "It's time for me to move on and forget Creed Ferraro. I'm sure he's already forgotten all about me."

Creed

It's only been three weeks since Zara left, which is about half as long as I knew her, and I'm still constantly thinking about her adorable freckles and long curls that bounce right back up when I tug on them.

I already struggle to remember the details in her face, where exactly those freckles were on her nose and her cheeks, the curve of her lips, the steel in her green eyes when she was pissed at me…

I should've taken more photos of Zara when I had the chance. Why the fuck didn't I? All I have are a few images on my phone of her and Oriana my guys sent and a photo taken right after our marriage ceremony. In it, I look annoyed, and she looks nervous.

I was an idiot who was too busy worrying about not being able to trust her that I pushed her away rather than pulling her closer.

"What are you going to do about Zara, you sad sack of shit?" Dre asks when him, Tristan, and Lorenzo barge into my office.

I rotate my chair from the sun setting on the city to frown at them. Standing before my desk, Dre's arms cross over the chest of his three piece suit as if I'm inconveniencing him with my misery.

"What the fuck do you mean, 'what am I going to do about Zara?' She's off in Italy, living her life. You should be worrying about your wedding plans, not me."

"We know where Zara is, but you've been a miserable *figlio di puttana* since she left, and I doubt that's going to change anytime soon. So, what are you going to do to fix it?" Tristan asks.

"Fix what, exactly? What am I supposed to do? Walk away from all my responsibilities here in New York for a woman I barely know? It's not like she can come back when Saint is about to start a war with the Sannas, and we'll be forced to choose sides," I remind him. "Oh, not to mention, we're going to take out Bowen Bertelli. And if we live through all that, it's only a matter of time before we're convicted of gun possession and sent off to prison for three-and-a-half years!"

"You don't think Zara would wait three years for you, or come see you during visitation days?" Lorenzo sounds skeptical, as if he's so certain that Zara would be up for that shit.

"No. I don't fucking know."

"You still don't trust her," he says.

"It's not about trust. Zara will always choose her daughter over me and the mafia lifestyle, and I can't blame her."

"Did you send her divorce papers?" Dre asks.

"Yes." Signing those papers was one of the hardest things I had to do. Killing people is a hell of a lot easier than signing away the marriage to the woman I love.

"Has she returned them yet?" Tristan questions.

"Not yet. It takes a while, though, for shit to come back from Italy."

"Really? You think that's why she hasn't returned them yet?" Lorenzo comments, his brow furrowed with skepticism. "It's okay to be happy, to live your life even if Carmine can't live his."

"Look," Dre starts. "I know Carmine wasn't just your brother, but he was your best friend, one of the few people who could give you hell without you blowing a hole through his head. I was jealous of how close you two were. And I know that if Carmine were here, he would tell you to suck up your pride and do whatever you need to do to be happy."

"That's basically what he said the night of the raid when Zara called me over to warn me, and I was being stubborn," I admit.

"You said Carmine told you to thank him in your wedding toast for not stealing her, right?" Dre says.

"Yeah, he did."

Lorenzo grins. "I'm not surprised he knew you would end up with her. And you did marry her. Then you shipped her off."

"The farther away from me Zara can get, the safer her and Oriana will be," I remind them. "This world of ours is too unforgiving for their innocent souls."

"I thought you said Zara was tougher than she looked," Dre remarks. "Did you ever ask her what she wanted? If she thought your world is too cruel? Did she tell you she didn't want any part of the mafia lifestyle?"

"No, but —"

"Then fuck off," he interrupts me. "Zara seemed smart and tough enough to make her own damn decisions, and you know it."

"She'd have to be both to endure seven years of abuse by the Rovinas. I don't want to cause her any more pain."

"Well tough shit!"

"Excuse me?"

"You're never going to stop worrying about Zara whether or not she's in your life, right? She could be in pain right now over in Italy, and you wouldn't know it nor could you do anything about it, which is what's going to drive you fucking insane. So why not just figure out a way to get her back, and not let a hypothetical war keep you from being happy for the first time in your life?"

Dre's not wrong.

I have been going crazy with worry. Not just about physical

harm, but how Zara is doing as she becomes a full-time mother to Oriana and how much she's probably doubting herself in the role. I wish I was there to see her and her daughter together, to reassure her she's an amazing mother. To confess, I'm so certain of that fact that I wanted her to be the mother of my children someday.

"So, you three think I should go to Italy and ask Zara what she wants?"

"Yes," they answer simultaneously.

I stare out at the city, thinking the idea over for several long, silent moments.

Finally, I turn back to Dre, Tristan, and Lorenzo. "Say I show up and ask Zara and her daughter to come back with me. Then what do I do when shit goes down with the families? Send them away every single time there's a problem?"

"You kept the peace in the city for ten years. Carmine's death was horrible, but it was the first in what, a decade or more?" Dre asks.

"Yes."

"You can keep the families from fighting, just like you have before. Lay down the law, no bloodshed, or they'll regret it," Lorenzo suggests while slapping a rolled-up magazine into his palm.

"Yes, I'm sure a threat from me will stop Saint from going after whoever he thinks killed his father and brother."

"Sure, there's a chance you fail," Dre replies. "But if you moved some of the guys to provide security and watch over Zara and her kid, they would probably agree. Besides, a woman and kid probably wouldn't get dragged into anyone's shit. Most families have lines they won't cross."

"That's a whole lot of probablies that could fall apart." I shake my head. "If anything happened to Zara or Oriana…"

"You won't let anything happen to them," Tristan declares.

"I couldn't protect her before," I remind him. "The damage Emilio did to her…"

"Will heal! Hell, it's probably healed up by now. She's been seeing docs, right?"

"Another probably from you too, really, Tristan?"

"Her injuries were bad, but she survived Emilio," Dre remarks. "And he only went after her because of their history. It didn't have anything to do with you."

"He tortured her to get her to confess that I killed Izaiah!"

"And she never ratted you out, did she? That is hardcore loyalty right there. I respect her for being so strong," Dre says.

Tristan chimes in, "Some men I know wouldn't be able to endure all that without breaking."

"None of the shit you just said makes me feel better for being responsible for her bleeding and scarring."

"Emilio hurt her before you came along, Creed. You saved her from him and Izaiah. They were her only enemies," Dre reminds me. "Now, they're gone. Zara and her daughter are finally safe."

"They'll never be safe with me."

"I'm going to book a flight to Italy," Dre huffs. "Either you can go, or I'll go my damned self to pick up those signed divorce papers from Zara."

I grind my molars. I don't want to see those papers ever again. "You sound just like Carmine, trying to light a fire under my ass."

Tristan flashes me a shit-eating grin. "So, our little pep talk actually worked?"

"Yes. I'll go see Zara and ask her what she wants."

"Finally," Dre mutters with a smirk.

"Why would she want to be my mafia queen when I can only offer her a future with infrequent conjugal visits? I doubt she want Oriana anywhere near me. We all know I would be a shitty father." It's one of my silent worries that's been on my mind since I was searching for the girl, that Zara wouldn't want me to be a part of her daughter's life.

"You won't be a shitty father, Creed. And if Zara loves you, then you two can get through anything," Lorenzo replies. "Any-fucking-thing, right?"

"I guess…I guess we'll find out."

"Good to hear. I brought you something to provide a little… comfort until you get her back." Lorenzo tosses the rolled-up magazine onto my desk.

I stare down at the title and image on the front. "A porno mag? Seriously? They still put out this shit and charge for it, even though the internet is free?"

"Turn to page thirty-four."

"Why?"

"Just do it!" Lorenzo huffs.

Picking up the filthy magazine, I turn the pages until I get to thirty-four. My jaw drops at the sight of the gorgeous woman dressed as a sexy Lady Liberty. Raising a torch in the air with one hand, her mint green robe is wide open, and she's completely naked underneath.

"Very patriotic, right?" Lorenzo asks. "It was a Fourth of July issue."

Slamming the pages shut, I glare at him. "Where the fuck did you find this?"

"I did a little digging into Zara's background after you married her," he replies while shoving his hands into his pants pockets, looking awfully smug for a man about to bleed out. "Emilio had some modeling contacts. He convinced her to do three issues just like that."

"I wish I could kill him again, this time with my bare fucking hands," I growl as I get to my feet. "While I'm gone, I want you to find every issue she's in, anywhere in the world, and buy it, no matter the cost. I'm going home to pack."

I take about two steps toward the door before I return to my desk and scoop up the magazine. There's one other urgent thing I need to do before I pack, thanks to that sexy ass photo. Holding the rolled-up magazine in the air, I ask Dre and Tristan, "Did either of you see my wife naked?"

"No, sir," Tristan answers. "We wouldn't dare disrespect you in such a way."

Dre punches his brother in the chest, hard enough to make him double over. "Lorenzo wouldn't let us. Not that I wanted a peek."

Shaking my head as I walk out the office door, I call back, "I want every *single* copy ever published before I get back, Lorenzo!"

39

Zara

"You look even more beautiful, sun-kissed and relaxed."

Turning toward his voice, I can't contain my surprise. "Creed?" Wearing a crisp black suit with a breathtaking view of Assisi behind him, he looks like death going on a relaxing vacation. And god, I've missed him. "Wh-what are you doing here?" I scramble off the lounge chair and wrap a towel around my wet one-piece bathing suit.

"Last I checked, I own this property, even if this is the first time I've stepped foot on it," he says as he glances around at the view, sunglasses covering his face. He looks pleased with the impulse purchase he made for at least three million, like a normal person grabbing a Snickers in the grocery store checkout line.

"How have you been?" he asks when he faces me again. I can't see his blue eyes behind the shades, but he must be checking me over, since he says, "You look well, and healing nicely."

Again, with the compliments while noticing Izaiah's name is still written in my flesh, it throws me off-guard. I am healing, at least superficially. When I shower and undress, I refrain from looking in the mirror at the angry, red marks that have run together in a jumble.

"I'm good. Fine. How…how have you been?"

"Good? Fine?" he repeats. His jaw ticks in annoyance. "That's all you have to say?"

"It's been great spending weeks with Oriana," I admit. "But only while I look for a job. In fact, we don't need this place. It's too much. You could at least sell or rent out the other house, since the girls and I are all fine living in the stables."

Ripping off his sunglasses, Creed glares down at me with blue eyes I've dreamed of every night. A glint of the sun draws my attention to the wedding band he's still wearing for some reason, even though he signed and mailed me divorce papers. "You're living in the fucking stables?"

"What? Oh. That's just what some of the locals told us it used to be before all the renovations." Shaking my head because we've gotten off topic, I tell him, "Look, Creed, what I'm trying to say is that we appreciate your… hospitality, but we'll be moving out as soon as I convince someone to give me a job. I worked full time as a manager for a discount store for years. I'm more than happy to do anything in town if I could just get a damn interview." I continue to babble, "Is employment handled differently here or something? Because the people I talk to in Assisi ignore me like they don't want to acknowledge me. And if they speak English, they won't say a word to me. Not that I can blame them. I'm a trashy American with no skills other than ringing up or stocking cheap groceries."

"You think people won't speak to you or give you a job because you're a trashy American?"

"Yes."

"No, *micetta mia*. They won't speak to you about a job because I put out the word to all the businesses not to hire you."

"Why in the world would you do that? And stop calling me *your pussy*. It's incredibly offensive." The truth is, I can't bear to hear the Italian phrase because it breaks my heart, knowing I'm no longer his anything.

"Why do you think I did it, Zara?" He ignores my complaint about the term of endearment.

"So I'll never be free of you? I'll just be trapped here for you to show up and taunt me? One second, you'll be right in front of my face, making me want you, and then missing you when you up and leave days later, going weeks or months without a word from you when you're back in New York!"

"No, Zara. I told them not to hire you because you deserve a break, to get to know your daughter and spend the days and nights with her. I did it because I love you, and I want you to be happy, to have everything you always deserved."

"You sent me away!" I shout, maybe a little too quickly, since it takes that long for the fact that he said he loved me to register in my mind. He's said it before, but when he told me I had to leave the country.

"You know why I did that too. It wasn't because I don't care about you. I sent you and Oriana away to keep you safe from me, my enemies, and my lifestyle."

"And I hate you for it, for not asking me what I wanted or listening to me when I told you not to throw us away."

"I didn't throw you away."

"That's what it felt like." I wave my hands toward the immaculate house thanks to the half-dozen servants who work here. "None of this or the fancy camera you sent with divorce papers can make up for that feeling either."

"I'm sorry," he says, his teeth grinding together as if those are his least favorite words. "I should've asked you what you wanted before sending you here. I still think it was the right decision to keep you safe. And that's another reason I didn't want you to work anywhere, telling people who you were, creating a trail of paper for the Rovinas or the NYPD to find you in case any bodies were to show up on the shores of the Hamptons."

"Oh," I mutter, since I didn't consider that angle. I assumed by living in a small town so far from New York, nobody would find us here. One of the Rovinas could potentially find out about Oriana and try to get custody. Or Izaiah could wash up or evidence like videos or DNA could be traced to me.

"And I came to see you today to finally ask you what you want."

I cross my arms over my chest to hold my towel in place. "Well, this isn't it. As nice of a vacation as it's been, it's beautiful but... empty."

"So, you want to return to New York?"

"Yes. Even though I know I shouldn't. I *can't*."

"What if I told you that I would do everything in my power to keep you and Oriana safe from the violence of my world?"

"I'd say you're full of shit."

"I'm not. I wouldn't be here, giving you the option to come back with me, if I didn't think it would work."

"How?"

"I moved a dozen of my soldiers to provide security around the penthouse and whenever you and Oriana go out. I've purchased bulletproof vehicles, which should arrive soon."

"Wow. That doesn't sound cheap."

"I'm also working on pinning Izaiah's murder on a drug dealer to take that heat off us permanently. There won't ever be a trial because the dealer will never be caught."

"What if he is caught, though?"

"He won't be. The guy recently ran off to Thailand, a few days after Izaiah was killed, and Emilio was tormenting all the dealers to question them. It turns out he was much safer in New York, since he got beaten to death in Phuket."

"You had a drug dealer beaten to death in a city called Poo-Cat?"

"No." Creed's lips nearly curve into a smile. "I just got lucky that someone else conveniently beat him to death for us."

"Sounds like you've thought of everything."

"I've tried to. I needed to make sure everything was in place before you could return with me. If that's what you want."

"I do. You know I do. But Oriana..."

"I'll spend whatever it takes to keep you two safe. I know I can't protect you and her from the entire world, but I can protect you from mine or die trying."

"It must be nice to be so rich and powerful that you can just snap your fingers and get whatever you want."

"I can't snap my fingers and get you, Zara, and you're the only thing I actually want in my life. Fuck the rest of it. Without you... I've been a miserable bastard since you left on that damn boat."

"You didn't even tell me goodbye," I whisper while trying to wrap my head around everything he's said when I still can't believe he's even here. "Do you know how much that hurt? To think that you cared so little for me?"

"I was a gigantic pussy. Is that what you want to hear? I should've said goodbye to you. I've regretted avoiding you that morning from the second I watched the boat pull away from the dock."

"You watched us leave?"

"Yes. Stupid, right? To be so close and not have the balls to speak a word to you?"

"That is pretty stupid." I smile, blinking at the most handsome man in the world through a blur of tears.

"So? What do you think?" Reaching into his pants pocket, he pulls out my wedding band, giant diamond ring, and a new, slightly smaller diamond. I thought I had lost my rings to Emilio. I should've known Creed would search his pockets when cleaning up the scene. "Am I worth the risk for you? For Oriana? I'll understand if I'm not. I can visit you both here..."

I don't let him say another word.

Throwing my arms around his neck, I slam my lips against his and kiss him the way I've wanted to since the night he kicked me out of his bed.

"Is that a yes?" he asks when his lips eventually move down to kiss my neck. His fist presses against my back with the rings inside.

"Yes."

"I have another question for you? Have you signed the divorce papers?"

"No." I silence any more questions by covering his mouth with mine again because I haven't had enough of his kisses yet.

I still find it hard to believe that Creed Ferraro wants to be with me.

In some ways, it feels like a gift for all the shit I had to endure over the past seven years, being practically sold to a mobster by my parents, being used, abused, and manipulated by two awful men. Having a child with a man I hated, then having her taken away from me so cruelly.

Spending my life with both my daughter and my ruthless husband seems too good to be true.

"I'm not him." Creed pulls away and gently brushes one of my loose curls behind my ears. "If you decide to come back and be with me, I won't ever force you to stay. Times will be hard. I'll be going away for more than three years, and I know it's asking a lot for you to stay with me through all that. I don't want you to be with me because you have to, though. If I'm who you want, then you get to make the choice to be with me every single day, without any coercion or manipulation."

"If you mean that, then I'll need my independence — a job to earn my own money."

"Okay."

"Okay?"

"I want you to be free to do what you want, what you love. And I hope you and Oriana will live with me. I want to be a father to her if you'll let me. Maybe even give her a brother or sister…"

"Whoa. Let's just take it one day at a time," I warn him with a smile I can't hide. I like the idea of him being a father and having his children way too much.

"One day at a time," Creed agrees with a devious grin I know means he won't make it easy to refuse him anything.

EPILOGUE

Zara
Two months later...

I fought falling even more in love with Creed, but it was impossible. And the more I fell in love with him, the more I wanted our little family to grow.

In fact, that's why I went to the doctor this morning before I enrolled in a photography class. I wasn't sure about leaving Oriana for a few hours in the afternoon, but Creed encouraged me to take a little time out of the day to do something for myself. Since he hired both Paige and Bethany to help, even going so far as to pay for them to live in the building, I decided to do it.

The class is three days a week from one to three, which is when Oriana is usually having a playdate and a nap.

I haven't found a job, but someday I'm hoping to earn a little money from freelance work.

And I'd be jealous Oriana insisted Creed tell her the last story of the night if I hadn't already tucked her in and read her four of them while she fought to stay awake.

Before Creed finishes reading to Oriana and comes to bed for the night, I search through our shared closet for one of his suit jackets to put on as a surprise. I haven't worn one since we got back from Italy two months ago.

As I shove hanging suits aside to find the perfect one, I discover two hidden boxes on a shelf underneath. One is long and white, and the other is a banker's box. Curious, I remove the longer one first and peer through the box's front window, finding a wedding dress.

My wedding dress.

Creed must have had it cleaned and boxed for preservation after we got back from the Hamptons. I didn't even know he brought it back with us, but I'm so glad he did. Oriana may not want to wear it, but it's still nice to have. The dress I married Creed in that smelled like garbage thanks to a long ride to the beach with a disgusting corpse.

Our life is definitely one of a kind, that's for sure.

Putting the dress box back on the shelf, I remove the banker's box that's so heavy, I have to place it on the floor. Kneeling next to it, I lift the lid to find two side-by-side stacks of magazines. There are advertisements on the backs that don't tell me anything, so I pick up the top one to flip it over.

"Holy shit on a stick," I gasp. Without having to flip the pages, I know it's the July issue from six years ago, which I posed for at Emilio's encouragement. I made that mistake not once, but three times while he and his friends in the industry assured me it would lead to more modeling jobs.

They were wrong.

But I'm not disappointed. I'd rather be on the other side of the camera, anyway, capturing little moments in life. Real life, not staged.

"Zara?" Creed calls out.

Shit. I took too long and ruined the surprise.

"In here!" I call out from the closet floor.

"What in the world are you doing?" Creed asks when he appears in the open doorway. I have to bite back my smile when I see he's wearing a super cute accessory, one I assume he forgot to remove after Oriana's bedtime story. "Uh-oh. It looks like you found my porn stash," he remarks with a grin.

"How do you have so many of these?" I hold up the one in my hand.

"Nobody gets to see my wife naked but me." He scowls. "Lorenzo helped me buy all the copies we could find."

"You found all these in the city?" I ask in disbelief as I toss the copy back into the box and put the lid on it, ready to bury that chapter of my life for good.

"In the world," Creed replies. "I bought every copy that was for sale on auction sites and any that could be traced to a purchaser."

"Wow." I get to my feet. "That's quite a feat. And I hate to break it to you, baby, but you're not the only one who gets to see me naked."

"What do you mean?" he asks, his voice several octaves lower.

"I went to the...um, lady doctor today."

"You did? Why? Is everything okay?" He comes into the closet and gathers me in his arms.

"Yeah, it was just a yearly thing," I lie. "I'm officially off my birth control shots. Way off them."

"Oh."

"Oh?" I repeat, following his unenthusiastic response. "I thought you were serious about wanting to give Oriana a sister or brother. You mention it, like, every other time you're finishing inside me."

"I know. And I do want to make a baby with you. That's all I fucking think about lately," Creed says.

"But?" I ask, since I can hear it coming.

"But, if I get you pregnant now, not only will I miss the birth, I'll miss the first several years of his or her life."

I swallow around the sudden knot in my throat. "You mean because you'll be serving your sentence for the gun charges soon?"

He nods. "The trial is less than four months away. Odds of a not guilty are so bad that my attorney thinks I should take a plea deal and get it over with, start doing my time."

"Wow. I didn't know that. About the plea deal, I mean. Wh- when are you going to enter the plea?"

"As soon as I give him the green light, Baxter's going to schedule it with the DA. Dre, Tristan, and Lorenzo are going to try and stagger their pleas for as long as possible."

"And you have to go in first?"

"The DA made it clear she isn't giving me any breaks, so yeah, I'll have to go first."

"I'm sorry." I reach and caress his face between my palms.

"No, *micetta mia*, I'm the one who is sorry. I hate leaving you."

"We'll get through it," I promise him.

"We will," Creed agrees. "And at least I'll get to attend Dre and Stella's wedding."

"Oh. Has she finally accepted a ring from him and agreed to set a date?"

"Not yet, but she will."

I smile despite the disappointing reminder of losing Creed to prison soon. "You know if she agrees to marry him it's probably only because Saint wants her behind enemy lines, right?"

"And Dre is only marrying her to fuck her while pretending we're all innocent. It's a match made in heaven." He grins. "Still, Dre thinks he can make her fall in love with him, despite the fact she won't accept his ring."

"That will be one hell of a trick. But every marriage has its problems, right?"

"Dre is a cranky son of a bitch on a good day. Having to give up all women while his wife tries to kill him may make him homicidal."

"It's going to be fun to watch him work for it."

"You'll have to give me updates on how it's going once I'm incarcerated." He pulls the dark cloud above us closer.

"I will," I promise him.

I decide to save my news for tomorrow.

Or next week.

Eventually, I'll tell him, just not when it feels so sad.

Pulling his face to mine, I kiss Creed hard enough to leave no doubt about how the rest of his night is about to go.

He groans in anticipation and lifts me by my bottom, my legs wrapping around his waist. As soon as he drops me on the bed and begins to unbutton his shirt, I stop him. "Don't move. Wait just one second."

"Why?" he asks as I crawl over to my side of bed where I plugged in my phone to charge it. I'd rather have my camera, but the phone will have to do for urgency's sake.

Quickly, I snap several photos of my mobster husband standing at the foot of the bed, tall, sexy, and intimidating in his partially opened black button-up, the front of his black slacks snug, barely containing his excitement.

"See something you like?" he asks with a smug grin as he reaches down to cup himself through the pants.

"God, yes." I bite my bottom lip. "I think I like your pretty pink princess crown the best."

His face falls a second before he lifts his arm and removes the crown he had obviously forgotten was still on his head.

"Fuck," he mutters as he stares down at the fake gems and tosses it on the mattress. "Oriana made me wear it while I was reading her Cinderella. She said we couldn't go to the ball until I put on the crown."

I laugh so hard I can barely get out the words, "She's a bossy little thing, isn't she?"

"Bossy like her momma." Crawling on the bed toward me, Creed asks, "How much is it going to cost for you to permanently delete those images from the Cloud?"

"Oh, these images are priceless, baby. I'm never, ever deleting them." I giggle. "The king of kings wearing a pink, jeweled crown..."

Creed makes a grab for my phone, and I squeal as I toss it on the floor. Once it's out of his reach, I tug my top off, grip his wide shoulders, and pull him down on top of me to try to distract him.

"Only you know the truth, that the king of kings is at the sole mercy of his beautiful queen." His mouth softly and slowly kiss the scars on my chest in sharp contrast to the urgency with which he jerks my pajamas and panties down my legs. "Now, spread your legs and let me worship you, *micetta mia*."

The End

Or is it?

If you want more of Zara and Creed, there's a bonus epilogue: https://BookHip.com/DLLHNLL

COMING SOON!

Thank you so much for reading **Filthy Little Games**!

If you want more of Creed and Zara then you can grab the bonus epilogue here:
https://dl.bookfunnel.com/2ss5q14j7r

Order Dre and Stella's book **Cruel Little Games** *to find out what's in store for the Ferraro family!*

Stella:
Andre Ferraro is everything I despise—arrogant, ruthless, and far too handsome for his own good.
I'd rather marry anyone else in the world, but my sick mother needs hope, my family needs the Ferraro fortune, and my brother needs allies to seek vengeance for my brother and father's deaths. There's no way for me to get out of this marriage to Andre unless I want to put the burden on my younger sister.
The crazy thing is, I don't want Andre, but I don't want anyone else to have him either.

COMING SOON!

Andre:

Stella Rovina has been my obsession since the moment I laid eyes on her, and now, she's going to be my wife.

When she offers me the deal of a lifetime—fake love for her grieving mother in exchange for one unforgettable night—I can't resist.

One night will never be enough for me, though.

I don't want just her body; I want her heart, her soul, her to be mine forever.

But I'm hiding a secret that could shatter her world.

If she uncovers the truth, our marriage won't just end—it'll burn everything to the ground.

Order your copy now!

ALSO BY LANE HART

If you enjoyed *Filthy Little Games* then you will love Savage Little Games, a dark mafia series that takes place in Sin City!

Start reading now: https://mybook.to/SLG

~ SYNOPSIS ~

In an ironic twist of fate, I've found myself entangled in Dante Salvato's world. The ruthless mafia king is no stranger to violence; but when he lays his eyes on my bruised and battered face, he's furious.

I thought my makeup was thick enough to cover the beating I suffered until my inappropriately flirtatious boss noticed. As a cocktail waitress in his casino, I've always been on Mr. Salvato's radar, but now he's obsessed, demanding to know who hurt me and why, intent on making them suffer.

When Dante discovers that my boyfriend Mitch not only owes money to another vicious Vegas mobster but is also cheating on me, he offers him one hell of a deal – Dante will pay off Mitch's debt in exchange for the one thing he wants more than anything – me.

Dante's offer requires me to spend the next seventy-six days and nights with him, one for every thousand dollars of Mitch's debt. When I refuse, Dante promises to kill Mitch right then and there for being the one ultimately responsible for my bruises.

Desperate to avoid bloodshed even after I've seen the evidence of Mitch's betrayal, I reluctantly accept Dante's deal with one stipulation. I warn the arrogant bastard that I will never, under any circumstance, sleep with him.

Now I just have to resist the mob boss for seventy-six days and nights while he uses every weapon in his arsenal to try and change my mind.

ABOUT THE AUTHOR

New York Times bestselling author Lane Hart lives in North Carolina with her husband, author D.B. West, and their two children. She enjoys spending the summers on the beach and watching football in the fall.

Connect with Lane:

Author Store: https://www.authorlanehart.com/
Tiktok: https://www.tiktok.com/@hartandwestbooks
Facebook: http://www.facebook.com/lanehartbooks
Instagram: https://www.instagram.com/authorlanehart/
Website: http://www.lanehartbooks.com
Email: lane.hart@hotmail.com

Find all of Lane's books on her Amazon author page!

Sign up for Lane and DB's newsletter to get updates on new releases and freebies!

ABOUT THE AUTHOR

Join Lane's Facebook group to read books before they're released, help choose covers, character names, and titles of books! https://www.facebook.com/groups/bookboyfriendswanted/

Made in the USA
Monee, IL
19 May 2025